SUNYATA
BOOKS

SEATTLE

HOLLOW FORTRESS

For information about permissions to reproduce selections from this book, translation rights, or to order bulk purchases, go to www.sunyatabooks.com.

Cover art by Anthony Hassett
Author photo by C.L. Canestaro
Edited by Regina McAskill Scherffius
Book design by Bryan Tomasovich at The Publishing World

Voorhees, B.L.
Hollow Fortress: Part I of The Four Gates series
978-0-692-16503-4

1. FICTION / Fantasy—Action & Adventure

Printed in the U.S.A.
Distributed by Ingram

SUNYATA
BOOKS

WWW.SUNYATABOOKS.COM

HOLLOW FORTRESS

PART I OF THE FOUR GATES

B.L. VOORHEES

To Jacqueline Phillips, with gratitude too long delayed.

PROLOGUE

Afghanistan
The Hindu Kush
August 3

"BEAUTIFUL COUNTRY," Jolly remarked.

Army Special Forces Lieutenant Nicholas "Nick" Herron grunted agreement. It was beautiful country, high in the Hindu Kush and largely untouched by the carnage that had ravaged the rest of Afghanistan.

Both men were lying prone on a granite outcrop above Bashar Hasem Pass, scanning the valley below through 100X Nikons. The SAT link had squirreled an hour before and they were forced to rely on direct visual contact with their quarry.

"Maybe they'll surrender peacefully," Nick said. Jolliteau gave him a wry glance.

Nick chuckled. He'd been with the team nearly four months but they had not yet engaged an enemy. He knew in Jolliteau's mind he was still on probation.

The big warrant officer suddenly tensed, the binoculars tight to his eyes. "There! They're in the open. That cliff wall. Seven, eight klicks."

Their target was a small group of Taliban, suspected of a recent raid on the police station at Dar as al-Ma'arri. At least they were thought to be Taliban. They'd gotten good descriptions from the villagers: seven young men, short beards, dirty robes, AK-47s, and black headgear. Taliban. Yet they were headed north, into the Pamirs. Taliban usually retreated to the southwest, to their hidden redoubts in the tribal country along the border.

So why north? North was high country, home of the mysterious Nuristanis, a people whose allegiance to Islam was questionable even by liberal standards.

And other behavior didn't add up. The usual Taliban MO was to kill or mutilate their victims, at least hold them hostage. After taking the station, instead of killing the cops this band had just tied them up and left them, alive. They took food, a little cash, and the station's two US-donated Humvees. Witnesses could recall none of the jihadist rhetoric associated with the Taliban. The vehicles had been found at the eastern base of the pass, abandoned where they ran out of gas.

It was telling. But what it told was anybody's guess.

Bashar Hasem Pass was low for the region, no more than five thousand meters, but their helicopter had developed mechanical difficulties early on. The team pushed ahead on foot, without rest for most of the day. *Diwangi*, mountain sickness, was not to be taken lightly. A dull throb at his temples alerted Nick to early symptoms. He broke open a cellophane pack of Diamox pills, washing them down with a gulp of canteen water, noticing Jolliteau's eyes on him as he did so.

Odd, he thought. First the bird, now the SAT link. Even their GPS units were acting up. Almost as if—

He stopped. Technology was technology, prone to failure at any time, more so in these ancient mountains. No reason to make it more than it was.

It was full summer and the valley below was surprisingly lush. It was warm for the altitude, close to eighty-five degrees. Nick loosened the checkered scarf around his neck, taking advantage of a cool breeze blowing up from the valley. He caught the unmistakable scent of citrus and jasmine blossoms. Three hundred meters below, the Abar River tumbled from high clefts into ice-blue pools as it wound its energetic way toward the plains of Bamyan.

Now that they were out of the shadows of the cliff, the men they followed were easy to spot. Seven of them, moving up the narrow trail that led to the mountain village of Bet al-Nuri.

Not good. No one wanted a firefight in a friendly village. Not with evening coming on.

A narrow and deceptively fragile-looking rope bridge spanned the gorge and the river below. Rico and Conagher, the team scouts, had already crossed.

"Finally some luck," said Jolly. "Looks like they've stopped."

Through the binoculars, Nick could see the men had halted in a small clearing just off the trail. From their animated gestures it appeared they were arguing.

"Time to move, Lieutenant."

Nick nodded and Jolliteau raised his hand in the "go" sign. Immediately the other eight members of the team scrambled to their feet and began working their way down the steep moraine, taking cover among boulders and fallen slabs of granite.

Nick holstered his binoculars and stood, swaying slightly as he did so. It was then that he heard the music, faint at first, then more definite, carried by the same soft breeze that had earlier perfumed the mountain air.

The music was foreign, unfamiliar, yet something about it compelled his attention. A reed flute. Drums. A man's voice, resonant and filled with longing, as though the singer called upon God Himself to deliver him of some great sorrow. His voice ran counterpoint to the flute's piercing demiquaver and the rhythm of the drums. As if in answer came a chorus of women's voices, clear and melodious. The music enfolded him. Nick found himself holding back tears.

The late afternoon sun reflected gold off the snowcapped peak of Tirich Mir, at more than seven thousand meters the highest mountain visible from their position. Without warning the peak flashed a brilliant green ray that lit up the sky.

For Nick the dual impact of the music and the light was startling. At that moment something opened in him, or opened to him. A memory, as faint and haunting as the music, agonizingly intimate. *If only—if only—*

If only—what? The thought escaped him.

"The light," he blurted out. "Did you see that light? It was—"

Jolliteau was staring at him, concern showing on his dark features. Concern, or something else?

The music had stopped. Nick looked back at the mountain. Once again the peak was gold, now darkening into a tarnished bronze. A sudden, agonizing sense of loss overcame him, followed by foreboding, like a dark cloud over the sun.

"You OK, Lieutenant?"

Nick steadied himself against a large rock. Breathe, he told himself.

The thin mountain air found his lungs, but he couldn't get over the feeling a door had opened to something higher, something vital, and he had missed it, and by missing it his life was about to take a very dark and dangerous turn.

Knowing that showing any sign of doubt or weakness at such a moment might mark him forever, he flashed Jolly a confident smile and straightened. "Let's do it."

CHAPTER
1

Oxfordshire
England
October 30

WILLIAM HAMILTON WINFORD III, Billy to his friends, Lord Winford to his neighbors, was busy coding in new instructions for King Leonidas when the doorbell rang. It was a real bell, pre–World War I vintage, made of resonant bronze that had to be manually struck. It had been hung in another age when servants had been expected to answer its call.

Billy ignored it. All his rooms were let and his lodgers had their own keys. He was engrossed in his programming.

What would motivate Leonidas? he thought to himself. Virtue? Duty? Glory? How could you program such indefinable things?

The bell ringer was insistent. "Go away," he mumbled, half to himself.

The ringing continued. A door inside the manor slammed. "I'll get it, you lazy sod!" shouted a reedy voice. "Play with your silly toys. Let an old woman do your work!"

Billy sighed. It was Meg, his oldest and most irascible lodger, and the only one with a room on the first floor. He would hear about this later.

He turned his attention back to the monitor. The battling figures froze on the screen. Motivation? Let's see. Selfless glory? Is there such a thing?

The computers were among the few artifacts in the house not from an earlier era. Eight boxes custom-built himself using the fastest processors available, running a stripped-down version of Linux for maximum number-crunching capability, hummed in an air-conditioned closet. The configuration accessed the Internet over a superfast fiber-optic connection to the same backbone used by nearby Oxford University. It was a perk for which he had spent a great deal of money.

On tables scattered around what was once the old manor's drawing room sat half a dozen thirty-two-inch monitors. Three screens displayed Greek and Persian soldiers doing their best to kill one another. A fourth showed the shifting numbers and icons of his code. On a wall, mounted between portraits of long-dead relatives, hung a giant OLED display waiting to show newly rendered sequences. A worn leather sofa and several equally abused chairs faced the screen, but for now it was dark.

How does one write an algorithm for virtue? mused Billy. What is virtue, the impulse behind it? Not talked about much these days. The Mahabharata went on about it. Plato of course. The Timeaus? No, that was more arcane, other worlds and all. The Greek word for virtue was *arete*, wasn't it? Valor in war.

He tapped the keys, studied the results, frowned. This was going to take time. Voices brought him out of his thoughts. A man's voice, oddly familiar.

Damn. Meg had actually invited the fellow in!

He lifted himself out of his chair, favoring his bad leg. Before he'd taken four steps the room's broad door swung open.

The light in the room was kept dim to better view the monitors. Billy's first impression of the intruder was that of a street person. Big, over six feet two. Well-muscled and dangerous looking. Unkempt dark hair, full beard, worn military fatigues. His right hand held a water-stained duffle. A rectangle of light from a hallway window had fallen on the duffle and Billy's eyes fixed on it. Tan canvas, a less faded area where the name tag had been removed.

Meg was hovering behind the man like an excited crow. "Don't just stand there like a piked fish," she cackled happily. "Don't you recognize your best mate?"

Best mate? Billy blinked and stared. "Nick? Nicholas! My God! Is that really you? You're supposed to be in Afghanistan! Why didn't you call?"

His friend's smile was peculiar. Thin and weary. Not like him at all. "Hello, Billy," he said quietly.

Billy wanted to rush forward and embrace him, but something held him back. Perhaps it was the wariness, an uncharacteristic reserve. "What happened to you, man? You look like you fell off a fishing trawler."

"Close enough."

Nick glanced around the room, his blue-green eyes expressionless. The monitors were all new, big flat screens, not the bulky old CRTs they'd replaced. He noted the images frozen there, the red battle cloaks, the armor and short-bladed swords.

"Greeks and Persians. Thermopylae?"

Honoring the change of subject, Billy pressed a key that started the battle going again. "Precisely. I've been programming different takes. If the Greeks hadn't kept retreating behind fixed fortifications after every battle, I'm certain they could have won."

Nick gave a disbelieving chuckle and shook his head. "Not likely. Leonidas had three hundred men. The Persians had over a million as I recall. Some said two million."

"Actually the Greeks started with six thousand men," Billy said, warming to the subject. He could almost forget that more than two years had passed since he and Nick had last sat in this very room, dissecting old battles, coming up with new strategies. It had been over four months since he'd last heard from his friend, a postcard from Kabul, a picture of a small, mud-walled mosque with an apricot tree in front. No real news. Only that he was enjoying the billet. Training mostly. He liked the Afghans, felt he was doing some good. Typically bright and optimistic.

"Leonidas sent the others back," he said. "All but his three hundred Spartans. What most historians overlook—what I think Leonidas overlooked—was that right up to the end the Spartans had dominated every battle. At one point they actually came within a few hundred yards of Xerxes himself."

"Great gods!" cried Meg. "You haven't seen each other in years and all you can talk about is some musty old battle! Can't you see the lieutenant is hungry?"

Billy blinked, startled to see Meg still standing in the hall, just beyond the doorway.

"Thank you, Meg. I'll attend to it." He stepped around Nick and closed the door. They could hear the old woman sputtering profanities as she shuffled off back to her room.

"Not much has changed, I see," said Nick, a glimmer of humor breaking through.

"Dried-up old cow. I should have booted her out years ago. I've lost more than one lodger because of her. You're the only one she ever liked, you know. Always wondered how you managed."

Billy stopped, apologetic as the truth of what Meg had said sunk in. "Sorry. You do look a bit peaked. What time is it?" He looked at his watch, a twenty-seven-jewel admiral's chronometer, its case carved from a single block of rose gold by Baume & Mercier in 1936. It had been his grandfather's, then his father's.

It was close to six. "I'd no idea it was so late. We can talk over supper."

Nick nodded, but his eyes were focused on the nearest monitor, where imaginary soldiers were still engaged in their endless battle.

"Nice animation. A-Life? They're making their own decisions?"

"Good eye."

"Why do you think three hundred men, or even six thousand, could defeat thousand-to-one odds?"

There was an edge to the question that told Billy it was motivated by more than polite curiosity. "Simple, really," he said. "The Persians couldn't bring their numbers to bear. Take Hannibal when he defeated the Romans at Capua. Worse odds, granted, but basically a similar situation. The Persian army had a top-down command structure. If the Greeks had kept on they could have reached Xerxes, cut the head off the snake. Weren't you the one who always argued odds didn't mean that much?"

A bleak sort of emptiness seemed to settle on Nick. "Did I? Must've been drinking. Besides, you wouldn't want to upstage the Oracle of Delphi, would you? Greece saved by its wooden walls and all."

Nick felt immediate regret. He knew how cynical he must sound. Lack of sleep. And he was hungry. Famished, really. He hadn't eaten a decent meal in days.

"You mentioned food?"

"Of course. You're staying, aren't you?"

"Billy, I, uh—I'm kind of broke right now."

"Don't be absurd. Your old room. Bed's already made up. But first, food. Let's see what's in the larder."

CHAPTER

2

WITH THE EXCEPTION OF THE COMPUTERS, little had changed in the old place that Nick could see. The kitchen, with its art deco appliances and large stone hearth, was exactly as he remembered. Most of the meals in the house were eaten at its large oak table, the formal dining room rarely used. Lodgers—currently five, Billy said—came and went at all hours and usually ate by themselves.

Nick's recent past was a nightmare, his future uncertain. But this moment almost brought meaning back to his life. He'd finished off his second bottle of beer and was chewing the last shred of meat from a cold leg of mutton when Billy finally got around to asking.

"So. Are you going to tell me about it?"

Nick put down the bone and wiped his hands on his napkin. "I left the army."

"I assumed that," said Billy, nodding at the bare spots on Nick's khaki shirt where his name and badges used to be.

"It wasn't a court-martial, if that's what you're thinking. Mind if I get another beer?"

"Help yourself. And bring that wine over here, if you would."

Nick grabbed the last beer from the refrigerator and an open bottle of wine from a nearby counter. Chateau Margaux 1987, he noted. He poured the wine into a glass and handed it to Billy. "Old times."

"Old times."

Nick drank straight from the beer bottle, reminded of happier days. His year at Oxford had been one of the few truly enjoyable years of his life.

"You were saying why you left the army," reminded Billy.

Nick frowned. Then after a pause, "We aren't the good guys anymore."

"We? You mean America? Western capitalists? The Corporatocracy? I thought we'd beat that beast to death." Billy was smiling but his eyes showed concern.

Maybe he has reason to be worried about me, thought Nick.

"No, we didn't kill the beast," said Nick. "Not really. We worked over policies, the politics. But we—me, at least—never really questioned the whole setup. The institutions. The system. The rhetoric that holds it all together."

Billy nodded. "An existential crisis, is it? Rather a profound one, I gather. Knowing you, I doubt it came about by reading Marx, or Ayub Qutub. You were never one for ideology. What was the tipping point?"

Nick took a swallow of beer and studied the beads of condensation on the bottle, surprised to find it already half empty. "We were trailing some Taliban. At least we thought they were Taliban. They'd raided a police station, stolen some food, couple of Humvees. Didn't hurt anybody. That was odd in itself, knowing how brutal they can be. We caught up to them the next day, a valley up in the Pamirs. Beautiful country. High mountains, like you see in dreams."

He stopped as a memory surfaced, the moment atop Bashar Hasem Pass when he'd heard that strangely affecting music, seen the flash of green light, felt the wholeness it had engendered, the feeling of loss and foreboding that had followed.

Why was he remembering it now? The beer, probably.

"Were they?" Billy asked. "Taliban, I mean?"

"Huh? Oh, no. Not really. Just a bunch of idealistic Muslim kids from Kashmir. They'd come to Afghanistan to fight the infidels, all right. Deserted after a couple of months when they realized the Taliban were little more than ignorant yokels, spouting things from the Qur'an that weren't there, twisting the words for their own purpose. Just kids, you know. The oldest was sixteen."

"And? What happened?"

"There were questions from the beginning. We were pulling out. Disengaging. My team's mission was mostly training Afghans. But then we got this order to track down this particular band of insurgents. Not kill them, mind you. Capture them, or at least as many as we could. No reason given. Colonel Burke, our commander, claimed even he hadn't been told, said the orders had come from higher up.

"A helicopter dropped us a few miles from where the insurgents had last been seen. Took us a day to catch up. We found them just before nightfall. There were seven of them. Kids, like I said. The bird that'd brought us had developed mechanical problems earlier. It was getting dark, so we figured we'd spend the night, wait for morning. Instead we were told another helicopter was on the way. That was unusual in itself. Flying in those mountains is difficult at the best of times, more so at night. But we didn't question it. Our prisoners didn't figure to be much of a danger. We'd taken their weapons, bound their hands with restraint tape. They were friendly, forthcoming. Almost as if they were glad to be captured."

Nick shook his head. Three months had passed and it still hurt. It would probably always hurt. He took another swallow of beer.

"Go on," said Billy.

"There was a village nearby, five klicks up the valley. Friendlies, we'd been told, but you never knew. We put out pickets, set up a cold camp, and waited. Shouldn't have bothered with the cold camp. After all, it was their valley. They knew we were there."

"Who? The villagers?"

"Yes. Big burly guys in karakul coats carrying Kalashnikovs. Five of them. At least the ones we could see. They hailed us, said they were from the village and wanted to talk."

Nick hesitated, remembering the men who'd shown up out of the twilight gloom that terrible night. "They were polite and courteous. Manly is a word that comes to mind, none of that silly schoolboy bravado the Taliban are known for. We had them stack their weapons outside the perimeter."

Billy took a sip of wine, set the glass down. "This isn't going to end well, is it?"

Nick seemed not to hear. He was back in the mountains. "They told us they didn't have any more use for the Taliban than we did. Bandar, their chief, said he'd fought with Massoud against them. Left when Massoud was killed. He invited us to their village. Us and the Muslim kids. He spoke excellent English, said he'd spent a year at Eton."

"You believed him?

"Strangely, I did. More importantly, so did my sergeant. But we kept our safeties off."

"Did you tell them a helicopter was coming?"

"I didn't want it to be a surprise. Bandar said they'd hang around till it arrived. I figured they were just curious. So I called it in, told command we had company. Five unarmed friendlies from the local village. 'Just wait for the chopper,' they said. So we built a fire, brewed some tea, passed around MREs and sat around talking: my guys, the Nuristanis, and the kids. We were cautious, of course. Our pickets stayed put. But I figured it was a good thing. Hearts and minds and all."

A log fell in the kitchen's hearth, sending embers across the worn tiles. Nick shifted in his seat. "Have you ever heard of the 'Salvador Solution'?"

Billy nodded. "A pyramid torture scheme. Torture one person until he or she gives you ten names. Doesn't matter if they're guilty or not. Odds are at least one knows something. So you torture those ten until you get ten more names and so on. I've been told it's quite effective. The CIA taught a number of governments in Central and South America the method. Argentina was first to use it, though it didn't become famous until El Salvador picked up on it. How does this fit in with your story? Let me guess. The helicopter."

"Helicopters. Two of them. Black, unmarked CSARs. Those new combat birds, originally designed for rescue work. An entire platoon of heavily armed contractors jumped out. There were others behind them. A full interrogation team."

"Ah. And you knew this how?"

"I recognized the man in charge. Balding, about my height, older by thirty years. He'd been pointed out to me in Kabul as CIA. One of the original Salvador Solution instructors. He asked for me by name, told me he was taking charge of our prisoners. He ordered me to split them into two groups and put them on the birds. My team and I were to remain behind. We'd be extracted in the morning."

"You agreed?"

"Hardly. I told him before I turned the prisoners over I'd have to hear it directly from my commander. Either that or see some duly authorized written orders."

"I imagine he wasn't too keen on that."

"Understatement. He was furious, threatened to have me court-martialed if I disobeyed."

Nick's face darkened, shadowed with a still-seething rage. "I'd always wondered how the Nazis were able to find so many sociopaths to do their dirty work. Makes you wonder about the human race."

"Try the wine," said Billy. "It's quite good." He pushed the bottle to Nick.

"Are you trying to get me drunk?"

"Absolutely. I suspect it will mitigate the self-pity. There's a glass behind you."

"Self-pity? Dammit, Billy, I—"

Nick stopped. Billy was right, he realized. He grabbed the bottle, filling the glass almost to the rim. "Long way from the village reds we used to drink," he said, noting the price tag still on the bottle. "You've moved up in the world."

"It came at great cost. I was forced to sell a good part of the estate to sort things out. That new mall they're building? Hideous thing. As a child I used to play in the woods there. There was a stream, and a cave in the hillside."

Billy held up his own glass for Nick to refill. He turned it in his hands, admiring the light from the hearth as it played on the crystal. He was remembering the woods. "It must have been a difficult decision," he said finally. "Giving those boys up to almost certain torture."

"Enhanced interrogation. Please."

"You haven't mentioned the Nuristanis. I've heard Afghans do not offer their hospitality lightly."

Nick nodded. "They were outnumbered and outgunned. But they'd shared tea with us. With the kids. It was a matter of honor, I suppose."

CHAPTER 3

NICK WOKE WITH A THROBBING HEADACHE and a sour taste in his mouth. He'd been dreaming of a green field bordered by a vast and forbidding forest. Animals lurked in its shadows and an alien sun shone overhead. Something about it was familiar. Beautiful and familiar and he hadn't wanted to let it go.

He glanced at his watch, an Army-issued Casio G-Shock Gravitymaster, the one thing of value he'd managed to hold on to during the journey from Kabul.

8:45. He'd slept nine hours, his first decent night's sleep in weeks.

He dragged himself out of bed and threw open the window curtain. Across the gables he could see the morning's distant traffic, stalled on the new Oxfordshire Motorway. There had been a time, not long ago, when the view from that window had been of a forested countryside. He wondered if his dream had been nothing more than a memory of that bucolic past.

When was progress actually progress, and when was it something else? Billy's careful leasing out of the estate's land to developers, painful as it must have been, had allowed him to keep his beloved manor. It had even made him a wealthy man, though you couldn't tell by the way he lived. Little had changed in that regard, save perhaps for the quality of his wine and the capacity of his computers. He certainly no longer needed to rent out rooms. Nick suspected he still took in boarders because he liked having people in the house, even old Meg, though he would never admit it.

The room was warm enough but he found himself shivering as he imagined a damp mist seeping through the windowpanes into his bones. Winter was approaching. The days were growing shorter. He had a disturbing image of the world closing in around him.

The thought was interrupted by a knock on the door. He opened it to find Billy standing in the hall. He was holding a large cardboard box. "Good, you're up. Found these in the attic. Thought they might be needed."

Billy pushed his way into the room and set the box on the unmade bed. He reached into a pocket and pulled out a rose-colored glass bottle. "Try one of these."

The bottle contained a number of large, multicolored pills. There was no label. Nick looked up, questioning.

"Go on," urged Billy. "Nothing addictive. Roots, herbs, and flower tops, I imagine. Elyse made them up. Good for headaches, hangovers, and jet lag."

"Two out of three. How'd you guess?" Nick popped a pill, swallowing it without water. "Who's Elyse and what's in the box?"

"One of my lodgers. Open it and see."

Nick removed the lid. It took him a moment to recognize the civilian clothes he'd left behind after he'd completed his master's studies: shirts, pants, shoes, even underwear. "You kept these?"

"Remembered them this morning."

Nick glanced down at the stained boxer shorts he was wearing. When was the last time they'd been washed? Weeks ago?

"I—I don't know what to say."

"A simple 'thank you' will be sufficient."

A young woman passing by in the hall stopped and peered in the room. Medium height, nubile, milky smooth skin, disheveled auburn hair. She was dressed for a night's clubbing: heels, waist-length faux fur coat and an expensive-looking silk shift, so short and clinging it was clear there was nothing underneath. "Letting out the room, are you Billy?"

The question was accusatory and Billy ignored it. "Just getting in, are you, Alice?"

The woman shrugged. "Twit left me at Kensington. Paid for the cabbie at least."

Pert nose, full lips. Under the streaked makeup Nick could see she was exceptionally pretty, quite possibly beautiful. Her brown eyes were full of mischievous humor. "You going to introduce us?" she said, pretending to notice Nick for the first time.

Her accent wavered between upper-crust gentility and East End Liverpool. Late teens or early twenties, Nick guessed.

Billy stepped between them. "Nick Herron, meet Alice Smith. Alice, meet Nick. Nick's a friend, and I'm not letting the room out. He's a guest. And you look like you could use some sleep. So on your way."

She studied Nick with a frankness that made him acutely aware of his dress, or lack of it. "Nick, is it?" Her voice dropped into an imitation Bacall, husky and theatrically seductive. "Well, Nick, I'm just down the hall. And call me Ally," she added with a sudden bright smile. "Alice is so very beige, don't you think?"

"You know the rules, Alice. No business here."

"Meanie."

The woman stuck her tongue out, gave a toss of her hair, smiled again at Nick and turned to leave. "Besides," she said, glancing back over her shoulder. "Who said it had to be business?"

Billy closed the door. "Student," he said as if it were an apology. "Second year French literature. Likes this room, says it has more light than hers. Pays her way by—well, you can guess. Her home life wasn't particularly stable. Father abuse and all that. Bright girl, though. Good heart."

He gave an exaggerated sniff. "You could use a bath, you know. There's a razor in with those clothes if you feel like shaving off the beard. Maeve might have some shaving cream in there. She won't mind."

Nick stroked his untrimmed beard. "Is that a hint?"

"Well. We wouldn't want the neighbors thinking I'm taking in terrorists now, would we? But if you insist on keeping it—"

"Not to worry," chuckled Nick. "Beards were all but required in the Stan. Something about being taken seriously by the locals. But I never liked wearing one. I would have shaved it off weeks ago if there'd been an opportunity. Who's Maeve?"

"Shared bath, remember. She lets the room opposite. Lead singer in an all-girl band, Celtic Maids. They're on tour in Wales for a month. Pubs and clubs, mostly."

"Maeve, Elyse, Alice, Meg. Billy, are all your lodgers women?"

"Only if you call Meg a woman. Frankly I rather like to think of her as a bat. Or maybe a crow. And no pop psychology, please. Wounded birds, how they make me feel more manly and all? The truth is women tend to be gentler on the old place. You do remember Nelson, don't you?"

Nick grimaced. He remembered Nelson all right, an odious giant who'd sat number five on the Oxford rowing team. He'd had the misfortune of sharing the bathroom with the man; drains clogged with coarse black hair, toilet always seemed to be filled with crap and never flushed, sweat-drenched workout clothes tossed about at random and a continuing stream of loud and unattractive women visiting at all hours of the night. Billy had finally given Nelson notice, an act that had taken more than a little courage. Nelson was known for having a short temper. Nick had waited nearby ready to jump in if things turned ugly. But Billy had stood his ground, bad leg and all. They'd celebrated the evening Nelson moved out.

"Remember that oath we took?" Nick mused. "What did we call ourselves?"

"Knights of the Blasted Heath," supplied Billy, straightening into a sort of martial salute. "Never lie. Stand up to bullies in all their forms. Loyalty to friends. Do the right thing even if it means death or dismemberment."

"And always behave honorably toward women," said Nick, smirking.

"Always. Though I take it by your tone you no longer agree with such sentiments?"

Nick forced down a sudden irrational anger. What do you know about it? he wanted to shout. Holed up in this bloody mansion, playing fantasy games where everything is black and white. The real world isn't like that!

But the anger subsided as quickly as it had arisen, leaving him feeling oddly ashamed, as if he'd disappointed not so much Billy but himself.

"The difference between a noble person and a commoner isn't birth," Billy had once said. "A commoner's first instinct is to drag everyone down to their level. A truly noble person recognizes real worth and does their best to raise everyone up to that level, themselves included. Sort of an 'I can be as good as any man' attitude rather than 'No one is better than me, whatever they pretend.'"

A rationale of the gilded class, Nick thought. Still, there had been a time not long before when he'd believed much the same himself.

"Breakfast will be ready when you're ready."

Billy left, closing the door behind him. As Nick sorted through his newfound wardrobe, he had to remind himself of the real reason he'd come to England rather than push on to the States. He'd spent all but his last few dollars in Gwādar, bribing the first mate on a Greek freighter, and he needed money. He was grateful to Billy. More than grateful, really. But Billy had already done enough just letting him stay there. Fellow Knight of the Blasted Heath or not, he wasn't about to ask him for more.

During his time at Oxford, Nick had put in a few months as a junior officer on a DOD procurement team to acquire human assets for specialized work in Iraq. Their contact had been a man in London. He had an appointment with him that afternoon. He hadn't seen the fellow in two years but they'd always gotten along well. He hoped some work would come out of it.

He picked out a pair of jeans, a tan shirt, and a blue cardigan from his old clothes. There was also an expensive pair of Armani loafers. The clothes had a faint but cloying smell of mothballs. Billy's doing, as if he'd known Nick would return someday and need his clothes back.

The bathroom had changed dramatically since the days he'd shared it with Nelson. Spotlessly clean, embroidered linens, jars of bath salts, scented candles, an entire shelf of boutique brand cosmetics. He'd spent far too much time consorting with the macho snake eaters in Special Operations, he realized. He felt like a bum who'd accidentally stumbled into a lady's boudoir. Which was close enough to the truth that he laughed.

He shaved while the tub filled, using his own razor. There was a jar of shaving cream on the vanity but he hadn't felt right using it, lathering instead with a bar of generic hand soap. He made sure to clean the sink when he'd finished, sweeping the remains into a plastic trash bag he'd discovered under the sink. He reminded himself to dump it before Maeve returned. He didn't want to be thought of as another Nelson. He turned off the tub faucets and eased into the steaming water. Whether the result of Elyse's herbal pills or the first hot bath he'd had in weeks, he couldn't say, but his headache was gone.

His thoughts drifted to Alice, Ally. Young, pretty, sexy, if a little slutty.

He smiled. A little slutty? She'd been about as subtle as a dock whore: Hey, sailor! Looking for a good time?

Unfortunately, at the moment, he couldn't afford the price of a kiss from a Barcelona streetwalker. Probably best. His limited experience with commercial sex had always left him feeling diminished somehow, less than the man he hoped himself to be.

What was it missing? The challenge? The mystery? Love? Had he ever been in love? An adolescent crush or two based more on physical attraction than anything deeper. What was love anyway? A clever marketing strategy, invented to sell lipstick, deodorants, and thong underwear.

How long had it been since he'd gotten laid? The German sisters in Athens, the Indian *bibi* in Peshawar. He'd had one date with that pretty NGO worker in Kabul but she'd been recalled two days later after a bombing had destroyed her clinic. As for the Afghans, forget it. Even to show interest in an Afghan woman was to risk a blood feud.

Four nights. Four out of a thousand and one. He'd have done better in a monastery. Best not to think about it, though musing on carnality was certainly healthier than dwelling on other, less pleasant events.

As he thought this, the memories abruptly returned. Vivid, as if he were reliving them:

The screams and shouting. "What are you standing there for, Lieutenant? Give the order! Give the order!" The staccato clatter of assault rifles, the strangely musical roar of the helicopter's miniguns. A Kashmiri boy futilely attempting to shield his younger brother. Jolly next to him, his head blown off. Cisco falling, then Lynsky. Smoke. The smell of cordite. The terrible silence.

There was nothing you could do, he thought. Nothing you could have done.

Dammit! He should have done something. Done what was right.

Even if it meant death or dismemberment.

The flashback passed more quickly this time than it had in the past, but still left him with residual feelings of impotence and anger. He took in a deep breath, let it out. The tension lessened. He was alive. He was thankful for that. It meant there was still time.

Time? Time for—what, exactly? He wasn't sure.

The bathwater had grown tepid. In his mouth was the sweet copper taste of blood. He'd bitten his tongue.

He toweled off and dressed. He found Billy in the kitchen, frying up a pan of scrambled eggs.

"Precisely on time," Billy announced, studying the eggs judiciously before shoveling them onto plates, one of which he handed to Nick. "A shave and some fresh clothes and you look both like the old Nick I knew and a new man entirely, if that's possible. Sit. Sit."

A platter of fried ham was already on the table along with a pitcher of fresh orange juice, biscuits, butter, and what looked liked a jar of homemade marmalade. A wisp of steam rose from the teapot's spout.

"Pill help?" Billy asked, joining him at the table.

"Headache's gone. Thanks."

"Thank Elyse when you meet her. Her concoctions usually do the trick. Tea?"

Nick nodded. Billy poured the tea into porcelain cups, adding a teaspoon of sugar in each. "Still insist on going to London? You're sure this fellow can help?"

"He was straight enough back then. He said the pay's up."

"Bugger the train, then. Take Isabel. She hasn't been out for a while, could use a good spin."

"Isabel? You're offering to let me drive Isabel?"

"I worry about her sitting too long. Oil gets mucky, tires get flat on the bottom, seals dry up. I'd drive you myself but you know how I hate London. Besides, this Leonidas thing has me snaveled."

Isabel was one of Billy's prides, a 1958 Jaguar custom phaeton inherited along with the title and estate from his late father. Billy's parents had both been physicians, unstintingly (Billy would say insufferably) zealous in their work for Médecins Sans Frontières. Billy had spent his childhood being dragged like unwanted baggage from one festering hole of humanity to another: Gambola, Ratanagua, Utter Gamesh, Pomadoji, places most people had never heard of and, if they had, were more than likely to avoid.

It was Pomadoji where Billy contracted a rare form of osteomyelitis, leaving him with a bad right leg and an intense dislike for foreign travel. He'd once said it was only luck he hadn't contracted Ebola or been killed by insurgents, which had been his parents' fate.

"Don't worry about petrol," he insisted. "Her tanks are full and insurance is paid. You'll be doing me a favor. Really."

CHAPTER 4

"SORRY YOU CAME ALL THIS WAY for nothing, Lieutenant. If I had known how to get hold of you I'd have told you not to bother."

Piers Pontson, owner and sole agent for World Specialized Services, folded his arms across his chest and leaned back in his chair. Not hostile, not exactly. But definitely not inviting. Three days earlier, when Nick had called to arrange the meeting, Pontson had been friendly and encouraging. "Young officer with your training and background? We'll find something to suit."

Unlike the large private military companies such as Constellis, Severus, and Falken, with their hundreds, perhaps thousands, of contractors and armies of lawyers and lobbyists, Pontson worked alone. He represented single individuals: ex-intelligence officers, engineers, scientists, and military specialists who, for one reason or another, preferred not to sign on with the better-known players.

Stocky and blunt-spoken, Pontson appeared to be doing well. He was wearing a tailored tan suit and he'd gained weight, yet despite the increased bulk looked healthy and fit. His office, new since they'd last met, took up a corner of the nineteenth floor of the Branson Building. Expensive afghan rugs lay over polished hardwood floors. The large oak conference table was covered with journals and trade magazines devoted to military and political news. Black-and-white photos of World War

II–era tanks, ships, and aircraft decorated the walls. A workstation with an array of sophisticated computer hardware covered an entire wall. The huge window behind his desk provided a spectacular view of the Thames; three of London's bridges were visible in the distance.

"You're saying there's no work available?" Nick said. He knew the answer but wanted the reason for the change in Pontson's attitude.

"Not for you. Considering your situation I'd be a bloody fool to take you on. Frankly I'm a bit miffed you didn't bother to mention it."

"Mention it? What are you talking about?"

"Come now. The little matter of your desertion, of course."

"Desertion!"

Pontson studied Nick's stunned expression with a curious frown. "Don't tell me you didn't know? After your call I did some checking. You're listed."

"It has to be a mistake. I resigned. I've been on terminal leave since I left Kabul." Nick fished two slim papers from his wallet and tossed them across the desk. "Here. My orders."

Pontson picked up the orders but made no effort to read them. "The missives say you deserted rather than face a court-martial. Refusal to obey an order during a live-fire engagement in which a number of men were killed."

Nick mouth tightened. "That's not how it was."

"The event happened."

"It did. But I never refused an order. Not a lawful one. I was the only legitimate US Army officer present. As for a court-martial, an open hearing is the last thing they want."

"You're saying it's a setup?" Pontson appeared to relax, as if an unspoken question had just been answered. "It does explain some things."

"What things? Where'd you hear I was wanted for desertion?"

"Sources. Dedicated sites. Nothing out on the net yet. Smelled a bit fishy, I admit. Too shaded, if you know what I mean. Frankly I'd like to believe you. You always seemed a levelheaded sort. Honest. Maybe too honest?"

Pontson gave Nick's orders a quick glance, then handed them back. "Easy enough to forge, of course. Proves nothing. I thought you said you were in Special Operations. Those were issued by someone in intelligence."

Nick started to reply, then realized he'd never studied the orders closely. There'd been no reason. It had all been worked out in Admin the day before. Pontson was right about the issuing authority: 24th Army Intelligence. The authorizing signature was unreadable; the name printed underneath was a light colonel he'd never heard of, LTC A. Bestair.

"We were transferred out of Spec Ops the minute we got back to base," he said, his mind racing. He searched his memory, trying to recall the sequence of events. "We never knew what our new command was. We'd been ordered to keep quiet, not ask questions. My team—what was left of it—was broken up, reassigned out of the country. I was told if I pursued the matter I could kiss my career good-bye."

"They wanted the incident hushed up."

"That was made very clear."

"So you resigned."

"I didn't see any other option. My commitment was up. An Army major I didn't know, Harriman or something, showed up at the BOQ with the orders." Nick held up the papers in his hand. "These orders."

"Hardly protocol, I would imagine."

"Hardly."

"And you didn't think that a bit odd?"

"At the time, no. I figured they were just happy to get rid of me."

Nick grimaced at his own naïveté. He should have been more skeptical. On some instinctive level, he'd known it wouldn't be that easy, that his resignation wouldn't end it. After he'd received the orders, the sense of threat had only grown stronger. It was the main reason he'd ignored the Space-A flight he'd been scheduled to take and hopped that convoy to Peshawar. He'd also wanted to be rid of the military. The sense of betrayal was too great.

But why the charade? The false orders, the charge of desertion? As he'd said to Pontson, the last thing they'd want was an open court-martial. If he were that big a threat, it would be easier just to take him out and shoot him. Blame it on the Taliban.

Of course that would have meant its own investigation. If they wanted him dead, better to do it off base. Somewhere outside the country—

His thoughts came to a sudden screeching halt.

Flights left Bagram every day, most with destinations closer to the US than Greece. Why had the major been so insistent that he be on that particular flight? Nick wondered if he were paranoid. But suddenly he was certain of it. Someone had been waiting in Thessaloniki to kill him. Only after he'd failed to arrive there had they bothered to charge him with desertion. They might as well have painted a target on his back.

But why? Why him? A junior officer—amend that. An ex–junior officer. What possible threat was he to anyone?

"All sorts come to me these days," Pontson was saying. "Ex-cops, bully boys, legitimate soldiers, and intel types. Even the occasional romantic, imagining themselves Beau Geste joining a Foreign Legion that exists only in their fantasies. The world being what it is today, if they're healthy and have some training I can usually place them. The difficulty here is that, while I'm inclined to believe you, I simply can't risk taking you on. Nearly all of my business these days involves the Americans."

He paused. "You do understand what I'm saying."

Nick nodded. "You can't upset your main client by taking on an accused deserter."

"I feel bad about it. Really. But for me it's not a matter of right or wrong. It's just business."

"I understand."

"Truth be told, I don't believe it would be in your best interest in any case. The minute you sign your name to a contract, someone, somewhere will know about it. Might as well send them an e-mail telling them where you are."

Nick nodded again. He'd been thinking the same thing.

Pontson lifted his bulk out of his chair and held out his hand. "You've my sympathies, Lieutenant. If you can take a bit of advice, I recommend you stay low to the ground for a while, let the thing die down. Then find an ombudsman, one you can trust. If you need money, which I assume you do or you wouldn't have come to me, I strongly suggest you peruse the want ads. There'll be work, though it may not be the sort you're used to."

He emphasized this last by an increase in pressure as Nick took his hand, as if the advice about the want ads was somehow more meaningful than it sounded.

Nick turned and walked out. The secretary barely acknowledged him as he walked past her desk to an open elevator. A man and a woman, both carrying briefcases, called out for him to hold the door.

He ignored them. The door closed with a pneumatic shush and he was alone.

He felt trapped, as if forces unseen were already closing in. Pontson seemed straight enough, but he wouldn't win any favors with his main client by not reporting the contact. There was a good chance he was already on the phone.

Why that useless advice about the want ads? He was in the country illegally. No visa, no work permit. As in most countries, there would be an underground labor market, but it was unlikely to be advertised. Maybe Billy could help him.

CHAPTER
5

NICK DROVE AIMLESSLY, collecting his thoughts. He saw a small park and pulled over. Leaving Isabel at the curb, he navigated through the nannies, prams, and joggers toward an unoccupied bench near a stone fountain. Dark clouds were building in the east. A storm, announced earlier by the BBC, was expected later that evening.

As he was about to take his seat, a passerby bumped into him, breaking his thoughts.

"Watch it!" he barked, needing to vent on someone.

The man disappeared into the crowd before Nick could make out his face. Slightly taller than average, grey woolen greatcoat, floppy grey hat. A newspaper, probably dropped during the collision, lay on the sidewalk. Nick picked it up.

The Times of London, today's date, folded in thirds, as though ready for a newsboy to deliver. He started to toss it in a nearby trash receptacle when something caught his eye. The employment section had been folded to the outside. One ad was circled in red ink:

TRAVEL & ADVENTURE

WANTED: Man, 20s to early 30s. Brave, honorable, in good health/condition, skilled in martial arts, particularly swordsmanship. Time of service TBD. Excellent pay and benefits. Contact S., Langton Manor, Langton Vale, by midnight Oct 31.

Nick looked around, half expecting to find someone filming him, their idea of a joke. But no one in the sea of humanity flowing through the park appeared to be the least interested, not in him nor the newspaper in his hand.

He read the ad again, then a third time. A prank. Had to be.

Irritated at himself for half believing, he again started to throw the paper away. Then, almost as an afterthought, he stuffed it under his cardigan.

CHAPTER
6

THE SUN HAD SET by the time Nick arrived back at Winford Manor. He left Isabel in the carriage house and went in through the servants' entrance. Meg was waiting below the stairs. "There you are, Lieutenant. Been wondering when you'd get back. Billy said to tell you he's out. Went off with Elyse. They should be back soon. He's a bit worried about you, you know."

"I know. I've got it sorted out, though."

Nick had a strange fondness for the old termagant, which surprised everyone, especially Billy. She spoke her mind right enough but beneath it all she had a warm heart. The truth was he found himself often agreeing with her sensibilities, however harshly expressed.

"I've a pot o' tea on."

Meg's room was really a suite, with its own bathroom and adjacent parlor. During his year at Oxford he'd often taken tea with her. She seemed to enjoy his company, regaling him with stories of living in London with "the major," her late husband, who'd lost an arm fighting in the Falklands. Nick had listened more than he'd talked, which was the reason, or so he guessed, that he was the one living person Meg had never spoken a harsh word to or about. That and the fact he reminded her of her husband, or so she'd said.

Clearly she hoped to talk now, while Nick wanted nothing more than to lie back in a warm bath and put all thoughts from his mind. "I had some fish and chips at a Harry Ramsden's on the way back," he said. "Later, perhaps."

"I'll keep the kettle warm. You've that look the major used to get when he was troubled. Sometimes it does good to talk things out. We close ourselves in, can't see the forest for the trees."

Had Billy broken his promise and said something? Not likely. More likely it was just him, ex-Lieutenant Nick Herron, wearing his trouble on his sleeve. He would have to watch that. No good involving others. He would work it out on his own.

Safe in his own room, he shed his shoes and began a series of martial art forms. He'd spent a summer in China after graduating from the Point, studying Yin Style Bagua with Grand Master He Jinbao. The workout had become a habit, almost an addiction, but in past weeks he'd been neglecting it. By the time he'd finished he was damp with sweat and breathing heavily.

Half an hour and sweating. He couldn't allow himself to go that slack again. He turned on the bathwater and did another ten minutes of Phoenix as he waited for the tub to fill, concentrating on the movement, stilling his thoughts as the form required.

He was interrupted by a knock. "Nick?"

"Come on in, Billy."

Billy entered, accompanied by a young woman. At first glance she didn't look over twenty. Petite, not over five two, with pretty features and flaxen curls. Her blue eyes were made larger by thick, horn-rimmed glasses. She wore a long, flowing print dress and sandals. Nick could easily imagine her with a garland of daisies in her hair.

Elyse, he decided. Maker of the remarkable headache pills.

Billy introduced them. He was smitten, Nick saw immediately. Well, good for him. It was about time.

"Had a pint and some chips at the Flying Dutchman," Billy said. "Walked the entire way." There was a note of pride in his voice.

"Walked? That's two miles!"

"Closer to three, actually. Elyse has been working on my leg. Getting around much better these days."

"Most of the problem wasn't the disease," Elyse broke in, with appealing earnestness. "It was compensations, the result of the disease. We've been releasing the contractions, strengthening the muscles. He's doing quite well."

She put her hand on Billy's arm. The movement was both prideful and affectionate, so subtly endearing that Nick felt a sudden rush of envy.

"I was about to take a bath."

"Oh, don't mind me. I grew up with four brothers. I'm off anyway. Women's group tonight I've got to manage. Pleased to meet you, Lieutenant Herron. Billy speaks very highly of you."

Her English was upper class with just the feathery hint of a dialect that Nick, who was good with languages, was unable to place. Not Irish. Northern Scotland, perhaps. Well educated, he guessed, older than she appeared. Twenty-three or twenty-four.

"Just Nick, please," he said.

"Nick, then. Good evening, Nick."

She turned back to Billy, standing on her toes so she could kiss him on the cheek. "Take a hot bath tonight with your salts. You did well today."

After she left Billy closed the door. "She asked to meet you," he said somewhat sheepishly. "She approved, though for the life of me I can't understand why."

"You could tell?"

"She's very open with her feelings. She'd let me know if you weren't right. She's quite intuitive."

"She's also very pretty."

Billy seemed pleased. "You think so?"

"Very. In a feyish, hippie, creature of the forest kind of way."

Billy laughed. "Certainly different than the society types my neighbors keep trying to set me up with." He glanced at the closed door. "I'm quite fond of her, you know."

Coming from Billy, the statement was a declaration of undying love. "How long have you known her?" Nick asked.

Billy pulled out a chair and sat down, stretching out his bad leg. "She answered my posting about six months ago. First time we met, she took one look at my leg and said, 'I can fix that.' I took her for one of those New Age twinkie people. Made me a bit angry, actually. I'd had my fill of therapies, you know. Lots of promises but nothing helped. But she worked on it, certain movements, a massage sort of thing she does. Gave me herbs, some exercises, makes sure I walk on it. Weight into the hips, feet flat on the ground."

He lifted the leg and dropped it again. "Bit played out now, I'm afraid. How was London?"

"Interesting."

"Interesting interesting? Or interesting like the Chinese curse?"

"More like the Chinese curse." Nick slumped back on the bed. "Billy, I'm, uh—I'm in some trouble."

"No work?"

"No." He hesitated, wondering how much he should say. "I'm leaving in the morning."

Billy had been kneading his leg. He looked up in dismay. "Morning? I'd rather hoped you'd be around a bit longer. I could use help with this Leonidas thing. Not quite sure how to go about it. If it's money?" He let the question hang.

"No. It's not money. Not just money. I learned something in London. It's best you not know. It could spill over."

Billy nodded as though not surprised. "I didn't mention it last night. You needed to talk. But I did feel you were being a bit simple about the whole thing. They wouldn't let you just go like that, resign your commission and walk off—unattended, as it were."

Once again Nick was surprised by his friend's keen intelligence. "The leave was phony," he said. "A setup. I've been declared a deserter. Not publicly, thankfully. Not yet. They'll want to keep it low-key."

"Makes sense. They would need to discredit you first. You will let me help? I'm not exactly without resources, you know."

Something in the way Billy said that last, the confidence, the absolute certainty, made Nick pause. Billy had changed since they'd last been together, and it wasn't just the improvement in his financial situation or the apparent healing with his leg. Nick had been so absorbed by his own problems he hadn't taken time to appreciate it.

The previous year, Billy had published *Asymmetrical Warfare in the 21st Century*. While it had sold barely enough copies to pay publishing costs, the book had earned him a respectable reputation in certain quarters, along with several consulting contracts. Billy never said who the clients were and Nick hadn't asked. But how many agencies and actors were there in the world interested enough in Billy's area of expertise to pay him good money for advice?

"I want you to promise me you'll forget I was ever here," Nick said.

"Pish. I won't do any such thing."

"Billy, these people—"

"Sorry. One for all and so forth. No use arguing."

Nick gave up. "All right. You asked for it. I'm relieved of all responsibility." But even as he spoke, he knew the words were a lie. Instinct told him he had put his friend at risk the moment he'd shown up at Winford Manor.

He told Billy the story of what had happened in Afghanistan, this time leaving nothing out. "Interesting," said Billy when he'd finished. "These contractors? CIA?"

"Not a clue. But I wouldn't be surprised. I kept asking who sent them, what their authority was. I was told my security clearance wasn't high enough. Had to be somebody high up, though, to suborn the chain of command like that."

"And no answer why they wanted those Kashmiri boys so badly."

"None."

Nick left Billy sitting thoughtfully on the bed while he went to take his nearly forgotten bath. He freshened it with hot water, but it remained lukewarm at best and he didn't stay long in the tub. He was getting out when Billy pushed into the room, the *Times* Nick had found in London in his right hand. "What's this about?"

"The newspaper?"

"It was on the floor. You circled an ad."

"I found it on the sidewalk. The ad was already circled."

"Really? You called, of course."

"No. Didn't bother. Must be a joke. Besides, look at it. No phone number. And the date? That's tonight. I don't even know where Langton Vale is."

"Two-hour drive north. Some sort of ancient battlefield thereabouts. Bit of a mystery. Wouldn't mind visiting the place myself." Billy looked at his watch. "Not yet seven. Plenty of time."

"You're not suggesting we go there? Now? There's a storm coming."

"Worth a try, don't you think? If nothing else it will get us out of the house."

"Billy—"

"No use arguing. Get dressed. After all, what do you have to lose?"

CHAPTER

7

NICK APPRECIATED BILLY'S AFFECTION for Isabel. The ancient Jaguar was as much a work of art as a machine. Her leather upholstery and burled walnut trim had been rubbed and polished so many times during her sixty-some years in the world they seemed to exude a warm glow. She cruised along at a stately sixty miles an hour, the sound of her 210-horsepower, straight-six aluminum-head engine little more than a soothing whisper.

With the traffic and some wrong turns, the drive took an hour longer than Billy had predicted. The hands on Isabel's clock read 10:47 when Billy finally spotted a sign, its faded letters barely legible even in the glare of Isabel's powerful headlamps:

Langton Vale
3 miles

"We'll make it," Billy said cheerfully. "We still have more than an hour."

Nick slumped back in his seat. He'd tried to catch some sleep during the long drive, but a growing and unaccountable apprehension was keeping him awake. The closer they came to Langton Vale, the more apprehensive he became. He tried to dismiss it as a general concern about his future, to no avail.

"You must admit the coincidence is intriguing," said Billy. "Finding the newspaper when you did. Particularly after that fellow Pontson's remark about looking in the want ads." He slapped Nick on the leg. "Come on. Full alert now."

Nick scowled. "I should never have let you talk me into this."

The night seemed to agree with his darkening mood. A full moon rose over the trees, its pale light in stark contrast to the black clouds of the fast-approaching storm. Clusters of houses began to appear, many with the half-timbered construction of an England two hundred years gone. Sporadic lightning flashes added to a sense of the unreal. A ground mist formed in the woods, flowing over the hedges and fields that bordered the road.

They hadn't seen another car since leaving the main highway. The sign at a two-pump Esso station was lit and Billy pulled in. "Luck to find a station open this late, " he commented. "Especially tonight."

"We out of gas?"

"She's still got a quarter but we might need it later. She's a grand old dame, but hardly a cure for global warming. Besides, we could use some directions."

The night was surprisingly warm and almost humid. An attendant emerged from the station and approached. He fit the quaint character of the village itself, dressed in knickers and shapeless wool.

"Petrol?" said Billy.

"We have that," the man muttered gruffly as Billy got out to stretch his leg. "How much ye be needing?"

"Whatever she'll take."

"A she, is she?" The attendant eyed Isabel appreciatively as he primed the pump.

"Good luck for us to find you open this late."

"Always open Samhain night, leastways till the women finish their doings. Sunrise, usually."

"Samhain?" Nick was just getting out on the Jaguar's far side.

"Halloween," supplied Billy. "Leastways its precursor. Full moon tonight. Some unusual astrological alignments this year. Elyse has got the others, Meg and Maeve, Rachel, Alice even, involved. They're doing some ritual thing back at the house."

Nick looked at Billy in disbelief. "Are you serious? It's Halloween night and you didn't bother to tell me!"

"I thought you knew, what with all the commotion around it."

Nick wasn't listening. "So that's what this is about? A ruse to get me out of the house so your boarders can chant at the moon?" Another thought occurred to him. "The ad. It's a Halloween prank!"

"Nonsense," said Billy, unperturbed. "I didn't plant that ad. The fact it's Samhain night should be irrelevant."

"Irrelevant!" Nick was at a loss. It was the girl. Billy had always been so logical, so sensible. Any other time and he might have said the change was for the better.

"Is there a Langton Manor around here?" he asked, turning to the attendant, half hoping the answer would be a negative and that would end it.

Instead the man nodded. "Aye. Two miles up the road. Can't miss it. Lies atop Battle Hill, it does. Gate to the property's locked when no one's about."

"No one's there?"

"Gerlach, the caretaker, disappeared July last. Some say with the family silver. Others not so sure. Me wife, for one. She's other ideas I won't repeat."

Nick shot Billy a look that said, "I told you so."

"Someone's there now, though," the attendant went on, seemingly contradicting himself. "Lights and such. Been seen walking odd hours about the downs. Wife says the squire's back."

Nick stood, trying to balance his emotions, the apprehension he'd experienced earlier mitigated by something approaching relief.

The attendant put the nozzle back on the pump. "Sixty-two quid, even."

Billy removed his wallet. "You're wife's in a coven?"

"Aye. She's Mistress," replied the attendant, taking the money. "We've a cottage adjunct Notting Wood. Druid stones there they use. And the woods themselves, of course. Good night to ye." The man touched a finger to his hat and disappeared back in the station.

"Coven?" Nick shook his head.

"Old Religion's common enough in these country villages," said Billy. "We'd better be on. Midnight's not far off."

The macadam road changed to cobbles as they entered the village proper. The shops were quaint and well kept. Neatly painted signs announced The Green Man Boutique, Wild Hunt Antiques, and Battle

Hill Crystals and Potions. Nick imagined that in daylight it would be charming and picturesque, a place for a weekend escape from frenetic city life. At night, this night at least, it seemed oppressive and medieval, with only an occasional street lamp lighting the way. Mist drifting in from the forest hung low to the road, curling up stairways and lampposts. Shadows prowled in the narrow alleyways.

They slowed as they passed the only building in town that was brightly lit. A wooden sign in front depicted a lion and unicorn, rampant. "Local pub," said Billy, stating the obvious.

The Lion and Unicorn. Nick found the name unsettling, though he was uncertain why. Through the pub's leaded windows, patrons could be seen crowded against a long bar, pints in hand. No women that he could see. Probably out in the forest, he thought cynically, dancing naked and throwing runes.

The road reverted back to a pale macadam as they passed beyond the center of town. A low round hill loomed to their left, separated from the road by a wide meadow. Atop the hill, silhouetted against the rising moon, stood a large and forbidding mansion, circled by a high stone wall.

It was another mile before they found the entrance. The iron gate stood open. The driveway beyond was lined on both sides with great shaggy oaks. A gust of wind, smelling of fall harvest and the threatening rain, filled his senses as Nick lowered his window for a better view.

"Gate's open," said Billy, again stating the obvious. For the first time that night he sounded uncertain.

Nick glanced at his watch. The luminescent hands read eleven minutes past eleven. The clock on Isabel's dash read exactly the same, 11:11. The second hand seemed to slow as it made its way around the dial.

The drive was narrow, built for an earlier time. Weeds, a foot high in places, clogged the cracks between the paving stones.

"No one's been up this in months," muttered Nick.

Billy shrugged. "Maybe there's another way."

Lightning brightened the sky, followed seconds later by the rumble of thunder. After the eerie silence, Nick found the sound oddly comforting.

The driveway continued its roundabout way for another quarter mile before coming to an abrupt end in a circular courtyard. The house loomed above, its gables and stone walls covered with dead and dying ivy and the patina of centuries.

Billy left the motor running and headlights on as they got out of the Jaguar. A gust of wind blew through the trees, causing leaves to drop.

"Spooky old place," said Billy as they approached the front door.

Nick thought he saw movement in an upstairs window. Probably nothing more than a curtain blowing in a draft. The light from Isabel's headlamps spilled sideways across the doorway, highlighting a large brass knocker forged in the shape of a lion's head.

Billy raised the knocker. "Wouldn't want to wake anybody." He hesitated, then said, "What the hell. Nothing ventured, nothing gained, as Elyse is fond of saying."

He let the knocker drop. A dull boom echoed inside as it landed on the strike plate.

Seconds passed. The wind was growing stronger. Nick was about to say something when there was a sound off to the right. Someone was approaching.

A voice came out of the gloom. "May I help you?"

Billy did a half turn in surprise, almost colliding with Nick.

A figure stood in the shadow of a nearby hedge. It was difficult to make out features: medium height, dark greatcoat, floppy hat of equally indeterminate color.

"I didn't mean to startle you," said the apparition. "I was out walking and saw the lights of your car. You're here about the notice, I presume?"

The figure moved closer, still hidden in darkness.

"Yes. The notice," said Billy, recovering quickly. "It's legitimate, then?"

"Quite legitimate, I assure you. I'm around the side. Cook's apartment. Follow me, please. Quickly, now. There isn't much time."

Without looking back to see if they followed, the figure vanished.

"Extraordinary," said Billy. "What do you make of that?"

Nick didn't answer. That enigmatic dread that had grown in him while nearing the village had returned with a vengeance. The feeling was so strong it took an effort of will not to grab Billy and bolt to the car.

Vexed with himself, he took a deep breath and shrugged. "Nothing ventured, nothing gained."

"Right," said Billy. "My thought exactly. Hold a minute, would you."

Billy returned to Isabel, switching off her engine and headlamps and pocketing the key. He returned brandishing a small flashlight taken from the glove box. "Ready."

A large drop of rain splattered the paving stones, then more and more. The long-expected storm had arrived.

CHAPTER
8

NICK FOUND HIMSELF in a curious state of heightened awareness. Sounds seemed louder, shadows darker, movement more precise and intentional. He felt as if the trees themselves were aware of his presence. And over it all a sense of immediacy he'd known only in that moment before battle. But this was no battle. In truth, the situation was so foreign to his experience he had no framework for comparison.

Imagination, he decided. The atmosphere was creepy enough to give goose bumps to a gravedigger.

A jagged fork of lightning lit up the sky, followed by sharp, crackling thunder. Rain clattered against the gutters three stories up and poured down on the paving stones. Billy led with the flashlight, following the path their host had taken, past stilled fountains, yews that hadn't been pruned in decades, and gardens gone to seed. By the time they rounded the corner of the house their coats were drenched.

Their host, outlined in a narrow lit doorway, waved to them. "Come inside. Put your coats on the rack there by the fire."

They were ushered into the warmth of a small but comfortable drawing room. A sofa and two overstuffed chairs circled a small stone fireplace. The room was lit by oil lamps. A grandfather clock in the corner chimed the half hour: 11:30. As their host shed coat and soggy hat, a shock of grey hair fell to her shoulders.

"I say," said Billy. "You're a woman!"

"Of course I am. Have been my entire life. I am Sianiave Langton, current squire of Langton Manor. Squiress, if you prefer. I placed the notice that brought you here. There's a teapot on the stove in the kitchen. Who is the applicant?"

"Applicant?"

"For the post. I believe the notice indicated one man. Singular. Which of you is it?"

Billy dropped the flashlight in a pocket of his coat and hung it up. "It's Nick, my friend here. I'm just along for the ride."

"Fair enough. Kitchen's through that door. Be a good fellow and brew up some tea while your friend and I talk, would you. China Keemun is all I can offer, I'm afraid." As she spoke, the woman began hustling Billy towards the nearest of two doors that led further into the house.

"Hold on a minute!" Without thinking, Nick grabbed the woman's arm and was surprised to find it as well muscled as that of a conditioned young athlete. She looked at his hand, not in annoyance, but as though amazed he'd had the temerity to touch her.

Apologetic, he released his grip. "Sorry. But before anyone goes anywhere I'd like to know what this is about."

"Impossible. There are aspects to the work that can't be discussed with anyone but the applicant."

"It's all right," said Billy quickly. He regarded the woman for a moment, then nodded. "You won't find better than him, you know."

She smiled kindly, with no hint of irony. "I suspect you're right."

Then, as though having said too much, she swept an oil lamp off a side table and shoved it into Billy's hands. "Take this. Electricity has been off. There's food in the icebox, cheese and crackers. Help yourself. I know I'm being short, but there really isn't much time.

"One caution," she added. "Stay in the kitchen. Under no circumstances are you to enter the main house. It's not—" She hesitated, searching for a word. "Safe."

"Right. Kitchen only."

Billy left, the door closing behind him. Nick faced the woman. "All right. You've got my attention."

"Please be seated. I have several questions for you."

Her tone, not demanding exactly nor rude, was of someone confident and used to being in charge.

He tried to profile her and came up blank. Her grey hair, full and straight, was simply arranged. She wore little if any makeup. A gold earring with a single blue stone hung from her right ear. Three large rings on her elegant fingers, one on her left hand and two on her right, were each set with a different stone: yellow, red, and green. Expensive leather boots, simple white cotton blouse, khaki slacks that could have come from any high-end shop in the world. Her English was so free of accent it was almost an accent in itself. Judging by the fine wrinkles around her eyes, he guessed she was in her sixties or seventies, though in the right light she might pass for younger. Perhaps much younger, if judged by the easy way she moved and the surprising strength he'd felt in her arm. Her nose was slightly crooked, as if broken and never set right, and there was a small scar to the left of her chin. Her eyes were a startling shade of emerald green. Other than a glint of sharp intelligence, they gave little away. One thing was clear. Here was a woman to be reckoned with.

He sat on the nearest sofa. The woman took a chair across from the fire, facing him. She removed a long-stemmed clay pipe from a wooden box on the coffee table and began packing it with tobacco of a type he'd never seen, grey shreds like desert sage. "Your name?" she asked.

"Nick Herron. Are you really a Langton? See-ahn-ah—?" He stumbled over the pronunciation.

"Correct, Sianiave. And yes, I am really a Langton, the last Langton actually. As for the work, it's exactly what the notice indicated. Since you've taken the trouble to answer it, I presume you meet the requirements?"

"They seem fairly straightforward."

"Your skill with a sword?"

"I was captain of both the fencing and archery teams at West Point, and I've studied aikido, bagua, and kendo since I was a child. Not that I—"

"West Point?" she said, interrupting. "An officer then? What rank?"

"Lieutenant, recently resigned."

"Your age?" She had irritating way of asking questions, abrupt almost to the point of rudeness.

"Twenty-six, more or less."

"More or less?"

"I was raised by foster parents. No one knows who my biological parents were. Or the exact date of my birth."

"An orphan. How intriguing. Well, Lieutenant Herron—or would you prefer I call you Mr. Herron?"

"Nick's fine."

"Nick, then. Isn't twenty-six a bit old to still be a lieutenant? One would assume a West Point man with any capacity at all would have risen to at least captain by now. Did you enter university late?"

"I was in Special Ops. Rank doesn't come easy."

"Of course."

The look of amusement on the woman's face indicated she understood exactly, or didn't believe a word of it.

A small flame seemed to sprout from a finger as she lit the pipe. Nick couldn't see a lighter. A match, probably, hidden in her hand. Neat trick. She took a puff and let it out. The smoke was grey but definitely not tobacco. Not sage or marijuana either. It had a pleasing, meadowy scent, nothing he recognized.

"One more question," she said. "Then it's your turn."

He braced for the question he knew must be coming, unsure how to answer. He couldn't tell her the truth, that he was a wanted man, wanted for desertion, even if it was a lie. Yet for some reason, lying to her was unthinkable.

The Squiress of Langton took another puff on the pipe and leaned back in her chair. As she exhaled, the smoke formed into shifting threads, like strands of DNA, that curled to the ceiling. Her fathomless green eyes caught and held his. The connection was almost physical.

"Have you, Lieutenant Nicholas Herron, ever asked yourself what compelled you to engage in such anachronistic martial pursuits as archery and fencing?"

The question was so oddly phrased, so different from what he'd expected, that for a moment Nick sat speechless.

§

Billy stood mesmerized both by the size of the kitchen and what it contained. Despite the flickering light cast from his lamp, much of the room was lost in shadow.

It was as if he'd entered a museum exhibit or wandered onto a movie set. The appliances were older than those at Winford Manor. The icebox was truly that, not just a figure of the old woman's speech, the sort in which a block of ice in a lower compartment kept the food cold. The gas range was a twelve-burner dinosaur, its center griddle massive enough for a large restaurant. Two ovens, each sufficient to provide for a small bakery, sat on either side. Utensils and copper pots hung overhead. Four large porcelain sinks and a huge woodblock cutting table faced a wall of cabinets with enough china to serve hundreds.

The squires of Langton had done some entertaining in their day, he thought.

He tried to place the mansion's current owner—if indeed she was the owner—in this context. If truly a Langton, she was undoubtedly the keeper of a great family's history, and its secrets. No great house was complete without its secrets.

His own family, the Winfords, had once been well-regarded members of the aristocracy. He prided himself on his knowledge of British history, military history in particular, which among the English was inseparable from the whole. But about the Langtons he knew little. A Stephen Langton had been advisor to one of the early kings. He couldn't recall which. Who were they? How had they gained their fortune? How had they come to build their manor on Battle Hill? And why did it appear the house hadn't been lived in for at least a hundred years?

An ancient battle had taken place nearby, reputedly on this very hill. The particulars were vague. Fourth or fifth century, Rome in decline. The period when the first tales of King Arthur emerged. Arthur, who in all probability had been a local patrician or tribal chieftain. Perhaps even Carodoc. Yet there was no mention of Arthur in tales associated with this particular battle. Nor of Romans, for that matter. Artifacts uncovered at the site were thought by most scholars to be of Celtic origin, though unique in design and workmanship.

In the late 1920s, a young German archaeologist named Pitr Dietrich claimed to have unearthed a magnificent sword in the area. Wrought of finely folded steel, the sword was still in relatively good condition. At the time, steel of any quality was assumed to be unknown to the Celts, much less steel that had managed to keep its integrity after being buried for fifteen hundred years. The archaeological establishment immediately labeled it a fake. Salted, in all likelihood. Suspicion fell on Dietrich, whose budding career came to an abrupt and humiliating end. Those same authorities dismissed the battle site as insignificant, a minor incursion by Norsemen, though in those days Viking raiders tended to stay nearer the coast.

Billy was convinced the battle was of more importance than those long-dead academics had realized. The actors and outcome might remain a mystery, but the effects had been lasting. Over the years, dozens more artifacts had been discovered, from brass spear tips to tarnished ax heads, turned up by local farmers tilling their land or children playing in the fields. Yet no skeletal remains had been discovered. Burned, perhaps? Or taken elsewhere for burial?

The Battle of Langton Vale was one of those queer historic anomalies reputable archaeologists avoided, much like Grail research or tales of Atlantis. "Career enders," they were called. Sir John Bingham had mounted the only serious excavation, in 1939. That ended with the outbreak of World War II and Sir John's untimely death a few months later.

Nothing since. A lost page in history.

"Intriguing," murmured Billy. "Very intriguing."

He set his lamp on the prep table. A copper teapot, half-filled with water, sat on the stove as Sianiave had said. It was one of the few pieces in the kitchen recently used. A tin of tea was on the counter along with teaspoons, a sugar bowl, slices of lemon, a box of matches, and three porcelain teacups and saucers.

Three? Almost as if she'd been expecting them.

He glanced at his watch: 11:44. Sixteen minutes to midnight. She seemed to be in a hurry. Why? The possibility others might arrive in answer to the notice was of small concern. Nick would be the best man for the job, he knew. Even if Nick didn't know this himself. But best for what, exactly? What was the job?

The Lady Langton was a presence, that was certain. Once she'd introduced herself, Billy had lost all doubt about her authenticity. He was relieved more than he cared to admit. It troubled him to see his friend in distress.

Answering the newspaper ad had been an excuse to get Nick alone for a few hours, to discuss possible courses of action. A loan, perhaps. Nick would refuse an outright gift. He could use some of the connections he'd made the past year, try to find out who was behind the desertion setup. The ad had seemed little more than a flight of fancy, though Elyse had pounced on it immediately as something to follow through on.

The thought of Elyse brought a smile to his face. Her openness to the unexpected, her faith in the extraordinary. She wouldn't question any of this. Not at all. She had a remarkable intuition about people. He wondered what she'd make of Sianiave Langton.

See-ahn-ah-vee. Celtic-sounding. Undoubtedly a great beauty in her youth and still a fine-looking woman. He'd immediately known he could trust her. It was the same feeling he'd had when he'd first met Nick. A solidness, an authenticity. He couldn't explain it, even to himself. He felt no need to try.

He lit a stove burner with a match. A five-gallon tank stood on the floor nearby with a line jerry-rigged to the stove's backside. No electricity, bottled gas. According to the man at the petrol, the mansion's caretaker had vanished some time ago under suspicious circumstances. Ms. Langton, it seemed, had not been long in residence.

His eyes were getting used to the dim light. While he waited for the water to boil, he wandered about, opening drawers, peering into cabinets. There was little enough in the icebox: a bag of ice, a block of cheddar, a loaf of bread, milk, a few other odds and ends including a half-eaten roasted chicken in a plastic take-out tray.

Was the job something to do with the house? Reclaiming the estate from dysfunctional relatives? Tracking down the caretaker who allegedly had purloined the family silver? Judging by the stash still in the drawers, he hadn't gotten away with much. Why was the ability to use a sword a requirement?

Billy put a single tea bag in each cup along with slices of lemon. The water was taking its time to boil.

Two large swinging doors on the far side of the room appeared to move, as though touched by a draft. Probably led into the main house. Couldn't hurt to look, he thought. Don't have to go in, just a peek.

Billy pushed open one of the doors just far enough to see into the hallway beyond. It was as dark as a cave. At first he had no desire to enter. Then a flash of lightning lit up the hall as if it were daylight.

"My lord!"

He stood transfixed. The flash had shown the hall to be exceptionally long, with a high, beamed ceiling and many doorways. The floor was a chessboard pattern of black and white marble. But the walls captured his attention. Wondrous things were mounted there: swords, shields, battle-axes, spears, and pikes, weapon designs he'd never before seen. They filled the hallway from one end to another, like a museum gallery.

Forgetting both the water boiling on the stove and his promise not to leave the kitchen, he almost stumbled in his excitement as he snatched up the lamp.

CHAPTER 9

"*WHAT COMPELLED YOU* to engage in such anachronistic martial pursuits as archery and fencing?"

Nick stared at the woman, struggling to hide his emotions. Why he reacted so strongly to this question, he had no idea. The moment she'd asked it, his heart had constricted into a cold ball, and a strange, almost painful throbbing gripped his head. The previous questions had been tailored to lead him along a certain line of thought, a technique straight from the pages of a military interrogation manual. Tease the subject with obvious questions. Then, when they least expect it, hit them with the kicker. Knock them off balance. Let them think you know far more than you really do, all the answers.

What answers? What was there to know?

Nick took a breath. The throbbing subsided. Without waiting for an answer, the woman took a puff on her pipe, her green eyes cool and appraising. "Your turn," she said.

The storm increased in fury, the lightning and thunder incessant. Buffeted by the wind, the rain sounded like a drum tattoo against the window. A loud crack echoed as a falling branch struck the house. Sianiave's eyes went to the clock. 11: 49. Eleven minutes to midnight.

Nick cleared his throat. "This job?"

"Bodyguard, of a sort. I've always admired a man who can use a sword well. It shows a certain strength of character."

"Is it you?"

"Excuse me?"

"Are you the principal? The body I'm to guard?"

"Heavens, no." She smiled as though the thought was absurd. "I'm just an agent. It's a woman, though. A girl, really."

"Is she coming here? You've been watching the clock."

"No. She's not in England. And I am concerned about time, very much so. We must be on our way shortly or we'll miss the, er, rendezvous. Therefore, since you appear to have the necessary qualifications, you have the job. You begin immediately."

"Hold it. I haven't said I'll take it. For one thing, what's the pay?"

"Pay? Of course. Five hundred a month, six-month contract. If the job ends sooner, you will be paid for the full six months. In the unlikely event it takes longer, all parties will be free to renegotiate."

"Five hundred what? Dollars? Pounds? Euro? That's not enough to—"

From somewhere she materialized a coin and flipped it to him. "Of these. Coin of the realm. I'm unsure of the current exchange rate, but whatever it is, I trust it will be sufficient."

Nick caught the coin and was surprised by its weight. It was crudely minted, but he had little doubt it was gold. Very fine gold. It reminded him of a doubloon, the engravings struck with hammer and die.

"That's crazy," he murmured, calculating the value of five hundred such coins. Energy costs, immigration, global warming, wars, and the growing public uncertainty about the world economy had combined to drive the price of gold north of a thousand dollars an ounce.

He turned the coin in his fingers. Heads showed a bust of a woman. The coin was worn, but the effigy still had a look of compassion and wisdom, like the Chinese deity Guanyin or the Tibetan Buddhist Green Tara. Tails featured a lion and unicorn rampant, the same image as the pub sign in the village.

Coin of the realm? But which realm?

"Where did you get it? And why the largesse?"

"You'll earn it, I assure you. As to where I got it, you'll find out soon enough."

She opened a drawer in the end table and removed a small leather pouch, which she tossed on the table in front of him. "There are ten more in that purse. An advance. Now, please, we must be going. Say good-bye to your—"

A scream from deep within the house cut her off. Nick jumped up. "What the hell!"

Sianiave was on her feet. "Your friend. I told him not to go in there!"

Nick, already halfway to the kitchen door, hardly heard. Sianiave hesitated a moment, then grabbed her walking staff and followed.

The storm was growing ever more violent, the lightning and thunder so frequent it was as if the house lay at the center of a pitched battle. Nick ran through the kitchen toward the double doors just as Billy came stumbling through, holding a sword.

"Billy! What's wrong?"

"We have to get out of here. Something's in there. A nightmare!"

Billy looked over his shoulder as if expecting the nightmare to appear at any moment. Shadow shapes cast by a shifting orange light danced across the walls amid an acrid odor of smoke. It took Nick a moment to realize what he was seeing. "Fire!"

Billy paled even further. "Bloody hell! The lamp. Wait, don't go in there. Nick!"

"The whole house could go up!" Nick bolted through the double doors.

Billy stood immobile, torn between his terror and guilt at his cowardice. Guilt won over. He was about to follow Nick when Sianiave stopped him. "What did you see in there?"

Billy's mind was already at work to rationalize the irrational, block out the unthinkable. "I don't know. Something. Something fearsome."

He weighed the weapon in his hand, suddenly unsure. "A shadow maybe. I don't know. I thought—" He caught himself, realizing she appeared neither surprised nor angry, just grimly purposeful. "It was real? You're saying it's real?"

The look on her face gave him the answer. "My God. Nick!"

Nick was in the dining hall struggling to pull down a burning tapestry when Billy and Sianiave arrived. The shattered oil lamp lay nearby, its flames spreading with improbable speed.

The room was huge, the ceiling easily thirty feet high. Tarnished suits of armor stood guard at the doors. The great table at its center was encircled by enough chairs for a company of soldiers. Tapestries, battle flags, and emblazoned shields decorated the walls. Doors opened on the far side into a second hallway that ended in darkness.

Nick gave up trying to save the tapestry. The oak paneling behind it was ablaze, the flames leaping from panel to panel as if alive. For the first time, he became aware of the sword in Billy's hand. "What are you doing with that thing? We have to call the fire department."

"No telephone service," said Sianiave. Her attention focused more on the darkness in the opposite hallway than on the burning wall.

"Do you have a cell phone?" Nick had left his new one back in his room. Billy had never owned one, considering them a modern horror.

"A what phone?"

"Cell phone. We need to—" He stopped. She clearly had no idea what he was talking about.

She turned away. "It's not important. We're late already."

"Not important? You'll lose the house, everything in it!"

Her lack of concern was both frustrating and unnerving. Did she want the place to burn? They might hold Billy responsible. "We'll have to drive to the village."

He took off running as Billy struggled to keep up. "Nick, I saw something in there. Honestly!"

Nick didn't answer. He was beginning to suspect that Billy might not be imagining things. It was clear the woman was hiding something. Behind them, she looked over her shoulder, alert. She seemed to be watching for more than the fire.

They ran through the kitchen and grabbed their coats in the drawing room. Outside, the storm was in full fury, the lightning flashes coming so close together it might as well have been day. Nick had to shout above the thunder and driving rain. "I'll drive. Where are the keys?"

Billy handed them to him without objection. Nick threw himself into the driver's seat, inserted the ignition key and pressed the starter button. There was no response, not a sound from the engine. "It's dead. You must have left the lights on."

"No. You saw me. I turned everything off."

"Where's the hood latch?"

"Hood? Oh, the bonnet. There. Down to your left."

Nick pulled the latch and jumped out of the car. Billy shined his flashlight into the engine compartment as Nick lifted the hood.

"What the—?"

The question trailed off into impossibilities. What had been Isabel's beautiful, polished engine now resembled a lump of grey wax melted over the undercarriage.

Nick glanced at his watch. Five minutes to midnight. Someone was having them on. But who, and why? More importantly, how? What could do that to an engine? Lightning? Must be, though some half-remembered lesson from Physics 101 told him it was impossible.

He fingered the coin in his pocket, shoved there when he'd heard Billy's scream. The pouch containing ten more was still on the table. An advance, she'd said.

Flames now flickered against the ground-floor windows. At this rate the entire mansion would be gutted in minutes. Billy put a hand on Isabel's fender. "Sorry, old girl."

The rain seemed to be easing. In the direction of the village not a light was visible.

"Where's the woman?" Nick asked.

CHAPTER
10

SIANIAVE APPEARED SUDDENLY around a corner of the house. The lightning and thunder continued unabated, but the wind had ceased and with it the rain. Instead of the greatcoat Sianiave wore a long wool cape, its hood thrown back, exposing her flowing grey hair. "Well, Lieutenant. Time is short. Do you accept the commission?"

Nick's thoughts felt suddenly and unaccountably leaden, disoriented, as though in an opium dream. "The fire?"

"Forget the fire! Do you accept the commission?"

He shook his head, trying to clear it. Billy elbowed him. "Say yes."

"But—"

"Of course he does."

Nick nodded feebly.

"Good enough." Sianiave shoved the bag of coins into Nick's hand. She must have grabbed them from the table. "The contract is agreed upon and witnessed. Now you must follow me. Your lives depend on it!"

She led them to a rusted iron gate hidden in the ivy. A stone path lay beyond, winding down through thickets of overgrown rose bushes. At one time the bushes must have bordered the path. Now gone wild, they covered much of the hillside. A streaming mist covered the dense foliage.

"Our car? The engine?"

"Dammit, man!" snapped Sianiave as she struggled with the gate latch. "Gather your wits! The creature your friend saw in there is real. It's working on your mind."

The words meant little to Nick, but Billy swayed as though he'd been punched in the stomach. "Real? Good lord."

"What you saw was only a thought form, otherwise you'd be dead. It's been trying to break through since last evening. The binding on the house is old, weakening. The fire will end it."

The latch snapped up. "There!" Sianiave cried. With the metallic grating of hinges long unused, the gate swung open. At the same moment, a horrifying shriek came from somewhere inside the house, slicing through the night like the cry of a banshee. The sound was savage and dissonant, so full of insane hatred Nick had to fight back nausea.

"It's through. Run!" Sianiave flew through the gate and down the path.

Nick gazed at the burning mansion as though entranced. His thoughts were sluggish. Nothing seemed quite real. He regarded the bag of coins in his hand, its meaning momentarily lost.

Billy grabbed his arm. "Nick!"

Billy's touch broke the spell. As if jarred awake, Nick came to himself. "I'm with you!" He shoved the bag under his belt and started after Sianiave, Billy close behind.

The path led down, its stones covered in moldy rose petals slick with rain. Billy followed in a stumbling gait, slipping more than once, the thicket's sharp thorns tearing at his clothes and skin. At first Nick easily outpaced him, but as he ran further, every step became an effort, as if the dullness that had attacked his mind had turned its focus on his body.

"Nick! Wait!" Billy crouched on the ground, breathing heavily, obviously in pain. "Give me a moment. It's this downhill thing. Hard on the leg."

"You can do it. We have to keep going." Despite his words, Nick stopped.

Above them, angry red flames had burst through the lower windows, shattering the glass, torching the trees and hedges, and engulfing the entire west side of the mansion. There was something both frightening and compelling about the sight.

"It's my fault," Billy said sorrowfully. "Such treasures there. Artifacts, weapons. All lost."

"Forget it!" cried Nick. "The fire spread too fast. Look at the flames. The color. Too red. It's not normal. Besides, our hostess didn't seem particularly upset about it."

Billy shook his head. "Whatever she's afraid of, it's real," he said. After a moment, he added, "You know, without Elyse I never would have made it this far."

"Marry her when you get back."

"She's certainly like no one—" Billy froze. "Look!" He pointed back up the hill.

A figure had appeared, silhouetted against the flames. It was humanoid in form, yet of greater size than any man. A splitting pain clawed at Nick's head. His stomach turned over in a queasy gurgle. Never had he felt such revulsion. "What the hell is that?" Nick cried. Billy was silent.

Hidden by the thicket and the gathering mist, they should have been impossible to see by anyone standing that far above. But slowly the creature's head turned in their direction, as if sensing their presence. With another unearthly scream it pushed through the gate and started down the path.

Nick helped Billy to his feet. "Time to go. Can you make it?"

"I'd bloody well better."

The path ended at the bottom of the hill in a meadow with a large standing stone at its center. Overhead, the storm clouds parted and the moon emerged. Its light reflected off the surface of the stone. Sianiave stood beside the menhir, bathed in the luminous glow. "Here!" she cried. "Here! It's almost upon you!"

Within that circle of light was safety, Nick knew, though why he knew this he had no idea. Close behind them, too close, he could hear heavy footfalls.

"Run!" shouted Sianiave.

Nick was within a few yards of the circle when Billy cried out again. He looked back to see his friend on the ground, clutching his leg and writhing in pain.

"Leave him!" cried Sianiave. "It's you the thing wants!"

Nick still couldn't bring whatever pursued them into clear focus. Now just yards away, it remained wraithlike, as dark and insubstantial as a shadow yet as real and inexorable as a freight train. Its labored breath stank of effluvium and decay. The features were a vague and malevolent distortion of the human: tiny pointed ears, a stub of a nose, a lipless gash for a mouth. It was hairless, with small reptilian eyes as pitiless as death itself. It slowed as it saw Nick. The spiked ball of a meteor hammer swung from a chain in its right hand, back and forth like a pendulum, teasing.

Nick moved to his right, hoping to draw the thing away from Billy, but the creature ignored the feint, stepping past Billy as if he didn't exist. Its attention was on Nick alone.

"Such a weak little monkey," it said in a rasping whisper.

The thing was evil. Nick had never thought in such terms, but it was the only word that fit. The creature reeked of arrogance, cruelty, perverse lusts, and a venomous hatred of all things human.

Nick stood, indecisive. Time seemed to slow. How do you defend against a monster wielding a meteor hammer? His revulsion had become stomach-twisting nausea. He started to back away, but it was like moving in thick mud. He could hear the creature's voice in his head, sly and seductive. "Weak. So weak. No hope. Weak—"

The hammer snaked out. From somewhere Nick found the will to duck, the ball missing his head by less than an inch. Instinctively he dropped into Crane Fights Snake, kicking out with his left foot at the creature's knee. But the move was too slow and lacked power. The creature shrugged it off as if it were a fleabite.

Again it swung the hammer. Spikes tore furrows of cloth and skin from Nick's shoulder. The ball continued, arcing with impossible speed. This time it struck his shoulder square, crushing bone and tendon and knocking him sprawling and bleeding onto the wet grass.

Just before he lost consciousness he heard Sianiave call out. The language was strange, though the words seemed familiar, part of the same distant and ephemeral memory that brought up images of lions and unicorns, and a woman's face on a gold coin.

Crazy. Everything was crazy. Just a dream, a dream only. Billy really ought to marry Elyse. He's a good man. True to a fault. He deserves happiness. Someone deserves happiness.

HOLLOW FORTRESS

If only–if only—

A blinding light.
Then darkness.

CHAPTER 11

NICK OPENED HIS EYES.

As a foster child, he'd spent seven years with a family of devout Christians, Dominionists who believed Armageddon would soon cleanse the United States of non-believers and Christ would reign supreme for a thousand years. The creature that had attacked him fit well with their beliefs. One of Satan's minions, if not the Evil One himself. But the feather bed on which Nick lay and the rock-walled room did not match their idea of hell. Nor heaven, for that matter.

Purgatory, perhaps?

He was breathing. He could feel his heartbeat, strong and steady. His vision was unimpaired. If anything, it seemed sharper than usual.

These facts told him he was alive, though it was possible he was dreaming. Still, the bed and bedding were tangible, solid. The room looked normal enough. If he were dreaming, it was the most realistic dream he'd ever had.

The room was unusual. Definitely not a hospital room, at least none he was familiar with. More like a granite cave, with a high ceiling and walls dressed by stonemasons, the corners rounded and uneven.

He was lying in a four-poster bed, its canopy tied in swathes to the posts. Hand-stitched sheets of white linen, fresh pillows, duvet thick and soft. Goose down, judging by a feather poking through.

The room's two doors were fashioned of heavy wooden planks banded in hammered iron. The door to the right was more substantial, with a dead bolt the other lacked. He assumed it led to the outside.

Outside? Where?

A heavy wooden table, several equally rough-hewn chairs, and a large dresser comprised the rest of the furnishings. Brackets bolted to the walls held unlit torches.

Where was the light coming from?

He raised his head. High above, a multipaned window cut through the stone in an uneven oblong. Sunlight streamed through.

Altitude. High altitude. He was in the mountains.

There had been rumors of a monastery high in the Pamirs, a cave system inhabited for millennia by monks reputed to have magical powers. A name came to mind: Abshar, meaning "falling water." Supposedly it had been in the very region where his team had encountered the Kashmiri boys.

Was he was back in Afghanistan? Had everything since that night been nothing more than a bad dream? It made a certain sense, but the details didn't add up. Instinct told him that wherever this was, it was not Afghanistan.

He sat up, his body obeying without argument. There was no stiffness, only a slight tenderness in his shoulder. He was dressed in an unbleached linen shift not unlike a hospital gown, but of finer cloth. He winced, remembering the pain as the creature's weapon had smashed into him. He pulled the shift open to find only yellowing bruises where the spikes had torn into his flesh.

If it were fantasy, where had he gotten the bruises? But if his memory were true, and a monster had slammed twenty pounds of spiked ball into his shoulder, how was there was so little damage? Training and hard experience had taught him something about the human body and the effects of trauma. The shoulder was especially delicate and complex. The blow had done serious damage, of that he was certain. Damage requiring surgery followed by months of therapy.

He rubbed his chin. Four, maybe five days' growth of beard. Where was he? Who had brought him here? Was he insane? Drugged? He considered the possibilities, rejecting them all. His mind felt clear—exceptionally so, in fact.

René Descartes: I think, therefore I am.

An image came to him: Descartes outside the gates of Prague the day the city fell in 1620. One of Nick's professors had used that legendary moment as a metaphor for the ascendancy of human reason. Until that fateful day, Prague had been a center for such vilified subjects as alchemy, mysticism, and magic. Descartes, of course, had gone on to become one of reason's greatest champions.

There was a logical explanation for everything.

The sound of the latch lifting on the smaller of the two doors brought Nick to alert. The door opened a crack and a face peered in, red-bearded and friendly.

"Good. You're awake." The man pushed open the door with his foot and entered, carrying a large tray. "Viands and drink, if you're up to it."

The fellow was one of the most extraordinary-looking individuals Nick had ever encountered. He stood perhaps five feet nine. But whatever he lacked in height he made up for in breadth. His chest was broad as a door, his limbs proportionate to his mass. He was dressed like a Viking yeoman, complete with sandals and fur leggings.

"Who are you?" Nick asked.

The man placed the tray on the table. "Aye. You have a great many, no doubt. Questions, I mean. Not many survive a morghul's blow, not to mention being yanked here without proper preparation. I'll answer what I can. But you'll be wanting a bite to eat first."

Nick swung out of bed, surprised at how easily his body moved. He felt twenty-two again, his age the summer he'd returned from China in the best shape of his life.

He stretched and yawned, languorously, like a bear awakening from hibernation. He regarded the loaf of country bread, four large red apples, and several thick slices of red meat on the table. Two huge tankards contained a dark liquid that might be cider, beer, or tea.

The fellow was right. He was hungry, ravenously so. "What time is it?" he asked.

"Late afternoon. Sianiave told me to pass on her regrets she was unable to be here when you woke."

Startled, Nick looked up. "Sianiave? She's here?"

"Left this morning. Back in a few days, she said. I'm not one to whom she confides all." He held out his hand. "I be Osmodon of Linsraden, Sianiave's liegeman."

Nick took the offered hand, his own almost lost in the massive paw.

The man's grip was surprisingly gentle. Nick had little doubt that had he wished, the fellow could have crushed his hand as if it were an egg.

"Nick Herron."

"Aye. Nicholas of Amra. She told me your name. I've sat watching over you for two days now, after Sianiave did the healing. If I'm to be your weapons instructor, I need to scry your mettle."

Amra? Scry? Healing? Morghul? Liegeman? Weapons instructor? Question after question, all hinting at a mystery Nick's reason told him could not be. For the moment he put them aside. Thirst and hunger trumped his need for immediate answers.

"Pleased to meet you, and thanks for the food. You'll join me?"

"Aye. Glad you asked."

Osmodon picked up a tankard and settled into a chair. "First rule of the traveler; never pass up a meal. Or the chance to drink good ale. One thing about the Lady Sianiave, she stocks the best." He raised the tankard. "*Y'ol bol'sun!*"

Surprisingly, Nick knew the toast. He'd first heard it from a Kyrgyz rug dealer in Kabul. "May there always be a road."

He raised his own tankard. Unlike Osmodon, who wielded his as easily as a pint glass, Nick was forced to use two hands. He drank, hesitatingly at first, unsure what to expect, then with dawning pleasure. It was ale, rich and heavy, better tasting than any he could recall.

"You're a traveler?" he asked, wiping his mouth with his sleeve.

Osmodon picked up a slab of mutton. "Aren't we all? Travelers on a journey into the unknown. But aye. Linsraden is many leagues off and I've been gone now these forty-four years. A pilgrim, teaching arms and fighting to the worthy and the willing. And to some not so willing, I admit. And perhaps not so worthy."

"Linsraden? Is that in the north countries? Sweden?"

"I've never heard of this Swe-Den. Linsraden is Linsraden, loveliest holding in all the world. Asgar's temple on the cliff above, white houses below, white-sailed ships in the harbor, and the blue sea beyond. Leastways, that's how it's still pictured in my mind. It's gone now, of course. Burnt by the Black Fleet, its people scattered, killed, or taken south as slaves and sacrifices."

Whatever Nick thought about the man's sanity, there was no denying the sadness that had fallen on him. "I took it on as a fault of mine," Osmodon went on, his shoulders sagging. "But I couldn't forswear my father. There'd been word of the fleet, but he didn't believe they'd come that far north. He refused my advice and led us inland to Danemar, on a goose chase, as it turned out."

The big man shrugged and bit into the mutton, devouring most of it in one gulp. "I've come to terms. My father is long dead, as are the others who rode with us that day. The women stay most in my memory. Warm, lovely things they were, as feminine as field flowers, but savage fighters when they'd a mind. They left their mark."

Nick tried to place the accent: a slight brogue, neither Irish nor Scottish. It reminded him of Billy's friend Elyse.

Billy! How could he have forgotten? "Billy. That—thing!"

"I was not present, of course," Osmodon said, unperturbed. He wiped mutton grease from his beard with the back of his hand and tore off a piece of bread. "Regrettably. But I hear you gave good account of yourself. Few can stand against a morghul without knowing the shields. Its foul thoughts cloud your wits and suck your will. Believe me, I know. Yet not only did you stand, Sianiave said you even managed a blow. As for your friend, once you were through, my guess is the beast simply left him and departed."

"Your guess? Billy wasn't five feet away, he must have—"

"Morghul's are vicious and evil, but never think them stupid. It was you he was after. Sianiave at least was not concerned."

Nick felt lost. All this was impossible, the very conversation mad. His eyes rested on the larger of the two doors, looking for an escape to a place of sanity. "What's out there?"

"Why, the outside, of course. It isn't locked. Sianiave has no need of locks. Not here."

It had been said as an invitation and Nick took it as such. He walked over to the door. Osmodon's eyes followed him, like a concerned father watching a child taking his first steps. After a moment's hesitation, Nick threw back the bolt and pulled up on the heavy latch. The door swung open to a draft of frigid air.

Outside was a small balcony, little more than a ledge. A low wall no higher than a man's knee was the only thing between the ledge and what must have been a two-thousand-foot drop to where a silvery ribbon of river wound through an impossibly steep canyon.

He fought down a momentary rush of vertigo. But it was not so great a shock as it might have been. He'd suspected they were in the mountains, but which ones? The peaks looked higher, more sharply angled and dramatic than either the Rockies or Alps. This might be Alaska, more probably the Andes or Himalayas.

How had they gotten him here?

Raptors circled in the distance—hawks, eagles, perhaps condors? With a slight tilt of its wings, one broke loose from the others, as if curious about this new thing that had appeared in its world. It soared majestically toward Nick's ledge.

As the dimensions of the bird became clear, Nick gasped in disbelief. "Holy—!" It was an eagle. But no eagle in the world could be so large. The thing was as big as a hang glider.

Reason no longer held. He fell back against the wall, his breath catching in his throat as he stared out at the impossible.

He felt a warning hand on his shoulder. "Best come back inside, lad," said Osmodon, not unkindly. "The eagles here aren't generally known to carry off grown men, but one can never be certain."

CHAPTER
12

Barad'An
Anor
April 17

PRINCESS GWYNDOLYN—Ren to her family and friends—
pulled back on the bowstring, stilled her thoughts as she'd been taught,
and released the arrow. It sped to the straw target, hitting the bull's-eye
with a gratifying thunk.

"By the gods!" cried Fletcher as he and Ren hurried closer to the
target to judge. "I believe you've done it!"

Ren had known the arrow would find its mark as soon as she'd let it
go. It had struck the very center of the circle, nudging against Fletcher's
own arrow a feather's width further out.

She lowered her bow, struggling with an undefined emotion.
Fletcher was captain-major of the wall guard and the greatest archer in
Anor. He had been her instructor for ten of her eighteen years. Now, for
the first time, she had bested him. She should be elated. Why did she
feel only emptiness, sadness?

This was a passage, she suddenly realized, one for which she had
not prepared. She'd come to the wall to keep her friend company, for she
knew how tired he got, standing the long vigils. The contest had been an
afterthought, a way to break the tedium.

Mabry Fletcher was no longer a young man. In less trying times, he would have retired years ago to his farm in Westing Garth. But his wife and sons were dead, his farm burnt along with the other outlying estates. After Artos left, taking the cream of the young knights with him, the incessant fighting bled away the rest, giving Fletcher little recourse but to continue in his post. She never could have defeated him in his prime.

The old man grabbed her up in his burly arms, his weathered face beaming with pride. "A great day! Truly a great day!"

"What?" she mocked, a lopsided grin hiding her true feelings. "That you were beaten by a girl half your size and a seventh your age?"

"Absolutely, child. Every teacher dreams of such a day, the day he knows the teaching is done, his skill and knowledge passed on." He set her down again and bowed. "I only wish I had prepared a trophy. This moment should be remembered."

Ren struggled to find a suitable reply, something that would lift the sudden sense of weight that had settled on her. But no words would come. She barely managed to hold back tears.

He pulled the winning arrow from the target. "I'll have it mounted."

"Now you're teasing me. Really, it was just luck—and only fifty paces."

"Six out of ten is hardly luck. As for distance, your strength will develop. I, for one—" He was interrupted by a shout from the nearest watchtower.

"Riders approaching!"

They ran to the parapet, the contest forgotten. In the distance a group of mounted men had emerged from the forest, riding at full stride for the city gate.

"It's the king!" shouted Fletcher. The tower watchmen took up the call. It was impossible to mistake Hellion, the king's great black stallion. At least three dozen horsemen, Uruks by their look, were in close pursuit.

Fletcher shouted orders. "Open the gate! Call out a sortie! It's Cuchulain and he's hard put!"

Battle trumpets sounded as the orders were passed down the wall. Slowly, with a twanging of ropes drawn taut and the grinding of wooden gears, the great gate began to rise. Ren watched the scene unfold below with mounting despair. So few.

Her grandfather had ridden out that morning with nine knights and five squires. She counted only seven men returning. She spoke their names aloud as she recognized their colors and horses: Cuchulain in the lead, followed by Aerindir and Abdelar, Bors, Prince Corwin, and Squire Carswell. Was that Old Knockpine?

Where were the others? She feared the worst. With fewer than fifty experienced knights and even fewer trained squires left in the city, every loss was felt, every death an irreparable blow.

"Archers prepare! Pikemen to the gate!"

Ren was old enough to remember when the land between the wall and Arden Forest had been a bustling city in its own right, with a shifting population nearly as large as Barad'An's. Makeshift shops, market stalls, tented pleasure pavilions, smithies, corrals, and forage barns, all servicing the once-vital caravan trade.

Gone now, burned by raiders or cleared for defense. Now there was just a mile of scarred grassland surrounding the ancient grey oaks that stood like sentinels marking the Great North Road. They had been planted the same year as the laying of the city's cornerstone. As yet, no one had the heart to cut them down.

The king was less than half a mile from wall and safety. The pursuers, Eastern Uruks by their dress, continued the chase on their wiry little steppe ponies. Did they think to attack the wall itself? Seven times in the city's long history the wall had withstood armies.

With the insight common to her lineage, a sight that, some murmured, bordered on the unnatural, Ren suddenly understood. They weren't after a king's ransom. They meant to kill her grandfather.

Why? Uruks were tribal nomads from the Blasted Lands, little more than bandits. What would the death of Cuchulain gain them, save more enmity?

A horse stumbled with an arrow in its shank, spilling its rider. "No! Get up!" Ren found herself shouting out loud, clenching her bow with white-knuckled hands.

"Belarane, Old Knockpine! Get up!"

She knew Belarane well. He had bounced her on his knee when she was a child, though he was aged even then. He always smelled of cinnamon.

As if hearing her words, the knight rose, sword drawn. Aerindir and Abdelar pulled up, their horses rearing as they turned back to help. Belarane waved them on. "Stay with the king!"

The enemy was upon him. Ren watched him fall, cut to pieces under sharp hooves and flashing scimitars.

"The sortie!" cried Fletcher. "Where's that damn sortie?"

Trumpets sounded as if in answer as knight after knight galloped out through the gate, many lacking battle dress. The Uruks wavered, then broke, flailing their curved swords and shouting curses as they retreated to the forest.

All but one. Riding at full gallop, a large Uruk with the bronze ornaments of a captain slid his bow from his shoulder, nocked an arrow, rose in his saddle, and let fly, all in one seemingly effortless motion. Ren watched in horror as the arrow arced towards the king with inhuman accuracy. It pierced Cuchulain's shoulder from behind even as he reached the safety of the wall.

"Grandfather!"

Throwing down her bow, she ran for the nearest ramp, past soldiers rushing up from the courtyard. Pages saddled nervous horses for riders hurrying to the field. Dogs barked while pigs, goats, and geese ran amok. Citizens stood rooted in fear as their bloodied sovereign passed through the huge gate, a black-feathered shaft protruding from his right shoulder.

Ren bullied her way into the throng. "Stand aside! Let me through!"

Cuchulain dismounted, staggering but doing his best to hide his pain. "Grandfather!" cried Ren.

The king turned away as she approached. "Keep back, child."

She started to object, but the words caught in her throat when she saw him sign to her silently: *Our lives are in immediate danger.*

Ren stood shocked. Never had she seen anyone use that sign, not since the High Priestess Saolin had taught her the hand language as a child.

Something was terribly wrong. It wasn't just the fallen knights or the arrow in her grandfather's shoulder. All of her senses snapped to alert. She searched the nearest faces for anything amiss.

"Bors!" called the king, motioning to the big knight by his side. "Help me with this bloody dart."

"Sire, we should get you to the healers—"

"Later," barked Cuchulain. Then, softly, "There's no time." In hand code he signaled *poison*.

It took all of Bors's long years of training to keep the emotion from his face. He glanced up at the knights mounted nearby, waiting for the king's orders. Had they noticed the sign? Their faces also gave nothing away.

Ren had seen it. Her eyes widened in alarm.

The arrow had penetrated through Cuchulain's shoulder. Only a grimace showed his pain as, careful not to touch the arrowhead, he broke off the end of the shaft. He dropped to one knee so Bors, using both hands, could take hold of the shaft and pull it free.

"There's bleeding, Sire. It should be bandaged."

"Let it bleed," grunted Cuchulain. He wrapped the arrowhead in a scarf and placed it in his saddlebag. He turned to Ren. "Find Saolin. Bring her to my chambers." Another hand sign, visible only to her and Sir Bors: *Trust no one.*

Cuchulain grabbed his horse's reins and mounted. "Carswell!" he called to his squire. "Bring the priest. Half an hour—no sooner and no later. By force if necessary. Corwin, Aerindir, Abdelar—attend me!"

With that the king, surrounded by the three knights, angrily spurred the big stallion and galloped away through the hastily parting crowd.

Concern for her grandfather was uppermost in her mind, but Ren also tried to make sense of his actions. The first signal he'd given was to be used only in dire emergency. Immediate danger—from whom? Why Saolin? Her grandfather hadn't spoken ten words to the old priestess in years. And what did that lying blatherer of a priest know about anything?

"Bors? What happened out there?"

The knight was close to exhaustion, his green and black battle dress stained head to foot with blood. He spoke softly, so only she could hear. "Best you obey the king. I fear you'll have answers soon enough." Taking up his reins, Bors swung back into the saddle. "Don't tarry, though. The dice are rolling." He turned his mount and rode through the gate to join the hunt for the Uruks.

She studied the crowd. Like her, it was fearful and uncertain.

CHAPTER
13

SQUIRE CARSWELL had his orders, and by his reckoning it was about time. "You two. Geoff, Pentwyn. Come with me!"

A hard man of no particular brilliance but deeply loyal, Carswell had been the king's squire for forty years, sacrificing land and a title to serve his sovereign. During the great rift he had allied with Artos. But after Cuchulain banished Artos from the kingdom, Carswell had stayed behind and remained steadfast. He'd never questioned that decision, though in hindsight it was clear Artos had been in the right. The squire's morality was simple. Remain true, even if it meant death. Even the death of a kingdom.

Carswell led the men-at-arms toward the church, though he didn't really expect trouble. Glays would never confront a tested warrior, certainly not the king's own squire. Despite the priest's pretentious title and claims to holiness, Glays was, in Carswell's mind, little more than a peddler selling charms and fairy tales to susceptible citizens. Carswell was of the old faith, sorely put out when Cuchulain had given Glays the Old Right Temple to be reestablished as a church to his strange religion and vengeful god.

As Carswell and his men approached, he saw twelve of Glays's ruffians waiting near the tower steps. Their clean white robes contrasted sharply with his own blood-soaked garments, so stained it was difficult to make out his colors of brown and yellow.

A slender, sallow man with the two gold stripes of a captain smirked as he moved to block the way. "Apologies, sirrah. The church is closed today."

"Stand aside. I'm here at the king's order."

"Squire Carswell, of course. I hardly recognized you under all that filth. Did you fall off your horse?"

Carswell knew the man slightly and had no use for him. He was one of the itinerant mercenaries Glays had hired to populate his so-called temple guard. Any other time he would have called out the insolent fellow for such rudeness, but he was on the king's business.

"Now you know me. Stand aside!"

The man didn't move. "I'm afraid not, good Squire," he drawled, his feigned courtesy belied by a sneer. "Church grounds are sacrosanct, as you know. Weapons are not allowed. You can leave your sword and dagger here with me. I'll take good care of them—and your men, too, of course."

"My men?"

"Certainly. The bishop will see only you. Your men must wait here."

"He expects me?"

"Of course." The man tapped his forehead meaningfully. "Divine sight, you know." It was clear the fellow didn't believe his own words, though several of the younger men in his troop raised their eyes skyward.

Carswell pondered his options. He had little doubt the three of them could handle this entire pack. Cuchulain's orders had been explicit: Use force if necessary. The squire's hand moved to the hilt of his sword. For a brief moment the smirk left the popinjay's face, and he took a step back.

Carswell hesitated. There were other issues involved. More than a small number of citizens stood nearby, watching the encounter. Cuchulain had not said why he wanted Glays brought to him, though he could guess.

"You've nothing to fear," said the man, again with mock courtesy. And then, as if challenging Carswell's courage, "The bishop is alone."

Carswell unbuckled his belt, handing it with sword and dagger to Pentwyn. A smaller dagger remained hidden in his boot. "Wait here. I won't be long."

He shoved past the captain and climbed the steps to the church entrance, though he thought of it still as a temple. Built in the old days on a hill within the city, taller than the royal palace, it was an almost exact replica of the Old Left Tower, the Temple of Yu'An Tara. That building, visible on a twin hill on the eastern side of the city, had been first. It was where the city drew its name, Barad'An: the Tower of 'An.

The priest's offices were to the right of the great columns and up another flight of stairs. Like most of the knights who'd remained with Cuchulain after the rift, Carswell was not young. He hadn't slept the previous night, and after the battle and chase he was near exhaustion. By the time he reached the door to the inner sanctum he was breathing heavily. He rested a moment. Then, irritated at his own fatigue, he pushed through the unlocked door.

The room was large and round, with a high, vaulted ceiling. Save for a few poorly rendered portraits of pasty men with yellow rings above their heads, the walls were bare. Carswell had been in the room when it served the old faith and the priest had not yet appeared. Shelves had lined the walls then, filled with manuscripts and leather-bound books.

Glays stood alone in the room, peering through a narrow window with a spyglass. From the window one could see the city below and the forest and hills in the distance. Divine sight, indeed. This was how the priest had known of his coming.

"Ah, Carswell," said Glays sociably. "Good of you to come. The sortie knights are returning. Without much success it would appear." He lowered the spyglass, turning to face the squire. "You were with the king. What brings you here?"

"You are to come with me. The king's orders."

Glays nodded agreeably. "Of course. I saw the arrow strike him. A nasty wound, I fear. I will bring my surgeon."

"I'd sooner put the king in the hands of the Uruk who shot him than that rat-faced magician of yours. You'll come alone—and now. The king awaits."

Glays wore a voluminous white robe, woven of silk and hemmed in gold. A golden cross hung from his neck on a matching chain, and jeweled rings decorated his fingers. His dress had been getting more elaborate with each passing month, Carswell thought dryly.

"Come, my good squire," murmured Glays. "You of all people wouldn't disallow our king the best medical help available simply because of personal dislike. Gothmog is really quite clever with wounds, you know."

Carswell was tired and losing patience. "Saolin will serve. Come."

"As you wish. But would you look through this first? I'd like to hear your comments," Glays said reasonably, proffering the spyglass.

The squire considered the request. The king was waiting, but only twice before had Carswell looked through a spyglass. Such artifacts were exceedingly rare, worth their weight in gold, as the art of their making was lost a thousand years before. What harm could it do?

Cautiously he took the tube and put it to his eye. Beyond the wall he could see the knights returning, as Glays had said. The glass brought him so close he could almost read the furrowed lines on Bors's face.

Glays moved closer. "And below, good squire? On the stairs? Tell me what you see."

"The stairs?"

Carswell lowered the glass. He didn't need its amplifying powers to see the calamity unfolding. Two of the white-robed guardsmen lay sprawled, their blood staining the marble steps. Pentwyn and Geoff stood back to back, pikes lowered, bleeding from a dozen wounds as the remaining guards circled in. A spear caught Pentwyn in the chest and he went down.

"What have you done?" Carswell shouted.

A long dagger appeared in the priest's hand. Carswell turned too late. He cried out more in surprise than pain as the blade found its mark in his side. He grabbed the priest's hand, to no effect. Glays was strong. The spyglass dropped to the floor, shattering.

Face twisted in malignant triumph, Glays used both hands and the weight of his body to drive the dagger through the squire's ribcage, its sharp blade cutting through bone and liver. "You half-wit!" he snarled. "Did you or your idiot king think to command me, God's messenger!"

Carswell struggled but knew he was lost. His grip weakened. As blackness appeared at the edge of his vision, he cursed his stupidity. Who would have suspected the priest to have such strength? He had failed in his duty, failed his king. That knowledge troubled him more than the certainty of his own death.

Then, as sometimes happens in that single moment before a man's life is snuffed out, Squire Carswell had a vision: the priest kneeling on a marble floor of intricate design with a knight standing over him, sword raised. The knight, unfamiliar to Carswell, was covered head to foot in blood, but the angles of his face showed strength and unrelenting resolve. A good man. The knight's sword swept down.

Carswell looked into the priest's maddened eyes. "You'll die beneath a knight's sword before spring is done," he said quietly.

A moment later the squire's hand slipped from the knife. A groan escaped his lips as the priest's weapon found his heart.

Glays held on to the hilt until he was sure Carswell was dead. The fool's last words had unnerved him. Not what he said but how it was spoken—in a voice neither frightened nor angry, as though stating a fact already known.

He shuddered. He'd have Gothmog perform a cleansing later. At the moment there was much to do. He looked down at the shattered spyglass. Shame, that.

He pulled the dagger from the body and turned back to the window. Men were dragging off the two dead pikemen, others washed the blood from the steps. Absently he wondered how many of his own had perished in the fight. No mind. Martyrs for the faith.

"Gothmog!" Glays exclaimed as a furtive figure in a black tunic appeared from behind a curtain, a slender dagger in his right hand.

"It went well, m'lord," the sallow little man said.

"Well enough." Glays studied the body bleeding on the floor. "Pity poor Squire Carswell. A brave and faithful man. Unfortunately he seems to have succumbed to wounds suffered earlier in battle."

Gothmog licked his thin lips. "I can use the heart, if it's not too damaged."

"Of course. Take the body away. Have someone clean up the mess."

Glays wiped the dagger on his robe, then tossed it on a nearby table. "I'll need fresh robes. Meet me in my chamber, and bring your bag. Our king awaits."

CHAPTER
14

SAOLIN HECATE, HIGH PRIESTESS of the Temple of Yu'An Tara, was already on her way to the king's bedchamber when Ren found her. A statuesque woman with flowing white hair, she was a severe beauty who had refused to succumb to either age or weakness. Two Sisters attended her. Each wore the blue robes of their order and carried small brass-bound chests that contained the tools and potions of their trade.

"Saolin! Wait!"

"Gwyndolyn. Good. You can help. I was told Cuchulain already removed the arrow."

Saolin was perhaps the only person, man or woman, who still called Ren by her birth name. "He believed it poisoned," Ren said, catching her breath.

The priestess frowned. "Since when do Uruks use poison?"

They rounded a corner, almost colliding with Aerindir and Abdelar as the brothers exited the king's bedchamber. Abdelar's usual good nature was dampened, his face set. "Ren. We were sent to find you. Your grandfather is failing."

Ren's heart fell. It was as she had feared.

Aerindir's jaw was clenched. His visage, hawk-like and intimidating at the best of times, was a portrait of controlled rage. "It was no common Uruk's arrow. He grows weaker by the minute. Unless you have something more in those boxes than datura and devilsbane, priestess, the king will pass within the hour."

"We shall see," said Saolin, moving past Aerindir. "Come, Sisters."

The pikemen guarding Cuchulain's chamber stepped aside as the Sisters approached. Abdelar caught Ren's arm before she could follow, pressing her into a nearby alcove. Aerindir stood guard.

Abdelar spoke urgently. "Ren, there's little time. Listen carefully. Your grandfather wishes to talk with you. But quit his chamber immediately afterward. Do not stay, much as you might wish. We must leave the city."

"Leave?"

"Your grandfather will explain. Aerindir and I will be waiting at the stables. Go directly there. Do not return to your rooms. Bring nothing and tell no one. Your life—and more—depends on it."

"Abdelar, what's happening?"

"Please." Abdelar grabbed her hands in an almost painful grip, his blue eyes frightening her with their intensity. "*Coriaen'ae al illi'ianath!*"

Ren's darkest fears were suddenly realized. The words were from a language so ancient it was no longer spoken in the halls of men. But meaning there was—dire meaning. It was half of a code phrase warning of mortal danger, a call for desperate action drummed into her since childhood: Abandon all.

She had never heard the words spoken in earnest, not even during the great rift when her uncle Artos had rebelled, leaving with his knights and the priests of the Old Right Tower.

Almost as though someone else was speaking through her, she heard herself reply, "*Illi'ianath ab desindre y ama.*" But abandon neither hope nor love.

Abdelar relaxed his grip. "We'll be waiting." He motioned to Aerindir and the two knights hurried off, neither looking back.

Ren's mind swirled with conflicting thoughts. Of all the knights in Barad'An, she was closest to Abdelar and Aerindir. Protective, loyal, and wise, they had always treated her as a beloved sister. She could never doubt them. And yet—Abandon all? Flee the city, the people she loved? Flee from what, and to where? What had happened out there in the forest?

She caught herself, remembering the teaching called Stilling of the Mind: Come to what is, come to the present. Put real effort to real effect. Ren closed her eyes, then stood straighter. She must see her grandfather.

The two pikemen guarding the door snapped to attention as she approached. Good men, though like so many left in Barad'An, both in their evening years.

Saolin and the two acolytes were stripping away Cuchulain's blood-soaked shirt. They wore thin lambskin gloves for protection. Prince Corwin, the only other person in the room, stood nearby, watching them work with quiet concern.

Her grandfather's face was ashen and soaked with sweat. Saolin turned him on his side to better reach his injuries. Blood, turned now to a black ooze, trickled from his wounds front and back. There was the foul smell of bile. Horrified, Ren imagined she could see tiny, wormlike shapes moving in the ooze.

"Carlyn, hand me the dragonsroot salve. Katrin, some water. And two of those poppy balls. Careful! Don't let that foulness touch your skin."

Saolin barked this last as Sister Katrin lifted up the shreds of the king's ruined shirt, carefully dropping them in a bedpan.

"Ren!" rasped Cuchulain when he saw his granddaughter. His voice was frail, dry as dust. "Thank the Fates. Come." He struggled to sit up, his body trembling with pain and fever.

Saolin steadied him. "Stay still, old man."

Sister Carlyn was from Eldemere. She had been Ren's playmate as a child. She barely acknowledged her now as she handed Saolin a jar of a greenish salve, which the priestess rubbed carefully onto the wounds. The ooze bubbled, then settled. The sickening movement in it stilled for the moment. The acolytes began a low chant, tracing healing symbols in the air with their fingers.

Cuchulain's eyes were steady with purpose. "Abdelar has spoken with you?"

Ren nodded. "Yes."

"You understand, then?"

"Save your strength, Grandfather. Please."

"There's little left to save. I'm for it. All Saolin can do is stave the pain."

"Don't say that! You're strong still."

Saolin shook her head. "This was no common poison, child. Dark work, woven by a master. Your grandfather is right. The best I can do is ease the pain."

"Not a small gift, old woman. There are things I've still to do."

"Swallow these."

Saolin handed Cuchulain him two green balls the size of olives. Ren fought back tears as her grandfather choked them down.

"Couldn't Sianiave help?"

"Perhaps, if she were here, but she's not." There was a hint of bitterness in Saolin's reply. She'd never gotten along with the sorceress, Ren recalled.

The poppy balls were taking effect. The tremor in Cuchulain's hand lessened. Color returned to his features and his voice steadied. "Saolin. You must leave. Go into the forest, take the Sisters. Glays hates women, the Sisters most of all."

"Glays?" Saolin stood back indignantly. "Leave? Because of that— that oafish swine?"

"He will be steward and regent when I pass. Have you forgotten?"

"How could I forget? You agreed to it against my advice."

"I had little choice. Artos left. Tradition demands that a man—"

"Tradition be damned! Your stubborn adherence to tradition caused him to leave."

Cuchulain sighed. There was deep regret in it. "This I admit. Which is why I must send Ren away, and you as well. Now."

"No!" cried Saolin.

Cuchulain ignored the outburst. "I can command my granddaughter, but of you, Saolin, I can only make entreaty." He stifled a cough as he reached for Saolin's hand. "Take the Sisters to Marduk. You'll be safe there, at least for a time."

Saolin drew back. "Nonsense. I won't abandon the tower. Certainly not to that loathsome creature. He would love to have Barad'An all to himself and his despicable god."

"It is not just his god who helps him in this."

"Not his—then who?" Saolin's face blanched with a sudden realization. "How do you know this? How could I not know this?"

"Glays has been patient, and they've planned carefully. You are not at fault. Until this morning, I was uncertain. It was Corwin who brought word. We can only hope the priest is not yet aware we know. For myself, there is nothing more. I beg you, leave the city!"

A violent tremor shook Cuchulain. He fell back against the pillows. The blood welling up from his wounds had turned dark again.

Saolin's face softened. She reached down and stroked his cheek with a surprisingly gentle touch. "Save a seat beside you in Velkela, my king. I feel I won't be far behind."

Were those tears in old woman's eyes? Clearly there was more between Saolin and her grandfather than she'd ever imagined.

Ren had known Saolin her entire life, but there was a barrier between them, a veil that precluded intimacy. Still, she respected the woman for her strength and wisdom, and for her dedication.

"Come, Sisters," said Saolin. "Gather your things."

She turned to Ren. "Farewell, child. You were always good student. I'm sorry we couldn't have been closer." The two acolytes took up their chests and followed Saolin from the room.

Prince Corwin, who had been watching, approached the bed. His handsome face gave nothing away. "I will also take my leave, sire."

Corwin had always been a mystery to Ren. Dark-haired, of indeterminate age, he had a strength that belied his slenderness. Of all the knights, save perhaps for Abdelar and Aerindir, he was the best at arms. He had come in and out of their lives for as long as she could remember, most often at times of crisis. No one, save perhaps Sianiave, seemed to know whence he came, and she never discussed his origins. Ren may as well have asked about the wind.

"Even you cannot stop this storm, my friend," rasped the king, his voice weakening as he spoke. "And you have your own work to do."

Corwin's smile was grim. "This is my work, sire. But in this matter I will follow your wishes, for I see no other course." From his boot he removed a dagger, lethal and businesslike in its lack of adornment, and laid it on the bed.

Cuchulain moved the knife out of sight under a sheet, near his right hand. With a nod to Ren and a look she did not understand, Corwin turned and left the room. Alone now, the dying man reached out to her.

"Grandfather, I—"

"Hush. There is little time. You must go to Ellohir, in Gallian."

"No. I won't leave you. I won't leave the city." They heard the sound of marching feet in the long hall outside. "Please, Grandfather—"

"Hear me out! Had I lived, I may have been able to hold the city, but this is not yet in your power. Glays will control Barad'An. You alone stand in his way. Ellohir can protect you. You will stay there until the time comes for you to return."

Ren could hear the guards outside arguing, barring the way to intruders. Her grandfather's voice was barely above a whisper. "Go! Aerindir and Abdelar are waiting."

The door opened and Ben Shafter, the senior of the two guards, peered in. "It's the bishop, sire. He demands to see you."

"Is Carswell with him?"

"No, sire. The bishop is accompanied by twelve of his temple guard. For your protection, he says." The old pikeman cleared his throat, uneasy. "He's brought his surgeon."

"Gothmog! That weasel. Grandfather, you mustn't—"

"Ben, escort my granddaughter to her chambers. When you are done, you are relieved of duty. Go home to your wife."

"Sire?"

"Now, Ben. Send Jorald home as well."

Ren felt the walls closing in around her. Why was he releasing his guards? Where were his knights? He seemed to be giving up without a fight.

Or was he? Glays did not act alone, he'd said. Clearly Saolin understood something Ren did not. Who or what could cause that obdurate old woman to flee?

Abandon all.

An elusive sense of knowing, the intuition that was both the bane and blessing of her lineage, engulfed her. Not the who or the how, but the why. Cuchulain, understanding his fate, was protecting those he most loved and trusted, sending them to safety.

Her grandfather was not fond of taking counsel; he could be unyielding as a stone. In his recalcitrance he had driven her uncle from the city, but it was this same stubbornness that for more than sixty years had allowed him to hold the city together against an ever-encroaching darkness. For all his faults, she loved him dearly.

He nodded as the understanding passed between them. Not trusting herself to say good-bye, Ren bowed and backed away. Ben Shafter escorted her from the room.

CHAPTER
15

GLAYS PACED RESTLESSLY in front of the door into the king's private chambers. He had waited ten years for this day, but now his patience was wearing thin.

An aged pikeman had stopped him. Twelve of his best guardsmen stood poised and ready behind him. He didn't count Gothmog, a weapon best used in the dark. The little magician stood there now, in the shadows, black bag clutched tightly against his chest.

The priest's eyes fell on his captain, Borson Brand. Young, predatory, ready to kill at a word, he'd acquitted himself well on the steps. They'd lost only three men while subduing Carswell's escort—not a mean feat.

He could end this charade now and kill them all, that miserable shell of a king and all his pagan lackeys. Except the girl, of course. He wanted her alive. But killing Saolin before he took charge of the city might provoke dissent. Too many of Barad'An's citizens still believed her puerile superstitions. When the time was right, he would hang her and the other witches from the great oaks in front of the city. That would cure the populace of their blasphemies.

Why delay? Brand watched him expectantly, waiting for the order, lean and anxious like a hungry wolf.

One factor alone made the priest hesitate, the same uncertainty that kept him waiting in the hall like a common supplicant. Aerindir,

Abdelar, Bors, and the other knights could be dealt with. Saolin and the Sisters he dismissed as irrelevant. But Prince Corwin was inexplicable, therefore dangerous. He'd once ordered Gothmog to conduct a ritual scry of the man, an attempt to learn what he could of this adversary. Gothmog selected a young girl as a proxy for the ritual, hanging her on hooks in his dungeon. But the attempt had failed disastrously. He'd encountered a shield so powerful it had blasted him from his circle. The brazier had begun a jerking dance, spreading hot coals across the floor. The girl had screamed madness about goblin worlds and machines that spit death—moments before her heart burst from her wasted body.

Gothmog had said that one wall, made of stone and four feet thick, had liquefied into a churning maelstrom, a malevolent labyrinth. He'd been so unnerved by the experience he'd lain useless in his bed for three days. Corwin seemed not only to have survived the sorcerer's assault unscathed, but also showed no sign he'd even been aware of it.

Glays stopped in mid-pace, remembering the look on the magician's face, a look of absolute horror. What had he seen to disturb him so?

When Cuchulain had ridden through the gate with the arrow in his shoulder, Glays had been so confident his time was at hand he hadn't bothered to consult his spies. It occurred to him he wasn't sure who was attending the king. The witch priestess and her acolytes no doubt, Princess Gwyndolyn of course. Bors?

He'd seen Aerindir and Abdelar leave, crossing the playing field. Where were they heading? Why would they leave the king's side? And why were there so few guards? Something was amiss.

Ten years. He'd been waiting for this day for ten years. He must use caution.

The heavy chamber door abruptly swung open. Ren emerged, eyes straight ahead, followed by the grizzled pikeman who'd challenged him at the door. Was Cuchulain already dead?

"Princess Gwyndolyn, you're leaving now? With the king so ill? I understand the arrow was poisoned." He placed a hand on her shoulder as though in condolence.

Ren looked at his hand as though it were an unsavory thing, struggling not to show her disgust. The priest had rings on every finger. One held a large ruby in a gold setting. His nails were long and carefully manicured, and the hand smelled of lavender.

She forced herself to meet his eyes. "Actually, Grandfather is recovering well," she said, pretending a calm she didn't feel. Lies did not come easily to her.

Anger, quickly hidden, showed in the tightening of Glays's mouth. He managed a nod. "Good news indeed, if such is the case. Our Lord is mighty. Blessed be our Lord. But there is a matter of some importance I would discuss with you. If the king is mending, as you say, I would have you wait."

Ren smiled. "Wait? For you? When there are so many more important matters to attend to?"

Filthy wench! The priest's fingers dug painfully into her shoulder.

Ren suppressed a grimace. The pressure eased almost immediately, yet his reaction gave him away. He was not master of himself. His emotions, his vanity, held sway.

More disturbing was the aggression he'd displayed. She was uncomfortably aware of her own vulnerability. Glays was easily a foot taller and a hundred pounds heavier than she, and now she was aware of his strength. His small, slate-colored eyes were windows on the arrogance, ambition, and cruelty that drove him.

Ren sensed something else, leering and possessive. She remembered the words of Meg, her handmaiden since birth. It had been the night of her first moon. "You are a woman now, and exceedingly beautiful. There'll be men who will want you for nothing more than that beauty. Not all will use flowery words or trinkets to win you. They'll try to take you. You must pluck the weeds before they take root."

"I can take care of myself, Meg," Ren had asserted. At that age, her visions of men took the shape of tall, handsome warriors, like Abdelar or Corwin, certainly not loathsome pigs like Glays.

Meg's wisdom was earthy, but often Ren found it far more practical than the obscure utterances of the Sisters.

Pluck the weed.

"Remove your hand," she said, using the voice of command taught to her by Sianiave, a voice without fear or doubt.

The priest blinked, staring down at the diminutive figure before him as though he couldn't believe what he'd heard. For a moment he appeared confused, but his anger quickly returned. His jaw clenched. Ren was sure he was going to strike her.

An amused chuckle from across the hall broke the tension. Glays looked up, eyes narrowing. Prince Corwin leaned against a pillar, his right hand fingering the pommel of his sword. "Problems, bishop?"

Behind Glays, Gothmog slunk further back into shadow.

"Certainly not." Glays looked at Ren. "We'll speak later, m'lady."

He turned away, as though dismissing her from his thoughts. "Captain Brand, wait here with your men. Come, Gothmog!"

Gothmog spat on the floor and followed the priest into the bedchamber.

CHAPTER
16

"WE'D BEST BE GOING" urged the old pikeman. For a brief moment, he wasn't sure the priest's soldiers would let them pass. He motioned to the other guard. "Jory, you're relieved. Go home. These fellows will look after the king now."

Jorald grunted in surprise. "You sure, Ben?"

"Go home. King's orders. I'll escort the princess to her quarters."

Jorald hesitated. The street trash the priest had gathered about him couldn't protect their hats in a calm wind. But Ben was as good a man as there was in the king's service, and with the princess herself standing there the order had to be obeyed.

He shrugged, lowering his pike. "If you say so, but I'm not liking it."

Corwin fell in behind as Shafter and Ren moved off. Once out of sight of Brand and the guardsmen, he stopped them. "Ren, there isn't much time. Your grandfather will stall as long as he's able."

"He has the dagger."

"He's very weak. I doubt his chance for success. I must leave you here." He put a hand on the pikeman's shoulder. "Keep an eye out, Ben."

"M'lord, why don't we just do him ourselves? Against us and Jory, that rabble couldn't—"

"I wish it were that simple, but this goes deeper than Glays. Until it's sorted out we'll follow the king's wishes. Take Ren to the stables. Aerindir and Abdelar are waiting."

"The stables?" Ben frowned as he realized the plan. Ren must be fleeing Barad'An. The thought troubled him deeply, but he saw the sense of it.

Benjamin Shafter of the Royal House Guard was old by any man's standards, both in years and experience. He'd served Cuchulain for over sixty years, and King Cymbromir before him. He'd survived many a battle, but none with so dark an outlook as this. The world had changed this past hour. That was the truth of it.

The king had given him his leave. He could retire with honor, spend his remaining days tending his garden with the missus, watch the grandchildren grow up—but in a world ruled by Glays.

He straightened. Whatever the future, he had one last task to complete before his oath was fulfilled.

Corwin took Ren's hands, leaning forward to kiss her cheek. "It's up to you now." He saluted Shafter and left.

Ren stood silent. She had beauty, rank, and a facade of strength, but she was little more than a child, one left to deal with matters beyond her experience. The weight of a kingdom would soon be on her shoulders.

"Come on, Ben," she said. "It seems we're on our own."

Ren set the pace. Ben settled into the loping battle run he'd learned as a young foot soldier. He took consolation in the fact that he carried his short pike that day instead of the heavier *cavalieret*, his horse killer.

He followed Ren across the Gathering Courtyard, skirting obsolete gardens, and down a broad stair overrun with hollyhock. As they crossed a weed-choked gaming field, Ren paused to study the ivied wall beyond.

"M'lady?"

Ben caught his breath. One thing he knew, this was not the way to the stables. Suddenly, Ren pulled aside a section of ivy to reveal a narrow, arched tunnel. Despite his years of service in the palace, he had never known of its existence.

"It will save us half a mile," said Ren. Sweeping aside cobwebs and spiders, she disappeared into the darkness. Head bowed to avoid the low ceiling, and against his better judgment, the old pikeman followed.

The tunnel sloped downward, growing ever darker. "Stairs here," whispered Ren. "Watch yourself."

Ben nearly tripped as his foot touched the first stair. Ren, surefooted as a cat, had already vanished. Thankfully, after twenty or so harrowing steps, there was light ahead. The stairs led to one of the many aqueducts that once irrigated the city. Now, it was dry and lichen-covered. Shafts of light filtered through overhead ducts.

They followed the aqueduct several hundred yards to another flight of stairs ending at a landing and a low oak door. Ren pulled open the door and they emerged into a grove of plum trees just west of the Moon Gate, smallest and least used of the four that led into the palace complex. The gate was open, and Ben saw no guards about. In fact they'd seen no one since leaving the king's quarters.

The market square lay on the other side of the gate. Its streets were crowded with people: shopkeepers and émigrés, soldiers, prostitutes, housewives, beggars, and artisans. All appeared to be staring up at the palace as though awaiting a sign. A woman and a young girl with worried faces stood aside as they passed.

Ren avoided the throng by cutting down the narrow alleyway separating the page quarters from the palace wall. From there it was only a few hundred yards to the east entrance of the stables.

Aerindir and Abdelar were leading three saddled horses from the staging paddock when they arrived. The knights had changed from their bloodstained garb into tough leather traveling clothes. Both were heavily armed, swords and daggers at their sides, full quivers across their shoulders, longbows in hand. The saddlebags were bulging and topped with bedrolls. The horses shifted, anxious in anticipation. Ren recognized them as three of the fleetest and sturdiest mounts in the city.

"Ren!" cried Abdelar. "Thank the stars."

Ben leaned over a hitching post, struggling to catch his breath and doing his best not to dishonor himself by throwing up. "Sorry, m'lady. I haven't had a run like that since the Battle of Neddley Vale, long twenty years hence."

"You did well, Ben," said Ren gently. She gave him an affectionate pat. "Your oath is fulfilled. Go home to your wife."

He rubbed the back of his hand across his mouth and straightened. "I'll wait to see you off, if you please."

Abdelar tossed Ren the reins to Light, a speckled buckskin gelding she'd ridden many times. She was pleased to find they'd brought her tournament bow from her apartments. It was a beautiful, deadly thing, fashioned of layered oak and ironwood, strung with catgut. Now it was attached to her saddle horn along with a full quiver. Her sword, Asin, along with a dagger hung there as well, on a sword belt that she quickly buckled around her waist.

"A troop of the priest's guard are headed this way," said Abdelar, mounting his own horse, a big roan named Glaerindor.

Aerindir steadied Stormcloud, a stallion named for the dark grey of his coat. He swung into the saddle just as the great horn of Barad'An sounded. The horn, set in an iron collar atop the Palace Tower, sounded only on two occasions: to warn the city of attack, or announce the passing of a king. Its mournful resonance echoed off the hard stones of the city. Ren knew it was the sign for which the people had been waiting.

"He's gone," whispered Abdelar, as if not quite believing it.

"Mourn later," growled Aerindir. "Now the priest rules in Barad'An!"

Ren had been well schooled, both in the martial arts of the knights and the subtle arts of the Sisters. Even so, a wave of grief threatened to undo her. Grief not only for her beloved grandfather, but also for a king, and for the city and people he'd ruled for more than half a century. Her city and people, which she loved with all her heart. And which she was about to abandon.

Light reared, almost pulling the reins from her hand. At the far end of the stables a double column of white-robed guardsmen was fast approaching.

"Ren!" cried Abdelar. "Now!"

She needed no urging. Light steadied as she leapt into the saddle. Without another word she spurred the gelding forward, out the paddock gate and down the cobbled road that led to the city's main gate, Aerindir and Abdelar close behind.

Ben Shafter watched until they vanished from sight. Those three are in for it, he thought gloomily, though half wishing he was young enough to join them.

By the time the three riders reached the plaza, the great gate was already grinding down. A platoon of guardsmen blocked the way. Ren didn't rein in until they were almost on top of them.

"Out of the way, you louts! Don't you know who I am?"

"Of course we know."

A bull-necked man stepped forward, a commander by his gold piping. This surprised Ren, for she'd never before seen him. How many others had Glays recruited into his private army unbeknownst?

"Aerindir and Abdelar, you are under arrest as traitors. Throw down your arms. Princess, you're to come with me."

Abdelar laughed. "Treason, is it?"

The two knights had slung their bows across their backs and drawn their swords, positioning their nervous mounts on either side of Ren. The priest's man stood unblinking, sure of himself. "No need for you to die here. Surrender and you'll be given a fair trial."

"Fair trial, my buttocks."

Sunlight gleamed off Abdelar's sword as it arced through the air. The man's head landed on the cobbles and rolled for several feet before being stopped by a guardsman's boot. The headless body collapsed backward, blood spraying those standing near.

For a moment the only sound that could be heard was the retching of a young recruit who'd been drenched in the ghastly shower. Another man, his face mottled purple in outrage, raised his pike and charged. "Murderers! You'll die for this!"

"Not today," said Aerindir. He twitched Stormcloud's reins. The stallion reared, its forehooves taking the man in the chest, crushing his ribs.

The other guardsmen moved in. "Kill them! Kill the heathens! God is great! For god and fellowship!"

Ren shoved her dagger through a man's eye as he tried to drag her from her horse. She broke another's thumb with a quick move, then sent him sprawling to the cobbles with a kick to his face. "The gate!" she cried, urging Light forward as she drew Asin. But too many blocked the way.

Battle horns sounded behind them. Ren parried a pike thrust, shoving Asin's point into her attacker's unprotected throat. Glancing back, she saw riders approaching, twenty at least. Her hope vanished when she saw the riders were all wearing the white cloaks of the priest's templars.

The gate was almost down. Aerindir and Abdelar had taken out half the original company of guardsmen, but those that remained and had pulled back to a position directly in front of the gate. There was no way to get through those pikes without risking the horses.

Suddenly the descent of the great gate stopped. Wooden gears shifted, slack ropes tightened. Slowly the gate began to rise.

"What?" screamed a guardsman. "Lower it! Lower the gate!"

The words changed to an incoherent gurgle as a white-feathered arrow struck his eye. Another man died with an arrow through his heart. One after another went down.

"Fletcher!" cried Ren. On the rampart above stood her aged mentor, bow in hand. Preoccupied as she was, she still marveled at his accuracy. Every arrow found its mark.

"Ride!" yelled Fletcher. "Ride!"

Ren and her protectors spurred their mounts through the gate to the open field.

§

From his perch on the wall, Captain Fletcher watched until they had crossed the field and vanished into the dark line of Arden Forest. A dozen or so white-cloaked riders, those who'd managed to escape his arrows, were at least a quarter mile behind.

A dozen? Aerindir and Abdelar would make stew meat of them, as would Ren. Better than anyone else in the city, Fletcher knew what she was capable of. He would have skewered more of the bastards but he'd run out of arrows. This and the fact his drawing arm ached as though a hot spike had been driven through it.

He removed a corncob pipe from a pocket under his chest plate, packed it with *suph* and lit it with a flint. Might as well have a smoke before they came for him. The dungeons, no doubt, unless they butchered him on the spot. Whatever way it went, it wouldn't be long. He could hear their footfalls coming up the nearest ramp.

He took a puff and sat down with his back to the stone parapet. Whatever his fate, he'd lived a good life, and he missed Helga, his wife, now long dead. His men would have joined him, but he'd ordered them off the wall. Politics wasn't his forte, and the sounding of the great horn had said it all. The king was dead. Glays would be steward, though it wouldn't be official until the conclave.

Ren was safe. All things considered, the royal archer of Barad'An was well pleased with himself.

CHAPTER
17

TRAVELING BY SLED in the mountains had proved exceedingly dangerous. Nick was glad to be clear of the ice flows, avalanches, and unexpected crevasses that had slowed their progress. They were making better time now. The snowfield at the skirt of the mountain sloped toward a broad expanse of forest. They had almost reached the tree line when, unexpectedly, Osmodon slammed down on the sled's brake.

"Hold up, Bear! Whoa, dogs!"

The big sled slid to a halt. The dogs, eleven of them, barked happily, tongues lolling, and settled into the snow. Bear, the big lead animal, looked back, puzzled by the stop. Nick wondered himself. The forest was less than a mile distant and several hours of daylight remained.

"A problem?" Sianiave asked.

"An odd sound," said Osmodon, jumping down from the rattan carriage. "Runner's my guess." He peered under the carriage, knocking away ice that had accumulated on the wooden runners. "As I feared, split near through. We'll be running on frame before long. Should've been quicker around that last snag."

Sianiave threw back her fur hood and removed her snow goggles, a piece of whittled wood with thin slits cut for vision. She used a hand to shade her eyes. "The snow's melting earlier than usual. You couldn't avoid them all."

Nick welcomed the break. Riding in the sled's carriage was more taxing than it appeared. Leg muscles constantly flexed and relaxed to compensate for the motion. They'd been traveling for three days and his legs were tired and sore.

"Can you fix it?" he asked Osmodon.

"It'll take time."

"We don't have time." Sianiave swung down beside Osmodon. "Will it make it to the forest?"

"If no more snags and luck is with us."

"Snow will be thinner under the trees. If it can't be fixed we'll walk. Ardendell isn't more than a league. Two at most."

Nick wondered at Sianiave's stamina. He was even more amazed at how much her appearance had changed since she'd arrived four days ago. When they'd first met he'd imagined her sixty-five, even seventy years old. She now looked twenty years younger. Even the color of her hair was different, not grey but silvery blond. He decided she was the most unusual woman he had ever met. Also the most irritating.

The change in her appearance was no more dramatic than the change in himself. Gone were his depression, his angst, the constant inner dialogue of impotence and guilt looping around in his head ever since that night in the Pamirs. Physically he felt stronger.

Not just felt—he was indeed stronger. Ten days of Osmodon's iron-handed training had put him into a shape he hadn't known since that summer in China. But that didn't explain half of his newfound strength. It was as though gravity itself was less in this world, gravity in all its manifestations, psychological as well as physical.

His hand fell to the sword at his side. The brass and leather scabbard strapped to the outside of his furs felt as comfortable as his combat rigging had felt in Afghanistan. Forty-four inches of razor-sharp steel, in quality the equal of a five-body *katana*. He could wield it as easily as he had the lightweight sabers and *épées* of his college days. In tests of strength he'd occasionally come close to besting Osmodon, surprising them both. On Earth, the Earth he'd known, he could imagine Osmodon competing in strongman competitions, tossing tree trunks, boulders, and blocks of pig iron around for sport.

"We'll camp in the trees tonight," said Sianiave decisively. She pointed to the forest below and a dark line of trees in the distance. "There's a river there, the Dunenwine. It flows to a large lake, the Dunenmere. Ardendell lies on its eastern bank."

Nick groaned inwardly. Ardendell was a way station for them, a village where Sianiave hoped to leave the sled and purchase horses for the remainder of the journey. The broken runner was a problem. A league or two, she'd said. He didn't look forward to hiking thirty miles or more in knee-deep snow.

"Let's go!" said Sianiave, clambering back into the sled. "We're already days behind."

"The mistress calls," sighed Osmodon, taking one last look at the runner.

Once onboard he let out a piercing whistle. With a jolt and renewed barking, the sled took off. Nick could now hear the sound that had alerted Osmodon, a thin abrasive hum coming off the right front runner that deepened in dissonance as they neared the forest.

Nick had learned a great deal since he'd arrived in this world. Tor Eyrie, the place where he first awakened, was a series of habitable caves high in a colossal range called the White Mountains. It lay just beyond the northern march of a kingdom named Anor. He'd learned this from Osmodon during his recovery.

From his experience in high mountains, he'd guessed Tor Eyrie's altitude to be near seventeen thousand feet, though the usual perceptions didn't apply here. The eagles were one example. As he'd watched from the terrace they soared overhead, graceful, majestic, improbably large and yet strangely unthreatening. The sky itself exhibited a similar contradiction. It seemed broader, more blue, yet somehow familiar. The thin air shouldn't have sustained him, yet he felt strong, even revitalized.

Some part of him remembered this place, this world where colors were more vivid, darkness darker, light lighter, the mountains higher, the very air more alive. During the day a glorious sun shone down on them. At night the stars twinkled like lamplights, scattered in constellations that were alien in ways he couldn't describe.

If the sun was king of the day, the moon was queen of the night. Though she carried the same markings as Earth's moon, here she appeared brighter and a good deal larger.

Since leaving Tor Eyrie, Nick had witnessed vast blue glaciers, frozen waterfalls a thousand feet high, herds of caribou as large as elk, and elk the size of Percherons. Other species he had never before encountered.

Once, they'd spotted a bear-like creature lumbering across the ice. Even at a distance it had appeared large enough to swallow a man whole. He had a nagging sense he should know about these things, indeed had known them. That taunting familiarity helped him accept it all.

In the end, it came down to observable facts. He still felt hunger and pain. Who was to say the world had come from wasn't the dream and this one the reality? If anything, this world actually felt more real.

He decided the sensible course was to take everything at face value. He'd been brought to a world not his own. Whether it was another planet, another dimension, or another time hardly mattered.

He was a soldier. He'd accepted a job. His clothes, including his coat, were missing, but they had given him replacements. In the pocket of his new fur coat, he'd found the bag of coins Sianiave had tossed him.

Sianiave had assigned Osmodon to be his counselor and weapons instructor. With little else to do, he'd thrown himself into the training with a fury. During breaks, Osmodon had answered what questions he could.

Tor Eyrie was only a small part of a network of connecting caves. Most were sealed, either intentionally or by time and the elements. It was said they'd once housed a great monastery. Water was drawn through a series of ingeniously engineered ceramic pipes. Hot water came from a mineral spring deep in the mountain to supply the kitchen and baths.

Merchants brought supplies to the tor from Ashar'Apu, a village in the river valley below. The villagers clearly held Sianiave in high regard, a regard they extended to her guests. They believed her to be descended from the ancient sorcerers who had once occupied the monastery.

"Do you think it's true?" Nick had asked Osmodon. "That she's descended from a race of sorcerers?"

"Can't say," he replied. "Some matters she doesn't talk about."

"How long have you known her?"

That question brought a rueful chuckle. "Met her at a tavern in Barad'An, if you believe it. She caught the eye of every man in the place when she walked in, but she sat at my table. Came directly to it, as though it were I she sought. I was a bit full of myself in those days. My only thought was to bed her.

"Bought her a drink," Osmodon continued. "Tried to soften her up, truth be told. Four flagons later I was dead drunk, and she still sober as a Sister. That's when she offered me a job. I was low on funds, not thinking too clearly. And she brought out this purse of empresses."

"Empresses? Coins?"

"Aye, ten of them. She wanted me to escort her to Minador, a city west of Barad'An, ten leagues maybe. Got in a skirmish or two, nothing difficult. Can't say the same for the next one, though."

"Next one? Another job?"

"Aye. That one nearly cost my life."

Osmodon seemed unwilling to say more, and Nick didn't press the subject. "You said you've been with her ten years."

"Ten, did I say? Seems more like a century. I may have mentioned, there's things she doesn't talk about, and much is beyond my ken. But she pays well and keeps me busy."

Nick had formed a picture of Osmodon and the woman who had hired them both. Osmodon was a good man. Sianiave had not only captured his loyalty, she'd provided him with a purpose. Exactly what this purpose was he couldn't or wouldn't say, but clearly he believed it noble.

Despite her sometimes thorny disposition, Osmodon had come to trust Sianiave, offering his fealty. "She earned it," he said, half jokingly. "Frankly I was surprised when she accepted, but knowing her now as I do, I suspect she planned it all along."

Osmodon claimed to know little about why Sianiave had brought Nick to Tor Eyrie. He never asked Nick where he came from, and Nick avoided the subject. In the end Nick simply said that Sianiave had hired him to protect a girl somewhere. Why she chose him he had no idea. He was just an ordinary soldier from another country.

When Osmodon heard this he let out a bellowing laugh. "Sianiave doesn't waste time with 'ordinary' soldiers. She has her reasons, believe it."

He'd paused, sitting back to study Nick thoughtfully. "Aye. Soldier you may be. But ordinary? I think not. For one, you've too great a skill with a sword." Nick had taken a moment's pride in the compliment, as Osmodon was a formidable swordsman.

The big man was also an enthralling storyteller. One evening after a brutal day of training, they'd tapped a keg of Sianiave's ale. Osmodon had filled the evening with tales of fighting, womanizing, and sorcery.

Barad'An was a city in the south, he'd explained, once the capital of a great empire, now fallen into hardship. Cuchulain, its king, was a fool; a brave man, but a fool nonetheless, reliving past glories while his kingdom fell into decay.

Artos, Cuchulain's nephew, was by all accounts strong and true, with a keen intelligence and an almost preternatural instinct that once had been the hallmark of his line. Osmodon had first traveled to Barad'An to offer his fealty to Artos, but he'd arrived a fortnight too late. Artos was gone, banished by his uncle. Jealousy, some said, or a disagreement over some matter; others whispered of treachery and sorcery. Ten years had passed and there had been no word of him.

Nick found Osmodon's stories fascinating, but assumed them to be little more than fairytales.

He related more easily to the villagers who lived below Tor Eyrie, at least those hardy few who traveled twice weekly up the narrow pass bringing supplies and food. Both in dress and manner they had reminded him of the Afghans he'd met in the Pamirs. Even their language seemed oddly similar, though when Sianiave had appeared a week later, she'd quickly dissuaded him from such ideas.

"What language are we speaking?" she'd asked when he'd brought up the subject.

"Speaking? Now? English, of course."

She'd looked amused. "English? Really?"

"Of course it's English."

"Try saying a word that describes something from your world. Something you don't see here."

Tor Eyrie was lit with candles, torches, and oil lamps. The image of a light bulb sprang to his mind, but when he tried to name it, no word would come, at least none that made sense. He tried speaking of computers, cell phones, airplanes, and automobiles, all with the same result. The more he struggled, the more the words—even the images—escaped him. His head ached with the intense effort.

Sianiave was sympathetic. "Don't fight it. Such things don't exist in this world. They can't exist in this world. You might be able to draw a picture, use written symbols, but I would advise against it. Words, images, and thoughts send out resonances. The effects, if not properly guided or applied, can be calamitous."

"We're speaking English now, I'm sure of it."

"No. You hear it as English, because that is what you know. But English doesn't exist in this world. No more than those other things you could imagine but were unable to name."

She grew serious. "There are correspondences between the worlds, of course. Otherwise you wouldn't be here. We couldn't be here. But they aren't the ones you think. That's why the appearance of the morghul in your world is so troubling. It knew the dangers, yet still it came. It risked more than you can imagine, just to get at you."

"Me?" Nick had winced at the memory, the revulsion he'd felt, the pain of the hammer slamming into his shoulder. "Why me?"

What was so special about him that some monster from another world would apparently take great risks to seek him out?

CHAPTER
18

THE RUNNER GAVE OUT five minutes into the forest, nearly toppling the sled. "That's it," said Osmodon surveying the damage. "It would take half a day's work to whittle a new runner."

Sianiave tossed a leather satchel on the ground. "Don't bother. This forest is too thick for the sled. We'll make better time walking."

She looked up through a break in the canopy where a half moon rose against a deepening orange sky. "It will be night soon," she added, frowning.

Nick sensed caution in her words. The first night out from Tor Eyrie they'd slept in a cave high in the mountains. The second night they stayed in the ruins of an abandoned temple, so old even Sianiave couldn't recall the god for which it had been built. This forest felt different, less protected. Nick remembered the eagles, and the bear-like creature he'd seen lumbering across the ice.

They made camp next to the damaged sled, under the branches of a towering willow. Nick collected firewood while Osmodon fed the dogs, tossing them cakes of the dried meat that had been their fare since leaving Ashar'Apu. Growling and barking, the dogs fought over the meal, but in the end all were satisfied.

Sianiave sorted through the supplies, deciding what to take and what to abandon. By her reckoning, Ardendell was still a good two days march south, but it could be more. She put items she deemed essential in a pile: bows, arrows, swords and daggers, oil and sharpening stones, flint, cooking utensils, and rope. They would keep their coats but do without the other furs, though pleasant to sleep on. They'd take the food, of course, though game was plentiful.

The coins she carried were heavy, but that couldn't be helped. They needed horses and tack. This far north neither would come cheap. Further south there would be more expenses. There were other means, of course, but sorcery drew sorcery to it, as light drew darkness.

The air beneath the trees was still and heavy. Drifts of snow had settled in the hollows and against the trunks. In some patches spring grass was already pushing up through the damp forest loam.

Twilight settled and the forest grew deathly quiet, as if the trees themselves were holding their breath. Even the dogs, chewing on the last of their meal, perked their ears as if they sensed something lurking in the darkness.

Nick dropped an armful of broken branches on the snow. "That should do it."

Sianiave barely glanced up from her work. "We need more for a watch-fire, enough to burn through the night. This is an old forest. It has little fondness for humans."

"That bear we saw, might it come for the food?"

"The dogs can deal with bears."

Her remark gave Nick pause. "Is there something you're not telling me?"

"Just keep your sword at the ready."

"Something's off," said Osmodon. "The dogs sense it. Forest's too quiet." He was carrying an armful of harnesses, which he tossed into a pile by the sled. "They won't be needing these. It's a long way back to Ashar'Apu."

"You're sending them back?" Nick had grown fond of the dogs, especially Bear, the lead. The journey seemed friendlier with them around, not to mention safer. At night they cuddled like puppies, keeping one another warm.

"They'll be of little use from here on. It's best we loose them. Come morning, I'll give them a good feed. Their home's in the mountains and Bear knows the way. They'll be safer than we, I ken."

Osmodon set about building the fire while Nick went to find more wood. His search for dry fuel took him far from the campsite.

A sound, a soft "hu," startled him. He looked up to see two large yellow eyes peering down from an overhanging branch. He dropped the wood he'd been carrying and drew his sword. Another "hu," low and inquisitive, was followed by the flutter of wings as an owl left its perch and flew into the night.

Feeling foolish, Nick sheathed his sword and began reclaiming his wood. To his left, a flickering light became visible through the trees. The light cast black shadows that seemed to move from tree to tree as if alive. Firelight, Nick realized with sudden relief. Osmodon had started the fire.

He weighed the wood in his arms. They had enough, he decided. If Sianiave wanted more, she could get it herself.

When he arrived back at the campsite the meal was ready: black tea, dried fruit, dried meat, and biscuits. They ate in silence. The forest had a way of dampening conversation. Even Osmodon, normally loquacious, spoke little.

Nick arranged his sleeping furs against the trunk of an oak. He lay back facing the fire, watching the embers as they rose like fireflies into the night. The pungent odor of burning wood and the crackle of the fire were comforting. The air was so still the smoke rose straight upward. The dogs had settled down.

Sianiave tamped leaves into the bowl of her pipe, lighting it the same way she had that first night at the mansion. Nick noticed neither she nor Osmodon faced the fire. Instead they sat obliquely, their eyes continually returning to the darkness between the trees, their weapons within arm's reach.

Nick shifted his own seat. Staring directly at a fire obscured vision. He knew better, but the comfort of the furs, the quiet pleasure of the fire, and the mysterious nature of the forest itself all had an intoxicating effect. It made him neglect the dangers that might lurk beyond the camp.

He looked around as he waited for his eyes to adjust. He noticed Sianiave watching him. The firelight reflected off her green eyes and golden hair. Golden?

He stared in fascination. Her hair, more silvery than blond that very day, now appeared full and golden. Her face looked younger, no older than thirty-five. The uncomfortable thought came to him that Sianiave was not only an extraordinary woman, but also an extraordinarily beautiful woman. The crooked nose and the scar on her chin only enhanced her beauty.

Had the appearance of age been an act, a disguise? If so, she was a master illusionist. Was this woman in the firelight her true self, or was this the illusion? If Osmodon was to be believed, she was indeed a sorceress. How many fairy stories had he read as a child warning of the sinister shape-shifting abilities of witches? That was before his foster parents had burned the books he'd brought with him from the agency, calling them satanic trash.

"You still believe this to be a dream?" Sianiave asked, smiling, as though aware of his thoughts.

"I'm no longer sure what to believe."

Smiling, she took a deep puff on her pipe, then let out a series of smoke rings.

"Don't tease the lad," growled Osmodon. "His answer was as sensible as any I've heard. Who can know the truth of such matters? Not even you, I suspect, with all your witch's knowledge. The desert people have a saying: 'Life is a caravan of dreams. Dogs bark, and the caravan moves on,' whatever our thoughts or beliefs about it."

Sianiave sent another smoke ring skyward. "A wise saying."

Nick had the uncomfortable feeling he was missing something of vital importance, but any thought he had on the matter was cut off by a searing cry deep from within the forest. It lingered, then trailed off.

"What in hell was that?"

"Quiet!" hissed Sianiave. Both she and Osmodon sat motionless, listening intently.

A second howl, this one much closer. Sianiave jumped to her feet. Osmodon grabbed his sword and battle-ax. "Keep your back to the fire, lad. They fear fire."

Nick stumbled as he buckled on his sword. "They? Who's they? What's out there?"

"Wolves," said Sianiave, sticking her sword point-first into the snow within easy reach as she took up a bow.

"You're worried about wolves and not bears?"

"Arden wolves, lad," said Osmodon as if that should explain it. He was peering into the forest as though intent alone could pierce the darkness. The dogs whimpered, all except Bear. He stood facing the direction from which the howls came, as if to protect the others.

Seconds passed. Something moved, or was it shadows playing tricks again? Nick rubbed his eyes. Red lights appeared in a line in front of the trees, glowing like malevolent fireflies. Was he imagining them?

Eyes, he realized with a shock. There were shapes behind them, wolf-like with fangs and snouts, yet larger than any wolves he'd ever seen. Their matted heads were disproportionately large, even for such massive bodies. He counted at least a dozen of the lean beasts.

"They're hungry," said Sianiave, nocking an arrow. "They're working up their courage. That big one by the oak. He'll come first. I have one shot, then it's blades."

"Their heads," said Osmodon. "Take off their heads." There was a glint in the big man's eyes and a maniacal grin on his face.

Sianiave drew her bow. "Beware an old man in a cloak."

"What do you—" Nick hadn't finished his question when Sianiave released her arrow. It struck the big wolf's eye just as it charged. The beast fell to the snow, snarling in agony but not yet dead.

The wolves attacked. Osmodon decapitated one with a stroke of his ax. Sianiave dropped her bow, taking up her sword in time to slice the top off a head. Turning quickly, she disemboweled another. Any other time, Nick might have enjoyed observing her skill, for she moved with lethal grace.

But the battle was on him. In the bloody minutes that followed, he lost all sense of time. He aimed for the heads, but often had to settle for quick thrusts and slashes at lesser targets.

Then from nowhere a beast leapt, grabbing his sword arm in its jaws, its weight throwing him back into the flames. With his left hand he drew his dagger and gutted the animal, rolling away just in time to avoid catching fire.

Then, as quickly as it had begun, the battle was over. The few wolves left backed slowly away, then turned and vanished into the forest.

Nick stood, breathing heavily. Carcasses, limbs, and heads lay about, along with a few dying wolves. Osmodon was covered head to foot in blood and entrails. "Well, that was a bit of fun," he said.

"Fun?" muttered Sianiave caustically. "Do you realize the danger if even one of us had fallen?"

Her eyes turned to the wolf she'd shot, still alive, the arrow embedded in its right eye. It snapped viciously as she approached. "I'm rather fond of wolves in general," she said. "But these things aren't really wolves, any more than trolls are human." With a stroke of her sword she took off the beast's head. "Foul, evil creatures."

She wiped her blade on the creature's fur. "How are the dogs?"

"The dogs?" Osmodon looked as though he'd been slapped. "The dogs!"

He ran to the tree where the dogs had been resting. Of the seven near the tree, not one remained alive; all were torn apart by the wolves. Seven of eleven, Nick thought. The other four must have run off or been dragged away by the retreating pack.

Osmodon was trembling; whether in rage or grief, Nick couldn't tell. He kicked at the body of a dead wolf. "Bloody damn beasts! The dogs got one, at least. Good and faithful creatures they were. I should have looked after them better."

"It's not your fault, Osmodon," said Sianiave with a surprising gentleness. "Dogs are no match for Arden wolves. We were lucky to survive ourselves. Perhaps some escaped. I don't see Bear."

Osmodon turned away as though he hadn't heard. With slumped shoulders he walked slowly toward the fire. Never had Nick seen a man look so forlorn.

"He has a soft heart," said Sianiave, sighing. "But we've other worries at present. We have to move camp. Wolves aren't the only predators in this forest. The smell of blood will attract even more evil creatures—wyverns, trolls, beings you don't want to think about."

"Wyverns? Trolls? I hope you're joking."

She flicked a piece of gore off her coat. "Do I look like I'm joking?"

§

It took them only minutes to pack. Osmodon helped, but said little.

Nick had shoved a last pot in his backpack and was tying the laces when a sound caught his attention, a moan or whimper. Barely audible, it came from the forest. "Do you hear that? It sounds like a wounded animal."

Sianiave closed her eyes to listen, then nodded. "That's no wolf."

"You can see about it," said Osmodon dully. "I don't have the heart otherwise. Call out if it's one of the dogs."

The fire still burned strongly, but beyond its light the forest was black as ink. On the far side of the willow, between darkness and dancing shadows, Nick found Bear, his head resting mournfully on the flanks of another dog.

"It's Bear!"

Bear wasn't hurt. The other dog, a young female, had half her stomach torn out. She lay on her side, barely breathing. Every now and then a soft whimper escaped. She barely reacted when Nick stroked her head. Bear glanced up, a plea in his eyes.

"I'm sorry, boy. There's nothing I can do."

Bear settled his head back against the female. Nick knew he should kill the dog, end her pain. Thankfully the decision was taken from him. She lifted her head one last time, nuzzled Bear as if to say farewell, then was gone.

"I'm sorry."

For a moment Bear lay unmoving. Then his head picked up, suddenly alert. He gave a low growl and leapt to his feet.

Someone was there, in the darkness between the trees. More shadow than substance, the person's appearance was so out of context Nick could only assume it to be one of his companions.

"Ozzy?"

This figure wore a cloak, face hidden beneath a cowl. If it had been Osmodon or Sianiave, Bear wouldn't be reacting as he was.

The specter stood silent, ominous. Nick suddenly remembered Sianiave's strange warning: Beware an old man in a cloak.

He glanced back at the camp. Sianiave and Osmodon were walking in his direction, oblivious to the figure in the woods.

"Who are you? What do you want?"

He heard the hiss of a dry chuckle. The specter was less than ten feet away. How had it gotten so close?

He drew his sword. "Stay where you are!"

Another hiss. The cloak seemed to shimmer, then dissolve, like black ink on black water. Nick found himself staring at the yellowed fangs and vulpine eyes of the largest wolf he'd ever seen.

He barely had time to raise his arm before the creature leapt on him, its weight driving him against a tree and knocking the sword from his hand. His forearm, protected by the thick fur coat, was the only thing between his neck and the beast's slavering jaws. He fumbled desperately for his dagger.

There was a sudden jolt, and the weight fell away. Possessed by rage, Bear had charged into the beast headlong, tearing at its flank tooth and claw. Nick grabbed up his sword just as the wolf regained its footing. The sharp blade cut deep into the creature's neck. Another swing and the head rolled free.

He fell back against the tree, shaken, while Bear continued to vent his fury on the headless torso. Sianiave and Osmodon arrived, blades in hand. Bear made one last attack at the bloodied body, then fell back panting.

"Big bloody thing," observed Osmodon, lifting a hind leg. "Two hundred pounds or more, even without the head."

Sianiave reached out to Nick's face. Her touch was cool and soft as she studied the cuts. "You were lucky. Little more than scrapes."

"You knew—" Nick could barely get the words out. "The old man?"

"A characteristic of Arden wolves is that the dominant male is always a shape-shifter. I thought the big male I killed was the alpha, but evidently I was mistaken."

"Shape-shifter? You mean a werewolf?" Nick was stunned.

"No. Those are rare indeed and don't travel in packs. Shape-shifters use a mind trick, an illusion. How's your hand?"

Nick flexed his fingers. "Looks worse than it is."

"Good. We don't have the time to spend on another healing. We'll clean those cuts. The gods know what filth it carried."

Bear walked up to Nick and dropped the wolf's gruesome head at his feet.

Osmodon grinned. "A gift for you."

CHAPTER
19

THEY SHOULDERED THEIR PACKS and started off, trudging deeper into the forest. Osmodon carried a small oil lamp and led the way. For Nick, the lamp's elfin light called up a dim, almost forgotten memory. He was lying in a bed, a woman looking down at him. She had long, dark hair and her lips were bright red. To his infant's mind she appeared exceedingly beautiful. She stroked his forehead, whispering, "Always remember, child. The darker the night, the brighter shines the candle."

His real mother? Nick didn't know.

Though Osmodon's lamp was barely the size of a pint glass, the dark forest magnified its light. He wondered whether it might attract the very beasts they hoped to avoid. Bear, trotting protectively alongside, seemed to share his concern, tracking back and forth, attentive to every scent and shadow.

"You've a bond now, lad," said Osmodon, commenting on the dog's vigilance. "Bear's taken you as family."

"How do you figure?"

"That female you found him with was Nettle, his eldest pup. Must have broken his heart, not being able to protect her and the others."

"Sounds like someone else I know," Nick said with a smile.

"Aye, mayhap. It's our job, you see, to protect those unable to protect themselves. By saving you, Bear regained his sense of purpose. That's why he gave you the thing's head—his way of saying, 'See, I can still do my job.'"

§

Nick had spent most of his childhood shunted from one loveless foster home to another. The longest he'd lived with a family was three years during high school with the Dobsons, a joyless and juiceless couple who'd tried without success to convert him to their tortured vision of Christianity. Miserable as he'd been, there had always been a dog around to comfort him, a stray or a neighbor's pet. Leaving the dogs had always been harder than leaving the families.

The Herrons, the last couple he'd lived with under the foster care system, were the sole exception. With their urging he'd taken their name as his own, though he'd known them less than a year. Those too-short months spent in their home in Newport had made up for the previous seventeen years of beatings, neglect, and empty promises.

During his sophomore year at West Point, the Herrons had left for Cabo San Lucas in *Jung's Dream*, their fifty-two-foot motorsailer. They never arrived. The Coast Guard suspected drug pirates, for the weather had been mild and Bob and Betsy were experienced sailors. Neither they nor *Jung's Dream* were ever seen again. It was as though they'd vanished from the face of the earth.

Osmodon, his lamp held high, led the way through the forest. "Bear's full name is Beonard," he said after a bit, breaking the oppressive silence and jarring Nick from his thoughts. "It means 'strength of the bear.' Your name, Nicholas, I'm uncertain of. But your clan name holds great meaning."

"My clan name?"

"Aye. Heron. A legend recounted to me as child tells the story of how, during The First Age, Horu, lord of the Anaki, decided that we rebellious humans were no longer worth the trouble to keep as slaves. So he ordered up a great flood to end the experiment. But his brother, Osir, was sympathetic to humans and disagreed. Hoping to save them he sent a heron, being a diving bird, to rescue a couple, a male and a female from the rising waters. These were Moste and Mara. Herons are still revered in places to this day."

"A common myth in many realms," murmured Sianiave.

"I thought there was no corollary here with—" Nick stopped, unable to find words either for "English" or "Earth" that made any sense.

Sianiave, following Osmodon, glanced over her shoulder. "I never said there weren't corollaries, only that they aren't the ones you imagine."

The answer was typical of her. "How can you know what I imagine?"

"Experience has to come first."

Just answer the damn question! he wanted to shout, but his irritation was short-lived. He remembered trying to tell Osmodon what it was like in his world. As much as it hurt his ego to admit, he was the child here, the innocent, though the longer he remained the more familiar the place became, even this gloomy forest. The memory of his world was fading.

Osmodon had stopped. He was studying a barely discernible linear depression that led off into the blackness. "What do you make of this? A path, I ken."

Sianiave moved closer. It was impossible to see beyond the range of the lantern. The darkness was near total. "It's going in the right direction. You've a concern?"

"Animals usually take the easiest route. Yet I see no tracks."

The forest had grown denser the further they progressed, cluttered with fallen trees and tangled undergrowth. To Nick the path looked inviting, its lack of animal tracks more plus than minus.

"Let the dog decide," suggested Sianiave.

"Good enough. Bear! Come here, boy."

The dog trotted up to Osmodon, tail wagging. Osmodon stroked his ears, then pointed. "This way, yes or no?"

With a bark Bear leapt over a fallen tree and disappeared down the path. Several minutes later he reappeared, barked twice, then ran down the path again for ten feet before he stopped, looking back at them.

"Satisfied?" said Sianiave. Her smile said she'd known all along what the answer would be.

Nick, for one, was glad to be on easier ground. They'd been on the march for over an hour, stumbling over roots and branches and struggling through snowdrifts. The fight had taken more out of him than he cared to admit. He was exhausted. His legs ached and the pack chafed his shoulders. Even Osmodon looked done in. Only Sianiave seemed untouched by the hardship, appearing to grow stronger the further they traveled.

They crossed a small stream. A paving stone was visible under the flowing water, with more stones further up the bank. They were following what appeared to be an ancient road.

When Nick pointed it out, Osmodon showed little interest. "Aye. Reckoned so, straight as it is. Question is, where does it lead?"

He turned back to Sianiave. "M'lady, shouldn't we be looking for a place to camp? It's been a long night, and I for one—" He stopped abruptly, raising his lantern. "Hello. What have we here?"

A two-story cottage stood in front of them, stoutly built of logs, slate, and stone. Broad stairs led up to a wide porch. Above it all towered a massive chimney.

As they drew nearer, Nick saw that skilled labor had gone into its construction. The stones had been carefully laid. The wood was grey with age but solid-looking and finely joined. Geometric figures had been carved into the window shutters—five- and six-pointed stars, triangles, and spirals. An octagon decorated the front door.

Sianiave gave a satisfied nod. "Good. We'll have a roof over our heads."

Nick's right hand moved unconsciously to the pommel of his sword. Sianiave, at least, had no such reservations. She was halfway up the stone steps. "Come along. It's safe."

"She's probably right," said Osmodon, obviously sharing Nick's concerns as he studied the building. "She usually is. Doesn't look like anybody's lived in it for years."

Dried vines covered one side of the house and weeds grew out of cracks in the foundation. Branches from nearby trees had worked their way under the eaves, pressing against the stone walls. A well in front had collapsed in on itself, and the porch was covered in a thick mat of dead leaves and drifts of snow.

Bear bounded up the steps after Sianiave. "Good," muttered Osmodon, his eye on the dog. "But I'm still keeping my sword handy."

Either the cottage door had been left unfastened or Sianiave was a master locksmith, for she had it open by the time the two men reached the top of the steps. The door was made of heavy timbers banded with iron. The latch and lock had been artfully forged.

Inside was a great room. A stone hearth dominated the far wall. There were several pieces of rough-hewn furniture and shelving but little else. A wooden staircase led to the upper floor. Firewood was stacked neatly in a corner. Sianiave dropped her pack and started tossing logs into the hearth.

The logs were so dry they didn't need kindling. Sianiave lit them as she lit her pipe, a trick Nick had yet to fathom.

"This was the ferryman's cottage," she said.

Osmodon looked up in surprise. "Ferryman? We're near Ostengarth, then. We've reached the river."

"You'll hear it in your dreams tonight. There are bedrooms upstairs but I think it best we sleep by the fire. There is a bath in back."

"I take it the ferryman doesn't live here anymore," said Nick, looking around at the empty room.

Sianiave explained. "Ostengarth was once the main crossing for the North Road. There was a garrison of border rangers nearby, a doughty lot. We'll see their tower in the morning, though it's undoubtedly in ruins now. It was tending that way the last time—" She suddenly stopped.

"When was that?" Nick asked.

Sianiave didn't answer immediately. "It's been a while," she said finally.

Osmodon set his ax and sword near the door, arranging his bedding in a corner near the hearth. "So the ferry's no more. How do we cross?"

"There's no need to cross." Sianiave found her pipe in a pocket of her coat and sat back in a chair in front of the fire. "We'll see the road in the morning. It parallels the river a ways, or used to. Cymbromir, Cuchulain's father, recalled the garrison eighty years ago. A week later forest bandits burned Ostengarth to the ground. This cottage was the only building left standing, and the ferryman the only person who escaped."

"This place is hardly a fortress," said Osmodon, settling down. "How did the ferryman manage to survive?"

"The ferryman was no Ostengarther. Nor was he really a ferryman for that matter. He was trained in Megida by the Brotherhood."

Osmodon looked up in surprise. "A wizard?"

"Aye. The year that Kosha Khan sacked Megida, he took refuge here and cast a binding."

"A binding. That explains the lack of tracks. It must have bled out onto the path." Osmodon gave Sianiave an accusing look. "You knew all along."

"What's a binding?" asked Nick. He set his pack down in a corner opposite Osmodon. The things Sianiave and Osmodon spoke about so casually mystified him. Despite recent experience, he still had trouble believing in wizards, or magic. He'd seen things that mystified him, but understood little of it.

"A binding is a spell," Sianiave said, "cast to protect a thing or place from, shall we say, disruptive forces."

"The manor house, when we met. You said the fire had weakened the binding."

"That was not a natural fire, as you may have guessed. And that house was older than it looked—far older. Of course, one must consider the strength of the original spell. The summoning of a binding as powerful as the one cast on this cottage is no spell for a novice. The ferryman was an adept. No one knows how old he was when he arrived here, but he tended the Ostengarth ferry for many years. He was a kindly fellow, but with little heart for his craft.

"A friend and I were once guests in this very house," she added. "The year the garrison was disbanded."

Sianiave had spoken offhandedly, but Nick sensed something else. Sadness, perhaps. Then he realized another implication of what she'd said.

"You said the garrison was disbanded eighty years ago."

Sianiave gave him a smile. "Let's just say I wasn't young, even then."

"That's impossible! That would make you—"

Osmodon sighed sympathetically. "Don't fret on it, lad. Imagine how I felt, realizing the girl I was trying to bed was old enough to be my great-grandmother."

"Enough," said Sianiave.

"Or great, great, great, great—"

"I said that's enough!"

With a look of amusement, Osmodon rolled over onto his side. "Don't wake me early. I haven't felt so done-in in years." With that he fell instantly asleep.

Sianiave tamped a mix into her pipe. Nick watched her, incredulous. Maybe time was different here. Maybe centuries didn't mean centuries. Maybe she and Osmodon were playing with him.

"Get some sleep," she said.

The fire eased the chill in the room. Bear curled up in front of the hearth. With his coat for a blanket and his pack for a pillow, Nick lay back. The last thing he saw before falling fast asleep was Sianiave seated in the chair by the fire, quietly smoking her pipe, lost in thought.

That night he dreamed, not of wolves and sorcerers, but of harsh lights and unfamiliar eyes of faces hidden behind green masks. He couldn't understand what they said, but their eyes showed concern, and there was a troubling urgency to their movements. In horror he realized they didn't see him. How could they help if they didn't see him?

He cried out in terror. "They don't see!" He repeated it over and over. "They don't see!"

A hand stroked his head, soft and comforting. A woman's gentle voice said, "Some see, child. Some see. You aren't alone. Trust me. All will be well again."

The images of lights and masks shimmered, changed, became sunlight reflecting off an emerald-green pool in a forest. A stringed instrument, a mandolin or lyre, played nearby. Amid the smell of pine needles and spring flowers, a beautiful girl with green eyes and golden hair swam naked in the pool, bathing under a waterfall.

CHAPTER 20

MORNING LIGHT FOUND A CRACK in the shutters and fell across Nick's eyes. Osmodon crouched by the fire baking biscuits as a pot of snow heated for tea and porridge. Sianiave was nowhere to be seen.

"Sleep well, did you, lad?"

Images of harsh lights and green masks, and the abject terror he'd felt, were now fading. What stayed with him was the image of the girl in the pool. "Very well," he said, and meant it.

He stood and stretched. His body was nowhere near as stiff as it might have been. Despite the growing rankness of his clothes and a foul taste in his mouth, he found himself in surprisingly good spirits.

Osmodon seemed to share his mood. "Right place, this cabin, spells or no. Sianiave's out collecting firewood," he added, flipping over a biscuit. "Said we should replace what we use. Took the dog with her."

"She's collecting wood and you're cooking? Interesting."

"She wanted to be by herself, I reckon. This place has some meaning for her, though I've no idea why. Ten years working for the woman and she's more of a mystery to me than when we met."

There were a dozen questions Nick wanted to ask, about Sianiave's age and the change in her appearance. What was this great purpose she pursued that Osmodon followed without question?

"No running water," grunted Osmodon. "Better outside anyway. No telling how many years a man wastes, pissing indoors."

Nick dug out the utensil Osmodon called a "bum brush" from his pack, along with the furred stick that served as a toothbrush and the powder that passed for toothpaste. As he walked outside, he noted the morning was surprisingly warm as the sun rose above the trees in the east. Bluebirds, jays, and robins were busy, and the air smelled of honey and pine smoke. New grass sprouted between patches of melting snow. All around the cabin, leaves budded green on the trees. It was an altogether different place from the witch's cottage he'd imagined the night before.

He breathed in a deep lungful of the crisp air and headed for the nearest tree. It was spring in this world, Nick knew. Early April, Osmodon had told him, though he hadn't guessed the exact day. It had been fall when he'd left that other world, October 31. Billy had called it Samhain, the time of witches, when the borders between the worlds were at their weakest. That bit of folklore had certainly taken on new meaning.

Sianiave entered the cottage several minutes later with an armful of wood and Bear at her heels. With a satisfied grunt, she dropped the wood by the hearth.

Nick and Osmodon, halfway through their breakfast, looked up in surprise. She had doffed her heavy furs, wearing instead tight buckskin pants and a brightly woven vest over a cotton shirt. She sported calf-high leather walking boots. Her golden hair, no longer hidden under a fur cap, was woven into a single braid down her back.

She is beautiful, Nick thought, even radiant. But it wasn't just her hair or clothes that caught him off guard. Nor were they the reason Osmodon, who'd seen her earlier that morning, was also staring open-mouthed.

Sianiave was smiling. Not the amused half-smile they were used to, or the sad smile of vanished memories, but a smile that glowed from the inside, bringing sparkle to her features. For the first time since Nick had known her, she appeared to be happy.

"I found a boat," she announced, ignoring their stares as she grabbed a biscuit.

"A boat?" Osmodon said, densely.

"A boat. Grounded by the old quay. I fear its owner met a bad end, judging by the bloodstains. Bit of luck for us, however."

Osmodon gave Nick a questioning glance. Both knew it would take more than finding an old boat to put her in such a mood. Perhaps it was the energy of the place, or the early coming of spring.

Osmodon asked, "And it's the finding of this boat that's brought such pleasure to m'lady?"

Sianiave looked up from her meal as if startled. "It's a fine morning, and that boat will save us two days at the least."

"We've been traveling at a good pace. Is it Gwyndolyn that concerns you?"

Gwyndolyn. A not-unpleasant shiver ran up Nick's spine. It was the first time he could recall having heard the name, yet it struck a chord, reminding him of forest pools, music, and green light.

"Of course I'm concerned about her," said Sianiave sharply. "Something's wrong. Events are in motion. We leave as soon as we finish eating." The smile had vanished.

"Is Gwyndolyn the girl we're going to meet?" asked Nick. "Is she a relative?" He was fishing. Neither Sianiave nor Osmodon had been especially forthcoming about the job he'd been hired for, though for different reasons. Osmodon seemed to know little more than he.

"Relative?" Osmodon's eyes crinkled in humor. "Now there's something I hadn't considered. Is she, m'lady? A relative, I mean?"

Sianiave set down her plate. "Osmodon, you've said enough."

"My apology." Osmodon looked only a little sheepish.

They left the cottage soon after, with Nick musing about the hidden meanings and secrets hinted at that morning. Sianiave led them down a gently sloping path that took them through the center of what had once been a sizable village. Here and there a broken wall or foundation peered out from the underbrush. A tall brick chimney was kept from toppling by the elms grown up around it. The stone arch of a doorway stood alone in a meadow, shading a jackrabbit as it nibbled at a cabbage plant. Birds and butterflies were everywhere. A fox watched curiously from its perch atop a fallen log as they passed. After eighty years, the forest had reclaimed its own.

The river itself was bordered by a thick tangle of alders, the path ending at the crumbling remains of a large stone quay.

"The Ferry Quay," Sianiave told them. "This is the widest part of the Dunenwine. The waters are slow and deep here. Crossing is almost impossible above, and not much easier below, at least until Ardendell and the Dunenmere."

She pointed to a line of weed-covered paving stones. "The Great North Road, or what remains of it. It follows the river south for a ways before turning again into the forest."

On the far side of the river, rising out of the trees, was a stone tower. Its parapet was blackened and fallen into ruin, giving it the appearance of a half-burnt candle. Sianiave regarded it for a long moment, then turned away without speaking.

The boat was lodged on a spit of sand built up on the high side of the quay. It measured eighteen feet long and was stoutly built, with a sharp keel and three plank seats. Its green and white paint was cracked and faded. A rust-colored substance stained its tiller and stern gunwales.

"Blood, right enough," judged Osmodon. "Lots of it. Whatever occurred more than likely had a mortal end."

The boat's oarlocks were in working order, but the oars were missing. Piles of flotsam—logs, leaves, and dead branches—had built up on the spit alongside the boat. Osmodon used his ax to fashion two logs into functional, if clumsy, paddles.

They stowed their packs in the center of the boat. Sianiave climbed into the stern. Osmodon had to coax Bear aboard, as the dog seemed to regard the water as more dangerous than wolves. Together Nick and Osmodon shoved the little craft into the eddy, then jumped in. Once in the central stream, Sianiave took the tiller.

The journey down the river was largely uneventful. However, at a point where the river narrowed, Bear leapt up barking, sensing something in a nearby thicket of trees. Osmodon had to pull him back to avoid overturning the boat.

By late afternoon the forest began to thin. The snow, save in the deepest shadows, was almost gone. Meadows appeared, rolling hills with wildflowers and new spring grass. Occasionally they would catch sight of the road, or a standing stone marking its course. Bear ate his meal cake for lunch. Nick, Sianiave, and Osmodon made do with their staple of dried meat and fruit. River water quenched their thirst. Nick found it pure and delicious.

"It comes from mountain glaciers," Sianiave said. "The river is still robust, but there's little agriculture in the region now, especially in the north. Sheep and cattle are in short supply; too many predators. I would guess there are fewer than nine thousand inhabitants left in all of Anor, where once there were ten times that. A family with three children is considered large. Most parents are grateful to have one."

"Plague?"

"Of a sort. And the constant raids."

Osmodon nodded. "The Uruks see nothing but empty land now, ripe for the taking. They've been bolder with every passing year."

"Uruks?"

"You've not heard of Uruks?"

"Perhaps by another name. Can you describe them?"

Osmodon grunted, "Aye. A tribal people, and fierce, they are. As for the rest, depends upon who you ask: drug takers, cannibals, worshippers of evil gods who decorate their tents with the heads of slaughtered children. They are ferocious in battle, merciless in victory; they murder the men and rape the women. Those who survive are sold as slaves, or put to work in the brothels of Nibur. Leastwise, so 'tis said. No doubt much is true, though I can attest to the fact Uruks are no more cannibals than you or I. Their ways are strange, harsh by our reckoning. I've fought them enough, and respect them, though I'd never admit to it, not with the way things stand these days."

"The Uruks aren't the problem, only the symptom," said Sianiave, steering them past a large rock.

"Symptom? Of what?"

Sianiave ignored the question. Nick had to content himself with listening to Osmodon's tales of his travels among the desert nomads. The stories sounded exotic and somewhat far-fetched, complete with dragons, djinn, and evil princes. But he was no longer the skeptic he had been. He was learning that, in this world, fantasy was reality more often than not.

CHAPTER
21

NIGHT HAD FALLEN when they finally reached Ardendell. The air had grown heavy, and a thin mist rose from the water. They'd paddled across a wide lake, the Dunenmere, its shores invisible in the darkness. Osmodon sat in the bow of the boat, lantern in hand, warning of the rocks and snags that appeared suddenly out of the mist.

As they debated whether to continue on in the darkness or find shore and make camp, the lights of the village appeared to their left. As they drew closer, the shapes of gabled roofs and a high wall appeared. A chill settled on them. The chorus of cicadas and bullfrogs that had been with them since sunset went silent.

"So few," Sianiave murmured.

"M'lady?"

"Ardendell is a well-populated village, or was. How many lights do you count? Fifteen? Twenty? There should be a hundred. And that wall wasn't there on my last visit."

A few strokes of the makeshift paddles sent the boat gliding into a long, narrow wharf. Bear leapt ashore. Osmodon set his lamp on a piling and tied the boat to a mooring post while Nick and Sianiave off-loaded the packs.

Even in the dim light of Osmodon's lamp, it was apparent the wharf was in deep disrepair. The few boats moored nearby were equally neglected, one only kept from sinking completely by its mooring line. The damp air smelled of rotting fish.

The wall was built of logs. A door through the stockade from the wharf was closed and barred from within. A crudely lettered sign read:

NO ENTRY AFTER DARK

"Not very hospitable," commented Osmodon.

Sianiave was thoughtful. "They feel the need to protect the town from the water side."

The water, black and still, reflected the light from Osmodon's lantern. The mist had grown thicker, drifting off the lake and rising through the cracks in the wharf.

"Makes my skin crawl," Osmodon muttered, staring at the inky water. "In Linsraden 'twas said grendels prefer such nights."

"Things are worse than I'd thought if grendels have come this far from the ocean," said Sianiave, shouldering her pack. "But you're right. If we have to sleep outside, it should be away from the lake. The road passes on the far side of the village. There'll be another gate."

"What's a grendel?" asked Nick uneasily, staring out at the mist-shrouded lake.

Sianiave was already moving off and didn't answer.

"I take it they don't have them where you're from," said Osmodon. "For which you should be thankful. They come out of the water at night while folk are asleep. What they do to their victims—that's not a conversation I would be having on a night such as this."

Hefting his pack and grabbing his lamp, Osmodon started after Sianiave. Nick took one last look at the lake, then quickly followed.

They followed the wall around to the far side of the village. There, as Sianiave guessed, was another gate. Large enough to drive two wagons through abreast, it was also closed. A small, unmarked door was built into the gate, a bell rope at its center. A peal sounded when Osmodon pulled on the rope.

A small port in the door popped open. A pair of bloodshot eyes peered out. "Who goes there?"

"Three travelers and their dog," growled Osmodon impatiently. "We've come a long way and have need of lodging."

"Come back in the morning." The port slammed shut.

"We'll pay," cried Sianiave. "With gold."

A moment's silence, then the port cracked opened again. "Gold, you say?"

Sianiave held up a coin so it glittered in the lantern light. The eyes widened. "Bless me! Is that an empress?"

"Yours, if you let us through."

"How do I know you aren't bandits, or worse?"

"Do I look like a bandit?"

"Fair to say you don't, m'lady. But those with you, bruisers they are, and armed, I see."

"Of course they're armed. Who travels these days unarmed? Come now. An empress, all your own. More than you make in a year, I wager—just for a kindness."

A moment's hesitation. "Pass it through."

Sianiave held the coin up to the port, where it was snatched in by skinny, arthritic fingers. After another moment, they heard bolts being thrown, and the door opened.

The watchman was a ferret of a man. He glanced nervously about as he waved them inside. "Hurry. I could lose my job. Work's hard to come by these days."

They passed into a small watch station. There were two chairs by a table holding a partially eaten loaf of bread and a jug of strong-smelling ale. A lantern hung from a bracket and a fire burned in a clay stove. A door stood opposite the one through which they'd entered.

Once the front door was bolted again, the gatekeeper relaxed, suspicion replaced by the crooked semblance of a smile. "You'll be staying at the Lion?"

Sianiave studied him. "Have we a choice?"

"Lion's the only inn still open. Holbert does right well, even with travelers so few these days. Head of the council, he is." There was accusation in his tone, and bitterness. "What's your business? Perchance I can be of help?"

"Our business is none of yours," grunted Osmodon, disliking the man.

"Of course, of course. Only, it's my job to ask such questions, you see. Names, business, destination, and the like. Council rules, you know."

"This is the way?" asked Sianiave, indicating the opposite door.

"Yes. But your names?"

Nick found himself staring at the fellow in utter fascination. It was if he knew everything there was to know about him. His lack of character, his greed, fear, cunning, the absence of anything substantial in his makeup—all was as clear as if he could read the man's mind. Accepting a bribe was common practice for him, and the gold coin had been far too much to pay. Nick also knew that once they'd entered the village, to curry favor he'd run and tell whoever the local power was about the new arrivals.

Feeling Nick's eyes on him, the man stepped backward as though physically threatened. "I've done nothing! Stay away from me!"

"Nick!" snapped Sianiave. She gave him a warning glance, then turned back to the gatekeeper. "We mean you no harm. We're here only for a meal and a night's lodging."

The man's shoulders slumped and he shook his head as though waking from a trance. "Of course, m'lady. The Lion it is. Tell Holbert that Old Bob sent you. Old Bob, it is."

After they left the guardhouse, Sianiave took Nick's arm. "I should have warned you. Try not to stare directly at people when the sight comes to you like that."

"The sight?"

"We'll speak about it later."

Nick turned to Osmodon for help, but the big man simply shrugged.

At first glance, Ardendell resembled another village Nick could remember, though he had trouble recalling a name. Wattle-and-daub construction, narrow cobbled streets, thatch and slate roofs, hitching posts in front of some of the larger establishments, an occasional covered well. A tallow candle burned in a nearby streetlamp. Others were dark.

The town's decline was clear in its fallen chimneys, boarded-up doors, and broken windows. Few houses looked lived in, though here and there a ray of light from a candle or lamp escaped from under a door or from behind a shutter. Over all hung the stench of decay.

Nick couldn't read Sianiave's thoughts, but he sensed both sadness and anger. "This way," she said. "The Lion isn't far."

A rat as large as a cat slipped under the door of a dilapidated building, disappearing inside. A faded sign over the door read:

Colm & Sons, Tinkers
Weapons Sharpened
Harnesses, Wagons and Kettles Repaired

Somewhere in the distance a dog barked. Bear turned his head, then ignored the sound.

"Fallen a bit has it, m'lady?" Osmodon commented. "I mean since your last visit."

"Yes," she said shortly. "More than a little."

She was sure of her way now, turning down a wide alley. The inn was at the far end, a large three-storied building with a many-gabled roof. Wrought-iron carriage lamps bracketed the front door. Smoke drifted up through a brick chimney, carrying the smell of fresh-baked bread and roasting mutton. Raucous laughter could be heard inside. Lights shone from the windows on the ground floor, but the windows on the upper floors were dark.

The inn was L-shaped, with a wing to their left. To the right, forming a courtyard, were the stables. Nick was taken aback as he stared up at a painted sign over the front door: a lion and unicorn, rampant.

"Don't read too much into the sign," Sianiave cautioned. "The inn here and the tavern back there have little else in common."

"It's an ancient seal," said Osmodon said, giving Nick an odd look. "Seal of the House of Ambergin. Must be known even where you come from." Nick kept silent.

At Tor Eyrie it had been Osmodon's job to train Nick. He soon discovered the lad's martial skills surpassed his own, something he hadn't thought possible. He himself had studied and taught the warrior arts for more years than he cared to remember. Yet in their sparring with swords and in hand-to-hand combat, he'd found his charge amazingly deft and using forms he'd never encountered. The young man's strength was astonishing for his size, and nearly equal to his own, though he hated to admit it. More than this, he sensed nobility in the fellow's character, and he respected him for it.

"No farmer's horse, that one," said Sianiave quietly. A horse in one of the stalls had caught her eye, a big grey with intelligent brown eyes and a blaze on its forehead. She moved closer for a look.

"No, ma'am," came a voice from behind them. "Greywind's a knight's horse."

A boy appeared. He had longish blond hair and his feet were bare. He carried a feed bucket. Nick guessed him to be about fifteen.

"You startled us," said Sianiave, though she didn't look startled. Nick suspected she'd known the boy was there. "A knight's horse, you say?"

"Aye, though Master Holbert has rights now. Are you looking to buy a horse?"

"Three horses, actually. I gather you're the stable boy. Have you any suggestions?"

"Master Holbert will sell those two there. He took 'em in payment." The boy pointed to an adjoining stall where two sturdy ponies stood watching curiously.

"Bill and Tarabald. Farm animals, but good for a day's work. And faithful. They keep Greywind company," he added, moving to the grey's stall and pouring oats into the feed bin.

"Greywind, you call him? How did an innkeeper come to own a knight's horse?"

The boy stroked the grey's head affectionately. "I found him wandering loose in the forest. Master Holbert took him in, hoping his rider might show up. But it's been over three months now. By law the horse now belongs to Master Holbert, but he's got no use for an animal trained for war, and feed costs dear. He'll sell him, right enough."

The boy regarded Nick. "Sir? Are you a knight?"

Nick turned. "Who? Me? A knight?"

"Greywind should go to a knight, and you have the look about you."

"He will not be used for farming," said Sianiave quickly, stroking the horse's neck. "That I can promise."

The horse snorted and stamped, but continued to chew his oats.

"Saddles and trappings?" asked Sianiave.

"Farm rigging for Bill and Tarabald, and battle gear for Greywind. It's how I know he belonged to a knight."

"What's your name, lad?"

"Will, ma'am. Some call me Wispy Will. I tend to daydream a bit, I guess."

Sianiave reached into a pocket, coming up with three coins that she gave to the boy. "Take these, Will. I'll trust you to have the horses saddled, fed, watered, and ready early, for we'll leave soon after dawn."

The boy stared at the coins in disbelief. They shone brightly, even in the shadowed courtyard.

"Hide them," she said, cupping the boy's fingers around the coins. "Tell no one. Even those whom you trust. Pay off your indenture. Promise."

"Ma'am?"

"Your indenture. Promise."

"By my heart, I promise! But—"

"You're doing us a service. Have the horses ready to travel in the morning."

The boy stared at the coins in wonder. As they moved towards the inn he ran after them. "The dog! Master Holbert doesn't allow animals in the inn. You can leave him with me. I'll see he's looked after."

"What do you think, Bear?" said Osmodon, scratching Bear's head. "Trust this boy?"

Bear barked once in reply and sidled up to Will.

"He's in your keeping, lad," said Osmodon. "His name is Bear, and he likes meat, and lots of it. We'll square it with your master."

CHAPTER
22

The inn's common room was crowded and homey, a welcome change from the cold night air and the grim streets of the desolate village. Tavern maids in bright blouses hurried about carrying trays of food and tankards of ale, brushing off groping hands and rude jests with the skill of long experience. An aged minstrel in ragged green cloak and dusty boots strolled between the tables, strumming a six-stringed lyre. The words to his songs were all but lost in the din. Sawdust covered the plank floor, and candles and hanging oil lamps lit the tables. A large stone hearth warmed the room. Every now and then a small boy would appear with a log and add it to the fire.

"Leastwise we know where the townsfolk are," commented Osmodon. "I was beginning to think the place bereft of people."

Nick studied the crowd. The "sight" he'd experienced with the gatekeeper hadn't entirely left. Despite the outward show of revelry, there was tension in the room. He noticed more than one man drop a nervous hand to his weapon, as if to reassure himself of its presence.

It wasn't a celebration that had gathered them here, Nick thought. These people were afraid. He saw it in their faces and heard it in their over-loud laughter.

As their presence was noticed, the laughter faltered. Even the minstrel stopped his strumming, turning to regard the new arrivals with curiosity. A rotund, balding man in a stained leather apron hurriedly approached, his brown eyes sharp and measuring.

There was a flicker of recognition as those eyes fell on Sianiave. "Welcome to the Lion and Unicorn, m'lady. I am Holbert Holbertson, keeper of this inn. I take by your baggage you're here for rooms?"

He spoke loudly, wanting others to hear, to get the matter of these travelers settled so the room could return to its pretense of normalcy.

Sianiave favored the man with a dazzling smile. "Thank you, yes. Three rooms if you have them, and a meal, if you will. We've come a long way and are tired and hungry."

Nick hid his surprise. Her smile had been enough to quicken the heart of a dead man. Its effect wasn't lost on the innkeeper. "Of course, m'lady. You'll have your pick of rooms. These are mostly local folk, and only five of my rooms are let. For all that, it's better than most nights. Not that I'm complaining, mind you, but we do miss the travel trade."

He stopped abruptly. "Apologies, m'lady. My troubles aren't yours. Three rooms, you said? There's the king's suite for yourself, and rooms across the hall for your companions. I'll give you a fair rate for the three."

"That's very kind of you."

The innkeeper's face reddened. "'Tis nothing. For a meal, we offer mutton, cheese, and bread. New-baked, of course. We still have flour, though fresh vegetables are hard to come by."

He looked toward a booth in the corner where a stout woman menaced a bearded man twice her size. Three younger men also sat at the table.

"You great hairy beast!" scolded the woman. "You're coming now, not tomorrow. Leaving your wife and daughter alone—you should be ashamed. And you three louts! What do you have to say for yourselves?"

"Big Nelly's wife," Holbert chuckled. "Come to drag him and her boys home."

The woman hauled the unresisting man away. The three sons, all with the same curly blond hair and bulk of their father, gathered up their weapons and followed, to the good-natured jeers of the onlookers.

"Maude! Mary!" Holbert waved over two tavern maids, and they quickly cleared the table. "Busy tonight, as you can see. You'll have to tend to your own baggage, I'm afraid, leastwise for the time being. I'll send a lad over, soon as I'm able."

"We'll manage," said Sianiave, giving him another glowing smile. "And thank you again."

"I'll see to your food myself." The innkeeper bowed, and almost tripped over himself as he scurried off.

"And ale!" bellowed Osmodon after him. "Don't forget the ale!" He slapped Nick's arm. "Did you see that, lad? Reminds me of when I first saw her in Barad'An. No doubt I acted as much the fool. Did that fellow actually bow?"

Sianiave sniffed. "He was only being courteous."

Osmodon laughed. "Courteous, you say?"

Whatever her motives, Sianiave seemed well pleased with herself. The atmosphere quickly returned to forced jocularity. A tavern maid arrived with three large tankards. She returned Osmodon's smile with a blue-eyed wink as she hurried back to the bar.

The ale was thick, dark, and strong. Osmodon finished his in one long draught and called for more. Nick's head was spinning after half a flagon. Waving off a refill, he looked around the room, his eyes falling on a table near the hearth. A young woman sat there alone. So far as he could see, she was the only lone female in the room who wasn't a barmaid. Even through the shifting throng and curling smoke he could see she was quite beautiful.

Why was she sitting alone? Was she waiting for someone—a husband, a lover? There was a tankard in front of her, but she didn't appear to be drinking, just lost in thought.

Her skin was as flawless as alabaster. A mane of black hair fell across her shoulders. Her rosebud lips were set in an enigmatic smile while her low-cut blouse revealed taut breasts. Nick guessed she might have been in her mid twenties, though something about her suggested she was older. She looked out of place. Despite her beauty, there was an unmistakable sense of menace about her, of darkness.

The longer Nick watched her, the more he wanted to stare. Heat seemed to emanate from her. He felt a magnetic pull, as though her body were singing to his, the song settling into his loins. She might have been the most desirable woman he had ever seen. Maybe it was the smoke in the room, but everything else around her began to appear hazy and unfocused.

A prostitute? Hardly. Every man in the room would have been at her table, slapping down coins and begging for favors.

Slowly, as if aware of his attention, she turned toward him. He realized he'd be caught staring, but he couldn't take his gaze away.

Their eyes met, hers black and fathomless. She smiled, just a small curling at the edge of her lips, knowing and full of promise.

"This should keep you for a bit!"

The arrival of the innkeeper with a huge tray broke the enchantment. He laid out platters of roast lamb, a loaf of bread, and a quarter round of ripe yellow cheese.

Neither Sianiave nor Osmodon appeared to have noticed either the woman or Nick's fascination, for which he was grateful. The effect she'd had on him was not a noble one, though Osmodon would certainly have understood.

He glanced back to find the woman gone, her table taken by three drunken farmers. The disappointment he felt was almost physical.

Osmodon had hewn a chunk of lamb with his dagger and tore into the bread with his hands. Likewise, Sianiave was making progress, though with smaller portions. Hungry as he was, Nick couldn't take his mind off the alluring woman. Could he find her again? And if he did, then what?

The innkeeper was still standing by the table. "M'lady, if I might ask—"

"Of course," said Sianiave, putting down a slice of cheese and reaching into her pocket. "How much do we owe?"

"Oh, not that. We can settle your account when you leave. It's just that you mentioned you've been on the road for a bit. It's been near on a week since we've had any news from the south."

"I'm sorry. We've come from the north."

"The north?" He seemed surprised.

"We are traveling south, however, and are in need of horses. We've been told you have several you might be willing to sell."

"Why, yes. Three, to be exact. But for the life of me, I can't think why would you want to travel south at such a time."

A tavern maid arrived, taking the tray from the innkeeper's hands and pulling on his arm. "Holbert! The tap is broken again. You'd best hurry!"

He shook his head sadly. "Third time this week, and with the coppersmith gone—please excuse me, but business calls. If you're serious about the horses we can talk later."

"That was a bit strange," said Sianiave as the innkeeper hurried off.

"How so?" asked Osmodon, pausing between bites.

"News from Barad'An can't be that hard to come by, even in these times. Yet our host seemed surprised we were even traveling in that direction. Something's not right, and it's not just the poor economic situation here."

Nick wasn't following the conversation. His thoughts kept returning to the black-haired girl. He looked up, realizing Sianiave had asked him a question.

"Sorry?"

"Is something wrong? You seem distracted."

"I'm fine. Just tired."

"We can all use some sleep. We're in for a long ride tomorrow."

CHAPTER
23

MIDNIGHT APPROACHED, its hour marked by a large water clock atop the hearth. The room emptied with unseemly speed, the patrons leaving in groups of three or four as if to give one another courage. Drunken laughter gave way to wariness as they headed into the night, crude weapons in hand.

The captivating woman was nowhere to be seen. Nick considered the possibility she'd been a hallucination, a fantasy conjured up out of his own tired and libidinous mind. Or maybe it was the ale.

No. She'd been no fantasy, no mirage. Somehow he was certain of that. Her effect on him had been too real.

The minstrel sat on a chair by the hearth, plucking a quiet lament on his lyre, lost in drink or sad memories, perhaps both. The barmaids went about their work, carrying off empty plates and flagons, replacing melted candles. Every now and then the blue-eyed wench encouraged Osmodon with a mischievous smile.

With a heartfelt sigh, Holbert joined them at the table, glad to be off his feet. With quill pen, ink pot, and a sheet of parchment, he proceeded to add up a column of figures.

"One hundred and seventy-three silver pennies," he announced with a flourish of his quill. "Three horses, their tack, three rooms for a night, this night's meal, heated baths for all, food for your dog, and breakfast for three in the morning. A bargain, I must say. The grey stallion alone is worth that if I'm any judge—a knight's animal by all accounts, with a fine saddle."

Nick knew little about the local currency, but considering how free Sianiave had been with her gold, the offer seemed a good one. From observing previous transactions, he estimated that gold was worth fifty times more than silver, and silver pennies were smaller than the gold empresses she'd been handing out. By that accounting, 173 silver pennies was less than the amount she'd given the stable boy.

Sianiave studied the innkeeper's tally. "A knight's horse? We've heard the story, Master Holbert, and while I do not doubt your ownership, what if by some happenstance we cross paths with its previous owner? Knights are known to be fond of their horses. As for the other two, they are farm animals, barely larger than ponies, and we have many leagues yet to travel."

"Have no worries there," insisted Holbert. "They are sturdy beasts, good for a long day's work or a long day's ride. As for the grey, I very much doubt ownership will be contested. There were no colors or crests we could find. The horse itself had several wounds, suffered in battle, no doubt. Healed now, of course," he added quickly. "It's probable, with the king's passing and events in Barad'An as they are—"

"What!" The table shook as Osmodon dropped his tankard. "What's that you say? The king?"

Sianiave looked stunned. "Cuchulain? Dead?"

Holbert reached out a hand as if to comfort her. "My greatest apology, m'lady. I thought everyone knew."

A complex series of emotions passed across Sianiave's features: anger, grief, uncertainty. The death of this king was a personal for her, Nick saw, though he had no idea why. Then, as firmly as if a door had been slammed, the practical woman he'd grown used to reasserted herself.

"As I said, Master Holbert, we've been in the north."

"Of course! Flog me if I've upset you. It's a sorry way to learn such troubling news."

"How?" growled Osmodon. "Not old age. That was a hard old man. He had years left in him."

Holbert shook his head sadly. "A Uruk arrow, they say. Tom O'Canter, the minstrel there, first brought tidings. Others have passed through since, but no news of late."

"With Artos gone, and Princess Gwyndolyn not yet of age." Sianiave had grown thoughtful.

"Aye," said Holbert, nodding. "The priest, Bleys or Glays, whatever his name, didn't wait a day before proclaiming himself steward. And high priest of both Right and Left Towers, if you believe it."

"Glays?" growled Osmodon. "That puffed-up ass? How in the hells did he end up on top?"

"Clever really," mused Sianiave. "By proclaiming himself steward and keeper of both towers, he not only gains control of the city, he becomes archon, and Gwyndolyn's sole guardian. The Sisters would never have agreed."

Holbert nodded. "It's said they had no choice. There's talk of some charter or other, signed between Cuchulain and the priest. Few knights were left to argue and the Sisters are no fighters. It's come out that the priest lured recruits into his employ for years, gathered an army about him. Those who oppose him, he either hangs or crucifies."

"Crucifies!"

"Nails them to the oaks and leaves them. You can smell the stench for miles, it's said, as a warning to others. I wouldn't have believed it, but we've heard it from more than just Tom."

Sianiave frowned. "How do people here stand?"

The innkeeper glanced over his shoulder, but only the serving maids, the fire boy, and the minstrel remained in the room. "A dangerous question."

"You have nothing to fear from us."

Holbert looked hesitant. "Well, I believed so, enough to sit and talk with you folk after hours, but living in fear can work on a man." He rubbed his head wearily. "If you travel south, as you say, you could end up facing the question yourselves, and from the wrong sort. Not that I would wish such a thing on you, or anyone for that matter."

Holbert leaned forward, his voice dropping. "There was a time when Barad'An was the heart and soul of Anor. The king's men protected the roads and caravans, guarded the borders. In Ambromir's day, it's said a virgin carrying a bag of gold could ride from one end of the kingdom to the other without fear. Well, sore be it, those days are gone, and have been for my lifetime. Barad'An is a hollow fortress now, walled up like an old maid's memories, hanging on to past glories."

"It doesn't trouble you?" asked Sianiave. "The king passing, this priest taking power?"

"Of course it troubles me. It troubles us all. But times change. We've got to mind our own. You've seen the town. Trade's all but disappeared. Travelers grow fewer every year. Even the weather's off—growing warmer, it is. A normal year there'd still be snow two feet deep. Bandits and wolves have the forest to themselves. People have gone missing, including children. Just last week Gef the Woodsman found a pit surrounded by rune stones and filled with bones—human bones, burnt and chewed upon. Uruks, some say, though Uruks rarely venture this far north, and they have naught to do with runes."

"Wildings?" suggested Osmodon.

"Or other creatures. Fairytales, some say. But the older folk, those that remember, know differently."

"Is this why the wall was built?"

"Aye, though I was against it. It won't hold against an army, or even a determined raiding party, but it makes some feel safer. There are few farms left. Burned out, or the people packed up and gone before they could be burned out. No fishing further than the end of the dock, though on bright days a few of the younger men will take a boat out. Some never return, even then. There's talk something evil has made its home in the lake."

Nick remembered the dried blood they'd found on the boat, the black stillness of the lake, and the uneasy feeling he'd had of being watched.

"I do well enough," the innkeeper went on. "But it's mostly local folk now. You're the first travelers from the north in more than a fortnight."

Then, as if making a decision, he dropped his voice to almost a whisper. There was anger in it. "You asked how we feel about the priest? We follow the Old Way here. For anyone to claim he speaks for the Mother as well as the Father, well, it doesn't sit well with us. Ardendell's a market town, or was. We know when someone's trying to sell us a bill of goods, especially since Princess Gwyndolyn was forced to flee."

"Ren is gone?" Sianiave exclaimed.

"Escaped with Abdelar and Aerindir by her side. They had to ride over a troop of the priest's guard to do it, leastways as Tom tells it."

Osmodon slapped the table and laughed. "Abdelar and Aerindir are with her? By Asgar, that's some good news, at least!"

Sianiave gave Osmodon a warning look, but the innkeeper didn't appear to notice. "Left a score of the priest's men lying dead by the gate," he said, grinning. "Tom claims he saw it with his own eyes. He's composing a song about it, sings the finished parts when he's a mind."

"Perhaps he'll sing it for us," suggested Sianiave.

"I'll ask him. It's good, the song I mean, if I do say so. It will travel. Little enough to ask for these days, but you take what you can get."

A shadow seemed to pass over the table as a tavern maid blew out yet another candle and disappeared into the kitchen. The minstrel's melancholy strumming stopped. For a time no one spoke. The fire had burned down to embers, and the room grew chill.

Nick shifted in his seat. His sword belt pinched his side and his feet ached. He knew he should pay more attention to the conversation. His companions' reactions told him important information was being passed. Cuchulain, Aerindir, Glays, Abdelar, Ren—these were names he should learn. But the image of the black-haired woman kept intruding into his thoughts like an enchantment. Where could she have gone?

Sianiave slapped four gold coins on the table. "We'll accept your terms, Master Holbert. The extra is for your kindness, and to expedite matters. Have the horses ready at sunrise, with enough bread, cheese, and dried meat to last the three of us a week. And send the minstrel over. I'd like to hear his story with my own ears."

"More than fair." The innkeeper reached for the coins. "But surely, after what you've heard, you're not still intending to head south? It's said the priest's men are stopping everyone they meet."

"Our travel plans are our own business. You're best not knowing them, Master Holbert."

"Of course. I'll send Tom over."

Holbert stood to leave, then turned back. "M'lady, it's not my usual policy to speak either politics or religion with guests. Certainly not with folk I've just met."

"A wise policy for an innkeeper, I would think."

"Indeed. Yet I wouldn't want you to leave you with the impression I have a loose tongue."

"You've a reason then, for speaking so candidly?"

"I do. Years ago, when I was still a boy and my father was keeper here, a knight arrived asking for a meal and a night's lodging. Tall and grim he was, and he carried a long sword. Much like your young friend here. It was summer, and there was a woman with him. Beautiful as the moon she was, even to my young eyes."

Holbert was watching Sianiave's face, as though looking for a reaction. When she didn't respond he went on. "I never knew who the lady was, but she and the man were close, for they took a single room."

"What has this to do with us?"

"M'lady, excuse me for saying this. But when you walked through that door tonight it was as if I was seven years old again. At first I thought it couldn't be, and put the thought aside. But as I look at you now—excepting that scar, you could be that woman."

Sianiave smiled. It was not an unkind smile, but Nick sensed there was more behind it, some emotion even her stern control couldn't quite hide.

"So you decided to trust us on a childhood memory?"

"The lady's face is as clear in my mind now as on the night they arrived."

Osmodon shifted uncomfortably, apparently finding something new to interest him in his ale.

"I suppose I should be flattered, Master Holbert. How long ago was this?"

"Eighty years it's been, as I will be eighty and eight this coming June. And you're right. I hardly understand it myself. But there was something else, you see."

"Oh? And what is that?"

"The knight was known to us. He had been a ranger at Ostengarth. His name was Cuchulain, and later he became king."

CHAPTER
24

THE MINSTREL, TOM O'CANTER, had grey, world-weary eyes. Although his instrument was missing a string and his fine features were creased with age, his voice was still deep and pure. He displayed a youthful exuberance in telling the story of Princess Gwyndolyn's escape.

"They had them till Captain Fletcher began raining arrows from the wall, and that was a wondrous sight. They rode out the gate, more than a dozen of the guard in chase. That evening only seven of the templars returned, and they weren't happy.

"They told the townsfolk that the brothers had kidnapped Gwyndolyn. All knew it was a lie, but templars sprung up everywhere threatening anyone who spoke against them. Executions began that very day, right in the street, on the least pretext. Most of the folk were dumbfounded, not believing such a thing could happen in Barad'An. But I've seen it too often before to think Barad'An immune to such evil. I was in Megida when the Kosha Sirdar wiped out the Brothers, before that in Marduk the day the count lost his mind and opened the gates to Uruk hordes."

Since he'd joined them at the table, Sianiave had been studying the minstrel as if to place him in her memory. The minstrel did his best to ignore the scrutiny, avoiding her eyes when he could. But at his last remark Sianiave nodded as though something had become clear.

Osmodon cocked his head in surprise. "Marduk? That was over 150 years ago."

The minstrel gave a rueful smile. "A hundred and fifty-eight, to be precise. I'm a bit older than I look."

Nick did a double take. The man didn't look over seventy. Earlier the innkeeper had claimed to be eighty-seven. Sianiave could easily pass for thirty now, or younger, and God alone knew how old she was.

How old was Osmodon? He appeared to be forty, forty-five at most. Maybe Osmodon's insistence on calling him "lad" was more than habit of speech.

"What happened to Captain Fletcher?" asked Sianiave. If she remembered the minstrel from some past encounter, she had decided not to mention it.

"They say he was taken to the dungeons."

"Alive?"

"At the time, though it might have been best were it otherwise. The priest has made his magician dungeon master."

"Gothmog?" snapped Osmodon. "That cockroach should have been daggered years ago."

"You speak as if you know the fellow."

"Only by sight. And that's close enough."

The minstrel grinned. Nick noticed that his teeth were straight and white for his age. "There was a song in Mirador, before the sack of course, called 'The Last Defender of Linsraden.'"

Osmodon brightened. "A good song?"

"Would you like to hear it? I think I can remember a few lines."

"I think we've heard enough for one night," said Sianiave quickly as the minstrel reached for his lyre. "Master Holbert, if you would show us to our rooms. We've a long way to travel, and must rise early."

"Of course. Your baths should be ready."

Nick stifled a yawn with a hand. The dark-haired girl was forgotten. He was tired, and the thought of a hot bath and a good night's sleep now dominated his mind.

"I'll be along," said Sianiave. As Nick and Osmodon followed the innkeeper, she turned to the minstrel, slipping a gold coin into his palm. "For your stories—and your silence."

The minstrel pocketed the coin. "Blessings, m'lady, but you've no worries from me, gold or none. I've little love of Bishop Glays, or his hateful creed. Poets are not welcome in such regimes. Neither poets nor artful women."

Sianiave nodded. "You know me, then."

"My eyesight isn't so far gone I'd fail to recognize the Lady Sianiave the moment she entered the room, though it was said you'd left Anor for good. I also recognized Sir Osmodon, though who your other companion is I've no idea. He has a formidable look about him, but he's in none of the songs I know. Still, he's young yet."

"An itinerant soldier who's offered his help." Sianiave pressed a second coin into the minstrel's palm. "Thank you, again."

"I also owe you thanks, m'lady, for we all have our secrets. I trust you to keep mine." The minstrel stood and bowed. "I wish you well on your journey. I've a feeling a great deal rides on its outcome, for all of us."

"Indeed it may," said Sianiave softly.

CHAPTER
25

THEIR ROOMS WERE ON THE THIRD FLOOR. Nick's was small and sparsely furnished, but the bed was passably comfortable, the mattress goose down, the sheets freshly washed with no sign of vermin.

A window looked out over the slated dormer of the room below, presenting a good view of the shore. The wooden stockade that encircled the village was closer than he would have guessed. In the darkness it appeared as ominous as a prison yard wall. Beyond the wall lay the mist-shrouded waters of the lake.

Their baths had been drawn, steaming hot. The boys who'd fetched the water were seated patiently nearby, copper kettles at their feet. When Osmodon asked whether they had other chores to do, the oldest boy replied that it was their job to remain at hand, in case more hot water was needed, and to fetch towels when the guests had done bathing.

There were questions Nick wanted to ask Osmodon, but the presence of the boys and the warm comfort of the bath itself subdued his more complex thoughts. Osmodon was equally disinclined to talk, lying back in the tub and humming a nameless tune.

"She's a comely one, she is," he said after a bit.

"Excuse me?"

"The wench who served us. Mary. The blue-eyed lass."

"Oh. That one." For a moment Nick had imagined Osmodon was

talking about the dark woman who had captivated him. "You know her name?"

"Aye. We had a meaningful talk."

So far as Nick could recall, Osmodon had barely said a word to the woman, much less a meaningful talk. But then his attention had been elsewhere.

"She has a friend," Osmodon said, soaping his armpits with a bar of rough soap. "The slender, flaxen-haired lass behind the bar."

Nick shrugged. He hadn't paid much attention to the tavern maids. "Morning is what? Five hours off?"

"Aye. But life is short and there's a long road ahead. We can sleep in the saddle."

"What about Sianiave?"

"She'd be the first to recommend it. She knows how antsy a man can get. If there was a fellow around to her taste, she'd be doing the same."

The thought of Sianiave with a man somehow made Nick uncomfortable. "Thanks anyway."

"As you wish. But I tell you, you're missing out on one of life's great joys. Who knows when we'll have a chance to lie with a pretty maid again? Do you good. Helps the juices flow."

"What my juices need is sleep. See you in the morning."

Nick stepped out of the tub and a boy handed him a towel. After rubbing down, he wrapped the towel around his waist, gathered up his boots and clothes and returned to his room. He didn't relish the thought of morning, when once again he would be forced to don his filthy clothes.

He tossed the towel on the chair, blew out the room's single candle, and lay face down on the bed, naked. The room was warm enough that a light woolen blanket served. Despite the warm glow of the bath, the late hour and his own exhaustion, sleep was slow in coming.

He would have stayed awake for the girl at the table. He tried to picture her face, but the memory had grown hazy. The image that came to him was constructed of bits and pieces of beautiful women he'd seen in the past. But the carnal ache, the hardening arousal, the certainty of her body calling out to his, these feelings had returned with a vengeance.

A noise outside the door brought him to alert. There was something disquieting about the sound; it was wet, ichorous, as though someone had dropped a large, sodden sponge on the floor.

Seconds passed and he began to relax. It was most likely Osmodon, returning from his bath, maybe stopping by in a last effort to fix him up with the barmaid. He smiled. Why not? Things had been so dark and strange, he should enjoy himself for a change, just for a night.

He rolled to his side, pretending to sleep, but the expected knock never came. Instead he heard another noise, the quiet metallic click of the latch being tested. He suddenly remembered he'd forgotten to bolt the door.

He sat up, his hand reaching for his sword. Whoever was on the other side of that door was not Osmodon. Nor would it be Sianiave. The surreptitious nature of the sound was that of a thief or assassin.

A bright moon had risen above the mist, shedding just enough light through the window that he could make out the latch as it lifted slowly off its catch.

He swung out of bed, sword raised, and pulled the door open. "All right!" he growled. "Whoever you—"

The challenge caught in his throat. Standing across the threshold was the woman from the common room. She wore an ankle-length white gown of a fabric so insubstantial it revealed rather than concealed an almost inhumanly perfect body. A slight breeze from the hallway played with the dress and teased her black hair. Her lips were red and parted in the same slight smile that he remembered.

She stood silent a long moment, waiting for him to speak. "Can I help you?" he stammered, feeling foolish even as he said the words.

"Has it been so long, Eanor?"

Her voice was soft, silken, at once innocent and lewdly intimate. Nick felt as if he had entered a dream. He was afraid to speak.

"You must invite me in." She said it not a question but a statement, as though reminding him of something he should have known.

A strange reluctance came over him. Again he felt foolish. Why was she there? Who was she? She'd called him a name. Ian something?

"You have me confused with someone else," he managed.

She looked amused. But her eyes darted to the sword in his hand. He sensed wariness, and a brief moment of doubt, even fear. "You have forgotten," she whispered. "I would not have thought that possible."

Nick was in turmoil, the dreamlike immediacy of the moment fighting a growing sense of unease. Why should he be afraid? It was all too obvious she was unarmed. "I'm sorry. Please come in."

He backed away, propping the sword against the nightstand and grabbing the towel, which he again wrapped around his waist.

The woman seemed almost to float towards him as she came into the room. He had the disturbing sense her feet didn't even touch the floor.

"And if you were not who I know you to be," she murmured, "would it matter so much?"

Nick's resistance was crumbling. What did it matter? A girl he'd been fantasizing about just moments before was standing in front of him, obviously willing. Why did he hesitate?

She continued towards him, her eyes locked onto his, swallowing him. He could smell her scent now, musky and exciting. Her skin was flawless, supernally so. Slender fingers reached out, touched his chest, sending an electric charge through his body.

He stood unresisting as she raised her mouth to his ear. "You remember."

Just before their lips touched she pulled away, teasing. Her breath smelled of saltwater and pomegranates. Her eyes led him down into deep places under the sea. A pale hand took the towel with which he'd been covering himself, coaxing it free.

All innocence was gone now. Her fingers moved to his groin with an unwholesome eagerness. "It's been too long. You've come so far. So hungry."

The warning voice in his head was a scream now, but he was no longer listening. He pulled her to him. Her tongue darted out, meeting his. They fell back on the bed, her dress seeming to vanish as if it truly had been woven from moonbeams. She flowed atop him, her mouth and hands growing ever more intimate. Warmth engulfed his groin. He felt a sharp pain as something probed his buttocks, then a pleasure so intense he thought he would explode.

Pain, as her teeth sank into his neck. He was beyond caring. Pleasure and pain had merged into an all-consuming rapture.

The moment of release, so close—

"Release him, you abomination!"

With a snarl of rage the creature that had been feeding on Nick lifted its head from his neck. It turned to see Sianiave standing in the doorway, her right hand holding a sword, her left a silver cross.

Nick opened his eyes to find himself staring up into a nightmare: mottled skin, like the corpse of an old woman too long underwater, white strands of hair, reptilian eyes, and a split tongue that flicked between needle-like teeth. Worse was the body entwined with his—a translucent sac, with long, sucker-covered appendages. Its thin, knotted legs were wrapped around him. The tentacle-like arms clamped over his groin and chest were as strong as iron, seemingly fused into place.

There was no pleasure now, only pain. Nick writhed in agony, unable to scream. The creature's malevolent eyes flashed angrily back and forth between Sianiave and him, unwilling to release its prey.

Sianiave spoke an unfamiliar word. A silvery light flashed out from the cross, lighting up the room.

"Begone, grendel! Back to the sea!"

The creature retreated as though struck by a brand. With a cry of frustration it separated from Nick, slid wetly to the floor and dove shrieking through the window glass to the dormer below.

It flowed off the roof and disappeared over the wall. Moments later there came a splash, as though a large fish had jumped in the lake.

"By Asgar, what the hells was that?" Osmodon stumbled into the room, sword in hand and wearing only a hastily wrapped towel.

He took it all in with a glance, focusing on Nick who lay unmoving on the bed. Purple welts were already forming where the creature's suckers and teeth had been at work. Behind Osmodon, eyes wide with fright and doing her best to hide her own lack of dress with a sheet, stood Mary, the tavern wench.

"What's all the noise? What's going on here?" Holbert appeared, carrying a metal-capped club. He stared at the shattered window, then at Nick lying curled on the bed. "Oh, my," he murmured, blanching.

"Bring water and salt," ordered Sianiave. "Lots of it, to my room. Quickly, man!"

"Of course. Right away. Right away."

The innkeeper took a last look at the broken window, frowned at the barmaid as if to say, "We'll talk about this later," and hurried off.

Hugging her sheet tightly about her, the terrified maid gave a cry of dismay and fled down the hall.

"Take him to my room, Ozzy," said Sianiave quietly. "That thing might come back. I arrived before it completed its desecration. They don't like to leave victims behind."

Osmodon picked Nick up as easily as though he were a child, carrying him across the hall to Sianiave's room. The room was several times the size of Nick's, with a larger bed, a table, four chairs, and a couch. There was even a fireplace, in which a small fire burned.

"A grendel?" Osmodon asked as he laid Nick on the bed.

"Yes. An old one. It must have come up the river from the sea. Our companion has been distracted all night. I was going to check on him when I saw its wet prints in the hall. It probably began its work on him even before we entered the inn."

"Why him, with so many others around?"

"An excellent question."

"Will he live?"

"We'll see."

For Nick the horror had momentarily retreated. He felt calm, as though none of this was real, inhabiting a state between wakefulness and sleep. His eyes remained open and the pain had diminished. But he was still unable to move.

Sianiave passed the silver cross back and forth over his paralyzed body, singing softly as she did so. Both the words and melody were unfamiliar to him. Nevertheless, they had an immediate soothing effect. He felt like a child again, Sianiave singing him to sleep with a lullaby.

Slowly physical sensation returned, and with it, pain. It grew in intensity until it felt as though his entire body were on fire.

"No!" The word exploded from him in one great spasm.

Sianiave gave a sigh of relief. "Good. You're back. You had us worried."

Holbert returned, carrying a bag of salt, a mug, and a large pitcher of water. Sianiave filled the mug, stirred in a handful of salt, and pressed it to Nick's lips.

"Drink it, all of it. They feed on the salt in their victims' bodies. A minute longer and there would have been nothing left of you but a desiccated shell."

With Sianiave's help, Nick managed to drain the mug. She repeated the dosing. After the third, he leaned his head over the side of the bed and vomited. Sianiave made him drink mug after mug until finally, weak and exhausted, he fell back against the pillows. The fire inside his body had eased, but the wounds where the creature had savaged him throbbed painfully.

"What was that thing?"

"A grendel, lad," said Osmodon cheerfully. "A real live grendel."

"The mind," Nick rasped, recoiling from the memory. "She, it—"

"Yes," said Sianiave. "It uses crude forms of desire to seduce its victims, attacking where they are weakest. Few survive a grendel's assault. Consider yourself fortunate."

Nick didn't feel fortunate. His throat was raw from salt and vomit, and his entire body ached. But worse than that was the humiliation, the self-disgust at having fallen into the monster's trap.

They attack where you're weakest. What did that say about him? How could he not have known, not have seen it for what it was?

Holbert paced anxiously in the background. "Nothing like this has ever happened here before. The Lion is known throughout Anor to be a safe hostel. If this were to get out—"

"I understand your concern," said Sianiave. "But I suggest you warn the council about what has taken up residence in your lake. Clearly the wall is no barrier. And, without doubt, it is still hungry."

The innkeeper trembled as her words sank in. "What's to become of us?" he mumbled dully. "What's to become of us?"

CHAPTER

26

Atha'amenth
Arden Forest
May 1

"SHE'S HOLDING UP WELL" commented Abdelar as he watched Ren at play in the pool below.

Aerindir was seated on a nearby rock, polishing his sword. "She'll do," he said. Abdelar chuckled. Coming from Aerindir, that was high praise indeed.

They'd been traveling for fourteen days, with little sleep, often eating in the saddle. Gallian and the safety of Ellohir's keep was at least another weary week off. In their flight from Barad'An they'd battled the priest's guards, then engaged a band of forest brigands who coveted their horses. Ren had acquitted herself as well as any knight, better then many. Ten of the bandits lay dead, the rest scattered into the forest. Two Ren had dispatched herself.

They'd spent the day camped near the mineral pools of Atha'amenth, a place once known for the blue-green of its waterfall and the warmth of its healing springs. It was lost to the memory of all but a few. The attending manor house with its many tiled spas had long ago fallen into ruin, overrun with brambles. But the turquoise waters still infused warmth into the pool in which Ren now swam.

Abdelar watched in pride and some wonder as she ducked under the waterfall, frolicking as though they were on a picnic, not fleeing from mortal danger into a lonely and uncertain future. Gods, what a woman she was becoming—fit to be queen.

Aerindir hadn't objected to a day of rest. They'd taken precautions, of course, scouting the nearby forest before setting up camp in a copse of alders. There was an animal trail as an escape route should one become necessary. Their weapons were always at hand, and when one bathed, two remained on guard.

The brothers had watched over Ren since her birth. They were loyal to her father, Prince Ilsidain, son of Ambromir and grandson to Cuchulain. That oath kept them from joining the knights who followed Artos into banishment. With Ambromir dead in battle, and Ilsidain's suspicious death during a boar hunt shortly thereafter, Cuchulain had become their liege lord. But in truth it was Ren to whom they gave their hearts, and of whom they felt most protective. Ren had been twelve at the time of her father's death, the same age as they were when their own father had passed.

Abdelar plucked a string on his lyre and began singing. He had a fine, clear voice, and was counted one of the best troubadours in the kingdom. His song told a story of lost love and the betrayal of a sacred city by its mad count. It was a sad and melancholy tune, and the story it told did not end well.

"Can't you sing something merrier?" groused Aerindir.

"I'm composing an ode to Cuchulain. There's a tonal similarity."

"Count Otho was a coward as well as mad. Whatever else you might feel about Cuchulain, he was a man."

"Aye," Abdelar agreed. "Though headstrong, and far too prideful."

Aerindir sighed. "A man, nonetheless, and a great warrior."

Abdelar nodded. "Hence the tragedy. A man who should never have been king, a great warrior, brought down by a Uruk's arrow and a conniving priest. Not grist for a merry mill."

Without waiting for an answer, Abdelar began to sing again.

"*With knights, nobles, and pikemen*
clutched about his bed,
and the Sisters and traitor priest
mumbling sugared phrases
in low and mournful tones,
Cuchulain, in all his glory, died alone."

There was a moment of silence. Aerindir grimaced. "Well? What do you think?" prompted Abdelar.

"In truth? It's dreadful. 'Low and mournful tones,' a cliché. I suppose Corwin is noble enough, but you left out Ren entirely. And anyway, how do you know who was there at the end, or what was said? We were ordered away, if you recall. By Ren's account Mother Saolin dealt quite tenderly with Cuchulain, surprising as that seems. Furthermore—"

"Enough!" laughed Abdelar. "I should have known better than to sing a song before it's fully rendered. But you're right. It is dreadful. Something or someone, a woman I'd wager, caused Cuchulain's heart to break early on, and therein lies the key to all his acts, and his failure. Being closed in heart, he was closed to his people, certainly to Artos. The truth of his life escaped him. A tragedy, and not just for a king. At least that's the theme as I see it."

"We all die alone," said Aerindir glumly as he studied the polish on his sword. "And a heart too open is an easy target for a spear."

"My brother, you've managed to summarize an entire philosophy in sixteen words—words I fear that are too well accepted in these dark times."

Aerindir grunted and fell silent. He had learned early on it was unwise to enter into philosophical arguments with Abdelar, who seemed to change sides and positions as easily as a bird hopped branches in a tree.

Perhaps that was his secret. Abdelar had always possessed the uncanny ability to see things as a whole, and to find meaning and hope even in the worst of situations. It was a gift he himself lacked, Aerindir knew.

Holding a fresh elm leaf over the edge, Aerindir let it drop. The leaf fell to the ground, cleft in two. Satisfied, he added a dollop of beeswax to the blade and burnished it with a chamois.

When this was done, he held the sword aloft, the midday sun reflecting off the blade. After forty years he still admired its stark and deadly beauty.

Drakulsyr, Dragonslayer, was its name. Its sister blade, *Daemonsyr*, Demonslayer, lay in its silver-banded sheath at Abdelar's side. Their father had given them the swords on his deathbed. Of all that he could leave them, he'd said, these two swords were the most valuable, the secret of their making lost to the ages. Extraordinarily light, they could cut through oak and iron as easily as other blades clove flesh.

Sheathing Drakulsyr, Aerindir stood to stretch his legs. Ren had come out from under the waterfall. She climbed toward a ledge overhead. How beautiful she was, long-legged, with golden skin and golden hair. She stood naked as she studied the water below, appearing for all the world like High Queen Gwyneth, or Yu'An Tara herself. She was their hope, he knew. Perhaps their only hope, fragile as it was. Not for the first time, he found himself wishing he had his brother's capacity to trust in destiny.

Ren arced into the pool in a perfect swan dive, surfacing moments later, laughing as she blew water from her nose. Rather than ease his worry, the very gracefulness of her performance reminded Aerindir that she was still little more than a child, and how very vulnerable she was.

Abdelar began another song, well known to Aerindir, for they had chanted it as boys for forty nights straight, part of their training as pages. It had been written by the poet Hafist and later put to music by some long-forgotten minstrel. In his indirect way, Abdelar was reminding him of something.

"*The warrior tames the beasts of his past*
So that the night's terrors
Can no longer break the jeweled vision in his heart.
The brave open every chamber in their past,
And banish all the mind's ghosts.
Only the warrior has the courage to slay the past giant,
The demons of the future.
The warrior wisely sits in a circle with other warriors,
Gathering the strength to unmask
Himself."

As Abdelar finished the song, a flock of sparrows broke suddenly through the forest canopy and passed over the falls. Abdelar's fingers clamped down on the lyre's strings, stilling them as the birds circled off toward the west.

He caught Aerindir's eye, then glanced at the horses. Moments earlier they'd been chewing placidly on bunch grass in a nearby meadow. Now their heads were up, ears pointing toward the trees from which the birds had risen.

Abdelar put down the lyre and stood, buckling on his sword and shouldering his bow and quiver as though nothing were amiss. Aerindir waved to Ren in a prearranged signal, but Ren was already pulling herself onto the flat rock where she had left her clothes and weapons.

Had she, too, seen the birds? Aerindir wondered.

He stowed the remaining gear in the bags while Abdelar saddled the horses. Both men moved about their business with a deliberate, deceptively casual efficiency.

Abdelar was tying his lyre to his saddle when Ren arrived, her own sword about her waist, her hair a tangled mess. *Enemies?* she queried in hand sign.

Abdelar nodded. "We've stayed overlong in any case," he said, voice low.

Unwilling to risk the horses on such uneven ground, they left on foot, Abdelar leading them down the narrow trail Aerindir had scouted the day before. The trail followed the base of the cliff, hidden from above and below by boulders, trees, and the overhang.

They traveled for perhaps an hour, seeing and hearing nothing untoward, when, unexpectedly, the trail ended. They paused, confronted by a sea of rolling grassland dotted here and there with islands of trees and forested hillocks. In the distance, half a league off at least, stood a single larger, cleared hill. The ruins of an old fort commanded its summit.

"Graylen Tor," said Abdelar. "A garrison once stationed there." This was for the benefit of Ren, who had not traveled these lands before.

Aerindir's sharp eyes scanned the horizon. "There," he said, pointing.

To their right, still several miles off, was a band of riders, perhaps twenty in all. They appeared to be milling around at the foot of the shallow canyon that led to the waterfall.

"Uruks?"

"My guess, though it's difficult to tell from this distance."

"It's us they're after," said Abdelar.

Aerindir nodded. "Cuchulain suspected the priest had contracted them. They've sent scouts to the pools, I'd wager, and are awaiting their return. They'll find sign of our camp and our trail."

Ren had been silent, her eyes closed. "We can't stay here," she said suddenly, as though something had become clear to her.

"The way we took will be difficult for them," said Abdelar, thoughtfully. "They will have to travel single file, and slowly, as we did. Perhaps we should wait here until dark."

Aerindir looked back up their trail. "Our pursuers may have split their force. It's what I would do. Even now some may be coming up behind. I say we go now."

Abdelar regarded their mounts, fighting nervously at their bits. "You're right. We have to trust the horses. We'll make for Graylen Tor. It may still be defensible."

Silently they mounted, the horses calming under their weight. With a nod from Abdelar, they started out at a canter across the open field.

CHAPTER
27

"SPLENDID VIEW," remarked Osmodon, as he climbed atop the ruined wall to sit beside Sianiave. "But I imagine it was a lonely billet."

Sianiave's attention was focused south, on the horizon. "The road was better traveled in those days," she replied absently.

Her knees were pulled up to her chest as she puffed on her pipe, golden hair hidden under a broad-brimmed hat. To Nick, struggling to undo the cinch on Greywind's saddle, she looked like a tomboy.

"You knew this place then?" he asked. He was still unwilling to believe her as old as he imagined, no longer able to see her as the grey-haired matron of their first meeting. Her starched personality had remained unchanged, though he was slowly beginning to appreciate the subtle sense of humor that lay beneath it.

"Before even my time, I'm afraid," she answered. "Old Empire. Graylen Keep was a link in a chain of defenses that ran from Monk's Haven on the western coast to Nuribor in the east."

The cinch finally undone, Nick wrestled the saddle off the horse and set it on a flat stone, once part of the keep's long-vanished tower.

Sianiave had paid for the horses and certainly had the right to claim the best as her own. Instead she suggested they draw straws. Nick had pulled the long straw, so the big horse was his. He'd come to the conclusion the game had been rigged.

Greywind was a warhorse, well trained and unusually intelligent. The animal was also grievously stubborn. Nick knew little about riding, and nothing about warhorses, and this one stood almost seventeen hands. The past few days had been a struggle, as if the horse were master and he the pupil. What's more, Greywind's tack, designed for battle, was far heavier and more complicated than the simple rigging of the two farm animals. Only recently had he learned to dress the horse himself, without having to ask Osmodon for help.

"Different in your land?" Osmodon had observed, watching Nick in his first clumsy attempt.

"Very," Nick had replied.

The ancient ruins of the keep lay about them. Only a small area of the old kitchen still held a roof. There they'd made camp. It was late afternoon, and dark clouds, heavy with rain, moved in from the east. The dog lay outside in the lowering sun, chewing on a stick. The horses munched on the clumps of grass that had all but replaced the stone floor.

Since learning of the events in Barad'An, Sianiave had appeared distracted, uncertain whether to continue to the city as planned or set out in another direction. Osmodon conjectured that she was looking for a sign, an omen.

Because of the approaching weather, Sianiave had decided to make camp at the ruined fortress, though two hours of daylight still remained and the trail up the hill was difficult. The view from the top was well worth the effort, Nick thought. The forests of North Arden were behind them now, and the surrounding countryside had turned emerald green from spring showers and was marked by seasonal streams. To the west a glimmer of sunlight could be seen reflecting off the Dunenwine as it continued its way to the sea. Southward, perhaps a league away, stood a line of low mountains. To the east, barely visible even from atop the tor, was a ribbon of ochre-stained hills.

It had been four days since they'd departed Ardendell. Nick's physical wounds had healed, but the disgust he felt for having fallen prey to the creature was still with him.

They attack you where you're weakest.

He'd invited the thing into his room. It had drawn its power entirely from his fantasies. It wasn't the first time he'd almost been killed by some monstrosity insinuating itself into his thoughts. The morghul, the wolf-thing in the forest, the grendel—all had drawn on his doubt, fear, and lust.

For Nick, the understanding of his culpability had come like a physical blow. It wasn't that these demons were stronger than he. Even at his lowest point, there had been a voice, some essential part of himself, that had known the truth, seen behind the curtain of illusion, known the danger. And yet the rest of him had refused to listen, lost in the enchantments.

His memories of the world he'd come from had grown increasingly insubstantial, though now one rose up sharp and clear: the summer he'd spent in China studying the martial arts. He'd lost a sparring match to a fellow student, a boy he should have beaten. His *sifu* had seen the problem immediately. Though naturally ambidextrous, Nick had found it easier to think of himself as right-handed.

"Balance is key to everything," his teacher had said. "To defeat an opponent, a clever warrior looks for imbalance, as indeed did that boy to whom you lost."

The rest of that summer his sifu had forced him to train as a left-hander. A month later he'd fought the boy again and won.

But that had been physical, and easily correctable. How did one correct an imbalance in one's own mind? He was loath to ask either Osmodon or Sianiave for advice. He was a soldier, after all, and a good one. He could work it out on his own.

As days passed, he came to realize that it was his pride, and fear of embarrassment, that kept him from asking for help he sorely needed.

On the evening of their third day out from Ardendell, as they camped near a stand of elms, he'd cautiously broached the subject with Osmodon.

"Ozzy, you once mentioned something about shields."

The big man nodded. "Shields against creatures like the grendel, you mean? Aye, but they're not like regular shields, lad. You can't just go in any armorer's shop and pick one up." He tapped his forehead. "You make them, here."

"How?"

"How do you learn to make anything? Experience, lad. By doing, by surviving and doing again. Teachers can help, but in the end it's you has to do the doing. In that regard you've managed rather well, I'd say."

"Of course, it must be experiences of a certain kind." Sianiave had been eavesdropping. "Experience for experience's sake is at best entertainment, useless for learning, even dangerous. And you must be prepared for it, or it won't take."

She'd pointed the stem of her pipe at Nick to make this last point. Was she accusing him of something? Weakness, perhaps?

"And how am I supposed to recognize the right kind of experience?" he asked dryly.

Sianiave smiled, as if reading his thoughts, then grew serious. "If you truly want to know, begin by remembering you're a stranger here. You can't learn if you're not present, and it's difficult to be present with all those little voices in one's head competing for attention."

Her words rang true, but the implication was unsettling and he'd let the matter drop.

Later that same evening, Osmodon had joined him as he relieved himself against a tree. "She offered you a gift tonight," the big man murmured quietly, unbuttoning his breeches and adding his own water to Nick's. "My advice would be to accept it."

"I've heard it before."

Nick spoke irritably. He remembered the mantras and techniques he'd studied in China and elsewhere. Even the army had mind control training. Don't pretend to be a tree, be the tree. When you aim at a target, be that target.

"If you'd understood what she told you," Osmodon said, "that grendel couldn't have gotten anywhere near you. Besides," he added with a good-natured wink. "It's not just the words, it's when you hear them. It's the timing."

Nick looked up. "Timing?"

But Osmodon had merely nodded, buttoned up his breeches and walked off.

CHAPTER
28

"NICK! OSMODON! Look there. Do you see?"

Sianiave stood on the wall, her attention focused on something in the distance. Nick followed her line of sight to a wooded area perhaps five miles off. At first he saw nothing unusual—treetops, shadows beneath. A light wind heralded the approaching storm. Beside him, Bear lifted his head, his nose searching the wind.

"There!"

Nick saw a flash of almost diamond brightness amid the trees, then another.

"Saddle the horses!" cried Sianiave, jumping from the wall and running to grab her saddle. "Quickly! You're about to earn your pay."

"What is it?"

Osmodon threw a saddle on his mount. "Sunlight off a sword blade. There's a battle our mistress means to join."

"Weapons only!" Sianiave shouted. She slung quiver and bow over a shoulder and vaulted into the saddle, spurring her pony down the hill without looking back.

Osmodon moved to help Nick, who was having trouble with Greywind's harness. "You'll soon appreciate that long straw you drew," he chuckled, buckling a chest strap. "My pony's a good-natured beast, but hardly fit for war."

After the slithery horror of the grendel, Nick almost welcomed the thought of a purely physical enemy. Bear barked, as if to hurry him on.

For once Greywind didn't fight his reins. The moment Nick was in the saddle the horse took off at a gallop, the dog close behind.

"Ho!" cried Osmodon, snatching up his weapons. "Wait for me!"

Nick soon overtook Sianiave. "Who are we fighting?" he yelled as he struggled to rein the big horse in. Greywind was faster than Sianiave's farm pony and wanted to run.

Sianiave's hat blew off in the wind, her blond hair flowing wild. Her face, tanned golden from the days traveling in the sun, was resolute.

"We'll know when we get there!"

Osmodon caught up with them at the wood's edge. The sounds of battle were clear now—curses shouted in a strange tongue, cries of pain, stamping hooves, and metal striking metal. Ahead in a clearing, two men and a young woman were holding off twenty or more attackers. They were swarthy, bandy-legged men with tattoos and *kohl*-rimmed eyes. The defenders stood with their backs against a large oak, the girl between them. Riderless horses milled about. The bodies of three other horses, riddled with arrows, lay nearby.

"Nick!" cried Sianiave. "See to the archers! We'll handle the riders."

Nick saw immediately what she meant. Twelve riders had pulled back, preparing for an assault. Nine others had dismounted and stood in a semicircle, sending volley after volley of black-shafted arrows towards the three by the oak.

With an almost supernatural display of swordsmanship, the two knights deflected the majority of the arrows, but more than one found its mark. Only the girl appeared untouched, as if the men were the archers' only targets. Her own quiver empty, the girl pulled a spent arrow from the tree behind her, nocked and released it. An archer fell, pierced through the neck, then another.

Nick gritted his teeth. During his college years he'd fought duels with épées, sabers, and katanas. But never had he fought for his life, and never from atop a horse. Greywind had no such misgivings and sprinted into the line of archers, knocking three sprawling and scattering the rest.

Nick recalled little of what followed, a violent fog of attacks, screams, and severed limbs. Two of the archers fell under his sword before they could cry out. Another lost an arm as he fumbled for his scimitar. Their crude leather armor offered little protection. One ran, but was brought down by Bear. Another managed to get off a bolt, but to Nick the arrow appeared to be moving in slow motion and was easily avoided.

Rearing and snorting, Greywind looked for more enemies, but the archers all lay dead or dying in the grass.

Close by, Sianiave and Osmodon had engaged the main body of attackers. Osmodon's opponents fell before him like leaves in a strong wind. With a powerful slash he disemboweled one foe, while with his left hand he pulled another from his saddle to be trampled by the maddened horses. Sianiave was no less lethal, fighting with both dagger and sword.

Led by a large Uruk on a black horse, in a last desperate effort six riders broke from the melee and charged the defenders at the tree. Despite wounds that would have crippled lesser men, the two guards stood their ground. The woman dropped her bow and drew her sword, skewering a rider who'd made the mistake of trying to grab her from his saddle.

Nick spurred Greywind forward. He took off an arm with a swipe of his blade, and knocked another attacker from his horse. The last to fall was the big captain who'd led the charge. Nick parried a wild blow, then reversed his grip, driving the point of his sword into the man's chest. He pulled the sword free, readying for another thrust, but it wasn't needed. A shudder passed through the rider as he toppled from his horse, dead.

The fight was over.

Nick took a deep breath and surveyed the carnage. The battle high was gone. Relief, fatigue, and an almost embarrassing sense of satisfaction swept over him. They'd won. The dead, the milling horses, all seemed oddly familiar.

Now on foot, Osmodon strode across the field toward him, a cheerful grin on his ruddy face, as though he'd just finished a pleasant walk in the woods.

"Where's your horse?" was the first thing Nick thought to say.

"None the worse for wear," Osmodon grimaced in disgust. "Had to leave him, though. Useless in a fight."

With the blood of half a dozen Uruks still dripping from the blade, he raised his sword as he saluted the three they had saved. "Aerindir and Abdelar, I presume. And Princess Gwyndolyn, of course. I must say the tales of your beauty and courage have not done you justice."

Gwyndolyn? Princess?

Nick saw the girl's face clearly for the first time. Even covered in sweat and blood, her beauty defied description.

Ren regarded them warily. "We are grateful for your help, sirs, but I would ask your names."

Neither she nor the two knights had lowered their weapons.

Osmodon grinned. "Of course. I don't blame you. I be Osmodon of Linsraden. And this tall fellow with the gaping mouth be Nicholas of Amra."

"Sir Osmodon? Sianiave's liege knight?" Ren's eyes widened in relief. "That is she, then? The other warrior?"

Osmodon sheathed his sword and hitched his ax. "Aye, here she comes now." Sianiave, leading her limping pony, was walking across the meadow toward them.

"It's been years," said Ren. "It was said she'd left Anor for good."

"Well met," said Abdelar.

With that he collapsed to his knees and fell forward into the bloodstained grass.

CHAPTER
29

BECAUSE HIS HORSE was both unharmed and swiftest, Nick took it upon himself to retrieve the packs left at the keep. At Sianiave's direction, Osmodon set about collecting a medicinal plant she called kingsroot; she'd noticed several of its familiar blue blooms in the meadow. Ren's and Aerindir's mounts had been slain, but the water skins on their saddles were untouched. The clothes in Ren's saddlebags were clean, and some of these she tore into strips for bandages.

A violent storm swept in just before sunset but was gone within the hour. The big oak, with its broad canopy of branches and leaves, served as a shelter for the others, but by the time Nick returned he was drenched and chilled to the bone. Osmodon had built a sizable fire, but before warming himself Nick first tended to Greywind, removing the saddle and giving the stallion a quick rubdown with a handful of grass. Then he helped Osmodon drag the slain Uruks to the meadow away from the camp.

The two knights had been stripped of their clothes and lay on blankets near the fire. Sianiave had removed the arrows—thirteen, Nick counted. The wounds were all in the front. Neither man had flinched from the fight or turned away.

Abdelar had gotten the worst of it. His skin was deathly pale, his breathing shallow. From the look of concern on Sianiave's face, he suspected there was little hope. But then he remembered his own shattered shoulder and how quickly it had mended under her care.

He squatted by the fire next to Osmodon, opposite where Ren and Sianiave ministered to the knights, cleansing their wounds, all the while chanting in an unfamiliar tongue. Otherwise all was quiet.

"Who are they, Ozzy?"

"Aerindir and Abdelar? Every minstrel in the kingdom sings of their deeds. Their father was Duke Ranulf of Caerlain, who died from wounds suffered in battle. They were just young lads at the time."

"Brothers?"

"Half. Abdelar's mother was a high-born lady of Caerlain. She died giving birth to Abdelar. Aerindir was born in Nibur to a nomad slave. The red fever took his mother on the journey back to Caerlain. The boys were raised as equals in Ranulf's eyes. It's said he loved them both greatly, though never could two men seem so different. In songs they call Abdelar 'The Fair,' always ready to sing or expound philosophy. Aerindir they call 'The Dark,' he being of grim visage and few words. Yet never one more faithful, or more courageous in battle."

"Orphans."

"Aye, like yourself."

Osmodon threw a stick on the fire and sighed. "The world has changed, that's the truth of it. You can't count on the old ways to hold any more. A man has to find his own footing."

A long moment passed.

"Osmodon, why did Sianiave bring me here?"

Osmodon chuckled. "I've wondered a bit on that myself. Leastwise until I saw you work today."

"But what I'm asking is, why me? I saw those two fight, the way they protected the girl, with not a thought to their own safety. With men like those—" Nick stopped.

"You think yourself less than they? Is that what bothers you?"

"Let's just say no one's written a song about me."

"Give them time. You're still young."

"Not that young. How old are you?"

Osmodon rubbed his beard. "Me? Let's see. My birthday is coming. May third, it is. I'll be sixty-seven. Some years to go until my dotage."

Sixty-seven! Nick wasn't sure if he found that encouraging or depressing. "And the girl?"

"Gwyndolyn? Not sure exactly, eighteen or nineteen. Years before her maturity in any event. Which is probably why the priest is so anxious to get his hands on her."

Nick felt an unaccountable sense of relief that she was genuinely young. "She's really a princess?"

"Aye. May be queen some day, if there's a queendom left to rule after this business with the priest. With Cuchulain dead and Artos gone, she's the end of the bloodline."

"This bloodline, it's important?"

"Sianiave believes so, as do most who give it any thought. The family has ruled for two thousand years and done a fair job of it, at least for the first eighteen hundred or so."

"You sound skeptical."

"Do I? Well, there's reason. But first let me ask you a question: In your land, what purpose does a king serve?"

"A king?" Nick started to say that the kings in his land served no real purpose. Then, after consideration, "They head the state, I suppose."

"Fair enough. And what is the state?"

"The people."

Osmodon slapped his thigh. This was a subject he obviously enjoyed. "Exactly! The people. And it's a king's job to rule his people, ably and justly. But too often they forget this. They begin to believe they are above us all. We are made of words, us mortals, and the stories and songs we listen to give the words meaning. Some stories say kings are divine, or at least come from the gods. So we get this doltish notion that people are here to serve the king, when precisely the opposite is true."

"You talk as though you've had experience in the area."

"My father was a baron, not a king. But I've seen how a land can be ruined by one man's poor decisions, baron or king."

Osmodon frowned, suddenly somber. "Being king has to be the scut work of existence. Few would accept it willingly, if they knew the load it carries."

Another long moment passed. The fire burned hot. Seated where he was, Nick couldn't see the two women, but could hear their chanting.

Osmodon shook his head as if waking from a dream. "In ages past, it's said the kings of Barad'An were chosen by both towers. They served at the will of the Tower Council for seven years only. That was the time it took for the disease of separateness to take hold, a sickness that isolates the king from the land and his people. Often the dethroned kings were put to death. It was considered an act of mercy, there being no one left who cared if they lived and most wanting them dead."

"This changed?"

"Aye. There was a king, Ambergin, who ruled well and wisely. Ambergin had the sight, but more importantly he never got the disease. He ruled for 150 years, this with the blessings of both towers. Remarkably, his offspring ruled for centuries afterwards, in the way that kings should, and the land flourished. The kingdom became an empire, by all accounts a fairly decent one. Though I myself am against empires on principle."

"I take it this was some time ago, judging by the ruins we've passed."

"Aye. Ages. Over time the blood thinned. But the line of kingship continued. The people shirked their own responsibilities in the matter. The kings began to think the power was owed them. The Tower Council lost the right to decide by squabbling among themselves over trivial matters. There were wars, plagues, fighting between the magisters and priests. Even the weather changed."

"And all this because the kings had lost their mystical connection with the people?"

"Not just with the people—with the land itself."

"Where does the girl fit into all this?"

"Sianiave believes the capacity to rule is primarily a learned thing. Both Artos and Gwyndolyn were trained from birth in ways few are privy to. Their blood makes them heirs, but their real birthright is in their training."

"Artos is Gwyndolyn's brother?"

"Uncle. By all accounts a doughty warrior and a just and honorable man."

Nick was thoughtful. He'd learned more in the past ten minutes than he had in the entire month he'd been in this world. It was clear Sianiave was working on a large canvas, though he wondered about his part in it. He had a sudden image of a great machine, like an elaborate clock: wheels within wheels, worlds within worlds, spinning and turning. It was a disturbing image and he shook it off.

Across the fire Ren stretched and rose to her feet.

She was gorgeous, Nick thought, graceful and glowing, though this may have been an illusion of the firelight. After Ardendell, he no longer fully trusted his own feelings in such matters. Yet the emotions he felt watching the girl were of a different order entirely—light rather than dark, heart rather than loins.

Had he been brought to this land to guard her? Would he give his life to that end as willingly as these two knights?

She glanced in his direction, but before their eyes could meet he turned away.

CHAPTER
30

REN HAD FAITH in Sianiave's healing abilities, but she sensed the sorceress was worried about Abdelar. Aerindir had improved, his color returning, his breathing steady. Abdelar was as pale as a ghost, his life signs hardly present.

Ren feared Aerindir would wake to find his brother dead, which would devastate him. More than brothers, Aerindir and Abdelar were like opposite parts of a whole.

Please, Mother Yu'An, Ren prayed. Let Abdelar live.

Ren had never told anyone, certainly not Abdelar, but there had been a time when she thought herself in love with him—and it was possible she still was. She might have pursued her feelings had it not been for her pride. Every girl in the kingdom imagined herself in love with Abdelar. Ren didn't want to be just another lovesick cow. And she was terrified that his code of honor would cause him to spurn her. A knight did not lie with his liege lady.

Yet she felt confused, for even as she bathed Abdelar's head, another emotion pulled at her, concerning the strange knight who had arrived with Sianiave. From the first moment she'd seen him, galloping recklessly into the line of Uruk archers, she felt something, an attraction almost frightening in its power. As though she knew him, and yet that was impossible.

She saw him watching her from across the fire when she stood, yet he looked away. "Sianiave?" she asked suddenly. "The knight with Sir Osmodon, Sir Nicholas."

Sianiave had finished bathing the brothers, and was now applying the salve she'd concocted from the kingsroot blossoms. "Yes?"

"Who is he? Where does he come from?"

"He comes from far away. A soldier."

"Only a soldier?"

"Why do you ask?"

"I'm not sure. There is something about him. I sense—"

"Yes?"

"Sadness, as if he does not know himself. As if he has never known his king or lady, if such a thing is possible."

Sianiave looked through the flames of the fire to where Nick sat talking with Osmodon, the dog at his feet. Her face softened. Ren imagined an unusual tenderness in that look but the moment was gone too quickly for her to be sure.

"Yes," said Sianiave finally. "Few in the place he has come from know whom they serve."

CHAPTER
31

ABDELAR DIED during the night, shortly before sunrise.

Sianiave had known the outcome almost from the first. One arrow had pierced his spleen, two others a lung. Even she couldn't repair such damage. It was a miracle he'd lasted as long as he did, long enough to see Ren safe. He'd died peacefully and without pain. She made sure of that.

Despite a heroic effort to remain awake, Ren finally slept. Sianiave didn't have the heart to wake her, or anyone else for that matter. They all needed as much rest as they could manage. They couldn't remain where they were, even with Aerindir injured as he was. At least one Uruk had escaped, perhaps others. If what she suspected were true, they would return with greater numbers.

She covered Abdelar with a blanket, placed another log on the dying fire, and sat back to smoke her pipe.

Things were not going well. Not well at all.

CHAPTER
32

A SOUND THAT WASN'T QUITE a sound brought Nick awake. At first he wasn't sure what it was, only that it tore at his heart and he wanted it to go away.

Then it came to him—grief of a depth he'd never known, worse than any physical pain he could imagine. He sat up, rubbing tears from his eyes. A dream, he thought. Or was it? It wasn't going away. He rubbed his eyes again and looked around. The fire had burned to embers and there was a comfortless chill in the air. A pale yellow light dawned over the treetops.

Ren sat cross-legged beside Abdelar. Her body was trembling, and silent tears ran down her face. The dog lay beside her, his head on her lap as if to console her. Sianiave was nowhere to be seen.

Then Nick understood. Abdelar was dead. It was Ren's loss he felt. But her grief was not for Abdelar alone. It was for her family and friends dead or left behind. It was grief for Barad'An, a vanished childhood, all she had lost. It was grief for life itself.

He wanted to put his arms around her, tell her everything would be fine, but he knew it would be a lie. He shook his head. How did she bear it?

Aerindir lay unconscious but still breathing. In the meadow, Osmodon stacked logs into the shape of a rough rectangle. A shelter? Were they going to stay here?

Wanting to console the girl, but knowing anything he said would be inadequate, Nick joined Osmodon.

"Abdelar's dead. Princess Gwyndolyn is upset. I don't know, maybe someone should—"

Osmodon shook his head. "Best to let her be."

Nick moved closer to the pile of Uruk bodies nearby. It seemed smaller than it had the evening before. There were pools of drying blood and drag marks leading into the woods opposite the camp. A paw print marked the soft earth; it was as big as a dinner plate, with six toes ending in long claws.

Osmodon came to stand beside him. "Aye. Something's in the woods, right enough. It's been watching us, and whatever it is, it has no qualms about what it eats. Must've dragged off two or more corpses during the night. If I'd known something that size was around, I wouldn't have slept so soundly."

"Where's Sianiave?"

Osmodon piled another log on the structure he was building, eyed it, then repositioned it. "She went for a walk, to look for herbs, I imagine, or to think. Things aren't going exactly how she planned, you may have noticed."

"She knew we'd find the princess here."

"A hope more than a knowing, I'd say. When she heard that Gwyndolyn and the brothers had left Barad'An, it wasn't hard to guess where they were headed. Gallian is the only place in a hundred leagues where the princess might be safe. They wouldn't take open roads, not with Uruks about. As it was, we were both lucky and unlucky. A bit sooner—" Osmodon shrugged, picked up another branch.

"Does she know about our friend with the big feet?"

"I may have mentioned it." Osmodon nodded toward a granite cliff perhaps a quarter mile distant, visible through the trees. "The trail leads toward that stony place. That's where it dens, I reckon. We can hope its stomach is full by now. Sianiave is safe enough. Whatever she decides, one thing's certain. We leave here after the funeral."

Nick suddenly understood. Osmodon wasn't building a shelter. He was building a pyre. "I'll give you a hand," he said.

"Good. We'll need more of these larger limbs, and underbrush for fill. But keep your sword handy."

Nick glanced warily around. He'd had enough of ravenous creatures.

Osmodon wanted a large pyre so nothing would be left to tempt predators. Much of the wood they'd found was damp, but Osmodon insisted this was not a problem, since he was mostly choosing chunks of maple wood, and another wood he called ironbark, for their flammable sap. He also had faith in Sianiave's skill with fire, though so far Nick had seen little evidence of it. If she was so adroit with fire, why hadn't she just blasted the Uruks with a fire bolt rather than risk their lives in a cavalry charge?

The sun was high over the trees when Osmodon deemed the pyre ready. Sianiave had returned and Ren had apparently worked through her initial grief, though Nick could sense the sadness hidden under her mask of determination. She spoke little, helping Sianiave fashion a travois out of aspen logs and blankets. Osmodon had guessed right. They would leave as soon as the pyre was lit.

"We'll continue on to Gallian," Sianiave announced. "According to Ren it was Cuchulain's last wish, and I've no better plan at the moment. Ellohir should be informed in any event. And I must consult with Bronwyn."

Nick and Osmodon laid Abdelar's body on the pyre. Ren placed his lyre in his hands, and his bow and dagger at his side. Sianiave kept Daemonsyr, wrapped in a blanket with Aerindir's sword.

Glaerindor, Abdelar's mount, had survived the battle, and Ren chose to ride him. They yoked the travois to Osmodon's pony. "He's better suited to that sort of work," Osmodon remarked. He himself had taken an Uruk pony, a buckskin somewhat larger than the other strays. The rest they kept as pack animals, and for Aerindir when he could ride again.

After a meal, they gathered in the meadow. Osmodon and Nick stood silent as Sianiave and Ren spoke a prayer. Then Sianiave gave a blessing and the ritual Call to notify the doorkeeper of Velkela, the Hall of Heroes, that one of their greatest was arriving.

Ren lit the pyre with an ember from the campfire, and Abdelar's body was soon engulfed. Without further word, they mounted their horses and started across the meadow toward Gallian.

CHAPTER
33

THEY TRAVELED EAST for nearly a week, encountering no enemies, human or otherwise. Woods and grassy hills gave way to arid land, flat-topped mesas, and wide expanses of tough yellow grass. The few areas of green they encountered usually meant a spring or water hole, where they would sometimes camp.

A massive herd of deer-like creatures passed to their left. Osmodon pointed out lions and packs of wild dogs stalking them. Occasionally they spotted a larger animal, always too distant to identify.

The weather grew warmer, and rain more frequent. They could see the grey curtain of a storm coming from miles away in an otherwise cloudless blue sky. Osmodon called it "walking rain," and it often missed them completely. The showers were short-lived and left the land smelling fresh and sweet.

Aerindir had not yet opened his eyes. His wounds had healed well enough, but it was not these wounds that concerned Sianiave.

One evening, as she and Ren bathed his body in a stream near their camp, she said, "He may be valiant in battle, but there is a part of him afraid to face the world without his brother beside him."

Anger, along with a steel-edged resolve, had replaced Ren's grief. "Is there nothing we can do?"

"Continue to tend him, is all."

They had made camp in a grove of cottonwoods beneath a low mesa. It was a dark night, the moon not yet risen, the sky speckled with stars. Their fire was barely large enough to boil water, but neither Sianiave nor Osmodon wanted to risk a larger flame. Along with the dangers that haunted the wilds, they considered it likely Ren was still sought by the priest's men. The Uruk band had not happened upon her by chance, and Ren thought she recognized the Uruk captain Nick had killed as the one whose arrow had murdered Cuchulain.

Conversation was muted, as it had been for much of the journey. Since Abdelar's death, Sianiave and Ren rarely spoke. That afternoon, before making camp, Ren had ridden alongside Nick for awhile and thanked him for his help. There was little he could say in way of small talk, so the conversation was brief.

Later, Nick drew the first watch. After the meal, Osmodon joined him and Bear on a ledge above the camp.

"You should be resting," Nick said, though he was glad for the company. Earlier, the dog had growled at something in the shadows. There had been furtive movement, and a clicking sound, like small claws scrabbling over stone. Bear lay with his head tilted toward the rocks, wary and alert.

"The less sleep I get, the harder it is to sleep," grumbled Osmodon, squatting down. "It's a fair night. Didn't want to waste it tossing and turning in my blankets. And Sianiave asked me to warn you that there's something out there. The horses have been restless."

"I've heard something, a clicking sound."

"Rock beasts, perhaps. Loathsome animals with sharp teeth and claws."

"Wonderful. How big?"

"Like a house cat, a bit larger. They travel in small packs and can strip a man to the bone in minutes. Though a man armed and awake, with a dog, shouldn't be troubled. They're cowardly creatures, really."

"All right, I get it. Stay awake if I want to avoid being eaten by rock beasts."

Osmodon chuckled. "I take it you don't have such things in Amra?"

"Our monsters are more of the human kind."

The clicking in the rocks had subsided since Osmodon's arrival. Nick was grateful the big man didn't seem in any hurry to leave. "What do you know about this place, Gallian?"

"Never been there myself. Was a barony of a sort, but independent now. Baron Ellohir rules with his wife, Lady Bronwyn. Both are well regarded by all accounts."

"How far is it and why are we going there?"

"From Barad'An, on a good horse by the Eastern Road, a man can reach Gallian in less than a week. Us, traveling overland, with Aerindir on a litter, difficult to say. Three or four more days at least. As to the why, I can only guess. Ellohir is known for his loyalty to the bloodline, and Gallian is said to be impregnable."

"Impregnable. Really. Is there such a place?"

"Never seen one myself, though Barad'An comes close. More than one army has been broken on its walls. But I reckon these days even Barad'An can be taken. Its walls are forbidding, but with Artos gone there aren't enough bodies to defend them properly."

Far away on the horizon lightning flashed. Seconds later came the dull rumble of thunder. In the east a full moon, or nearly so, was rising over a distant mesa, its bright light casting sharp shadows among the rocks.

"Why me?" said Nick after a long silence.

"You're still chewing on that bit of fat? A liegeman such as myself has certain duties and obligations, mind you, discretion being one of them."

"I understand if you can't talk about it."

"I can talk about it. She's never forbidden me that. But the truth is, I know little more than yourself, though I've certainly pondered on it."

"You've an opinion then?"

"I have. First off, it doesn't take a soothsayer to see you're no common soldier. It was proved to me back there in the meadow, the way you fought. I've never seen its like."

"You held your own."

"I'm a good infighter. Built for it, you might say. Gang like that, undisciplined and unprepared, can't bring their numbers to bear."

Nick looked up. "Numbers to bear" struck a chord of memory, but it faded away.

"Wasn't much for us, really," Osmodon continued. "But the way you and that horse worked together was a thing of beauty. By the gods, busy as I was, I almost stopped to watch."

"But Sianiave?"

"Aye. Sianiave. Why bring you here when the princess has protectors aplenty in Barad'An? Could be a foretelling, her knowing you'd be needed at the meadow, and maybe later. Except if she'd had foresight of that battle, she kept it well hidden. When that innkeeper let it drop that Cuchulain was no more, and the princess gone from Barad'An, I could see it threw her mightily."

"So, if I'm not here as a bodyguard, then—" Nick grew exasperated.

Osmodon held up his hands. "Hold there. I'm not saying you aren't here to look after the girl. But Sianiave never does anything without having at least six reasons for it."

"One good one would do," Nick grumbled.

Osmodon studied Nick in the darkness for a long moment, stroking his beard. "It's only a guess," he said finally, smiling. "An opinion, mind you. But I reckon she might be matchmaking."

"What?" Nick rose, almost dumping his sword off his lap. "That's crazy!"

"You asked."

Nick took a deep breath, his mind spinning. "Tell me how you came to this, this opinion?"

"Of course. First off, it's plain you're high born. You can't hide something like that. It's obvious in your manner, in the way you speak, think, carry yourself. Secondly, as you yourself have wondered, why else would Sianiave go to such lengths?"

Nick shook his head. He felt threatened by the idea. "Ozzy, you're way off. I'm about as far from high-born as you can be. I'm an orphan, for God's sake!"

Osmodon nodded. "Then you never knew your parents?"

"I know what you're thinking. But believe me, it's impossible."

But even as Nick objected, he wondered if Osmodon were right. It certainly would explain the loneliness he'd always felt in that other world, and the uncanny familiarity he felt with this one.

What compelled you to engage in such anachronistic martial pursuits as archery and fencing?

Worlds within worlds, puzzles within complexities, like an elaborate Chinese box. If any of it were true, it would mean Sianiave had known him beforehand. Which led to the conclusion that Sianiave, or someone, had been keeping an eye on him, possibly for his entire life.

You are not alone.

How dare they? How dare they play with his life like this?

He chose his next words carefully. "You're suggesting that I was spirited away from here as a baby? For what possible reason?"

Osmodon glanced away, then looked back. "I'm not saying I know it for fact, but you could do worse than throw a rose or two the girl's way."

"Ozzy—"

"I know you favor her, lad. I've seen it in your eyes when she's near. She doesn't hold your liege, if that's what's troubling you."

"She's a child, not to mention a princess!"

"Hardly a child. You saw the way she fought. As for being a princess, she's also a woman, and I'd bet a good sword she's a randy one at that. I've seen the way she looks at you, lad."

"She hasn't spoken ten words to me since we met."

"She's had other things on her mind. But she's interested, no doubt. You can't see it yourself, perhaps, but Sianiave's certainly noticed. Little gets by her."

Osmodon stood to leave. "Give it a go. What's to lose, after all? If nothing else it'll make this journey a bit more pleasant. Now, don't forget the rock beasties."

Nick was speechless.

Osmodon ambled off. Bear rumbled deep in his throat, then lay his head beside Nick's knee. Absently, Nick scratched his ears. Rock beasts were the last thing on his mind.

CHAPTER
34

THE VOICES WERE SOFT, SOOTHING.

Sleep. Sleep is good. You are tired, so tired. Rest…Sleep…Sleep….

Nick's hand tightened on the pommel of his sword. He'd almost dozed off. He had no idea what time it was, but the moon was full overhead.

Waiting….

He shook his head. It had been no dream. He could still hear the voices whispering, expectant. He looked about. A half dozen pair of jewel-like eyes peered down at him from the rocks, their movements accompanied by a sinister clicking of claws on stone.

One beast had crept down and was standing less than six feet away. In the moonlight it appeared to be a sort of monkey or ferret, with sharp, slender claws and a mouthful of needle-like teeth. When it saw he was awake, it chittered and disappeared among the rocks.

The voices stopped, the gleaming eyes vanished. Bear, who had fallen asleep at his feet, lifted his head. "It's all right, boy. They're gone."

"Congratulations. You've earned your first shield." Sianiave emerged from the shadows, sword in hand. "Get some rest. I'll keep watch. They won't be back," she said.

"The rock things? I heard their voices. Bear was asleep."

"Don't blame the dog. They work as a pack with a group mind. They can be more powerful than a grendel when their prey is tired. But the enemy can't get at you that way again."

"Enemy? You speak as if there's only one."

"One and many. The morghul, the weir-beasts, the grendel, these creatures are real and dangerous in their ways. But we cannot name the One—not in the dark, with its creatures still about."

"You mean the priest, Glays?"

"No, not Glays. He's just another creature under its thrall. Wait until we reach Gallian. For now, get some sleep. We've still a ways to go, and we enter the badlands tomorrow."

Badlands? Nick wanted to question her more, but at the moment found the idea of sleep far more attractive. He would wait. Maybe in Gallian he could get some clear answers. Bear followed as he made his way back to camp.

"Sleep well," Sianiave called after him. "There's a binding on the camp. Not strong enough to attract the hunters, but enough to keep these little monsters at bay."

CHAPTER
35

THE FOLLOWING MORNING Aerindir opened his eyes and sat up. "Welcome back," said Sianiave matter-of-factly. "How are you feeling?"

The knight looked around and asked, "Where are we?"

"Two days out from Gallian, three at most."

"Gallian? How long have I—"

"A week."

"A week." Aerindir closed his eyes again, then with an effort he put an arm back, rolled to his side and attempted to stand. Ren moved quickly to steady him. "You should keep still. You'll open your wounds."

"I'll manage." He looked down at the travois, then turned to Nick, who was packing up his bedding. "Sir Osmodon I know, but forgive me, I do not know your name."

"Nicholas. It's good to see you feeling better."

"I owe you my life, Sir Nicholas. Those archers overwhelmed us."

Nick knew then he was aware of his brother's death. There was an awkward moment of silence.

"I'll fetch your clothes," Ren said.

Nick returned to his bedroll, watching from the corner of his eye as Ren brought the knight his clothes, helping as he dressed. Intimate as the act was, neither expressed any self-consciousness. Like family, Nick thought.

"Cheer up, lad," said Osmodon, putting an arm over his shoulder. "Nothing strikes a woman's heart more than a sick puppy or a wounded knight. He's her friend, after all."

Nick's feelings were more complex. It was hard to deny a certain jealousy, though he was sincerely pleased by the knight's recovery. There was something about the man he could not help but like, a courtliness, an indefinable charisma. Behind Aerindir's forbidding looks and grim demeanor, Nick recognized him as a knight in the best sense of the word, the sort he and Billy had imagined themselves to be only after many beers: courteous, courageous, honorable, ready to lay down their lives for something higher. Women loved them, men admired them, minstrels sang songs about them. But with the admiration also came envy.

Osmodon had described the arduous years of a knight's apprenticeship, with instruction not only in the martial arts but also in the ways of honor and virtue. Few completed the training. Those who failed out often became mercenaries or sheriffs.

Nick had confidence in his own martial abilities. It was the concept of virtue that troubled him. Men like Aerindir lived in a world that understood such ideals, venerated them. He, on the other hand, came from a place where such notions were all but lost, considered quaint and romantic, suited to eccentrics and sentimentalists but of no actual value in the "real world."

Greywind shifted his legs, snorting, as Nick tied his bedroll to the saddle. They had gotten along much better since the fight in the meadow.

Give it time, like Osmodon said. He was still new at this.

Though still weak, Aerindir refused the travois, preferring to ride. Nick suspected he courted the physical pain as a way to avoid a greater one. The others saw this as well, for no one argued with him, although at times it looked as though he might fall from his saddle. By early the next afternoon he was sitting upright, his strength much improved. Still he spoke little, and Ren often rode beside him.

They made better time without the travois. Savannah grass, scattered trees, and flowing streams gave way to sandy washes and desert sage. The days had grown warm. Monsoon rains arrived like clockwork, leaving rainwater in sinkholes, gullies, and rocky depressions. Wildflowers of all colors abounded and cacti bloomed red, yellow, and blue.

Nick was riding behind Osmodon when the big man reined in. A troop of horsemen was visible in the distance, sixty or more, also riding east. Sunlight glimmered off their shields and the bronze tips of their lances. A line of oxcarts followed behind, with people walking alongside.

"Uruks?"

"No. They carry lances. And their shields are metal, not leather. Besides, Uruks would never ride in a column like that, or use oxcarts. Hard to make out their colors, though."

Aerindir stood in his stirrups to see better. "Ellohir's men, I'm certain."

"Pick up our pace," said Sianiave, spurring her pony forward. "We'll be in Gallian before nightfall. I for one would appreciate a hot bath tonight."

Nick looked over to see Ren beside him. "Have you been to Gallian before?" he asked.

"I have," she replied. "Twice, as a child. I visited there with my grandfather. He and Ellohir were great friends."

"We can get a hot bath there?"

"More than a hot bath, I would say." Ren grinned impishly, then spurred her horse forward to join Sianiave.

Nick gave Osmodon a questioning glance; he shrugged. Aerindir smiled. "Ellohir has nine daughters. Only two are married, so be warned."

Osmodon laughed as he rode after the knight. "Nine daughters? Aerindir, tell me more!"

Nick was last to follow. Being close to their destination cheered the others, but he was having the opposite reaction. It would be good to get back to civilization, to a real bath, clean clothes, and fresh food instead of dried cheese and stale jerky. But their arrival might also mean the end of his service.

Gwyndolyn would be safe. Aerindir would be there, not to mention Osmodon and Sianiave. Much as he would have liked to believe in Osmodon's notions about romance, deep down it didn't feel right.

He found that he dreaded the thought of leaving. What was back in the other world for him? A life on the run, if he was lucky, or prison, even death. His memories of the world that had been his home had grown dim and nightmarish: endless wars, worsening climate, burgeoning population, and meaningless technology. People there lived in fear, laziness, and greed. Who in their right mind would choose to return to such a place?

There was Billy, of course. He owed him. Maybe he could bring Billy to this world. It would suit him, and Elyse as well. They could work as teachers and healers.

He would ask Sianiave about it.

CHAPTER
36

"HALT AND DECLARE YOURSELVES!"

The mounted warriors had appeared like ghosts out of a field of broken boulders, lances at the ready. The challenge had come from their captain, a tall, lean man with the scowl of a lifelong soldier. His scrutiny passed from Osmodon to Nick, lingering for a moment on Ren and Sianiave, as if to place them. Bear gave a low growl and bared his teeth.

"Greetings, Beothyr," said Aerindir. "We saw your column from afar and thought to join you."

Recognition came slowly. "Aerindir? By the gods, man, I didn't recognize you under that beard!" The captain's scowl was replaced with a wide grin as he signaled the other riders. "Raise lances! It's Aerindir of Caerlain!"

A ripple of relief passed through the company. Aerindir was obviously well regarded by them, for which Nick was grateful.

"We've heard rumors." Beothyr turned to Ren. "Then you must be— my deepest apologies, m'lady! I should have known you."

"I would have been surprised if you had, Captain," replied Ren courteously. "I was a child when last we met."

"Ellohir told us to look for you. It was said Aerindir and Abdelar would be with you. But no one mentioned the Lady Sianiave, or your other companions. And where is Abdelar?"

"He fell nine days ago," said Sianiave. "Uruks."

"Abdelar? Dead?" Beothyr looked stricken "This is sore news, sore news indeed. Aerindir, I am sorry."

Beothyr's men were covered in dust and weary, their dress stained with blood, helms and shields battered. The news of Abdelar's death seemed to darken their mood. Aerindir nodded in acceptance but said nothing.

"You've seen recent battle yourselves," said Sianiave.

"Aye. Uruks. They laid waste to Rumstock. We crossed the band responsible this morning, at Talisyr where the rivers meet."

"The oxcarts? The people on foot?"

"The lucky ones, women and children mostly. We're escorting them to Gallian. No other place is safe. Not since the war started."

"War?"

"You haven't heard? Sabbat Khan, Kosha Khan's son, has taken power. He's rallied the tribes, promising land and booty—our land. He means to carry out his father's purpose, gathering an army in Nibur. Knowing our weakness, the Uruks have been growing bolder. Rumstock was a slaughter."

Beothyr's lips tightened in anger, and he looked away. "Now is not the time to speak of it. We have a patrol to keep, by Lord Penthys's command," he added, as if to explain.

Aerindir frowned. "Penthys? I'd assumed he retired to his estates years ago."

"You'll find many good men who'd thought they'd seen the last of it back in battle dress. We can no longer count on Barad'An for support."

"We have some knowledge of this," said Sianiave. "But as you say, we'd best speak of it later."

"Certainly, m'lady."

Beothyr motioned to a freckle-faced squire with blue eyes and a shock of red hair visible beneath a dented helm. "Miklos will have to accompany you. Battle protocol is in effect. Lord Penthys insists."

Sianiave gave a short laugh. "Say no more."

"Aerindir! We'll tip a cup in Gallian soon, gods willing." With that Beothyr swung his horse around and disappeared up the wash, his men close behind save for the young squire.

Nick and the others followed him through the cactus and up another gully. A dozen riders broke from the column as they approached, galloping out to confront them. "Halt!" shouted their captain. "Word of the day!"

"Fortengyn!" answered the squire. "Squire Miklos, of Beothyr's scouts, escorting the Princess Gwyndolyn, the Lady Sianiave, and their company."

The formal protocol made Osmodon roll his eyes and Aerindir shake his head in wonder.

"The princess and the Lady Sianiave can proceed," answered the captain. "The others to the rear."

"We will stay together," said Ren.

"Captain," said Miklos uneasily. "It's the princess."

"I see that. But Penthys would have my head if I disobeyed an order, even for a princess. Even for you, m'lady," he added with a glance and a slight bow to Sianiave.

Sianiave nodded. She turned to the others. "You'll be fine in the rear. Lord Penthys is a good field general, but you'd have better conversation with a brick. Will you take us to him, Captain?"

"I will. Miklos will return to the scouts."

The young squire looked disappointed, but saluted without complaint and rode off without looking back.

Ren was miffed. She felt like baggage. She respected Sianiave, emulating her in many ways. But she'd grown up in a city dominated by strong-willed men and equally strong-willed women and managed to hold her own. She felt she'd earned a little respect.

She preferred to remain with the three knights, men she considered friends, if not more. Aerindir was recovering nicely, but he still needed her ministrations. She was his liege lady, after all, and there were obligations. Osmodon was immensely capable, funny, wise in the ways of the world, and a wonderful storyteller. But it was Sir Nicholas she was most taken with, and that was troubling. They weren't close, but it was if they'd known each other before. Her feelings were deeper and far more complex than lust. The thought that it might be love had crossed her mind.

Who was he? She'd given him every opportunity to talk about himself, but he'd always backed away. At first she wondered whether it might be some fault in herself, but she sensed the attraction was mutual. Perhaps a vow of chastity, or to another woman?

Men could be such fools. She would talk to Sianiave.

Lord Penthys was a hard-faced veteran whose frame, though thinned with age, was still formidable. As they approached, he sat straight in the saddle, his dress as bloodied as any of his men. His helm bore the raven crest of his estate, several leagues to the north of Gallian.

"Princess Gwyndolyn," he said, addressing her with a formality that annoyed her. "I'm glad to see you safe, though your appearance is not unexpected."

"You had word, I'm told."

Ren remembered the old knight from a visit he'd made to Barad'An years before. He had been distant even then. The years hadn't changed him overmuch. In his youth he'd been counted among the greatest of field commanders, considered honest, hard on his men, and uncompromising in his sense of duty, if rather abrasive. In many ways he reminded her of her grandfather.

"Refugees from Barad'An brought accounts of the king's passing and your escape."

Penthys regarded Sianiave, his demeanor showing neither warmth nor welcome. "There was no mention of you, m'lady, or your two companions. And I understand Abdelar is absent?"

Penthys despised unnecessary conversation, so Sianiave was brief. "Abdelar was killed in a Uruk ambush. Their purpose was to capture Ren. I, and my companions, came across the fight. We dispatched most of the attackers. Unfortunately, some few escaped."

The old warrior frowned. Ren couldn't tell if the expression was one of sorrow at Abdelar's death or disapproval that Uruks had escaped.

"Abdelar was a good fighter," Penthys remarked. "A league back our scouts reported seeing a band of Uruks, but they ran before we could take them. The princess must be protected, of course. You and she will ride with me."

It was an order, not an invitation. Ren started to protest, for the last thing she wanted was to ride behind this harsh old man, but Sianiave stilled her with a look. "A gracious gesture, m'lord."

Either the old knight hadn't heard, or had chosen to ignore, the slight edge of sarcasm in Sianiave's reply. Ren looked back, but could no longer see the rest of their party.

§

"Look's like we're the baggage," grunted Osmodon as Sianiave and Ren rode off with the captain to the front of the column.

"Sianiave is right," said Aerindir. "We're better off here. Companionable, Penthys is not."

Nick was preoccupied with observing Lord Penthys's troops, appreciating their formidable discipline. They kept a tight formation, sitting straight in their saddles despite the recent battle. They rode in a double column, with flankers on either side, men riding point, and a rear guard. Along with the scouting party they'd run into, he figured the total strength of the company to be nearly a hundred.

The men carried long wooden lances tipped with bronze blades, capable of either piercing or slashing. Their helms and shields appeared to be bronze also, and they wore body armor of lacquered leather over quilt padding.

Nick and his companions joined the refugees at the rear of the column. The blank, shocked faces were like many Nick had seen in Afghanistan. They had witnessed the slaughter of family and friends, the destruction of their fields and houses. In time, grief would come. But for now they just struggled to survive.

Oxcarts rumbled along with whatever valuables they'd salvaged. There were few wounded, which spoke both of the Uruks' cruelty and efficiency. Penthys's soldiers had been even more efficient, for they appeared to have suffered few, if any, casualties.

A dreary procession. Grim reality dampened conversation.

§

The road on which they traveled was very much like the road between Ardendell and Graylen Tor. Some sections were well preserved, others broken or entirely washed away. Not a few times the column was forced to slow when the carts bogged down in sand.

They began a long descent into a shallow canyon, in the center of which stood a solitary flat-topped mountain shaped like a wedding cake.

"Gallian," said Aerindir.

Osmodon looked skeptical. "That's Gallian? Where's the keep?"

"The mountain is the keep."

The road branched, one branch continuing east, the other north toward the mesa. As Nick studied the surrounding geography, he began to suspect the nature of their destination. Imposing cliffs with watchtowers on the rim rose before them. Not until they were in the shadow of the cliffs could he make out an opening, little more than a seam in the red rock wall.

Horns sounded at their approach. Nick sensed rather than saw soldiers among the rocks and watchtowers as the column proceeded into the seam.

The seam became a tunnel, high enough for a mounted man but barely wide enough to accommodate the carts. The tunnel floor was paved with cobbles and deeply worn. Oil lamps bracketed the walls. The sound of hooves, creaking saddles, and wooden cart wheels echoed off the cool stone walls. It was a quarter mile before they saw natural light again.

When they emerged into the open, Nick could only stare in wonder. His guess had been correct. The mountain was what remained of an ancient volcano, high cliffs forming its outer wall. But the view that greeted him was beyond anything he had imagined.

CHAPTER
37

THEY WERE GREETED by a panorama of green surrounded by near-vertical rock walls in shades of umber and brown. The valley was perhaps five miles across. A sizable river ran through its heart, fed by a half-dozen waterfalls cascading from the cliffs. On the far side of the valley, seemingly carved into the cliff itself, was an imposing mansion.

It was nearing sunset. The caramel light of the lowering sun bathed the cliffs and reflected onto the mansion, as though it burned with a golden fire. "It's enough to make one forget Linsraden," murmured Osmodon.

A brick road curved through well-kept fields. The main column turned right, following a trail below the cliff. Riders dropped back as they led the refugees on another trail to the left.

"The legion barracks are there to the right," Aerindir explained, "hollowed out of the cliffs. The barracks on the left haven't seen use in half a century. I imagine that's where they'll house the refugees."

Ren and Sianiave galloped to the rear of the column, accompanied by Sir Penthys. "You will continue on to High House!" barked the old man. "There will be a council in the morning. I trust you will be there."

Without so much as a good-bye, he galloped off to rejoin his men.

"Pleasant fellow," remarked Osmodon.

Ren laughed. "You had the best of it in the rear, even with the dust."

"To his credit, he is a gifted military commander," said Sianiave, though she was as relieved as Ren to escape the old man's stifling formality.

"His is a well-earned reputation," said Aerindir.

"Is it?" Osmodon asked skeptically. "Well-earned, I mean, or merely well-repeated?"

Aerindir started to answer, then caught himself. He was recalling what Abdelar had sung that afternoon by the pool: "Only the warrior has the courage to slay past giants."

Most understood the line to mean that a true warrior had to vanquish emotion. Emotional energy, while powerful, was short-lived and easily spent. So they had been taught. But Abdelar had said there was more to it. To be truly effective, whether in war, lovemaking, or life in general, a certain amount of emotion was essential.

Abdelar had kidded Aerindir about his apparent lack of warmth. Aerindir had never told him it wasn't his lack of feeling that was the problem, but its overwhelming presence. He imagined what Abdelar would say about Penthys. Can a child grow up straight and healthy with an emotionally aloof father? Can a warrior rise to his full potential with an emotionally aloof commander?

Such thoughts were new and troubling for Aerindir. He'd always left the charm and philosophy to his brother, with his more agile wit.

For Nick the ride through Gallian was a journey through a dreamscape. How could such a place exist in the midst of a desert? A lake shimmered in the distance, or perhaps it was a mirage. Two dogs herded a dozen goat-like creatures toward a pasture gate. A large, tidy farmhouse stood nearby. To their left was a small village, with houses, shops, corrals, barns, and what looked like a multi-storied inn. But it was the cliff palace that caught and kept his eye. Its dazzling colors changed as the sun set, from white gold to burnished bronze to a glowing burgundy. High House, Penthys had called it.

As they drew closer, Nick saw signs of military activity: tents on a parade field, hastily built corrals and barracks, forges tending to all manner of ironwork. Soldiers, quitting their drills as dusk settled, moved aside as the small group passed by. Some were grim, battled-hardened veterans, others fuzzy-cheeked boys who would have looked more at home behind a plow. There were a surprising number of women among them, many carrying bows nearly as tall as themselves.

A stone causeway swept up toward the palace, wide at the bottom but narrowing as it neared the gate. Its supports were slender and elegantly curved, giving the causeway a deceptively fragile appearance. But Nick saw immediately its graceful beauty belied a more practical purpose. It would be impossible for massed troops to storm.

"Can't starve 'em out," mused Osmodon, thinking along the same lines. "There's plenty of water, and they grow their own food. Take a year to dig under the mountain if it was even possible, and how would you feed and water your army in the meantime? Not in that wasteland outside. It would have to be taken from within, by treason or sorcery."

Aerindir grunted. "You have a devious mind, Sir Osmodon."

"Habit of an old soldier, I'm afraid."

"In two thousand years, Gallian's been threatened but once," said Sianiave, "by the sorcerer King Paracelsor in 1273. Gallian lay under siege for eight months."

"Saolin has told me something of this," said Ren. "A dreadful tale, but with a proper ending."

Sianiave nodded. "As Osmodon has guessed, it was betrayal and sorcery. Banothyr was the younger brother of Baron Antoris, Ellohir's great-grandfather. During the siege, Paracelsor promised him the title for his betrayal. There were other reasons as well. Banothyr was said to be enamored of a certain concubine, who presented him the scheme.

"Banothyr slipped a potion into the evening meal, incapacitating Antoris, his wife, and seven of his children. But Arn, the eldest son, was late to dinner that night, having been in training as a page. The boy arrived to find his uncle in the dining hall, covered in blood, the dagger he used to perform his grisly business still in hand. With his training sword as his only weapon, Arn managed to kill his traitorous uncle. He was not yet sixteen. He lost a hand in the fight, and became known as Arn One Hand, and he ruled well and wisely for over a hundred years."

"As great a baron as Gallian has ever had," remarked Aerindir. "Save perhaps for Ellohir."

"What happened to this sorcerer fellow and his army?" Osmodon asked.

"Barad'An sent knights to break the siege. Later Paracelsor was killed in a duel. His land now lies in waste."

"I thought he was a sorcerer," said Nick. "Yet he was killed in a duel?"

"The duel was with another wizard, a Megidian. Neither man

survived. When it was over, it's said there was nothing left but a shattered hall and two bloody puddles on the floor."

Osmodon grimaced in distaste. "Dangerous calling, sorcery. Give me a good horse and an honest sword any day."

Aerindir nodded agreement, but Nick saw Ren exchange an amused glance with Sianiave as if to say, "Men!"

As dusk fell, lights came on in the palace above. Boys carrying burning wicks ran down the causeway, lighting its many lamps. Across the valley, a maroon sunset lowered into night. Lights winked on in farmhouses, barracks, and the village.

The immense wooden gate stood open as they rode into the courtyard. An old man came out to greet them as grooms hurried to take their horses. The man was tall, nearly Nick's height, with short white hair and kindly patrician features. He wore a simple grey robe, but he carried himself with authority.

"Lady Sianiave!" he cried. "Princess Gwyndolyn! Such an honor. We're delighted to see you safe. Aerindir, my boy, we heard the news of Abdelar's passing. I am truly sorry. A great loss for us all."

Aerindir nodded shortly, but once again said nothing.

"Membrion is Ellohir's chamberlain," explained Sianiave, "as he was to both Ellohir's father and grandfather. Membrion, this is Osmodon, my liegeman."

The vizier took Osmodon's hand in a warm grip. "Sir Osmodon, delighted. You were in Nibur when last Sianiave visited, I recall. But we've certainly heard word of your exploits."

"The honor is mine," returned Osmodon politely.

The old man turned his attention to Nick, and for several moments didn't speak. His grey eyes bore into Nick's.

It was Sianiave who finally broke the silence, and with it the old man's gaze. "This is Nicholas of Amra. A soldier, and our companion."

There was an odd inflection in the way she said this last, but it may well have been his imagination. Nick felt a sense of relief when the old man turned away. A feeling of almost physical pressure was gone.

"Good, then. I'll see you to your apartments. Don't worry about your baggage. The house folk will see to it. You've had a long journey and baths are waiting. Ellohir is cleaning up after a day in the field. Dinner is at seven. You are all invited to attend. This way. Follow me, follow me."

CHAPTER
38

DESPITE ITS IMMENSE SIZE, there was an appealing homeliness to High House. As with Tor Eyrie, much of it had been tunneled out of rock, but there was an artistry here that Sianiave's retreat lacked. High ceilings were set off by fluted columns and handsome arches. Tiled stairs led to different levels. Paintings and finely embroidered tapestries covered its walls. In sitting areas, fountains and fireplaces were encircled by luxurious divans, and all was brightly lit by a multitude of lamps.

Nick was the last of his companions to be shown to his apartment. There was a spacious sitting area with chairs, table, and a large fireplace. The massive oak bed was dressed with a colorfully embroidered comforter and down pillows. A large window overlooked a garden where a veil of shimmering water fell into a tiled pool.

From that height the valley resembled a dark sea speckled with starlight. Campfires and village lamplights glowed in the distance. The window was open. A warm breeze gently played across the curtains, carrying the scent of exotic flowers and the sound of a woman singing. Nick couldn't make out the words, but the melody was haunting.

"The baths are down the hall," Membrion said before leaving. "If you need anything, just ask one of the house folk. We hope to see you at the morning council. Your arrival has caused quite a stir."

The old chamberlain stood for a moment as if wanting to say more. Then, appearing to think better of it, he bowed and left.

Nick stood by the window for a long moment, captivated by the woman's song and the night breeze. From the moment they'd entered the valley his spirits had lifted. Gone was the weariness from days in the saddle. There was a sense of timelessness to the place that was strangely familiar, as though he should know it, had known it.

Fighting a sudden and inexplicable urge to weep, he turned from the window. Membrion had told them dinner was in an hour. With a bath waiting, that didn't leave much time.

Osmodon and Aerindir were already at the baths, soaking in separate tubs when he arrived. Four young women attended them, none looking older than nineteen. Their hair was cut short and they wore simple blue linen shifts. The eldest of them took Nick's clothes before escorting him to a tub.

The water was pleasantly warm, almost hot. A second girl scrubbed his back with a long-handled brush while the first kneaded soap into his lengthening beard and matted hair. It was all done with gentle professionalism.

When they'd finished, the women left the room "Lovely lasses," Osmodon murmured contentedly. "Do you think they'll be around later?"

Aerindir laughed. It was first time Nick had heard the sound from him. "They're Sister initiates. This service is part of their training, so don't get any ideas. They're sworn to celibacy, leastwise till they've earned their robes."

"Sisters?" Osmodon frowned. "How unfortunate."

"Working in a men's bathhouse seems an odd sort of training for girls," Nick commented.

Aerindir smiled again—a strange smile, both amused and rueful, conveying deep sadness. "What better way to learn about men? Women are not allowed into the mysteries of the Right Temple, any more than men are allowed into the mysteries of the Left Temple. There are exceptions only for those who show great capacity. Abdelar was one such, though he never completed his training. Sianiave is familiar with both, as is Lady Bronwyn."

Osmodon looked over in surprise. "Lady Bronwyn is a sorceress, you say?"

"Of high degree. Surely you've felt it in the energy of this place. It's not in small part due to her presence."

Before Osmodon could respond, the initiates returned carrying clean towels.

"You'd best finish your baths," said the senior girl. "You still have your massages, though just quick ones tonight. Dinner will be served shortly thereafter."

The three men were toweled off and led to padded tables in an adjoining room where the girls rubbed them down with scented oil. When they'd finished, they gave the men clean robes and lambskin sandals to replace their own travel-worn garments, which had, at least for the moment, vanished.

"That was a bit of all right," sighed Osmodon as the three stepped back into the passageway, closing the door to the baths behind them. "Have to visit here more often."

A number of guests were already present when they entered the dining hall. Nick immediately sensed a not-so-subtle tension in the room—not the fear he'd experienced in Ardendell, more a common though unspoken concern. More women were present than men, a surprising number of them exceedingly attractive. He stood beside Aerindir, who seemed to know the names of most of those present.

Bronwyn's and Ellohir's daughters were introduced: Griselda, Katrina, Gwynith, Niobe, their names coming too fast for Nick to remember. A dark-haired beauty with lavender eyes stood back, her attention on Aerindir alone. As she started to move forward, a burly, red-bearded man stepped between them. "Aerindir! We've heard about Abdelar. Terrible loss. Terrible."

"Lord Crespin. What are you doing in Gallian?"

"Bran's Well was sacked in an Uruk raid. The sheriff was killed. The south holding is in a frenzy. I came with a troop to help sort things out and met one of Ellohir's scouts. He told us he'd seen you with Princess Gwyndolyn and the sorceress. We arrived ahead of you by several hours, I would guess. What happened in Barad'An? We've heard only rumors so far. Has the king really passed?"

"He has. But we'd best leave the telling until tomorrow, at the council. You'll be there?"

"Yes, of course. War is upon us, like it or not. Without Barad'An, how can we—"

"Tomorrow. We'll speak about it tomorrow."

Crespin gave Nick a searching glance, then, seeing someone else across the room of apparently more interest, nodded and left. Aerindir had already turned to the dark-haired woman, only to be interrupted by a matron in a flowing gown. "Aerindir, my dear boy. We're so sorry to hear about your brother."

The matron kept looking at Nick as she talked. Aerindir introduced them. "Lady Conseltrane, Sir Nicholas of Amra. Lady Conseltrane is Lady Bronwyn's aunt," he added, his tone giving nothing away.

Nick had given up denying his knighthood. Apparently if you carried a sword and rode in such company as he, everyone assumed you were a knight. "A pleasure, m'lady," he murmured politely.

"The pleasure is mine," gushed the woman. "We all have so many questions. It's said you're Sianiave's new liegeman?"

"I'm afraid not."

"Oh, but you must tell me—"

"At the council," said Nick, following Aerindir's example and pulling himself away. He looked around for Osmodon, finding him in animated conversation with one of the daughters, a buxom blonde. Griselda, he thought.

"They'll bore you to death," said a small voice beside him.

"Excuse me?"

He looked down to see a young girl staring up at him. Her large brown eyes were disturbingly straightforward. He guessed her to be about ten. "They're good folk," the girl went on. "As you can no doubt see, since you have the sight."

"The sight?"

Nick guessed immediately she was referring to his intermittent ability to see into people, to read their character. Since arriving in Gallian, his ability had been improving. So far he felt none of the greed, fear, and envy he'd perceived in Ardendell. The people he'd met here were who they appeared to be: strong, self-reliant, and good hearted, even the overly curious Lady Conseltrane.

"Don't bother to deny it," the girl continued firmly. "I won't tell anyone. I have it myself. It's my specialty, you might say. And I do love my sisters, but unless you enjoy talking only of men and their deeds, they'll bore you to death. Only two are married, you know."

She nodded at the dark-haired woman who was now engaged in conversation with Aerindir. "Yseult is the only one besides myself who qualified for training, and she has her heart set on Aerindir."

Nick was at a loss.

"Qualified for training? You mean for the Sisterhood?"

The girl sniffed. "Only if we don't measure up."

"Measure up?"

"To the standards."

Standards for what? The child's mother was a sorceress. It might be expected that one or more of her daughters would follow in her footsteps. Apparently the Sisterhood was only a stage in women's initiations.

"No doubt you're wondering," continued the girl seriously, "whether I can read you, which I can't. Just as you can't read me, or Sianiave, or my mother. Everyone's been very curious about you since hearing of the mysterious knight accompanying Sianiave. Sir Osmodon has never been to Gallian before, but we've heard the songs. He is as great a knight as any, it's said. Without a king or even a holding of his own, he is a perfect liegeman for Sianiave. But I overheard you with my auntie, Lady Conseltrane, and if you aren't Sianiave's new liegeman, then who are you, and why are you here? And why, if you're of any importance at all, which I assume you to be since you do have the sight and you came with Sianiave, are there no songs about you?"

Nick stared down at her, speechless. This precocious child had cut to the heart of his being. Who was he? Why was he here? She showed such clear-headed awareness, he wondered if he might not be talking to a midget. The girl looked up at him, eyes wide and guileless, waiting for an answer.

"Who did you say you are?"

"Oh, I'm sorry. I should remember my manners. I'm Kaitlyn, the youngest daughter. Kate, if you please. I thought you knew. But then, how could you, since this is your first time here?

A rustling among the guests saved Nick. Sianiave and Ren had entered the hall. They were dressed in identical sleeveless gowns of ivory silk, and looked like sisters. Their hair, highlighted by weeks in the sun, had been washed and woven into braids and set with jeweled pins. An aura of light seemed to surround them.

Another woman accompanied them, more petite even than Ren but striking nonetheless. Her short hair was silver and covered with a silver mantle adorned with tiny blue stones. It was impossible to guess her age. Her face was both young and old. Her eyes were silver grey, the color of dawn just before sunrise, her skin flawless. She wore a pale yellow gown embroidered with blue and silver filigree. Despite her diminutive size, she carried such an air of command Nick knew at once this must be Bronwyn, Baron Ellohir's wife and mistress of High House.

"Please take your seats," she announced. Her voice was soft, yet carried easily throughout the large hall. "My husband sends regrets he will miss this evening's dinner. There is a matter he must attend to. All of you know Lady Sianiave. Her beautiful young companion is the Princess Gwyndolyn of the house of Ambergin, who has asked that everyone should call her Ren as when last she visited us years ago."

All conversation ceased. The guests took their seats. Nick held back, uncertain of his place. The seating appeared to be determined by some etiquette of which he knew nothing. Soon he was the only one still standing, uncomfortably aware that all eyes in the room were on him. Other than Baron Ellohir's empty chair at the head of the table, only one other seat was vacant, immediately to the right of Bronwyn and facing Ren and Sianiave. It was clearly a seat of honor. Osmodon, and even Aerindir, were seated further down. Having little choice, Nick took the vacant chair.

Bronwyn acknowledged him with a nod and tapped a silver bell. Immediately boys and girls dressed as pages entered carrying decanters of red wine, which they poured into ceramic wine cups placed around the table.

"To Abdelar," said Bronwyn, raising her cup. "A great and good knight, and a friend to us all. He will be sorely missed. May he find peace in Velkela."

"To Abdelar!" Solemnly everyone raised their cup and drank, even little Kate, Nick noted.

The wine was heavy, with a sweet taste akin to honey. Glancing around the table, Nick saw that many had tears in their eyes, and some openly wept.

The cups were refilled. Bronwyn raised hers again. "To our guests: Lady Sianiave, Princess Gwyndolyn, Sir Aerindir, Sir Osmodon, and Sir Nicholas of Amra. They have survived a terrible journey. May they find safety and rest during their stay with us in Gallian."

"Hear, hear!"

Again the cups were raised and emptied. More wine was poured. A second group of servers arrived, carrying trays of game hens, sweetmeats, fruits, breads, cheeses, olives, and vegetables. The dinner had begun.

Belying her small stature, Bronwyn had drained her second cup with one swallow, pouring herself a third as she turned to Nick. "How do you find this land of ours, Sir Nicholas? Not too strange, I trust?"

She smiled, her eyes twinkling in amusement. Across the table Sianiave watched with an equally mischievous grin.

She knows! Nick thought with a shock. Sianiave must have told her. He wasn't Sir Nicholas of Amra, but Nick Herron, a disgraced soldier from another world.

The idea left him feeling exposed, and not a little intimidated, though the wine helped. He was already feeling a pleasant buzz. It had come on quickly. He'd never been particularly susceptible to alcohol. Then it occurred to him that it might not be wine at all. He only assumed it because of the color. "It's been—interesting," he said, in response to Bronwyn's question.

"I can imagine. I travel only rarely myself. Sianiave has told me of your land. By her description, it sounds rather horrifying."

"Don't tease him," said Sianiave. "He's come a long way."

"Has he? Well, we'll see."

Nick knew there was more to the short conversation than the obvious, but what that was he could only guess.

A warm glow settled over him. He raised his cup again only to find it empty. Bronwyn refilled it herself. "Thank you, m'lady."

M'lady. He liked the formal courtesy here.

The mistress of High House laid a small hand gently on his and leaned forward. Her lips were so close to his right ear he could almost feel their soft touch. "Tonight is a night for enjoyment, Sir Nicholas of Amra," she whispered. "Not for pondering."

Surprised, Nick looked at her, but she had already turned away to speak with a server. He glanced across the table, first at Sianiave, then at Ren. Both were astonishingly beautiful, radiant. But it was Ren who captured his attention. She looked back at him, a questioning smile on her lips. He forced himself to meet her gaze, unsure of what he would find.

The moment their eyes met was so intimate that it shocked him to his core.

So far as he knew, he had never been in love. The feeling was unknown to him. The fact of it was as unexpected as it was unmistakable. It came as a wave of joy, and he saw it mirrored in Ren's eyes.

He looked quickly away. The wine. It had to be the wine. He was being too bold.

No. It was true. He was in love. He'd known when he'd first seen her across the meadow that fateful afternoon. He'd just been unwilling to admit it. It was far too frightening, and beyond all reason. It was life-changing.

He looked to her again, but Ren was in caught up in conversation with the man next to her, the red-bearded fellow who'd spoken with Aerindir earlier, Lord something-or-other.

Was Osmodon right? Were he and Ren meant for one another? Was that the reason Sianiave had brought him here?

Tonight is a night for enjoyment, not pondering.

Bronwyn's words were prophetic. Never had food tasted better, nor conversation been brighter. He lost count of how many times his cup was filled. Musicians arrived, a man playing a flute and another a harmonium. An assortment of drummers entered, joined by a singer, a woman whose voice was undoubtedly the one he'd heard earlier from the window of his room.

The music washed over him like warm honey. The night seemed to go on forever. At one point he looked up from his wine cup to see Sianiave, Ren, and Bronwyn watching him with the same knowing smiles he'd seen earlier. For a brief moment he imagined every woman in the room was staring at him with smiles in their eyes and on their lips.

The drumming grew louder, the wild strains of the flute more intense. Guests swayed to the rhythm of the drums. A man began calling out—Membrion, he thought—and the women responded with a chorale so haunting and beautiful the sound penetrated to Nick's very soul.

And then a green light engulfed the hall.

§

Much later, at sunrise, Nick found himself alone in his bed, remembering little about how he'd gotten there. He fell fast asleep, a wide smile on his face.

CHAPTER
39

"SO," GROWLED ELLOHIR. "It's true. Barad'An has fallen to this pig's ass of a priest, and Cuchulain never suspected?"

"His sight was always on external threats," said Aerindir.

"The priest fooled everyone," said Ren. "Even the Sisters. A petty man spouting nonsense. No one took him seriously."

In appearance, the lord of Gallian was the exact opposite of his wife. Bear-like in stature, with flaming auburn hair and piercing blue eyes, he looked at Ren seated across the council table from him and smiled. She's a fighter, by the gods, despite her youth, he thought. And will make a good queen, if she lives that long.

"Cuchulain may have been shortsighted," he said with a gentleness that belied his formidable appearance. "But his last act was to see you safe, child, and that is no small thing."

Bronwyn nodded.

Nick, fighting a dulling headache, listened with only half an ear. What was he doing there? A page had woken him from a deep sleep early that afternoon. Everyone else had been seated when he arrived. He felt like an interloper.

Relative to the rest of the palace the council room was small, no more than twenty feet across, with three tall, lead-paned windows facing east. The table at which they all sat was circular, inlaid with multicolored woods set in a nine-sided geometric pattern. Each of the nine points matched a chair, one each for Ellohir, Bronwyn, Membrion, Penthys, Aerindir, Crespin, Ren, Sianiave, and himself.

Nick was seated more or less opposite the baron. Aerindir was to his right, Crespin to his left. Ren sat to the left of Crespin, away from his direct line of sight, for which he was grateful. He couldn't remember what happened at dinner, but he was sure he'd made a fool of himself.

God, what must she think of him? Wine had never affected him that way before. He'd apologized when he'd arrived, only to be met with amused smiles. Ellohir's reaction in particular baffled him.

"Sorry I missed it," the baron said, his eyes sparkling with humor. "I've always enjoyed Bronwyn's dinners. I tend to forget sometimes, what it is we fight for, us men."

Nick nodded. Maybe he'd missed something. The headache made it hard to think clearly.

Across the table Crespin fidgeted with a button on his tunic. "We've always been able to count on Barad'An's help. With the Uruk tribes marauding, and this new *sirdar* in Nibur with an army ten times the size of ours, what hope have we?"

"Barad'An was in no position to come to Gallian's aid even before the priest's treachery," said Sianiave. "Or am I wrong in that? What say you, Aerindir?"

Aerindir nodded. "It's true. This year we have been at battle constantly, yet barely managed to keep the borders to our own shire protected."

"I find it difficult to understand," said Sir Penthys, "how Cuchulain allowed things to come to such a state."

"We know your mind on this, Penthys," said Ellohir, irritably. "Whether we agreed with him or not, he was our king. I'll not hear him belittled."

"I'm sure Lord Penthys meant no disrespect, my husband," said Bronwyn calmly. "If discussion of a man's missteps can help us better understand our situation, it is only wisdom to listen."

Ellohir opened his mouth as if to reply, then sighed. "You're right of course, my dear. My apologies, Penthys. Cuchulain's death sits poorly with me. Can we at least agree we've lost an ally?"

Penthys gave a short nod. "Of course."

The exchange, brief as it was, gave Nick an insight into the political dynamics in Gallian. Ellohir and Bronwyn were as different as two people could be, yet they functioned as one. Ellohir was the protector and strongman, Bronwyn the voice of practical wisdom.

"Good," said Ellohir. "Our scouts report that the sirdar's army plans to march in ten days."

"Ten days!" blurted out Crespin. "So soon?"

"It was to be expected," remarked Penthys, unperturbed. "Any later, and he would have to contend with the full heat of summer."

"Yes. Certainly. But ten days! He will be at our gates in a matter of weeks. We've hardly time to call in the outliers."

"That's already been done," said Membrion. "But there's another matter. It seems the sirdar has found a morghul to lead his army."

Crespin paled. "A morghul!"

"Posh," sniffed Penthys. "Morghuls have never aligned with men. But even if true, the creatures are hardly known as strategists."

"What need is there of strategy when one has an army seventy thousand strong?" Crespin said.

"Someone's thinking for them both," said Ellohir. "Barad'An is their objective. They will bypass Gallian."

"And leave an enemy in their rear?" Crespin said.

"Hardly a threat," said Penthys. "Why waste resources when a single brigade could close Gallian off like a cork in a bottle? It's what I would do."

Nick's headache had lessened, and he found himself listening with interest. At the word morghul, a sharp pain cramped his left shoulder. He fought to remain calm, but soon his distress began to show.

"Something troubles you, Sir Nicholas?" asked Bronwyn.

"Nothing. An old injury."

"Sianiave told us of your encounter with a morghul."

"You did battle with a morghul?" Aerindir regarded Nick with amazement.

"Hardly a battle. It nearly killed me."

"Yet you survived. I wouldn't have thought it possible," said Aerindir.

"Yes, tell us about it," said Crespin eagerly, as though Nick's encounter somehow offered hope. Even the aloof Sir Penthys showed interest.

Sianiave came to his rescue. "Whether the morghul Sir Nicholas fought is the same creature who leads the sirdar's army is irrelevant. The Uruks, the morghul, even the sirdar, are pawns. Another force moves them."

"The priest?" Crespin asked.

Sianiave dismissed the thought with a wave. "Hardly. As Ren said, a trivial man, barely capable of seeing past his own nose. Whoever or whatever lies behind our travails is far more of a threat than the priest."

Penthys looked unimpressed. "Any thoughts as to who this 'other force' might be?"

"I've suspicions, but I'd rather not voice them until I know more."

"But, surely—"

"First things first," interrupted Ellohir. "The sirdar's army will be on us in less than four weeks, sooner if they're pushed. We must decide on a plan. Sir Nicholas, Sianiave has told us you have some knowledge of warfare. What are your thoughts?"

Nick looked up, startled to have the question directed at him. In the past few weeks he had, unwittingly perhaps, absorbed a great deal of knowledge about this world. Something about the political situation was familiar, though he had yet to place it.

"Four weeks to prepare?"

"Or less."

"How many men can you muster in that time?"

"We can gather a hundred knights, perhaps. Two hundred mounted soldiers, a thousand trained foot soldiers, another thousand untrained, mostly farmers and shopkeepers. But they'll fight."

"Allies?"

"Expect less than twenty knights from the outliers," said Penthys. "Though it might be possible to raise another thousand soldiers, mounted and foot."

There was a long silence. "Have we forgotten the desert people?" asked Membrion. "They've no love for the sirdar."

Crespin snorted. "Their politics are a madhouse. We could never get them to join us."

"They're good fighters," said Osmodon. "If they can be convinced the sirdar is a bigger threat than the other tribes, they will join us."

Nick was thoughtful. "Saying it's possible, how many could we count on?"

"If their *madhias*, their wise women, declare for it? Three thousand mounted, at least," Membrion said.

"We are also forgetting Artos," said Sianiave.

"Artos?" scoffed Penthys. "There's been no word in a decade. Even if he lives, what makes you think he would ally with us? He made his loyalties clear."

"His argument was with Cuchulain, not Barad'An."

"And if he were available?" asked Nick. "How many would he bring?"

"Two thousand mounted, at least."

Nick looked up to see all eyes upon him. "So," he said. "If my numbers are right, even if the desert people join the fight, Artos is found, this priest dealt with, we're still talking less than seven thousand men. This against an army ten times that number?"

Ellohir nodded. Crespin shifted in his seat. Even Penthys looked subdued as he absorbed the bleak prospects.

A memory came to Nick, so vivid and full of meaning it could almost be said to be a vision: Billy standing in his drawing room surrounded by scenes of battle, saying, "Weren't you the one who always argued odds didn't mean that much?"

Nick smiled. His headache was gone and he was suddenly feeling much better. "Well," he said cheerfully, "Others have triumphed against worse odds. Much worse, really."

CHAPTER 40

DINNER THAT NIGHT was a very different affair from that of the previous evening. Ale replaced the honey-tasting libation. The atmosphere was quiet and sober. Bronwyn and Ellohir did their best to keep the conversation light, but the topic of war was on everyone's mind. Beothyr, the scout captain, attended, as did the ruddy-faced mayor of the local village.

Penthys and Crespin had left immediately after the council meeting, as both faced long rides back to their own estates. Aerindir was also absent, as was Yseult, the dark-haired daughter. The coincidence did not go unnoticed.

"Abdelar would certainly have approved," said Ellohir, cutting into his steak. "He encouraged Aerindir to show more interest in women."

"Yseult is often said to be the fairest of our daughters," added Bronwyn. "Certainly the most gentle."

"Does she really fancy Aerindir?" asked Ren.

The question might have come from a curious and protective sister. Still, Nick wondered if there might be a note of jealousy behind the concern.

Bronwyn sighed and nodded. "Yes. Since she first laid eyes on him—when she was twelve, I think—Yseult has thought only of Aerindir."

"They're kindred souls," said Sianiave. "Pure and giving."

"You know my opinion," growled Ellohir. "Hers is a gentle nature. The training would do her good."

"You would have our daughter spend her life in a cloister?"

"I would not see our daughter disappointed. These are dark times. Too many knights do not return to their wives."

"Yet, here you sit," said Bronwyn, patting Ellohir's calloused hand affectionately. "In any case it's a moot point. Yseult has made her decision. I do not think we need worry about it overmuch. And I do not think Aerindir will be easily killed."

"Yesterday I would have said the same about Abdelar," Ellohir muttered gloomily. He took a long draft of ale and fell silent.

Nick was fascinated by the conversation. He glanced at Ren, their eyes briefly meeting before he looked away. Kindred souls?

The council meeting had gone on most of the day. Nick had been surprised by the weight they'd given his views. Even Sir Penthys had listened without interrupting, afterwards asking some pointed questions.

Why? This was always the question. Why was he here in this world? Why was he at the council meeting? Why was he, a simple soldier, being treated with such respect? Sianiave must have said something, but what? What were her real reasons for bringing him to this world? Had she made a mistake?

During the meeting he'd felt more self-assured. He did have something to offer. His years in the other world, many spent studying military strategy, had given him understanding, expertise, and knowledge they lacked here. His memory of that place may have diminished, but the knowledge was there.

He also learned that his job here was not yet done.

§

After dinner, Nick returned to his room to pack. He and Osmodon planned to leave before dawn to find the desert people. Another long journey lay ahead, and he wanted to sleep.

He was almost finished when there was a knock at the door. He opened it and was startled to find Ren, in a thin shift of light green silk, standing there. Her hair was loose, and a determined set to her jaw gave him the mistaken impression she was angry. He half expected her to stamp her foot while pointing an accusatory finger.

But she surprised him. "It would appear you were going to leave without speaking to me," she said. "So I decided to come to you."

Nick was at a loss. "Would you like to come in? I've got nothing to offer you, some water. There's a cup." He stopped, embarrassed.

Her laughter, sweet and genuine, broke the tension. "Would you join me for a walk?"

Nick, startled, glanced at his kit on the bed. There was still some packing to do.

What was he thinking?

"I would like that very much," he said, surprised at his boldness, but also pleased with himself. It was a relief to speak honestly for a change.

"Good," she said, taking his hand. "It's a beautiful evening."

They walked together down the curving stairway that led to the garden below. Whether by design or chance the falling waters caught the lamplight in such a way as to create a rainbow. The faint sound of a lyre drifted on the breeze.

"It's a courageous thing," said Ren as they stood watching the play of light on the water, "to volunteer as an emissary to the desert people. The dangers are legend."

"Osmodon has traveled there before."

"Aye. A doughty warrior and a good companion, though I find it curious he is not going with Sianiave."

"I think Sianiave wants to go it alone for a bit. Osmodon guesses she's planning to use sorcery to locate Artos."

It was difficult to keep the skepticism from his voice at the mention of sorcery, but clearly Ren had no problem with the idea. "In any event, I'm glad you're traveling together. I wouldn't want harm to come to you."

"You wouldn't?" Nick stopped. A sudden understanding came over him. "That night, at dinner—that was real?"

"Of course. I'm surprised you doubted. I was quite disappointed when you didn't speak with me afterwards."

"I thought I was imagining things, that it was the wine."

Her smile was gone, her eyes locked onto his. "That was not wine. That was the sacred *haoma*. Unlike wine, haoma does not lie. It opens the heart. You experienced the unveiling, a vision of all that is real. Did not you feel it?"

"I didn't realize."

She's shaking, Nick thought, then realized it was he who was shaking. They stared into one another's eyes, then came together, their lips meeting.

They backed away, as if in surprise, then laughed, and kissed again. Sweetness, joy, and a growing excitement took them both.

Time seemed to stop. A maidservant saw the couple. She smiled to herself and did not interrupt.

§

Before the sun was up, Nick kissed Ren gently on the forehead, rolled out of bed and dressed. She appeared to be asleep, and he hadn't the heart to awaken her.

In the light of the waning moon, he gazed down at her body, naked beneath the sheet. Her knew he would give his life for her. Nothing was more important or more precious. Their lovemaking had been unlike anything he had ever experienced, bringing ecstasy he hadn't known to exist. Her soft skin, her breasts, the curve of her thighs and the secrets between them, her smell, her taste—everything was perfect, as though he and she were two parts of one being.

It took an effort of will to turn away.

Ren, only pretending to sleep, watched as he took up his kit and closed the door quietly behind him. She struggled with her feelings. He was a good and kind man, with greatness in him. Of that she had no doubt. She wondered whether her feelings were love. But she sensed a void at the center of his being, some terrible wound that terrified her. She wanted to help heal it, but had no idea where to begin, or what might have caused such horrendous pain.

What if he never returned?

A great ache arose in her heart. Yet painful as it was, she knew it was only a fraction of the pain that Nick must always feel. She wanted to run from it, from him, avoid that pain at any cost. But she also knew that at the center of that emptiness lay a great and valuable secret.

The pitiless voice of her ancestors, the bloodline, rose in her mind. *To be a true queen, you must know this.*

"No!" She cried the word out loud, clutching at her pillow as tears streamed from her eyes. I'm not ready. Not yet. Please.

But the voice was relentless. *It is your destiny, Gwyndolyn. You will know.*

CHAPTER
41

Barad'An
May 16

MILFORD ANASTIS GLAYS, Lord Steward of Barad'An, Archon of Anor and Guardian to the Crown Princess, was in a rage. "You imbecile!" he ranted. "How could you allow her to reach Gallian?"

Gothmog cringed under his glare, though inwardly the little magician was seething. He'd had enough of the priest. If the fool had listened to his advice in the first place, the girl wouldn't be a problem. But the priest wanted to wed her, to give him the legitimacy he imagined he still lacked. As if real legitimacy was based on anything but raw power.

There was more than politics behind Glays' desire, Gothmog knew. The man's lust for the child sickened him. A shallow imitation of the ecstasy he himself knew—complete release, without the disgusting taint of animal rutting.

The cleansing of the city was nearly complete. The last of the knights were either dead, imprisoned, or in exile. The Sisters were gone, their tower turned into barracks. What resistance remained was scattered and weak. So many bodies hung from the oaks bordering the Great Way that crosses had been erected on which to suspend more victims. The crows had feasted for weeks.

The smell of their decay blanketed the city, making its way even into Glays's chamber. It excited Gothmog, nourished him. "All is not lost, m'lord," he murmured. "The princess can be retrieved."

"Retrieved!" The priest's swung his scepter, shattering a vase. "She's in Gallian, you dolt. You imagine your Uruk hirelings can take Gallian when an entire band was undone by three warriors?"

Gothmog shifted uneasily. The arrival of three unknown warriors at such a moment could not have been coincidence. Descriptions provided by the two Uruks who'd survived the rout left no doubt in his mind as to their identities, at least two of them. When years ago the witch had vanished, he'd thought her gone for good. Now she was back. Along with Prince Corwin, Sianiave was one of the few people he truly feared.

Glays studied the red jewel atop his scepter. Gothmog suppressed a smirk. The scepter once belonged to the imperial herald, an office vacant for well over a century. The priest had found it in the treasury. Imagining it kingly, he'd claimed it as his own.

"So," growled Glays. "Capture her, you say? From Gallian?"

The scepter swung again, shattering another vase and missing the magician's head by inches. "And how will you accomplish this, might we ask?"

"M'lord," cried Gothmog quickly, cringing at the close call. "We have her nanny, and others beloved by her. She will be concerned about their welfare."

"Welfare?" Glays weighed the idea, and a slow smile spread across his thick features. "Yes, of course. Excellent. Pen an invitation. Be sure she understands the consequences of refusal. Send a messenger, someone with flair, and provide him with a fast steed. It's a long ride to Gallian. We'll hold the wedding immediately upon her return."

"Wedding? M'lord, isn't that a bit precipitous?"

Glays appeared to gloat. "The sooner the better. It will help to quiet the rabble." He waved at the broken pottery. "Have someone clean this up."

"Yes, m'lord."

Gothmog bowed and left the room. Since he'd taken office, the smallest slight sent the priest into a rage. His sermons, now attended by mandate, had become rants, but his fixation on the girl was the most worrisome.

§

A stairway behind a bolted door in the administrative wing of the palace led to the dungeon. Gothmog knew every one of the 148 stairs by heart, counting them in his head as they spiraled down into a darkness lit intermittently by wax torches. In the past, the dungeon had held only the most dangerous offenders. Common criminals were kept in the citizen's jail beyond the palace walls.

When Glays had appointed Gothmog to the position of Holy Inquisitor, all that had changed. The magician wasn't interested in pickpockets, thieves, and drunks. Even murderers were of little concern. Let the templars deal with them, sever a hand or foot, hang them as they saw fit. But the dungeons were his domain now. Once, they housed fewer than half a dozen prisoners at any given time. Now they held well over a hundred, and the number was growing. Recalcitrants, traitors to the regime, wives and children useful as hostages, all were his playthings now, to do with as he pleased.

The winding stairway ended at a large oaken door secured with an iron lock. A bell hung nearby. Gothmog rang twice in quick succession. There was a grinding sound as the lock turned. A huge, slope-shouldered brute holding a lantern and a ring of keys acknowledged Gothmog with a grunt.

Radlik, the keeper of Barad'An's dungeon, had been taunted as a boy by the other children. They called him a troll's bastard, for even then he looked more troll than man. And, like trolls, Radlik had a taste for human flesh.

Gothmog had discovered Radlik in a dungeon cell, awaiting execution for the rape and murder of a farm girl. Gothmog appointed him keeper. As a safeguard against indiscretion, he had Radlik's tongue cut out. Radlik didn't mind greatly. He rarely spoke as it was, and he enjoyed his new status. He took up residence in a large office cell near the dungeon door. The dank atmosphere had turned his skin a maggoty white, and his long grey hair was falling out in patches.

Save for the occasional moan, the shifting of chains and the unrelenting drip of water, the dungeon was as silent as a tomb. Prisoners had learned to expect the worst if they attracted the keeper's attention. Occasionally one of them would go missing. Radlik was clever enough to avoid taking anyone whom his employer might still find of some use.

"Is it ready?" Gothmog asked.

Radlik grunted affirmatively. He led the magician past rows of cells inhabited by emaciated prisoners who looked quickly away when the keeper cast his baleful eyes in their direction.

They turned a corner into another vaulted passageway, following it for some distance before stopping at the door to a cell-like room Gothmog called the Summoning Room. Inside were shelves of manuscripts and leather-bound books, the colored bottles and vials of powders and potions necessary for the calling. A large cabinet was the single item of furniture, its drawers filled with thumbscrews, needles, razor-sharp knives, and other implements of torture. These were not essential to the ritual, but he occasionally found it amusing to put them to use.

One wall was bare of shelves. A boy, no older than twelve, hung there, chained spreadeagled, his feet a foot off the stone floor. His shirt had been torn from his torso and his dark hair hung over his bloodied face. A six-inch drainage hole in the floor nearby was covered with an iron grate. The grate, the wall behind the boy, and the floor were stained a mottled rust.

"Please!" cried the boy, his voice hoarse with pain and terror. "I didn't do anything wrong. Please!"

The boy had been arrested for speaking ill of one of the priest's men, though he pleaded innocence. For Gothmog the boy's guilt or innocence was irrelevant. In the past, he'd been forced to utilize runaways and orphans, nits and scabies who would not be missed. No longer. He had his pick of the city's youth now, and the templars knew his preferences. The practice he was about to engage in had been banned for over a thousand years. His obsession with it had been the cause of his banishment from the academy at Megida. The imbecilic fools! He still chafed at the memory, the shame.

He checked the boy's chains, then looked to see that the proper ingredients had been placed in the brazier. He retraced the containment circle Radlik had drawn on the floor with chalk, leaving the pentagram intact. He'd taught Radlik well, but in this work, one impure ingredient or a mispronounced word could be disastrous. His failure with Prince Corwin had undoubtedly been due to such an error, or so he'd convinced himself. Since then he had been even more rigorous in his procedures.

Satisfied that all was in order, he donned his robe and, with a wave of his hand, lit the brazier. The robe was woven of black silk, with red embroidery that gleamed in the torchlight. Though it had been soaked in the blood of a thousand victims, it never needed cleaning.

He removed a stone from a felt-lined drawer. The stone was black obsidian, ancient beyond reckoning and said to hold the souls of the people it murdered. Its cutting edge was so fine as to be translucent when held to the light.

Radlik left to stand guard in the hall outside. The boy was babbling now, repeating himself over and over. "Please don't. Please don't. Please—"

Ignoring the entreaties, Gothmog emptied his mind of thought. A minute passed, then another. Then the moment came upon him and he began the invocation. "*Nazghat'ul ishka'mar kh'en, nazghat'sul, ishka'mar ch'en, nazghat'ul esha'mar sya'nif.*"

The words echoed against the stone walls. The torches flared and dimmed. The room grew dark, illuminated solely by the coals glowing in the brazier.

A corona of black light began to form above the boy's head, pulsing like a living thing. Gothmog traced the requisite pattern in the air, watching it hang fluorescent in the darkness for a moment before vanishing. The acrid smell of sulphur filled the room. "*Nazghat'ul esha'mar gha'anif, nazghat'asul, esha'mar atua'hul. Shammat!*"

The boy moaned and spittle flew from his mouth. The pungent smell of urine filled the room as he voided himself.

With the skill of long practice, Gothmog brought the stone down in a vicious arc, slashing open the boy's chest. The boy stared at him in a sort of reproachful disbelief as the magician reached into the open cavity and tore out his heart.

Gothmog placed the still-beating heart in the brazier. "Come, my master. The way is open. *Nazghat'ul esha'sul, nazghat'ul sensa'nul.*"

The black circle of light expanded, shaping itself into a globe. For a brief moment the globe floated in the darkness, black and shimmering. Then, with a terrible urgency, it poured itself into the boy's open body.

The head jerked erect. The eyes, no longer blue, were filled with an alien blackness. The lips formed into a grotesque grin. "Servant, what have you for me?"

Gothmog could not stifle a small moan. The ecstasy was close. "Princess Gwyndolyn escaped, master," he rasped. "I believe the witch Sianiave is responsible. They are in Gallian."

"I know this." The voice coming from the boy's mouth was hoarse as it fought to control unwilling vocal chords. "A small matter. A fortress can also be a prison. When Barad'An has fallen the sirdar's general will install a permanent garrison outside the cursed place."

"The army is on the march?"

"It is. They will pass Gallian in eighteen days." There was a brief pause. "I am concerned with the witch. She has companions."

"Two, it's been reported," replied Gothmog. "The Linsraden mercenary, and one other, whom I know not. He is tall, dark-haired, and uncommonly skilled with a sword. So was the description."

"Mark him well. This one may be more dangerous than all the rest."

"A warlock, master?"

"Possibly. The witch has taken great efforts to bring him here."

The boy-thing gagged, spitting out blood. It licked its lips. "What of the priest?"

"He decays. His self-importance grows daily. He refuses the steward's seat, instead taking the throne. He uses the royal 'we' when he speaks. I fear he will not honor the agreement. He is obsessed with the girl."

There was a long silence. The boy-thing spat out more gore.

"Master?"

A loud gurgle escaped the body. The boy-thing's eyes bulged as if any second they might burst from its head.

"This body grows unstable."

"Master, it was healthy—" But the black light was already gone from the dead boy's eyes, the head collapsing on his ruined chest.

Gothmog stepped back in frustration. He hadn't achieved his usual release, in fact felt unaccountably drained and exhausted. The boy must have had health problems he was unaware of.

He replaced the stone in its case and doffed his robe. Radlik would clean up the mess. The dungeon baths emptied into the city sewers, which in turn emptied into an underground river. Where that river flowed Gothmog had no idea and didn't care. All he knew was that it was a good way to dispose of garbage.

Radlik refused to eat the corpses, considering them tainted.

CHAPTER 42

Gallian
May 21

REN FINISHED READING the letter the emissary from Barad'An had brought and passed it to Bronwyn. Bronwyn held the letter up, reading the words aloud:

Felicitations to Crown Princess Gwyndolyn Ambergin

My Dearest Child:

With the Lamentable passing of your Great-Grandfather, King Cuchulain Ambergin, and the recent finding by the Court that your Uncle, Prince Artos Ambergin, now ten years absent, is to be stricken from the Roll of Ascension, it stands now that you are the sole heir of the line of Ambergin.

Furthermore, upon your maturity at the age of thirty-three years, you will ascend to the Throne as Queen, ruling over the Kingdom of Anor and the Imperial City of Barad'An. Until that time of your ascension, and in the absence of any relations of sufficient means and standing as to be able to care for you in the manner befitting your Station, the Court has ordered you to be placed under the guardianship of the Lord Steward of Barad'An.

We urge you to return to Barad'An and take up your rightful duties. But, should you choose to deny this request, We cannot assure the safety of your property, or those citizens in Barad'An to whom you owe allegiance.

Your immediate return will do much to forestall Havoc and Distress upon
these good persons.
>*Your Servant,*
>*Milford Anastis Glays*
>*Lord Steward of Barad'An and Archon of Anor*

Bronwyn lowered the letter. Sianiave, seated nearby, said nothing. Ellohir regarded the emissary with a careful eye. "You said your name was Gaskel. Were you privy to the contents of this letter?"

"Of course," said Gaskel, ignoring the frown that darkened Ellohir's features. "It's plain enough. I assume the princess will wish to leave immediately. You may provide a reasonable escort, though as personal representative of Lord Glays, it will of course be under my command."

Captain Gaskel of the Temple Guards had been raised a privileged son of a wealthy Meridorian merchant and knew something of court protocol. It was why he had been chosen for such an important mission; that and his appearance, about which he had little false modesty. He was tall and well set up, with a long mustache and curly locks of brown hair. He'd joined the Temple Guards early on, seeing it as a way back to the station he considered his due. As emissary to the Barony of Gallian, he represented Barad'An's highest seat. He intended to make it clear that Ellohir had no say in this matter.

He gave Ren a slight bow and a roguish smile. A princess, yet still a woman. He knew Lord Glays planned to marry her, but she would be in his keeping for a nearly a fortnight. The prospects were intriguing.

Bronwyn handed the letter back to Gaskel. "A bit presumptuous, not to mention overwritten, Emissary Gaskel? All those capitalized letters, the childish use of the royal we."

"Excuse me?" said Gaskel, surprised. "Overwritten? Childish?"

"Exactly so," agreed Sianiave. "It seems more the sort of thing a petulant boy might pen. Why not just say what he meant: return immediately or he will have every man, woman, and child Ren ever loved put to death. Straightforward. No temporizing."

Gaskel flushed with indignation. In Barad'An such disrespect would be cause for instant death.

He had arrived at Gallian the night before after eighteen hours in the saddle, nearly killing the horse. He may very well have killed it, for all he knew. Despite his fatigue and the softness of the bed, he'd managed little sleep. He sensed immediately that something malignant lay behind Gallian's deceptive beauty, something that threatened to undo his very manhood.

Now he knew the source of the threat. These women, in particular the one called Bronwyn. Ruling side by side with her husband. Intolerable.

Without thinking, his right hand moved to the pommel of his sword. "I would not treat this matter so lightly, m'lord," he said, speaking directly to Ellohir and ignoring the women.

"No?" asked Bronwyn prettily. "And how should we treat it, Emissary Gaskel?"

"Yes," agreed Sianiave. "Tell us, Emissary Gaskel. What is the proper way to treat such threats?"

It was their scorn that did it, their condescending amusement. Amused by him!

"Enough!" he cried. "Gallian is a vassal holding. You have read the letter and seen the seal. I'm taking the girl back to Barad'An. Escorted or not, she leaves with me. Now!"

He lunged forward to grab Ren from her seat, but Ellohir stepped between them. Enraged at the man's temerity, Gaskel drew his sword. "You dare to interfere?"

Too late he realized his mistake. With a speed that belied his girth, Ellohir swatted the sword from his hand, sending the weapon flying across the room.

"We do not deal with regicides and traitors," said Ellohir evenly. A twitch under his left eye was the only sign that he was struggling to control his anger. "Nor with their lackeys."

Gaskel stared, unbelieving, clutching his damaged hand. Ellohir had disarmed him with the casualness of a father taking a spoon from a child. He looked for a way out of what was fast becoming a dangerous situation. His sword had landed some ten feet away.

He realized that his hand was broken. Even if he managed to get to the sword he would never be able to use it.

"Well," said Bronwyn, unperturbed. "It's Ren's decision."

Ren nodded matter-of-factly. "I'll return, of course."

"Return?" Ellohir turned in amazement. "To Barad'An, to that weasel of a priest? Even if he doesn't have you throttled the moment you enter the gate he'll lock you in a cell and parade you around like a pet!"

"The priest has other plans for Ren," said Sianiave.

"Other plans? What other plans? She's all that stands between Glays and the throne."

"He plans to marry her."

"Marry her?" Ellohir was dumbstruck.

Bronwyn nodded in agreement. "Ren is eighteen. That gives him only fifteen years to act in her stead as guardian until her maturity. But were he to marry her and father a child, it would cement his legitimacy."

Ellohir nodded as understanding came. "Of course. I'm a fool. But that still leaves the question of—"

They were speaking as though he were invisible. Holding his broken right hand with his left, Gaskel began to have hope. The girl would return. He just needed to be patient.

"It's decided," Ren said firmly.

"It will be a grand wedding," said Sianiave, nodding. "As befits the archon of Barad'An."

"Difficult to find time alone with the groom," suggested Bronwyn.

"It will need only a moment," said Ren. "The blade must be poisoned, to be certain. Fitting, as it was how Grandfather died."

Gaskel's hope turned to dismay. Bantering as they might at a quilting, these women were plotting to assassinate the lord steward of Barad'An.

There was still time. He could get away, warn—

"What about this worm?"

Startled, Gaskel realized the girl was speaking about him.

"Oh, him?" Ellohir waved negligently. "I'd almost forgotten. Gaelin! Robby!"

At Ellohir's command the door flew open. Two men, dressed in black sheriff's garb and carrying long daggers, entered. A third man stood quietly in the background. Gaskel had seen him before, the knight Aerindir.

They'd been waiting, he realized with a shock. He thought the royal seal would protect him. He'd been a fool.

"Wait!" he cried, his pride forgotten. "I can help you!"

"As I mentioned earlier," said Ellohir dismissively, "we don't deal with traitors." Then, to the two men, "Squeeze what information you can from him, then toss him off a cliff."

"With pleasure," said the larger of the two.

"You can't do this!" screamed Gaskel as the two deputies grabbed his arms. "I'm an emissary. The covenants!"

"You broke the covenants when you drew your sword," said Bronwyn.

"You bloody witch! You did this!"

"Take him away," said Ellohir, disgusted.

"Get your hands off me, you oafs! You'll see, you'll be hanging from the trees, all of you! Outland scum! Witches!" His curses echoed down the hall even after the door had closed.

"Pleasant fellow," murmured Ellohir dryly. He turned to Aerindir. "You heard, of course."

"It's as expected."

"You'll accompany Ren?"

"I will."

Ellohir stroked his beard and sighed. "I envy you. Sir Nicholas and Sir Osmodon face unknown dangers in the Great Desert, Lady Sianiave travels alone in search of Artos, and you return to Barad'An and possible death while I have to remain here like a rabbit in a trap."

Bronwyn put her hand on Ellohir's. "You will not be alone, my husband."

CHAPTER
43

NICK STIFLED A CURSE as he looked around. The oasis, which had been both their destination and their hope, was a blackened charnel house.

"We won't quench our thirst here," remarked Osmodon, his voice dry from the heat. "The water appears to be tainted."

An understatement, Nick thought, as he studied the bleached skeletons and rotting carcasses that surrounded the pool. He recognized camels, hyenas, and what he took to be lions, though larger than those he knew. Other remains could have been cattle of some sort. There was the horned skull and bleached rib cage of some huge beast whose identity he couldn't even begin to imagine.

He passed his tongue over cracked lips, recalling what he'd learned in survival training about how to make use of succulent plants, condensation pits, even the blood of their horses. The desert was an oven, easily 110 degrees in the late afternoon.

"Who would have been so cruel as to poison a *wadi*?" Osmodon sounded genuinely aggrieved. "Wadis are sacred to the nomads, politics and fighting are *haram* there. Forbidden."

"Could it have happened naturally?"

"Not likely. Wadi Nuri was known for the purity of its water. Now even the sand looks afflicted."

Osmodon was right. A black stain circled the pool, and everything within its circumference was dead.

Greywind fought his bit as Nick backed the horse away from the tainted pool. Whatever had poisoned the oasis was virulent and quick to kill. He was glad they'd left Bear back in Gallian.

"What now?"

"Abu Mesina is still four days off. We won't make it without water." Osmodon was thoughtful. "I remember the nomads talking of another wadi, a small one half a league east of here. Bistami, it's called."

"Do we have a choice?"

"We can go back."

"The last water we passed was three days ago."

"Aye. But I'm not sure Wadi Bistami even exists. And it also may be tainted."

Nick looked at the water skin sagging against his saddle. There was barely enough to last a day, much less three. However bad it got, he would not slaughter Greywind for the horse's blood.

He pulled off his makeshift headdress, shaking out the dust and sand. They were surrounded by a desert the like of which he'd never seen—blasted earth and scorched salt flats, sand dunes as high as small mountains. The sun seemed to take up half the sky.

Ren had called him brave. When he agreed to travel to Abu Mesina as Ellohir's envoy to the desert people, he'd had no idea of what lay ahead. Volunteering had been a way to extend his service, to remain in this world and near Ren, for he knew now she was the center, the very heart of it. The thought of leaving her, of returning to the dreary place of his past, still troubled his sleep.

"I'm going on," he said, replacing the headdress. "You coming?"

Osmodon sighed and nodded. "Your decision, lad. I do my liege lady's business, and apparently looking after you is that business."

"I appreciate that."

"Man's oath and all, you know."

Laughing, though with little enough reason, they turned their reluctant horses and headed into the desert. After the desolation of the oasis, the desert seemed absolutely cheerful.

They rode on the rest of that evening and through the night. The following day, when it again became too hot to travel, they stopped, setting up camp under the cornice of a windswept dune. There they ate a meal of hard bread, dates, and dried meat, drinking only a mouthful of water each to wash it down. They saved what remained for the horses. They spoke little, their mouths dry and their lips chapped and bleeding. Eventually both men lay back in the thin shade of the cornice and slept.

Nick was awakened by a thumping sound. He opened his eyes to find Greywind pawing the sand by his head. He sat up and dusted himself off. The sun was low in the west and Osmodon was nowhere to be seen. A line of footprints led from their small camp up the slope of the dune. He found Osmodon lying prone on the sand, staring intently at something in the distance.

Osmodon cautioned him with a wave. "Keep down. Their scouts have eyes like hawks."

Nick dropped to his elbows and shimmied forward. Perhaps a mile away, silhouetted against the dying sun, marched a long line of camels, with white-robed people herding goats alongside.

Osmodon spoke quietly. "The camel bells woke me. Thought it my imagination, but there it is. Must be over a hundred animals. See how they circle? They're setting up camp for the night."

"Why are we hiding? They'll have water, won't they?"

"Aye. They'll have water, and food as well. Trouble is, they're as likely to murder us as give us a meal. No telling with them."

"How long did you live with them?"

"Six months, and that was in Abu Mesina. A rich sheik hired me to train his sons with the sword. If these are Bani Faisal, or from a tribe allied with the Bani Faisal, it's our good fortune."

"And if not?"

"Could mean our heads unless we do some fast talking. Alliances between tribes shift about more than this sand."

"And we're asking them to be allies?"

"The nomads have a saying: 'Me against my brother, my brother and I against our cousins, our cousins and us against the world.' Terrific fighters. They're honorable, in their way, not like the Uruks. Give 'em a common cause and they could conquer the world. Almost did once, or so the stories go. And they hate the current sirdar. They still remember when raiders from Nibur stalked the trade routes and ravaged their caravans. Gallian protects their western border. If Barad'An falls, so will Gallian. Leastways that's the argument we'll give."

"Why wait? Let's give it to them now."

"Abu Mesina welcomes travelers. Caravans in the open desert tend to be more suspicious. They may think us spies or bandits."

"I'd rather trust desert hospitality than our chances of surviving two more days without water."

Nick moved to stand, but Osmodon grabbed his foot. "Wait until they set up their tents. They'll feel safer then, less apt to spike us on sight."

The sun had vanished behind the horizon when Osmodon finally deemed it safe to move. On their approach they were immediately surrounded by riders, young men robed in grey-trimmed black and wielding scimitars.

"We've gotten into something," said Osmodon quietly as the riders surrounded them. "Caravan masters use mercenaries as guards. These fellows are house guards."

"House guards?"

Before Osmodon could answer the leader of the riders called out. "*Estopa haena! Min? Min wa'en?*"

Surprisingly, Nick understood. He'd been fluent in Pashto and Arabic in that other world. The same concurrencies in language must hold, he decided.

"Stop here!" the troop's captain had said. "Who are you? From where do you come?"

"Greetings!" Osmodon called out in a halting version of the same language. "Peace be upon you. I am Osmodon of Linsraden and this be Nicholas of Amra. We travel to Abu Mesina with a message for the *loya jirga* from Lord Ellohir of Gallian. We claim the right of travelers. Whose caravan is this?"

The man who had hailed them was a handsome, dark-skinned youth. He prodded his horse forward. "From Gallian? This is true?"

His dark eyes had a look of fierce intelligence, but Nick sensed Osmodon had caught him by surprise.

"By the gods and my honor, it is so. Can you take us to the caravan master?"

"This is no merchant caravan," the man said, smiling for the first time. "Emir Malik bin Abdulafaiz al Shah is lord here. I am his son, Bandar bin Malik al Shah."

Nick started. A memory surfaced. Bandar was a common enough name in the east, and the man before them bore little resemblance to the Nuristani chieftain he had met that terrible night in the Pamirs. Still, the name had shaken him. That Bandar had been older and larger, with grey eyes. This fellow was young and bearded, his eyes the color of night. What the two did share was an almost mocking sense of self-awareness.

Osmodon bowed. "Beg pardon, your highness. We saw your caravan and assumed—"

"Apologies are unnecessary. I will take you to my father. If you are who you say you are you will be welcome. Follow me."

The caravan was larger than they had first thought. Nick guessed there were over a hundred tents, with twice that many camels. It was well protected, with numerous armed men about. Their guide's father was obviously a man of some stature.

The camp had been set up with military efficiency. The livestock had been herded into rope *kraals*, the camels tethered, the cook fires fueled by camel dung. Women and children turned from their tasks and called out, "O Bandar! Who are these prisoners? Are we in for an execution?"

"They aren't prisoners," responded their guide, laughing. "They are guests, and I'm taking them to meet my father."

The easy informality with which their guide was met made it clear the young man was well regarded among his people.

Bandar led them to the center of the encampment, where a large tent of pale orange canvas stood. A boy took the reins from the prince as he dismounted.

"A moment, please." The young man pushed open the tent flap and vanished inside. Several minutes later he reappeared. "My father will see you. It is customary for guests to leave their shoes and weapons outside.

"Your horses will be well cared for," he added, seeing Nick's hesitation.

Nick and Osmodon left their boots with their swords and daggers by the entrance. Inside the air seemed cooler, the tent insulated from the heat by thick cotton panels tied to the walls. The interior was lit with brass oil lamps. Richly woven carpets covered the floor. A portly man with a trim white beard and a purple-and-gold headdress sat cross-legged in a circle with six other men near the rear. The mouthpiece of a large hookah was being passed between them.

An old woman in a black *chador* sat cross-legged to the right of the entrance flap. She wore no veil, and appeared to be studying a pattern of cards on the rug. It was impossible to guess her age. She looked as old as the desert. Her thin hair was dyed black with kohl, her face burnt brown by the sun, her wrinkled hands little more than claws.

Apparently oblivious to both the men in the circle and the new arrivals, she took another card from the deck, placing it carefully with the others.

Something about the old woman bothered Nick. And then he saw. She was blind. Her eyes were solid white, the disturbing milky white of a boiled egg. How could she read the cards? Yet read them she did, studying the patterns emerging before her with a peculiar intensity.

Ignoring the woman, Bandar bowed toward the white-bearded man seated across from him in the circle. "My father, these are the travelers of whom I spoke. They bring a message from the lord of Gallian to the council of tribes in Abu Mesina."

"Peace be upon you, O travelers," murmured the emir, bowing his head in formal greeting. "You have journeyed a long way. Come, join us."

The men moved aside to create room for them. Bandar bowed again to his father, nodded at the two travelers, and left.

The hookah's mouthpiece was passed to Nick. It was carved in the shape of a dragon's head, from bone or ivory, he guessed. It was yellowed with age, attached to the pipe by a tube of woven silk. He nodded thanks to the man who handed him the mouthpiece, and took an experimental puff.

The smoke was surprisingly mild and pleasant, even familiar. If not the same herb Sianiave was fond of smoking, it was certainly related. Rather than making him feel lightheaded like some other leaf he'd smoked, it produced a sense of clarity and calm. He took another puff, deeper, and then passed the mouthpiece to Osmodon.

"My son is unable sit with us," explained the emir. "As a captain of my soldiers he is quite busy. These are troublesome times. The desert has grown more dangerous for everyone."

"We are grateful for your hospitality, O Prince," said Osmodon, exhaling a cloud of the mild smoke. "Two days ago we arrived at Wadi Jami to find it poisoned. This afternoon we gave the last of our water to our horses."

Nick admired his friend's finesse. In one brief sentence, he had described their plight, alerted the emir to the poisoned oasis, and demonstrated their good character.

A murmur of dismay passed among those seated. "Forgive me!" cried their host, motioning to a servant. "Sabry! *Gibli moiya! Bisora!* Bring water for our guests."

"We are in your debt," said Osmodon.

"It is we who are in your debt for bringing us news of Wadi Jami, for it was to be our next stop. Those who would poison a wadi . . . May their souls wander the desert without respite."

There were nods of agreement from the circle. A boy hurried over with a two cups and a pitcher of water. Trying not to appear greedy, Nick drained his cup in one swallow. After the third refill his thirst began to slake.

"The people of the desert have always been on good terms with the people of Gallian," observed the man next to Nick.

"Indeed," agreed the emir. "They were once *Saharim* themselves, before they chose to settle, or so it is written. My son tells me you bring a message."

"We wish to present it in Abu Mesina," said Osmodon. "It concerns all the tribes."

"All here have seats on the council. Emir Abu Salim, my uncle, sits at its head. Can you not tell us something?"

Osmodon considered for a moment, and nodded. "I don't see why not." He paused, then said gravely, "The sirdar's army prepares to move against Barad'An. It is said a morghul commands."

"Of this we know," said the emir. "They are already on the march."

Osmodon leaned forward in alarm. "This is troublesome news indeed. When, may I ask?"

"Five days ago. We've just received word ourselves, although we have known of the sirdar's plans for some time. We head for Abu Mesina to discuss the matter, and are moving our people south to safety. The sirdar's agents must have poisoned the wells. Wadi Jami is not the first such atrocity to be committed."

"If their goal is Barad'An," snapped a sharp-faced man across from Nick, "what matters it to Gallian, or to the desert people, for that matter?"

Osmodon barely glanced at the man, his attention on the emir. "If Barad'An falls, where will this army go next? Gallian will be surrounded, a prison to those within, unable to protect its borders, or yours."

"What need have we of Gallian?" said the man. "The desert will protect us, as it has always done." There were nods of agreement.

Osmodon faced the man who spoke. "A desert with poisoned wells will not protect you. Once this army has taken Barad'An, it will turn to Abu Mesina, whose walls are not nearly so strong."

Silence greeted this announcement, and Osmodon pressed his point. "The sirdars have always been jealous of the desert people's hold on the caravan trade, and your seaports to the south. The son of the sirdar they called 'The Butcher of Megida' has openly declared his intent to succeed where his father has failed, to build an empire that will stretch from the sea to the mountains."

"Other men have had this dream," said a white-haired man quietly. "All have failed. Only the desert abides."

"They've failed because people rose to fight them."

"Is this the message you bring?" cried the hatchet-faced man angrily. "You wish us to join with this mad priest who rules Barad'An, to fight against an army that, with all the tribes together, we cannot hope to equal? Why do you think we go south? If we thought there was any chance of defeating the sirdar's army, I would offer my sword gladly. But I say to ride to Barad'An is foolishness."

There were nods and murmurs of agreement. To Nick the sentiment of the group was clear. They knew about the coup in Barad'An. It wasn't a surprise. To their way of thinking, the priest must pose as great a threat as the sirdar's army.

If he and Osmodon couldn't convince the men seated here, Nick knew they would have little success in Abu Mesina. But what argument could convince them to disregard the safer course, and agree to ride to possible death in a land not their own?

Osmodon was having difficulty coming up with another approach. "When they attack Abu Mesina, what then—"

Nick put out a restraining hand. Osmodon stopped in mid-sentence. Nick handed his cup to the tea boy and stood. "How many times in the past has a large force been defeated by a smaller one? With your people and ours allied, we can defeat this army. As for the priest, he will be gone. This I promise you."

He sat down to silence. He didn't know why he had stood and spoken, but it felt necessary. Unfortunately, with the sirdar's army already on the move, he knew it might already be too late.

One of the men confronted him. "How can you promise such a thing? Are we to risk our lives and the lives of our families on the desperate promise of a *ferengi*? A stranger? A man we know nothing about?"

"Abdul asks a fair question," said the emir, frowning. "Who are you to make such a promise?"

He'd gone too far, Nick thought. What had caused him to promise such a thing? Even Osmodon was giving him a questioning look. Before he could think of an answer he was interrupted by a shout from the old woman sitting in the corner.

"Malik! Listen to this man!"

"*Dol amrick*? Your highness?"

With astonishing agility, the old woman leapt to her feet, pointing at Nick with a bony finger. Her glaucous eyes, sightless as porcelain, seemed to bore into his soul.

"Listen to this one. He speaks truth. Listen to him, for he has been sent to us!"

No one argued. Even Osmodon nodded, as though her words were irrefutable. Only Nick seemed to question the old woman's statements. The rest of the company stared at him, their faces displaying wonder, even awe.

"The *Mahdi*?" whispered one, half question, half hope. But the question went unanswered, and the name was not repeated.

CHAPTER
44

LATE AFTERNOON OF THE FOLLOWING DAY, Nick and Osmodon stood watching as the caravan receded into the distance. A light breeze, hot enough to have come from an oven, blew in from the east. Nearby, rising out of the sands, stood a great stone obelisk, its bleached and pitted face inscribed with lines of cuneiform that neither Nick nor Osmodon could decipher.

"Go west from the stone," the old woman had said. "You will come to a road that will lead you to the ruins of an ancient city. Khagad'Oth it is called, though once it had a different name. Do not remain there after nightfall!"

Her sightless eyes held Nick with a singular avidity. He gave his word they would leave the place before dark, though Osmodon appeared reluctant. They would save two days by taking this route, the woman told them.

"Mad as a mud hen," grunted Osmodon, shaking his head.

Nick studied the obelisk. He imagined he could hear voices emanating from it, and the horses shied away. Osmodon liked the stone no better than the horses did, but was more concerned about the promise Nick had made.

"You seemed to agree with her readily enough yesterday," Nick said.

Osmodon shrugged. "Why not, if her delusions gain us an alliance?

But Khagad'Oth has an evil fame. They say *effretes* abide there. Mothers use the name to frighten children."

"You're afraid of an old wives' tale?"

"And if I am?"

Nick looked at Osmodon in surprise. The big man was truly worried.

"Makes my skin crawl," Osmodon admitted. "That old woman, those eyes, like milk left too long in the sun, staring like she can see right through you. Now we're on some cursed road heading to a cursed city. For what, to save two days' travel?"

He pointed at the obelisk. "You noticed how the caravan kept shy of it? Have you touched it? How can stone remain cold in this heat?"

He's right, Nick thought. The stone was cold when it should have been scorching. And the shadows it cast seemed to move.

"Too late to back out now."

"She's a crazy woman. Wait till they're on the other side of that dune. We can head back the way we came."

Nick was tempted. A sense of anxiety had been growing in him ever since the old woman had spoken the name Khagad'Oth. The whole matter disturbed him in ways he couldn't put words to.

A commotion in the distance caught his attention. A lone figure on a white horse was riding towards them at full gallop.

"The emir's son," observed Osmodon, squinting against the glare.

Reining in his rearing horse, Prince Bandar greeted them. "*Uma o'rabia* asked me to tell you that the Bani Attar will be with you at Barad'An in one month. She said you must hold until then, by any means. She said others will come, that you are not alone. May Ahriman be with you."

Without waiting for a response, the young prince spun his horse around and galloped back to the caravan.

"A month," muttered Osmodon darkly. "The Bani Attar can muster at most five hundred men. And we're supposed to hold? Hold what? I told you the old woman was mad."

You are not alone.

Nick, remembering similar words from a man in another world, shrugged. Yet the old woman's message did little to allay his concern.

Without further talk, they mounted their horses and headed west from the obelisk, in the direction of the lowering sun and a line of low chalk hills. For a time they rode in silence, until the sky began to darken. Osmodon had turned uncharacteristically pensive.

"What do you really know about this place?" Nick asked, trying to lighten the mood.

"Enough to avoid it."

A glum silence followed. Stars appeared in the east.

"It's said that Khagad'Oth was once a center of great learning," said Osmodon suddenly, as though he had been turning the thought over in his mind. "It was known as Ain al Arif then, 'The Magnet of Wisdom,' a place of sorcerers and healers. There was good in their knowledge, but even greater evil."

"Anything to the stories?"

"When I worked for the sheik in Abu Mesina, a rich merchant visited. He told us that once, as a boy, while searching for a goat that had escaped from his father's herd, he'd stumbled upon the place. I still remember the way his hands shook when he spoke of it.

"'Don't leave the road at night,' he said. 'To leave the road at night is death. Should you ever have the misfortune to visit the place, under no circumstances should you remain after dusk, for it is then the horror awakens.'"

"More or less what the old woman said."

"Aye. Last night the emir called her *dol amrick*, your highness. Bandar called her *uma o'rabia*, which means mother number four. Whoever she is, she certainly has them under her thumb."

At first the road beneath them was little more than a vague suggestion in the sand. But as they continued forward they began to make out cracked and pitted paving stones. The breeze picked up. Sheets of sand swirled across the stones, but even in the dimming light the road's outline had become remarkably clear.

Nick felt a tingling sensation down his back as he urged Greywind forward. It was a strange mix of dread and anticipation. The horse must have felt it as well, for it had begun to shudder, the shaking not stopping until all four of its hooves were set firmly on the paving stones.

Osmodon looked down, studying the stones. He opened his mouth as if to speak, then closed it. He might treat werewolves and Uruk war parties with equal aplomb, but talk of anything that smacked of the supernatural clearly made him edgy.

The sun settled behind the chalk hills, only its glow remaining. The wind changed directions, bringing with it an unusual chill. At first it was a welcome relief from the stifling heat, but it soon grew uncomfortable and both men donned heavier clothing.

They continued on until the moon was full overhead. The road reflected its light, a white ribbon in a timeless sea. They stopped, dismounting near the remains of a weathered oxcart half buried in sand. Osmodon made quick work of the cart with his ax, using the wood to build a fire in the center of the road.

They ate a quiet meal, each caught up in his own thoughts. The wind had settled into a steady breeze, blowing the smoke from the small fire eastwards, away from the hills. The horses chewed a sparse meal of grain and misshapen desert weeds. Nick lay close to the fire, his back against his saddle, a blanket wrapped tightly around him.

If their directions were right, Khagad'Oth should lie in a shallow canyon just beyond the hills. Osmodon sat, his eyes intent on the desert, sword in hand and ax nearby as if he expected attack at any moment.

Just before he fell asleep Nick imagined he could hear voices in the soft whisper of the wind, calling him into the desert. But he'd heard such voices before, and they no longer had power over him.

CHAPTER 45

NICK WAS AWAKENED BY VOICES.

The fire was little more than embers. A low fog covered the desert in thick patches. The horses stood quietly nearby, their eyes closed as if asleep.

Osmodon stood at the edge of the road. He appeared to be arguing with someone further out in the sand. Nick could almost imagine another figure there, shrouded in mist.

Alarmed, he started to call out, but some sixth sense warned him to keep silent. A battle was raging, though of what kind he had no idea. But he was certain that to call out would be his friend's undoing.

Osmodon's face was a mask of anger and pain. "You wasted the best of us in a goose chase!" he cried out. "You gave us to our enemies."

The shape in the mist seemed to answer, a low whisper, like silk pulled over sand.

Osmodon leaned forward, fists raised in defiance. "You have no right to accuse me. I kept faith. It was you who failed! You who betrayed your people with your greed and arrogance. You led your people to their doom, and I'll hear no more!"

With obvious effort he turned his back on whatever was hidden in the mist. For a time the ghostly voice continued to speak, softly, soothingly, then with increasing anger. Osmodon ignored it and returned to the fire.

With a shriek of rage, the mist-thing dissolved, and there was silence.

Osmodon let out a great sigh and his body slumped. Perspiration dripped down his broad brow, droplets glistening in the moonlight. He looked up to see Nick watching him. "Terrible things," he said, "these ghosts."

"You all right?" Nick asked.

Osmodon thought about that for a moment, then nodded. "Never stood up to my father when he was alive. Perhaps if I had, things would be different now."

CHAPTER
46

THE MIST AND COLD were gone with the first glimmer of dawn. Osmodon did not speak of his encounter, and Nick didn't ask, but the big man seemed calm, as though a great tension had left him.

They attack where you're weakest, Sianiave had said. Why had Osmodon been singled out? Nick wondered. Was it simply that he'd slept closer to the edge of the road?

They ate a quick meal and broke camp, anxious to leave that haunted desert behind. The sky was cloudless, the air hot and still. An hour passed, then another, when suddenly the road ended at a cliff. Below lay the fabled ruins of Khagad'Oth.

From their viewpoint, Khagad'Oth appeared little more than a series of broken walls and featureless piles of stone. Much was covered in sand, and the mounds that remained revealed only a hint of human design.

Near the center of the canyon, a number of larger buildings still held their form. Nick tried to envision the city as it once had been. The canyon itself was not large, about three miles long, and narrow. Khagad'Oth existed in striking contrast to the natural forms of the landscape. Its man-made structures, what remained of them, had been laid out in geometric patterns. He sensed a purpose to the design that went beyond aesthetics.

The road had almost completely eroded away where it dropped into the canyon. What remained was little more than a goat track etched into the side of the cliff. Any other time Nick would have turned back, but to do so now would add days to their journey, days they couldn't afford.

"Have to walk the horses," said Osmodon. He looked as unhappy at the prospect of descending that broken path as Nick felt.

They started down in single file, Nick in the lead. Stones dislodged by their passage fell several hundred feet before hitting the valley floor.

Petroglyphs marked the cliff walls, pecked into the stone. They reminded Nick of the carvings at the ferryman's cottage at Ostengarth, and the patterns he'd seen in the tilework and tapestries at High House.

Near the bottom, the trail passed between the cliff and a large slab that had broken away from the main wall. As he entered the gap between them, Nick felt the same frisson he had experienced when Greywind had first set foot onto the ancient road.

This time Osmodon felt it too. "A binding," he announced. "There are places that have them natural. This is no human sorcery."

Unlike Gallian's crater, the canyon was not enclosed. Its western wall was a series of tablelands with openings between them. A shallow wash ran through the canyon's center. In ages past it might have been a running stream, but now its bed was choked with thornbushes and stunted trees.

They rested in the shade at the bottom of the cliff where the road was in better repair. A pair of ravens passed overhead, their glossy black heads cocked towards the intruders. Their caws sounded both welcome and warning.

The horses drank a small amount of water from their cupped hands, then Nick and Osmodon drank some themselves. When they were refreshed, they mounted and continued on.

As they approached the city, they saw the structures were in better condition than they appeared from a distance. Streets and alleyways could be made out. Walls protected from the elements still displayed much of their original plaster, though any color had long ago been bleached white by the sun. Nick felt a rightness and harmony about the place completely at odds with its evil reputation. He doubted its architects were the sinister magicians of legend, or that evil brought the city to its end. More likely it was the changing weather and the encroaching desert, though some might argue evil and man-made decay went hand in hand. It wouldn't have been the first civilization to end this way.

"This is something," remarked Osmodon.

They had come to a central square with a five-sided obelisk in the middle, its top half lying broken at its base. Fallen walls surrounded the square, though one structure, larger than the rest, appeared almost intact. Its domed roof was at least thirty feet high. The facade was wide and windowless. Marble steps led to a broad gallery lined with broken columns. Two massive metal doors, one partially open, guarded its entrance.

The building was so large that Nick wondered why they hadn't noticed it from above. "A temple of some sort," he mused.

Osmodon nodded. "Likely. Those doors are bronze; must be worth a king's ransom. Wonder why no one's carted them off?"

"They must weigh tons." Nick wiped a sleeve across his forehead. The heat was intense, reflecting off the sand and bleached stones with the ferocity of a forge. The sun was directly overhead. Even the ravens had sought shelter from its pitiless glare.

The open door of the building looked inviting. It would be cooler inside. They could rest until the stifling heat had subsided.

"We've guests," said Osmodon suddenly. He nodded towards a series of indentations in the sand. They were clearly footprints.

Nick felt it now, eyes watching them. The horses had grown skittish, their ears cocked. The road was the main access to the square, east and west. If someone was hiding behind those walls, then they had been observing them for some time.

"Through that arch looks clear," suggested Osmodon .

Nick hesitated. If they had to flee, west through the arch would be the obvious direction to take. Too obvious. But what were the options? They couldn't go back.

Maybe no one was out there. Maybe the feeling of being watched was nothing more than the effect of the heat. Maybe those dimples in the sand had been left by a wandering mountain lion.

A blood-curdling cry came from somewhere in the ruins, cutting off Nick's thoughts and any hope that they were alone. Osmodon drew his sword. The cry was followed by a second, then more and more, until Nick could no longer count the voices.

They appeared like ghosts, men in ragged robes and blue headdresses, standing on walls and in alleyways. Ten at least blocked the way to the arch. Their faces were strangely distorted, scarred by disease and marked with tattoos. Their teeth were filed to sharp points.

Behind them, atop a high wall, stood an old man, his face so corroded it was difficult to make out his features. Only his eyes stood out, gleaming black and malevolent.

The ululating cries became a cacophony. Then, at a gesture from the old man, the noise stopped. The man raised both arms over his head and shouted, "*Yala al fehudin! Al ferengi al mat!*"

"The temple!" cried Nick, drawing his sword as he spurred Greywind towards the steps. He felt a sudden sharp pain in his side, but was too busy staying in the saddle to worry about it.

The opening between the bronze doors was just wide enough for a horse. Spears, arrows, and rocks followed them like a hailstorm.

Nick was first through, followed closely by Osmodon. He leapt from his saddle, slapping Greywind on the rump to move him away from the deadly rain of missiles.

They were in a large antechamber of some sort, its recesses shrouded in darkness, the floor covered in mounds of grit. A rock skinned Nick's ear, and he ducked behind one of the doors. The door moved as his shoulder fell against it.

"Ozzy! Give me a hand!"

Immediately Osmodon ran to his aid. With both their weights against it, the massive door gave way, swinging shut with an echoing boom. The room was pitched into shadow, the impenetrable darkness of a tomb.

"Too easy," said Osmodon. "You'd think someone oiled the hinges."

They heard a strange rustling sound above them. Nick looked up, but in the darkness could see nothing. The air was bitter with the caustic odor of ammonia mixed with the smell of sheared copper. Outside they could hear the muffled cries of their attackers, the ringing thumps of their weapons hitting the metal doors.

There was one last, trilling cry, then silence.

"They're leaving," said Nick, with more hope than confidence.

"Probably the smell," muttered Osmodon dryly.

Nick had his own conjectures. Was there another entrance? Were their attackers even now stalking them in the dark?

The horses shifted nervously. Nick put his hand on Greywind's shoulder. They're frightened, he thought. What are they afraid of? Trained warhorses wouldn't be afraid of the men outside. What is that eerie rustling?

There was a flash and a metallic snap as Osmodon struck his flint. With the third spark his traveling lamp came to life. "A little light on the subject does wonders, as my nanny used to say."

The first thing Nick noticed was the floor. The mounds of grit weren't sand. The substance was damp and stuck to his boots. It was also the dark rose color of dried blood.

He suddenly remembered where he'd encountered that smell before. A cave somewhere, on a training mission.

"Bats!"

"These aren't bats," said Osmodon grimly. He held the lamp higher. Above, clustered against the dome of the ceiling, were hundreds of huge, tick-like creatures. Birds, insects, or animals, Nick couldn't tell. Whatever they were, they made the hair on the back of his neck stand up.

"Blood kites," said Osmodon.

"Are they dangerous?" Nick knew it was a foolish question even as he asked.

"If a thing that flies in swarms large enough to blacken the sky, and can pick a camel down to bone in a matter of minutes, isn't dangerous, then I don't know what is."

Osmodon lowered the lamp. "Kites only feed at night. Explains why our friends outside aren't trying harder. Probably figure us as good as dead."

Every now and then one of the kites would lose its grip and drop, floating in the air for a brief moment before fluttering upwards to find another hold.

Osmodon handed Nick the lamp. "Hold this. Let's get that arrow out of you. Makes me uneasy."

"Arrow?" Startled, Nick looked down to see the shaft of an arrow sticking just below his rib cage.

Osmodon studied the arrow for a moment, then, with a single quick movement, grabbed hold of the shaft and yanked it out.

"Ow! You might have warned me!"

"Don't be a goose. It wasn't deep. See, clean. No poison." Osmodon held the arrow up. The head was chipped obsidian. Blood covered no more than an inch.

He tossed the arrow aside and rummaged through his saddlebag, bringing out a small jar. "Beeswax and goat grease, with some of Sianiave's powders thrown in. Lift that shirt up."

As Nick held his shirt up, Osmodon rubbed a sticky green salve on the wound. "Not much bleeding. I've patched worse with this stuff. Be right as rain in a day or two."

When he finished, he put the jar back in his saddlebag and retrieved his lamp. Nick lowered his shirt. The salve had stopped the bleeding. What pain there had been was gone.

The kites were becoming more active. Their eyes and eel-like mouths were on the underside of flat, heavily veined bodies with barbed tails. For the moment at least, they seemed to take no notice of the men.

"Our friends outside will want to be in their caves before nightfall," said Osmodon, thinking out loud. "Kites hunt by scent. It's been windy the past few evenings. If we ride with the wind we should be safe enough. We'll have to wait till dusk."

"Maybe there's another way out. There's a passage."

"Fair enough."

The horses in tow, they crossed the room and entered into a long hallway. Once out of the kite chamber, the horses seemed to calm. Nick saw that the floor of the passageway, though coated in inch thick dust, was free of dung.

Out of habit, he counted his steps. At eighty, the passage ended at the top of a narrow flight of stairs leading down into more darkness.

"Doesn't likely lead to a back door," commented Osmodon doubtfully.

"Can't hurt to look. Besides, we've got a few hours till dusk. It's better than sitting in a pile of kite dung, waiting for them to attack."

"You have a point."

They left the horses at the top of the stairs. Nick counted twenty-nine steps set with black marble. Near the bottom he smelled the improbable, though not unpleasing, scent of lemon, a relief from the dung heaps. The silence was almost total.

They entered another vaulted room. As Osmodon raised his lamp to get a better look, Nick had to fight a sickening impulse to bolt and run.

"Hold there, lad," said Osmodon, grabbing his arm. "What's wrong? You look like you've seen a ghost."

Nick took a breath and let it out. "No. No, it's all right, I'm fine." But he wasn't. He was as close to panic as he'd ever been in his life.

The room was perhaps thirty feet in diameter, with no other way in or out, and no place for an enemy to hide. Like the kite chamber it had a domed ceiling, though this one was a vibrant blue. The marble floor tiles formed a large enneagon, identical to the one on the council table at High House. The figure was enclosed in a border of alternating black and white tiles.

Nick's panic began to ease, though he had to force himself to take a step forward. Each step took increasing effort as he neared the center of the room, as if a physical force was attempting to hold him back. But with each step came an increasing sense of expectancy, of something momentous about to happen.

He put a foot on the green tile marking both the center of the room and the center of the enneagon. Relaxing, he took another deep breath and turned back to Osmodon.

But Osmodon was not there. Instead he faced a blinding pillar of light, so ferociously bright the pain of it drove him to his knees.

"No, no! It isn't time! I'm not ready!" Whether he screamed out loud or just thought it he had no idea.

The searing light vanished, and with it the pain.

In time, he opened his eyes. Had they been closed?

He floated weightless in an ink-black sea under a dark sky littered with stars. It was impossible to tell where the sea ended and the sky began.

A small constellation of stars, set at the apex of the dome, drew his attention. The stars drew together, merged into a lattice, a tetrahedron pulsing with color. It descended, engulfed him with light, and lifted him up.

This was death, and yet not death. He felt no fear. He was on a craft, a chariot that was carrying him through time and space.

He saw terrible things: battles through all of time, visions of death and destruction, men killing with stone axes, mobs fleeing burning cities, sailors throwing themselves into the sea as fleets of ships were destroyed by cannon fire, squadrons of flying machines using beams of light to boil the oceans and turn the earth into molten slag.

And just as the images became too much to bear, the landscape altered once again. Nick looked down on Khagad'Oth, seeing it no longer as a ruin, but as it had been: a timeless place, hidden and protected from the world, perfect and eternal. He saw himself at the center of a great pattern, a labyrinth whose luminous lines reached out into the infinite.

And as he followed these lines back to the stars, the stars merged into a singular point of radiance that took the form of a woman.

But before she revealed her face, a shadow descended.

CHAPTER
47

West Arden Forest
May 25

SIANIAVE WAS TROUBLED. Things had been going amiss ever since the morghul had appeared at Langton Manor, and she wasn't sure why. She considered that they were moving through an amorphous cusp. She was old enough to have experienced the previous one, when arid reason became the predominant mode of thought. There had been unrest then as well, but nothing to equal the difficulties they now faced.

The ethereal world was out of balance. Reason and logic seemed to be stuck on the same narrow path, at the risk of losing it all. But Sianiave suspected a deeper and darker cause, a shadow player using Reason for its own purposes, manipulating its weaknesses of arrogance and gullibility.

Waning sunlight cast amber beams through the trees. She'd been nineteen hours in the saddle, twenty the day before. Her recuperative powers were far beyond those of most people, but even she had her limits, as did Phaeton, the white stallion Bronwyn had provided for her journey.

She was still two days from Marduk, the only place on the continent where the dragon lines met in the appropriate configuration. She found herself thinking of that other Earth and its technological marvels that could have whisked her there in an hour.

Such clever technology was, of course, impossible here. And she was concerned with the rapid and unexpected advancement she'd witnessed on her last visit. She'd had the distinct impression the science was being seeded. If so, who was doing the seeding, and for what purpose? Better to give a five-year-old child a bucket of gunpowder and a box of matches.

She doubted it was the lizards. They were evil brutes. Just the thought of them turned her stomach. But they were also slow to change and relatively crude in their thinking. Such a refined strategy as she sensed here was beyond them. In this they were a great deal like the morghuls.

Shared patrimony? She'd heard stories, of course, the legends and myths, had read many of the ancient writings. When she had more time, she would look into that.

Should she fail here, that other Earth might have to be written off. The thought saddened her. Despite the growing foulness that engulfed it, there was much about it she would miss.

The ancient track she'd been following passed through a meadow where a small stream ran. She dismounted, allowing the stallion a long drink before tethering him to a tree near some long grass. She removed the saddle and travel bags, then rubbed him down with the saddle blanket.

Phaeton was an extraordinary horse with fire in his grey-green eyes. Even in her long life, she'd seen few to match him. Bronwyn had been generous in offering him, but then Bronwyn was as aware of the stakes as she. Gallian couldn't stand alone.

She built a small fire and cooked a wild hen she'd killed earlier. When she'd finished eating she set out her blankets, stuck her sword and dagger in the soft earth within easy reach, and lay down. This night she was determined to get a good night's sleep.

Time passed, yet sleep eluded her. None of the mind-quieting techniques she knew helped, even her personal favorite of matching names to the stars overhead. Eventually she gave up.

She withdrew her pipe, tamped the dried suph into the bowl, and lit it.

A wolf howled in the distance. The cry held no menace, for it was not one of the shape-shifting kind. Moments later its call was answered by its mate.

Pebbles rattled in the stream. A brace of rabbits hopped past, searching for cover. Moments later the dark shape of an owl passed overhead. Nearby, Phaeton continued to chew quietly on the grass.

An omen, owls. Psychopomps, like ravens and coyotes. Messengers from the netherworld, worshipped in some cultures, considered evil in others, harbingers of death.

So many years she'd been at this. And now it appeared all was drawing to a climax. Did this include her own life as well?

It was worth considering. Part of her early training had been to travel to the moment of her own death. She'd forgotten much of what she'd seen that night so long ago, though she knew when it was time the memory would be there. At this moment death did not feel particularly imminent, for what that was worth. The way things were changing there wasn't much you could count on anymore, even mystical visions.

Sianiave rarely dwelt on the past. There was too much pain, too many people, places, and times once loved that now were gone. Yet the memories were there, many of that other Earth. Sitting on the steps of the Parthenon, debating virtue with that wise little man Socrates; that year in old Jerusalem, learning the secrets of the *merkaba* from the Brothers of the Chariot; the warm evenings in Baghdad's House of Wisdom, smoking hashish and discussing the nature of reality with the savants of Harun al-Rashid. In Toledo, she recalled the ecstasy of the Mirror Dance; years later in the orient, the satisfaction of studying the martial arts with such incomparable masters as Hokosai, Dr. Xie, and Sensei Ueshiba.

Some of her most prized memories, however, were of more commonplace things. Lunch on the Left Bank in Paris, drinking a good house red and watching the throng pass by; late nights at the old Blue Note, listening to Charlie Parker practice his riffs.

It had always surprised her how very little she had changed over time. Her essence hardly seemed to have changed at all.

She still enjoyed life's pleasures. And she still loved, which was perhaps the greatest surprise of all. She'd had countless lovers, most gone from memory. But she'd been in love only three times, and those loves were etched deep in her soul.

She leaned back against the oak to which Phaeton was tethered, inhaling a lungful of smoke. A meteor arced overhead, its blue-and-gold trail vivid against the onyx sky. Another omen?

A fish jumped in the stream. A warm breeze, smelling of pine, tickled the tree leaves. Phaeton snorted contentedly. For a moment, everything seemed at peace, all too rare these days. The binding on the Earth world was broken. Chaos was in the shifting winds.

She found herself mouthing the words to a poem:

Turning and turning in the widening gyre
The falcon cannot hear the falconer;
Things fall apart; the centre cannot hold;
Mere anarchy is loosed upon the world,
The blood-dimmed tide is loosed, and everywhere
The ceremony of innocence is drowned;
The best lack all conviction, while the worst
Are full of passionate intensity...
The darkness drops again; but now I know
That twenty centuries of stony sleep
Were vexed to nightmare by a rocking cradle,
And what rough beast, its hour come round at last,
Slouches towards Bethlehem to be born?

Was she right in this pursuit? Artos had left Barad'An with a formidable force. Such a large company did not just vanish without word or sign.

She'd known him in his youth, knew of his dream of a new city, a new kingdom safe from the encroaching storm. Cuchulain had ridiculed him, calling his dream unmanly, even treasonous. Because of her close relationship with his uncle, Artos had distanced himself from her as well.

She missed Osmodon, and she was anxious about Nick. But Nick must face his challenge alone, without her support. The ordeal that awaited him was beyond the capacity of most to understand.

Had there been time, had she taken time, the shock could have been lessened. The depth to which that Earth had fallen in just forty years had caught her off guard. Its tools of mind control had grown unbelievably more subtle and efficient.

Phaeton snorted again, stamping his hoof as if to distract her. Even from so distant a place as this, she knew her thoughts could reach Nick and interfere.

She took another puff of the calming smoke and began naming stars.

CHAPTER
48

"BREATHE!"

The word was simple, yet primal in its power. Nick took a deep breath, choked, and opened his eyes. A face formed amid the emptiness of space, and with it recognition. Osmodon.

"Thank you," was all he could say. Or perhaps he didn't say it, only felt immense gratitude to Osmodon for bringing him back from the desperate loneliness of non-being.

"You had me worried, lad. You stopped breathing there for a time."

They were in the kite chamber. Osmodon must have carried him there. The rustling of the kites had grown noticeably louder, and the light through the now open door was grey and dim. Nearby the horses were saddled and wary, anxious to leave.

"We haven't much time," said Osmodon, helping him stand. "Our friends outside have left."

To Nick, the world still did not seem quite real. Looking around, he imagined he could actually see through the building's stone walls. Dusk was settling outside, and the ancient streets were empty. A hot breeze blew sand across the cobblestones. Greywind nudged Nick with his head, as if to hurry him up.

"The kites are waking," whispered Osmodon. "Can you ride?"

Nick hesitated. Could he? His body seemed to be functioning well enough. "Yeah. I can ride, a little woozy is all."

He took the reins. Osmodon caught him when his foot slipped in the stirrup and helped him into the saddle. "The wind is right, out of the east. If we survive this I'll give a year's tithe to Asgar."

Even as Osmodon spoke a kite dropped from the ceiling with a blood-chilling screech and landed on his back. He ripped it off before it could sink in its fangs, slicing it in two with his dagger, then quickly swung into his saddle.

"Time to go."

Another kite dropped from above and fastened its claws into Greywind's neck. Greywind screamed and Nick tore the creature free, slamming its squirming form against the doorway as the big horse bolted through.

Greywind took the lead with Osmodon's mount close behind. They passed down the steps and through the ruined city at full gallop. Dusk was lowering into night and overhead stars were appearing. Behind them came a sound like a great wind, but Nick didn't look back. It took all of his effort just to stay in the saddle.

They rode flat out until the horses began to tire. Only then did they slow their pace. When Nick did look back, it appeared as if a dark cloud was rising out of the ruins. But it was headed northeast, away from them.

Osmodon straightened in his saddle. "Asgar will get that tithe I promised."

The horses were heaving, their mouths foaming. "What now?" asked Nick. "The horses are done in."

"I suggest we keep on, riding easy. I would be quit of this canyon. I reckon if the horses could talk, they'd agree."

"You'll get no argument from me, not if it gets us to Barad'An sooner."

"Barad'An?" Osmodon looked over in surprise. "Shouldn't we return to Gallian with the news of the alliance with the desert people?"

"Barad'An. Ren's there."

"Ren? Why would she go back? How could—" Osmodon studied Nick's face a long moment, then nodded. "Barad'An it is."

CHAPTER
49

Men'leth Hills
South Arden Forest
June 5

NICK NEEDED REST. It had been over a week since they'd fled Khagad'Oth, riding hard with little sleep. He said almost nothing about his experience there. Much of it was beyond words.

Five days ago, they'd seen a dust cloud rising in the north. Osmodon guessed it to be the sirdar's army, already nearing Gallian. He estimated it would be no more than three weeks before Barad'An itself was under siege.

The Great Eastern Road lay to their north. To save time and to avoid the sirdar's army, they'd ridden directly west from the ruined city, following a little-used trail the desert woman had described. That morning they'd entered the Men'leth Hills, marking Arden Forest's southern border. There the trail had grown vague and steep, often forcing them to walk the horses.

"You know," said Nick after a difficult incline. "I never asked what you saw back there, before you woke me up."

"You screamed. You were tearing at your face like the kites had you. I started to help and—" Osmodon looked puzzled. "That's all I remember.

I must have fallen asleep. When I awoke you were on your knees, staring at what I couldn't say, but no longer fearful, more in wonderment. I hauled you up the stairs, threw you across Greywind, and hurried back to the kite chamber. By this time the kites were waking, and the horses were going mad. I had to wrap their eyes so they would mind me."

"I saw things, Ozzy, terrible things—"

Nick stopped. The trail had suddenly veered to the left, then leveled off. They had reached the summit.

"Barad'An?"

"Aye," said Osmodon quietly. "The old lady herself."

They stood for a long moment, not speaking, for the sight was breathtaking. Beyond the mountains and forest, circled by a plain of emerald grass, stood Barad'An, once empress of the world. Her massive walls appeared to be seamless and sloped slightly inward, with battlements at the top and watchtowers at regular intervals. The outer wall stretched four miles in either direction from a central gate, which was standing open.

The sun was setting and high clouds cast a reflected glow on the city. Nick could imagine her walls to be made of pure gold. Beyond, he could see the towers and tiled roofs of palaces and temples, hostelries, and public halls.

The North Road had been laid straight as an arrow to the great gate. It was bordered with oaks and appeared to be paved with multicolored stones.

Osmodon sighed. "She's beautiful, right enough. But don't be taken in by her looks. That field that surrounds her was once a town in itself, destroyed by raids, warfare, and dwindling trade. Her walls are still high and strong, but not as they once were. A keen eye can find many faults. Skilled masons are in short supply, repairs costly. But her greatest weakness is the lack of defenders. Forty-eight towers once housed 108 men each. Now they're empty, or mostly so."

"How do you suggest we get in?"

Osmodon grinned. "The gate's open, lad. Should anyone ask, we've come to offer our services. I assume the priest will welcome new recruits, especially two good fighting men such as ourselves."

The mounted their horses and started down the narrow trail. "There's an inn," Osmodon said. "The Golden Dawn. Has the strongest ale and prettiest wenches in Anor, and also the best gossip. If you're right, and Ren is here, we'll find out soon enough."

It was late afternoon by the time they reached the road. The air stank. "I've no good feeling about this," muttered Osmodon. "I know that smell."

Nick too recognized the smell, the cloying stench of death. Its source soon became evident. The great oaks that lined the road were filled with corpses, some spiked to the trunks, others hanging from the limbs like some hideous fruit. Many appeared recent, while others were clearly weeks old, their skulls stripped of flesh by the swarms of squawking crows. What from a distance Nick had assumed were multicolored paving stones he now saw to be grey, but stained with blood and offal.

Osmodon's face was a mask. "I can't abide this stench. Let's ride in the field."

The air was still. Even in the open field, the smell followed them. Grim purpose had settled over both men. For Nick the walls before them no longer looked golden, but red and bloody.

No trumpets sounded their approach as they neared the gate. No soldiers came out to greet them. They were halfway through the gate tunnel when the first challenge came. "Halt! State your allegiance and your business."

An aged pikeman in a tattered white cloak blocked the tunnel. A red cross decorated his breast. Half a dozen white-cloaked ruffians lolled against the walls, their garments hastily fashioned of dirty cloth. Several carried tankards, which they passed back and forth with ill-natured humor.

"We've come for employment," said Osmodon. "We've heard you're in need of good fighting men."

"Pike, 'em, Willy" cried a sallow-faced drunk. "Send 'em to hell with the rest of the heathen trash!"

"Yeah, Willy," cried another. "Show us that pike work you're always bragging about."

"Mercenaries, are you?" growled the old man, ignoring the taunts. "Be ye heathens or believers?"

"Oh, believers, most certainly," replied Osmodon agreeably.

The old man squinted, clearly skeptical. "Be ye heathens, ye will burn in hell. If ye speak the truth, there'll be a place for ye. But ye won't get an audience until after the occasion."

"Occasion? And what occasion would that be?"

"Why the wedding, of course. Ye haven't heard?"

"Not a wit."

"Ye haven't come for the drink, then? Perhaps ye be true after all."

"Aye, true we are. But this wedding? Someone high-born, I take it?"

"The highest." The old man squared his shoulders. "The Lord Glays is to wed Princess Gwyndolyn come morning."

Nick blanched. "Wed? Ren? That's impos—"

"A great occasion, indeed," interrupted Osmodon quickly, shooting Nick a dark look.

"Aye. Lord Glays has ordered three days of festivities, free drink to all off-duty templars." The old man cast a frown of disapproval at the soldiers lining the walls. "Though it's become impossible to say who's off duty and who's on.

"Perhaps ye know something of soldiering yourself, sirrah," he added quietly to Osmodon. "You've the look." Then, louder, "Enter, if ye will. We've orders to be lenient to travelers during the festivities."

Nick, still choking down his outrage, followed Osmodon into the city. "It can't be true. Ren would never—"

"Enough," grunted Osmodon without turning his head. "We aren't out of it yet. Look around you."

They had entered a large square. Cobbled streets branched from it in six directions. Templars were everywhere, drinking in doorways, leaning against walls, seated on fountains where no water ran but their own.

Coarse laughter echoed from the taverns and alleyways. A few of the more sober-appearing men regarded the pair with narrowed eyes. Others gave them an incurious glance before continuing with their drinking. Most were armed with daggers or pikes, though many carried nothing more than clubs or rude spears.

The cobbles were littered with refuse. The windows in dozens of shops were shattered, the shops looted of wares. Feral dogs pawed through garbage, occasionally breaking into fights over a piece of stale bread. What few of the citizenry they saw were either old women or men too stooped with age to be of use as soldiers.

"Look at the bright side," whispered Osmodon. "We've made it into the city, and we know for certain she's here. Not that I doubted, mind you."

"But I tell you, Ren would not—"

"Of course she wouldn't, not willingly. There's something we're missing. In any case, it seems we've arrived just in time."

Osmodon was thoughtful. "Look at them. Undisciplined, untrained, and ill-armed. Do you see preparations for a siege? The priest must know the sirdar's army is headed his way. Does he think the walls enough to save him?"

Nick was forced to agree. There was a commotion among half a dozen templars gathered around a chandlery as a fight broke out. It ended quickly when one man smashed his tankard over another's head, knocking him unconscious.

They turned off the main street and down an alley so narrow the opposite walls could be touched with outstretched arms. A block later the alley opened up on another square. Judging by the wooden booths at its center, Nick guessed it had once been a marketplace. Now the booths were as empty as the streets with not a soul in sight, not even a drunken soldier.

The streetlamps remained dark. With lengthening shadows, the streets had become sinister. What few lights there were shone from behind closed shutters and curtains. It reminded Nick of Ardendell, though on a far vaster scale.

They came to a five-story building just off the square. Wooden balconies hung below the upper windows. The sign over the front door showed a sunburst, its face and rays painted in gold leaf against a maroon field. They had arrived at the Golden Dawn.

A smaller sign, handwritten and tacked to the door, read:

Closed. No provisions. The Management.

Swearing, Osmodon dismounted. "Hells! Probably the first time in a thousand years the Dawn's doors have been closed."

Nick had been looking forward to a good meal and a night's rest. "What now?"

"There are other inns, though none so hospitable as the Dawn. It's where I met Sianiave, you know. I still remember—"

"Who speaks of the Lady Sianiave?"

The hoarse whisper startled them, coming out of the darkness as it did. Nick drew his sword, turning to see a man standing in the shadows. He carried a long sword with an easy familiarity.

Osmodon drew his own sword and dismounted. "Who asks?"

The man gave a sudden laugh and stepped forward into the light. "Osmodon of Linsraden! With that block of a body, it can be no one else."

"Bors?"

Bors sheathed his sword and grabbed up Osmodon in a great hug. "Gods, it's good to see you, Osmodon. Of all of us, you were the last I expected to come."

"Bors, why are you here? We'd assumed every knight worthy of the name had left this place, or is on the oaks yonder."

"You're not far wrong. But first things first, the priest's spies are everywhere. We're lucky tonight that most of them are drunk." The knight eyed Nick. "Your companion? He can be trusted?"

"With your life."

"It is with my life, and the lives of many others. Come with me. We'll attend to introductions later. Quickly."

The knight led them to a small door near the larger stable doors. He knocked three times, the knocks evenly spaced. The door opened immediately, and they were quickly guided in by several hands. Someone struck a flint, and a lantern flared to life.

They found themselves in a large courtyard with a stack of hay in the center. Stalls made up three of the four walls. Three other men were present, a stoop-shouldered man who carried the lantern, and two teenage boys, who took the reins to their horses.

"Andy and Adelph will see to your horses," growled Bors. "Grab your kits. We can talk inside. By your looks you could use could use a drink and a bite to eat."

"The sign said the inn was closed."

"To keep the soldiers away. Buffoons they may be, but they're raiding the city. Gastain was taken. He refused service to anyone wearing the white cloak. Giselle hung the sign the same day."

"Gastain taken? Dead?"

"We don't know. Many are hanging on the oaks. Others are taken to the dungeon. I'm not certain which is worse."

They followed Bors and the old man through a door, then down a hall and into the common room. There were two lamps alight but much of the room was still in shadow. There was a bar and numerous tables, all empty.

Bors seated them at a circular table under one of the lamps. The old man hung his lantern on a nearby hook and vanished, returning moments later with three tankards of ale.

"Gregory has worked at the Dawn for ninety-three years," Bors explained once the old man had vanished again. "He'll bring food. In the meantime, we'd best trade tales. Your friend here, to start."

"Nicholas of Amra, meet Sir Bors Graalwyth, one of the greatest knights of Barad'An and a good friend."

"Honored," said Nick.

"I've not heard of—Amra, did you say? A land to the south?"

Osmodon took a long drink of ale, wiping his beard with the back of his hand. "Sir Nicholas is from beyond the White Mountains."

Bors looked at Nick in surprise. "Beyond the White Mountains? A long way to travel, indeed."

"Indeed," said Nick. He drank. The ale was good, delicious after the long journey.

The knight regarded him for a long moment, opened his mouth as if to say something, then, thinking better of it turned back to Osmodon. "You received the word, no doubt. Tell me, is Sianiave with you?"

"She is elsewhere. The lad and I have been traveling. It's been weeks since we've heard word of anything."

"You're serious? Then why have you come here, to the Dawn, on this day and at this time?"

"Happenstance, it would appear. Though I suspect your waiting outside in the dark has something to do with it."

"Aye. Though I was not waiting outside. The boys saw you coming and summoned me."

"You were expecting someone?"

"'Hoping' is the better word. You have heard of the marriage the priest has planned for the morrow?"

Nick tensed, but held his tongue.

"Only this evening," said Osmodon, nodding. "When we entered the city. It seemed unlikely, to say the least."

"Ren arrived a few days ago with Aerindir. He was arrested immediately and taken to the dungeons. We've heard nothing of him since, though I suspect he's still alive, at least until the wedding. Gothmog, that rat-faced magician of Glays's, runs the dungeons now. What tales we hear would give nightmares to a crow."

"She came willingly? Ren, I mean?" asked Nick.

Bors gave him a curious look. "Willingly enough, though when Aerindir was dragged off she fought. It's said the priest threatened to kill her loved ones unless she returned."

Osmodon nodded. "It's as we thought."

"We can't let it happen, of course. I put out the word that all knights still loyal and free should meet tonight, here at the Golden Dawn."

"How many have arrived?"

Bors hesitated, then clapped Osmodon on the arm and said, "So far? Two."

CHAPTER

50

"AERINDIR'S DONE NOTHING WRONG."

Ren spoke evenly, though it was a struggle to keep her raging emotions in check. "Release him and I'll give you no more trouble. At least allow him to attend the wedding."

Glays lowered the scroll he'd been reading and looked at her in surprise. "Done nothing wrong? My dear, he's a traitor. How would it look if he were to go free?"

His puzzlement appeared so sincere that Ren wondered if he'd begun to believe his own lies.

She knew it was hopeless when she came to him, but she had to make the effort. She'd heard the rumors about conditions in the dungeons since the magician had been given charge. She suspected she'd been meant to hear them, to keep her in line. Aerindir wasn't the only one she knew who was being held in that foul pit.

"It can do you no harm. He's been a faithful friend to me, and I'll keep my word."

She hated having to lie, but it was a small matter considering she intended to kill the man. She remembered one of the Sisters' aphorisms: "The definition of a fool is someone who tells the truth to a liar."

Glays appeared to lose interest in her pleas and set the scroll aside. "If he's found innocent, the proceedings will have a favorable outcome.

When you commence your wifely duties, we can discuss the matter further."

Wifely duties! That was it. Ren's control broke. "You arrogant, evil pig!"

She struck at him, but Glays caught her hand inches before it reached his face. He twisted her arm, forcing her to her knees. As she struggled to free herself he landed a blow that sent her sprawling backward to the floor.

"Speak to me again like that and I'll have Gothmog cut off Aerindir's feet. You both can watch while the dogs have them for play." He spoke equably, without apparent anger, but Ren did not doubt he would do exactly as he said.

"Spare her face, m'lord," remarked Gothmog dryly. "There is a wedding in the morning, if you recall."

The magician had been watching from the doorway. It mattered not to him if the fool cut the girl's throat, but there was more involved. If this farce of a wedding were to play out correctly, it wouldn't do to have the bride's face looking like stew meat. Nor did he think Belliol would appreciate it. For some reason, the master wanted the girl delivered unscathed.

Ren remained still. It wasn't the blow that had shaken her as much as her lack of self-control. Giving vent to her anger was a sign of weakness. He'd provoked her, of course. The question was, had he done so deliberately? Was his off-handed manner an act designed to force her off balance? Was he that clever?

She took a trembling breath. So much depended on her. If she'd known in Gallian what she knew now, she would not have returned.

Tomorrow. Tomorrow it would be ended, one way or another.

The thought gave her strength. She wiped blood from her bruised lip and struggled to her feet. She lowered her head, not in deference, but so he wouldn't see the hatred in her eyes.

"Apologies, my—lord." The words threatened to choke her. "It's only that Aerindir has been a good friend, and I wish no harm to come to him."

Glays stared at her as if trying to gauge the truth of her words. He pursed his lips, then finally nodded. "Good, then. In any event you'll have new friends, my dear. But be a good girl and we may consider your friend's release. It would not be seemly should you have to visit him on the oaks."

Ren had seen the bodies of the poor wretches along the road. She hadn't looked too closely for fear she would recognize someone she knew.

She'd sworn to kill this man, or die in the attempt. But her confidence was shaken. They'd taken her dagger when she arrived, but the poison meant for its tip was hidden with her toiletries. A knife, a needle, anything with a point or an edge would do. That was her task now, to find a weapon.

Glays clapped his hands. A woman appeared, bowing. "My lord?"

Her name was Nadwyn. She had been introduced as Ren's new handmaiden but was, in truth, her jailer. Meg, her handmaiden since birth, was in the dungeons with the others. This woman was as tall as a man, with short black hair. She wore a stern grey dress with a black stitching. Her narrow black eyes regarded Ren's bruised lips without comment.

"Take the Princess Gwyndolyn back to her chamber. She's had a fall."

The priest picked up the scroll again, as if his mind were already on other matters. The woman took Ren's arm, her strong fingers digging painfully into muscle. "Come with me, Princess."

Ren detested her. She had no doubt she could best her in a fight, despite the woman's formidable appearance, but now was not the time. Feigning weakness, she allowed herself to be led from the room.

After they'd gone, Gothmog stepped forward. "She'll murder you first chance she gets," he said.

Glays appeared to be honestly amused. "Oh, come now, Gothmog. You just don't understand women. Their deepest need is to subjugate themselves to a man's strength. She fights it now, like a young mare fighting the bridle. But she'll learn."

"If you say so, m'lord."

The magician kept his judgments to himself. The priest was oblivious to the danger the girl presented. His assumptions, his ideology, his very self-image made it impossible for him to take any woman seriously, much less a nubile teenager.

He was glad that playing counsel to the man was a dwindling concern. In three weeks, or less time if the stars were favorable, he would no longer have to put up with the preening dolt. He'd accomplished what he'd set out to do. Barad'An was damaged beyond repair. Success was at hand. In a very short time, the priest would be a non-issue.

"I trust the preparations are on schedule?" Glays asked, picking up another scroll. A list of wedding guests, Gothmog noted.

Since Cuchulain's death, the priest had grown ever more aloof and self-involved. Other than wedding the girl, little seemed to interest him. He made no effort to attend to the affairs of the city, leaving such matters in the hands of newly appointed deputies. With his recent talk of an alliance, rather than the agreed-upon vassalage, it was unlikely he planned to honor the bargain, yet he'd done nothing to prepare for the city's defense. Maybe he truly believed this god of his would save him. More likely the priest was slipping into madness.

For Gothmog, it made no difference. Either way it would end the same. If Glays honored the bargain to turn the city over to the sirdar's general, so be it. If he chose defiance, what matter? With Barad'An so weakened, it would be impossible to mount a serious defense.

"Preparations for the wedding are well in hand," Gothmog said aloud. "The hall is being readied as we speak."

"Musicians?"

"Three local groups."

"Excellent. Come with us, then. We wish your opinion on a new robe acquired for the wedding. It's from the east."

Gothmog dutifully followed Glays to his dressing chamber, though in his mind he was already anticipating nightfall. Templars patrolling the forest had brought in a young man, a stable boy from the north. He was strong, naïve, and, most importantly, in excellent health.

Gothmog had decided his last subject must have had some disease he'd missed. This new one should be perfect.

CHAPTER 51

THE GOLDEN DAWN boasted a common room easily twice the size of the one at Ardendell's inn. Much of it was now hidden in darkness. Light shone from behind the kitchen doors, but Gregory had not yet returned.

"It began the day the king was murdered," said Bors, glancing over his shoulder toward the kitchen. Nick couldn't tell whether he was concerned that he might be overheard, or impatient for food.

"They call it the 'cleansing,' a nasty name for butchery. Those unwilling to pledge their allegiance to the priest and his god are either imprisoned, or—" Bors stopped, his jaw tight. "You've seen the oaks, no doubt."

"We have," said Osmodon. "How many knights still live?"

"Difficult to say. A few survived the assassins and escaped into the forest. Belarane, the squire, Lord Claymore, Yvon Branch and his sons, Dorset, and Banks, all are dead. You now tell me Abdelar has also passed. A grievous loss. He was the best of us."

"You say some are held captive."

"It's impossible to know how many rot down there. Parsifal, Pelidon, Granvyl, and Thorson were taken, along with a dozen captains. Aerindir most recently."

"Where is Ren now?" Nick tried not to let his worry show.

"Prisoner in her own chambers, by accounts." Bors slammed his fist on the table. "Dammit! You know she's our last, best hope."

Nick and Osmodon exchanged glances. "You hinted you've a plan," said Osmodon.

Bors picked up his tankard, then set it down again without drinking. "Aye. Such as it is. We were hoping for more than the two of you to show tonight."

"There's time yet. How many men does the priest command?"

"Three thousand at least, with more arriving every day. Greedy for spoils mostly, though perhaps half also believe his fairy tales."

"How many can we count on?"

Bors looked at the two men, then smiled. It was not a pleasant smile. "Let's just say your arrival has more than doubled our current complement of knights."

There was a moment while this sunk in. Then Osmodon laughed. "We're it? We three?"

"Bleak odds, admittedly. But not so bad as it appears. There is support among the common folk, like these you've met here tonight." Bors clenched the handle of his tankard, and he drank.

The kitchen door opened and Gregory finally arrived with a pot of dense beef stew and a platter of bread and cored apples. A boy followed carrying bowls, napkins, and spoons. For a moment conversation abated as the bowls were filled.

Nick sorted his thoughts. Three against three thousand. Bors was neither as tall as himself nor as broad as Osmodon, but the man exuded strength. Balding and sunburnt, with a large, ragged cicatrix down the right side of a muscular neck, Bors appeared to be in his late forties. Though from recent experience, Nick had learned not to make assumptions about age.

Bors tore off a piece of bread, passing the loaf to Osmodon. "Few of the templars are real fighting men. They're farmers, dandies from Meridor, brigands, and freebooters mostly. With this holiday the priest declared, half are drunk, the other half doing their best to get that way."

"What of the sirdar's army?" Osmodon asked. "It will be at the gate within a month. They aren't prepared. The wall is unmanned, the soldiers poorly armed. Is the priest unaware of this?"

"He appears to be unconcerned. The true believers say his god will protect him."

Osmodon dipped his bread into his stew and chewed. "Sounds like Megida to me."

"Who's Megida?" Nick asked. The name seemed familiar, but he couldn't place it.

"Not who, lad, what. Megida's a city, or was. Its walls were not nearly so great as Barad'An's, yet still it was thought to be impregnable. It was the seat of the House of Seven Worlds, where the sorcerers of the Brotherhood were taught. Yet this current sirdar's father took it as easily as picking ripe fruit."

"It's always been suspected it fell to treachery," said Bors.

"The priest's magician, Gothmog, was an acolyte then," mused Osmodon, taking another bite of bread. "Sianiave said he was banished for practicing necromancy. It's why she holds him in such contempt. That and the general fact he's an evil little worm."

Bors nodded thoughtfully. "Necromancy? That puts a new light on it. If the magician is allied against humankind with some morbid demon, it's possible the priest isn't our biggest worry."

"Does this affect your plans?"

"Let me ask you this. When you arrived, did you notice any blue robes among those hanging from the oaks?"

"Sisters?" Osmodon stared at Bors in surprise. "I don't recall, though admittedly I wasn't looking too closely."

"There are none. The priest declared them traitors, and Saolin herself the architect behind Cuchulain's assassination, as if the Sisterhood hasn't protected the Ambergin line for over two thousand years. Yet when Glays's soldiers arrived to arrest them, they found the Tower empty, all 216 Sisters gone. Vanished. It's said Glays was beside himself for days, for he hates women, the Sisters most of all. He's turned their tower into barracks for his guard."

"Interesting. But how does this apply?"

"You may not know—few do—but like Abdelar I was once chosen by the Sisters, though I never completed the training. Still, a vow was required never to reveal what we learned. But there are vows and Vows. And a vow, after all, is only words, is it not?"

He stopped, as if waiting for a reply.

Osmodon nodded, closing his eyes as he searched his memory. "Men are made of words, and stories give meaning to those words."

Bors smiled, obviously pleased. "Good. I am released." He leaned forward, his voice dropping. "According to the Sisters, Barad'An was originally built over a series of granite caves. People would retreat to them for protection during times of crisis. But over time, as the city grew to its present size, the caves were forgotten. They became part of the sewer system, for a river flows through them."

"The Sisters escaped through the sewers?"

"So I believe. The Left Tower is the oldest structure in the city. A door must still exist."

"Useful knowledge. But unfortunately, we're not trying to escape."

"Think on it, my friend. Barad'An's dungeons must also be part of that cave system."

There was a moment of silence as this sank in. Then Osmodon slapped the table. "Forgive me for a dunce. Of course!"

Nick stared at the two men uncomprehending, then caught their meaning.

CHAPTER
52

"OPEN! OPEN IN THE NAME of the Prophet Glays, or we'll break the door down!" A loud banging shook the inn's front door.

The boy who'd helped them in the stables came running in. "Sir Bors! Guardsmen!"

Bors was already on his feet. "We heard. How many?"

"Ten by count."

"Warn Gregory and the others, then hide yourselves. Hurry!"

"We can fight."

"Let them have the tavern tonight. You can take them in the morning, when they're too drunk to stand. Remember, first light in the old stadium. Tell the others. Go!"

The boy ran toward the kitchen. Outside the clamor grew. "In the name of the prophet! Open or die!"

Osmodon stood, sword drawn. "Only ten? Why wait?"

"No!" Bors was already moving toward the back of the room. "Follow me."

Reluctantly, Osmodon sheathed his sword and followed the knight. Nick was close behind. There was more cursing, then a loud crash. The soldiers had a battering ram.

Bors led them through a door at the rear of the common room, which he barred behind them. "They're looking for ale, not us. This way."

They hurried down a narrow hall to a door. Behind it were crates and shelves full of plates, mugs, and utensils. Bors pushed aside a rack of wooden bowls, revealing the narrow opening to a tunnel. A lamp hung from a spike on the wall. He lit it with a flint and motioned them to follow.

Heads bowed, holding their scabbards to keep them from clattering against the walls, they continued for several hundred feet before the tunnel came to an abrupt end at a stone wall. At the bottom of the wall was a drainage hole, barely large enough for a man to crawl through.

"Every city has its underworld," Bors observed.

He unhitched his scabbard and dropped to his knees. "No talking from here on. The last one blow out the lamp." With that he disappeared into the hole.

Osmodon looked doubtful. "I'll plug it like a cork in a bottle."

"I'll go first," Nick offered.

"No. I may need a push from behind."

Sighing, Osmodon removed his sword and dagger, his belt and his leather vest, shoving these before him as he squeezed his bulk into the hole and crawled forward.

Nick waited until he could no longer see Osmodon's feet, then blew out the lamp and followed.

The tunnel was at least twenty feet long, its walls slick with mold. He reached a cistern where Osmodon hoisted him into open air.

They stood in a deserted alleyway that stank of urine and rot. The only light came from behind the shutters of a nearby second-story window.

They buckled on their weapons. Bors replaced an iron grate over the hole. "This way," he whispered, motioning to their right.

Osmodon hesitated. "Isn't the Left Tower the other direction?"

"You forget. The tower is a templar barracks now. Besides, it might take us days to find that door. Trust me."

They followed Bors down a wider street that was lit by bonfires fueled by broken furniture and wood torn from market stalls. The city, which had appeared so wondrous from a distance, had become dark and alien. Harsh laughter echoed in the distance. A woman screamed. A soldier with a tankard in his hand glanced in their direction but said nothing.

From alleyway to open street to yet another alleyway, they traveled for what seemed like miles to Nick before Bors finally stopped. They had come to center of the city, the Common Green. The park was now little more than a wild patch, a dense and dark forest in which one man or many could easily be lost.

A path led into the trees. "This way," Bors whispered.

Nick kept up by using his sense of hearing rather than sight. Deep into the park Bors stopped, lighting an oil lamp he'd removed from behind a bush. Before them was a large fountain, easily twenty feet high. It was crowned by a marble statue of a lion and unicorn, rampant. The fountain was in disrepair, empty of all but rainwater.

Bors led them to the far side of the fountain, where he revealed a grate hidden beneath a cloak of branches. He kicked the branches aside and lifted the metal frame.

"Down there you'll come to the main tunnel. Follow it to your left. Continue to follow it left whenever it branches. The way is marked with the rune for 'forward,' a trident, like this."

The knight held up three fingers, then turned to leave.

"Wait!" cried Osmodon. "Aren't you coming with us?"

"No. I'm to join the city folk gathering in the stadium. They need one of us to lead them. Have faith. Keep to the left and follow the runes. You'll come to a wall. In this wall, you'll find a stone door with an iron ring. Pull on the ring. The door should take you into the dungeon."

"Should?" Osmodon shook his head in disbelief. "By the gods, Bors! You haven't tried it, have you?"

"An old man I located who worked in the sewers told me about it. I trust him."

"An old man? Bors, this is no plan. It's a wild hope!"

Bors grinned. "Come, my friend. You're famous for your courage, and your friend certainly doesn't appear shy. If you're unable to locate the door, return the way you came. We'll meet at the stadium. The wedding begins at the dawn hour in the Ceremonial Hall. We have men inside who will see the doors are opened when needed."

Osmodon peered into the dark hole. "Well and good, but—"

"Take this lamp. There are torches at the bottom of the shaft for when the oil runs out. If you should meet the magician, dispatch him quickly. His helper is a half-breed troll by accounts, immensely strong but dumb as a brick. You should have no trouble."

"Just the two of them?"

"Aye, though there may be guards at the top of the stairs. Good luck." With that Bors turned and vanished into the darkness.

Osmodon stood, holding the lamp. "Well, damn my eyes. What do you make of that?"

"You don't really mean to go down there, do you?" asked Nick.

"Not my first choice," replied Osmodon glumly. "But like the man said, if we can't find the door, we can always come back."

Nick peered down into the black hole and sighed. "Right."

CHAPTER
53

Gallian
June 5

BRONWYN FOUND ELLOHIR sitting on a veranda, gazing at the valley below. There had been no word from Sir Osmodon and Sir Nicholas, nor from Sianiave.

The night was warm, and the scent of frangipani and roses hung in the air, flowers she'd cultivated herself. She took a seat beside her husband, enjoying the peaceful moment, which she knew to be achingly ephemeral.

The sirdar's army had passed by Gallian three days before, leaving behind three brigades to guard the entrance. The army was larger than first reported, at least eighty thousand strong. There was no doubt that a morghul commanded. Bronwyn had sensed its poisonous thoughts even as the army approached.

After a long silence, Ellohir spoke. "Ren is the key," he said slowly, as if the thought was new to him. "Without her Barad'An is nothing but an empty fortress, without heart or soul, not worth the life of one of our folk."

Bronwyn remained silent. She knew this was hard for her husband.

"Do you the think the priest knows this of her?" he asked.

"He has no understanding at that level, I think."

"If she were not at this moment in Barad'An, we would remain here, in Gallian."

"But she is there."

"Aye. But—"

Ellohir stopped, unable to continue with the idea, for it was deep, and he had not yet thought it through. Bronwyn could see this, and was proud of him for understanding as much as he did.

"We must go to Barad'An," he said finally. It was half a question.

"Yes," she said.

Ellohir stood, and a great weight seemed to have lifted from his shoulders. "Good. I'll give the word."

"And the brigades outside?"

"We'll leave through the caves. A messenger can advise Penthys and the others. We'll meet at Graylen Tor. Perhaps we can surprise even this morghul general."

CHAPTER 54

Western Coast
June 5

WHEN SIANIAVE SAW THE OCEAN, tears fell down her cheeks. It was not because her long search was almost ended, though it was a clear day and, less than twenty miles distant, she could make out the white cliffs of the island that was her destination.

No, not the island but the sea itself touched something deep within her soul. The waves crashing restlessly against the sandy beach, the moist touch of the salt air, the cry of the seabirds in their ceaseless search for food. The Mother: patient, eternal, healing.

The tears caught her by surprise. She promised herself that when she completed this task, she would find a house in that other world, by the sea. She would remove her amulets, the stones and crystals, and embrace the forgetfulness, erase her long past.

The memories would return, of course, when she was needed.

It had been too long since she'd let go. Her emotional reaction to seeing the ocean told her it was time again. Her body could replenish itself endlessly, but her soul needed care. She had known others who had not taken such precautions. Over time, they had simply faded from existence.

She spurred Phaeton down onto the sand, in the direction of the little village that nestled under the cliffs at the far end of the beach. They would have boats to take her to the island.

CHAPTER
55

Barad'An
June 5

OSMODON LACED THE LAMP to a belt loop, then tested a handhold with his weight. Muttering imprecations, he slowly began to descend. Nick counted to twenty and followed, pulling the grate back over the opening as he did so.

The shaft dropped straight down; how far was impossible to tell. Even with Osmodon's lamp to light the way, they couldn't see the bottom. Some of the handholds were so worn they offered no grip at all. These they inched past by pressing their backs against the opposite wall.

It seemed like an eternity, though it had probably been no more than fifteen minutes, when Nick finally heard Osmodon call out. "Watch it here, lad. Don't lean back. The shaft opens into the main sewer."

Then, "I see the bottom. Pile of torches there. Almost down."

There was a muffled thump as Osmodon dropped to the floor, followed by the sharp sound of breaking glass as the light went out.

Osmodon swore. "Damn. Broke the lamp. Hold on."

Nick had an anxious moment while Osmodon fumbled in his pocket for a flint. There was a spark, and a torch burst into flame. Nick quickly let himself down, dropping the last few feet.

They were in a vaulted chamber. Arched tunnels opened in all directions. Effluent trickled through the shallow culverts in the center of each tunnel toward a large central drain. The air was dank and musty but smelled more of moldy leaves than sewage, for which both men were grateful.

The stone floor was covered in black, grainy silt and littered with debris. Nick counted eight torches left by Bors, nine including the one in Osmodon's hand.

"Bors said to go left," said Osmodon, turning in a circle. "But left of what?"

Three tunnels led off the chamber, each of similar size. Nick pointed to a trident-shaped rune carved on the right side of the nearest opening. "There."

Conversation was short. They continued left whenever the tunnel branched. Even their whispers seemed to echo. Osmodon's torch cast ghostly shadows on the rounded walls. At times they found themselves struggling through knee-deep piles of debris—leaves, branches, the rotted carcasses of animals, and things even less wholesome.

When they stopped to get their bearings, they heard other sounds: the rustle of small creatures scurrying for cover, the quick slithering of a snake as it disappeared into a tangle of dead leaves. More disturbing was the dry, ominous chitter of rats. The sound had been with them for at least the past half hour.

More than once, Nick had glimpsed the sharp face of a gigantic grey rat staring out from the darkness, its red eyes bright with menace. He mentioned this to Osmodon, for he had the unmistakable feeling it was actually stalking them. He imagined he could hear its thin, malignant thoughts. *Patience, brothers. They're strong now, and armed. But we'll have them soon. Patience.*

The darkness became more oppressive the further they traveled. One rat—Nick was certain it was the same one that had been following them—scurried past and stood unblinking in the passageway ahead. Only after Osmodon threatened it with the torch did it leap to the side. There it remained, out of range, continuing to glare at them with feral intensity.

They had burned through all but two of their torches, still with no sign of the door Bors had spoken of, when abruptly they came to another large chamber, off of which three tunnels branched.

Osmodon's torch had burned almost down to his hand. He touched the dying flame to one of their two remaining torches and tossed the shard into the culvert. "We'd best find that door soon. I don't fancy being caught down here in the dark." It was an unpleasant thought.

"We can burn driftwood," Nick suggested.

"Aye. Though it burns too quickly." Osmodon gave a nod over his shoulder to where there were now rows of red eyes peering at them from out of the darkness. "They've been gathering."

"I've noticed," said Nick.

He studied the openings to the three tunnels. He could find no rune to point the way. Bors had said keep left, but the tunnel furthest to their left held little appeal. Smaller than the others, its entrance was covered by an enormous spiderweb. Bones of a dozen small animals hung in its weave.

Osmodon handed the torch to Nick and drew his sword. He swung at the web, but the blade stuck to the thick strands and only with difficulty was he able to pull it free. "By Asgar, it's like pitch! Try the torch."

Nick held out the torch so the flames touched the web. It resisted momentarily, then with unexpected suddenness flamed into ash. On the left side of the wall behind the web, they found the rune.

The sinister chatter of the rats grew louder. Dozens of the vermin were now gathered behind them, the smallest the size of a house cat. *Almost time. Almost time.*

Osmodon's sleeve caught on a loose strand of web. As he pulled his arm free, a spider with a body the size and color of an eggplant dropped onto his shoulder. Its six segmented legs were as long as Nick's forearm, the bloated abdomen as shiny black as polished ebony. Osmodon turned his head to see six opaline eyes staring back into his own.

"Gods!" He shrieked, twisting and reaching for his dagger as he tried to shake the creature off.

"Hold still!" cried Nick. He swung the torch against the spider, knocking it from its perch. As if made of the same flammable stuff as its web, the spider abruptly caught fire, scuttling like a living torch back into the tunnel. Its screams sounded eerily human. They echoed for a long moment before finally trailing off.

The rats paused, breaking ranks as many fled back from where they'd come.

"Gods," muttered Osmodon, again brushing his shoulder. "The size of that thing!"

Nick looked back at the rats. "We'd better go. Our friends seem to be regaining their courage."

They moved off down the tunnel at a near run, Nick in the lead. Unlike the previous tunnels, this one had no center culvert to channel water. Even the walls were different, more natural and cave-like.

"Listen," said Nick, pausing. "You hear it? Water. Lots of it."

"The river, you reckon?"

The tunnel curved to the right, coming to an abrupt end at a deep fissure, the other side of which was a smooth stone wall. The fissure was at least twelve feet across, and out of the crack came the sound of rushing water. At one time a wooden bridge had spanned the break, but the bridge had long ago fallen away, and now only the stone bolsters remained.

On the opposite wall, Nick could make out an iron ring embedded in the stone, and the thin outline of a door marked with a trident rune.

"By Asgar!" muttered Osmodon. "I was beginning to lose faith in our friend Bors."

"Just in time," Nick said quietly.

He lit their last torch, dropping the stub of the previous one in the fissure, counting the seconds before the flame was extinguished in the torrent below.

"Fifty feet," he observed.

"I'm more concerned with the width of this crack," said Osmodon as he unbuckled his sword belt. "Never been much of a jumper. Need a running start to make it. And once over, doesn't look like we'll be able to get back. Not with so little room there."

"I'll go first," Nick offered.

Osmodon shook his head and smiled. "Sorry, lad. Age before beauty. Toss these to me when I'm over." He handed Nick his sword and dagger.

Before Nick could object, Osmodon had sprinted forward. His leap was poorly executed, and he came up short of the landing, barely managing to catch the far lip of the fissure with his hands. Nick held his breath as the big man struggled to pull himself onto the ledge.

"Nothing to it," he declared, dusting himself off as he stood. "Stay where you are. No use us both getting trapped here if I can't get the door open."

He took hold of the iron ring and pulled. The door gave several inches, then held. "It'll open, I reckon. But I may have to pry it with my sword."

"Hold on," said Nick. "I'll give you a hand. I'm not going back alone. Not with those rats waiting."

He tossed Osmodon's weapons across, along with his own, then the torch. Osmodon set them against the wall and braced himself to catch Nick.

Nick took a long running jump, landing well on the ledge, but something slick underfoot caused him to lose his balance and send him skidding painfully into the wall.

"Serves you right for trying to show me up," laughed Osmodon, helping him to his feet.

"Like you said," grimaced Nick. "Nothing to it."

They buckled on their weapons and faced the door. Both took hold of the ring and Osmodon counted, "One, two, three!"

With a grinding of stone against stone, the heavy door inched slowly outward. Then, abruptly, it broke free, swinging open with such weight and speed Nick barely managed to avoid being thrown backward into the fissure. As he scrambled to save himself, his right foot caught the torch, sending it spinning across the floor. It teetered at the lip of the chasm for a brief moment, then disappeared over the edge.

CHAPTER
56

REN WAS NEAR EXHAUSTION, but sleep was out of the question. Morning was only a few hours away, and she had yet to find a weapon. A long needle would do, or a shard of glass.

The problem wasn't the lack of such implements. The problem was the woman, Nadwyn, and her two helpers. They never left her side.

She had originally planned to kill the priest soon after the ceremony, when they were alone. But now she knew she could not wait that long. She would never take the marriage vows.

Bronwyn had hinted at this before she'd left Gallian, reminding her that marriage was a sacred pact, particularly for one of the high-born, symbolizing the divine balance. The power and potency of symbols and ritual, of sworn word, had been drummed into Ren since childhood.

She had to strike before the vows were exchanged. That left only a short time for her to act. She never would have thought herself capable of killing with such cold conviction, but her duty lay heavy on her and, after the horrors she'd witnessed since her return, her compassion was in short supply.

Nadwyn reached out to touch her swollen lips. "That bruise is healing nicely. A little powder and gloss and no one will notice. Now you must get some rest."

Ren started at the touch, but something in the woman's eyes, a subtlety in her voice, gave her pause.

Desire. Nadwyn had hidden it well.

Ren had been told of certain individuals, a few in the Sisterhood itself, who were known as the third sex. Such people were rare and generally revered. They had an innate, intuitive understanding of the nature of balance. They often made excellent magisters and healers.

But there was another sort, like Nadwyn, who knew little of balance. They identified with only one side of the great scale, and in doing so allowed themselves to become agents of corruption. Ren suddenly knew what she must do.

Smiling with a shyness she didn't feel, she placed her hand on the woman's. "Your hand is cool," she murmured, using the voice to mirror the woman's own desire. Nadwyn was cruel and naturally suspicious. Ren knew she would have to use every device the Sisters had ever taught her about seduction.

"I can't sleep," she said.

"You need your rest. You are to marry the most powerful man in the kingdom in the morning."

"Men do not interest me." Ren's voice was low as she looked directly into Nadwyn's eyes. "Not in that way."

Her fingers touched Nadwyn's wrist lightly. She felt the pulse quicken.

There was a long moment of silence, Nadwyn's instinctive caution fighting a growing desire. "Leanna, Portia!" she barked suddenly. "You are free to go."

"But Nadwyn—"

"I will attend to the princess. She needs her sleep, and she won't get any with you two lurking about. Leave us!"

"Of course, ma'am."

The one called Leanna bowed and left. Portia, a stout girl with sallow skin and a distinct pout, stood her ground. She glared at Ren, her resentment obvious. Jealousy, Ren saw.

"Nadwyn—"

"Go!" the handmaiden snapped.

The girl opened her mouth as if to retort, then abruptly closed it, and with a venomous glare at Ren, stomped off and slammed the door behind her.

Nadwyn's mouth came close to Ren's cheek. "If I had known—"

"There's time."

It was the only encouragement Nadwyn needed. She drew Ren to her in a powerful embrace, forcing their lips together. Ren's hand fell to Nadwyn's thigh. A dagger was hidden there under the woman's dress, as she suspected.

Nadwyn carried Ren to the bed and laid her down, disrobing her as if she were undressing a doll. When Ren was naked, she removed her own clothes, letting the dagger drop to the floor. Ren lay pliantly, pretending to enjoy the attention but inwardly picturing what she must do.

Nadwyn fell on top of her, kissing her mouth and neck, her right hand stroking her thigh. Ren groaned and allowed her right arm to fall back, as if in pleasure, near where the dagger lay.

Almost.

Nadwyn raised her head.

In a movement so quick Nadwyn had no time to react, Ren jerked the dagger from its sheath and drove it straight into Nadwyn's eye. The woman shuddered once, and lay still.

Quickly Ren shoved the body aside and staggered from the bed, her breath coming in great gulps. Shaking, she took hold of the dagger's hilt and pulled it free.

She had a weapon now. She must calm herself. There were things to do: hide the corpse, get rid of the bloody sheets, wash herself, come up with a story to explain Nadwyn's absence.

Slowly her breathing returned to normal and the trembling grew less.

CHAPTER
57

NICK SWORE UNDER HIS BREATH. "What now?"

"Give me your sleeve," said Osmodon. "The linen will burn easier than my leather. Steady now."

Osmodon used his dagger to cut a length off Nick's right sleeve, then wrapped it around the blade. Nick heard the sound of a flint, and for a brief second the tunnel was ablaze with light as the makeshift torch almost exploded into flame.

"Damn!" cried Nick, jumping back. "What did you put on that?"

"Polishing oil. Let's go. It won't last long."

The door opened on a narrow passageway. The stench was overpowering. They had entered a charnel house. A stream of blood ran down the center of the passageway, the awful ooze that had caused Nick to lose his footing.

Swords in hand, they moved quickly down the passage. Within a hundred yards the torch began to sputter.

"Your other sleeve," said Osmodon.

As Nick tore off his remaining sleeve, some sixth sense caused him to lower his head. There was a whooshing sound as a spiked club the size of a fence post smashed into the wall behind him, missing his ear by less than an inch.

A nightmare stepped out from the gloom with a face that seemed a bloated mockery of a human's. A bloodstained apron girdled his waist, and a large ring hung from his belt rattling with iron keys.

"Gods," muttered Osmodon, removing his sword. "A bloody troll. What next?"

The creature belched. His teeth were stained and rotted. Nick noted the tongue seemed to be missing. He moved to the creature's right. The monster appeared not to notice. His attention was on Osmodon, who still held the faltering torch.

"I take it you're the one responsible for the mess on the floor?" said Osmodon.

Bellowing in rage, the monster swung. Osmodon jumped backward, barely avoiding the club. Seeing an opening, Nick shoved his dagger into the creature's ribs. It grunted and jerked away, the dagger still locked in his side.

Radlik bellowed in pain, his slow mind just now beginning to grasp the precariousness of his situation. Who were these men? Did they work for the priest?

"By Asgar, you're an ugly one," taunted Osmodon, moving closer.

Still Radlik hesitated. He must warn Master Gothmog.

Osmodon thrust with his sword, piercing Radlik's right shoulder. Radlik wailed, bringing his club down, but Osmodon had already stepped out of reach.

Blood poured from Radlik's wounds. He lashed out again with the club. Nick swung his sword and severed the creature's left wrist. Radlik bellowed again as the warted hand fell to the floor.

"Go, lad!" cried Osmodon. "I'll finish this fellow!"

It was clear the fight would soon be over. Nick recalled Bors's warning: If they should encounter the magician, kill him quickly.

"Go!" yelled Osmodon again.

Nick slid past the creature's flailing club. The beast's grunts had become a pitiful mewling. It would be over before the torch Osmodon still held died.

There was light ahead where an iron door stood open. A voice echoed down the corridor, a chant of some sort. "*N'ash ash iskan gashsa. Nash ash ishkan hasha….*" It seemed somehow familiar.

Not the words, Nick realized. It was the feelings they evoked: cruelty, hatred, lust.

There was no time left. He did not know how he knew this, only that he had to end that awful chant before it reached its conclusion.

The door was unlocked and he burst into the chamber. A small, ferret-faced man stood near an open brazier. He was dressed in a dark robe and held a black stone above his head. A boy, stripped to the waist, was chained to the stone wall.

Nick took this in at a glance. What held his attention, however, was not the man, who had turned toward him enraged, nor the look of abject terror on the boy's face. It was the small circle of blackness above the boy's head, vivid against the wall. The anomaly in the air was not just black, but utterly and completely devoid of light.

Nick had known evil in his life, had even lived with it as a foster child. He knew the black void that can engulf a person when life is bereft of meaning and hope. But never had he encountered anything so profoundly foul as what hovered in that black circle.

"Get out!" screamed Gothmog, the stone held like a weapon as he lunged.

The stone cut through Nick's leather jerkin as cleanly as a razor, but drew only a thin line of blood. Nick pivoted, his own blade sweeping downwards, skinning the left side of the magician's face and lopping off an ear.

Snarling in maniacal fury, Gothmog threw himself on Nick, his teeth sinking into Nick's forearm. Nick smashed a fist into the mess he'd made of the magician's face, sending him sprawling across the room. With a shriek that sounded much like the spider he'd flamed in the sewer, Gothmog scuttled sideways and disappeared through the open door.

"Sir, please. Sir Nicholas, help me!"

Hearing his name, Nick turned in surprise. The foul halo had vanished. He looked closer and with a shock recognized the stable boy from Ardendell.

"Will? How in heaven—"

As he looked around for a way to release the boy from his chains, Osmodon appeared in the doorway.

"Try these," said Osmodon, tossing him Radlik's key ring.

"The magician ran. Be careful. He's quick."

The lock on the boy's shackles was small, and the smallest key opened it. Nick caught him as he collapsed forward. "Let's get you out of here."

He carried the boy into the corridor and set him down with his back to a wall.

"Please, sir. Don't leave me here."

"You'll be all right. I'll be back." Nick hoped he sounded reassuring, but he could already hear the distant clangor of alarm bells.

He caught up with Osmodon in the main dungeon. It was lined on both sides with overcrowded cells full of hollow-eyed prisoners.

"The keys!" cried Osmodon. "Open the cells! The bloody magician got away. There'll be guards down here any minute."

Aerindir was in the first cell Nick unlocked.

CHAPTER
58

AERINDIR HAD LOST WEIGHT and color, but his eyes blazed with a savage intensity as Nick unlocked his chains. "Well met, Sir Nicholas! How many are you?"

"Just me and Osmodon. Bors is with a contingent above. We came in the back door."

"Two only?" Aerindir staggered slightly as he stood, but soon found his footing. "The magician ran past as though the hounds of the seven hells were after him. He sounded the alarm."

"Here! Help us, let us out!" The clamor from the other prisoners grew. His fingers fumbling as he searched for the right key, Nick unlocked cell after cell. Prisoners surged out: men, women, even small children, perhaps a hundred in all, many barely able to stand or even speak.

There would be a fight, he knew. Retreating through the sewers was out of the question. Aerindir, with Osmodon's help, quickly sorted out those who appeared fit enough to fight, twenty in all. The rest were women, children, and men too old, weak, or sick. Nick wondered how many soldiers were on their way.

"Weapons?" asked a tough-looking old veteran. "Have you weapons for us?"

"Fletcher!" cried Aerindir, grabbing the old man in a bear hug. "All this time you were here? By the gods, after your stand on the wall we thought you done for."

"Aerindir, my boy."

Fletcher held up his arm. A dirty bandage covered the stump where his right hand used to be. "I'll never pull a yew again, but my left hand can still wield a sword."

"Follow me," said Aerindir. "There's an armory."

Aerindir led them to nearby door that Nick opened with a key. Pikes, daggers, triflects, and swords lined the walls in orderly racks. All were covered in the rust and dust of ages, probably unused in generations, Nick thought. Aerindir drew a sword, checked its edge, then balanced it in his hand. "It's not Drakulsyr, but it's still sharp. It will do."

"Hurry," someone said. "They're coming!"

The weapons were quickly handed out. The heavy clatter of hobnailed boots could be heard as they neared the bottom of the stairway. No formation or discipline there, thought Nick.

"We can fight!" shouted a tall, buxom woman. "Give us weapons."

She stood with several other women, their dresses torn, faces filthy with grime. Some were middle-aged, one appeared no older than fourteen, but all wore looks of fierce determination.

"Maewyn," said Osmodon, recognizing the woman who had spoken. "She's a wench from the Dawn."

The woman drew herself up to her full height, which topped Osmodon's by a good two inches. "Was a wench, until I slapped one of their kind and blasphemed their puking prophet. Do you decline the help of an honest serving maid?"

Osmodon laughed and tossed her a sword. "To the contrary. I'm just glad it's them you're to face and not me."

The soldiers had reached the bottom of the stairs. Nick counted eight as they pushed their way into the dungeon. Their leader was a big, bleary-eyed sergeant in a stained templar robe. "What the hells goes on here?" he blustered, angry at having to cut short his drinking. "Get back in your cells, you bloody scum. All of you! By the prophet, you'll suffer for this!"

The sergeant seemed unable to understand the situation. He strode forward, his pike lowered. He stopped when he saw Nick. "Who in the bloody hells are you?"

The words were hardly out of his mouth when Nick's sword flashed and the sergeant's head tumbled to the stone floor.

"Good answer," remarked Osmodon dryly.

The fight that followed was brief. Nick's anger had been growing ever since he'd entered the magician's workshop and found Will chained to the wall. At that moment, in the circle of black light that had hovered over the boy's head, he had recognized something so alien and foul it was impossible to put words to it. All he knew was that it was the embodiment of all that he hated, everything he had fought against his entire life. Now that anger was growing into something else entirely, a rage of a kind he'd never experienced, subsuming all rational thought.

Nick killed three of the soldiers. The others were done in by Aerindir, Osmodon, and Maewyn. More guardsmen came clattering down the stairs. Nick met them at the bottom, cutting down the first man, then two more in quick succession. How many died under his blade he never knew, for his rage blocked all else out but the killing. The priest's ill-trained soldiers stood no chance.

The landing was soon running with blood. His boot slipped, and he almost went down. Osmodon's strong arm steadied him. "Easy, lad. Let others have some of the fun."

Nick pulled away and started up the stairs as more guardsmen descended. He parried a pike thrust and took off a leg. The man toppled and fell screaming down the stairwell to join the bodies piling up below. More thrusts, more parries. Time ceased to have meaning.

And then it was over.

Nick found himself alone at the top of the stairs with little memory of how he'd gotten there. He stepped into a high-ceilinged room, looking sharply about for more enemies. Instead he was greeted by the sight of a weathered old man seated at a tall, narrow desk. The man was writing on a scroll with a quill pen. A candle burned nearby. He wore a high-collared black coat, and long white hair fell to his shoulders. A scrivener or clerk was Nick's first surmise, though the idea that a scribe would be there at that place and time of night was absurd.

He appeared unaware of the fighting that had just taken place. He looked up from his work, frowning as he saw Nick. Or was the frown an illusion caused by his craggy features and odd appearance? Beneath his shaggy eyebrows, his eyes actually appeared to twinkle. "You'd best hurry," he said. "It's almost dawn, you know."

The meaning of the words struck Nick like a blow. Dawn already?

Forgetting the old man, Nick sprinted toward an open door. The chill of the morning air took his breath away. The sun was not yet up, but its first light painted a golden sheen over the city. Somewhere a cock crowed.

A huge, temple-like structure several blocks away stood out. Its walkways and windows were ablaze with torches and lamplight. There was little doubt this was the hall where the wedding was to take place.

Nick turned back, but the old man was gone. His desk, chair, pen, candle, and inkwell had also vanished. Osmodon, Aerindir, and Fletcher were standing where they had been. Why were they staring at him?

He shook his head as though waking from a trance. He hadn't slept in many hours and fatigue was setting in. There was a painful throbbing at his temples and his sword arm burned as if with a fever. He remembered the magician's bite. It had seemed inconsequential at the time.

He looked down at himself. He was covered head to foot in blood. No wonder they stared.

A blare of trumpets sounded from the Ceremonial Hall. Blind rage had been replaced by another emotion, the overriding sense that time was running out. "Follow me!" he cried.

"Hold up, lad!" said Osmodon. "The stadium's the other direction."

"There's no time!" shouted Nick over his shoulder.

"He's right," said Aerindir. "The wedding has already begun."

CHAPTER
59

THERE IS NO NOW BUT NOW. All is part of the Whole. Even at the center of a whirlwind there is stillness.

A small hand tugging at Ren's sleeve interrupted her meditation. "M'lady, the horns—"

"I have ears," she snapped.

She looked down to see a flower girl staring up at her, a look of hurt surprise on her small face. She held a basket of brightly colored impatiens.

"I'm sorry," said Ren, immediately contrite. "You're Semy, aren't you?"

"Yes, m'lady."

The girl's voice quavered. Ren stooped until their eyes were level. "Well, Semy," she whispered, "I didn't mean to bark."

Semy brightened. "It's all right. It's sad you have to marry that hateful man."

Ren blinked. She wanted to hug the child, but the wedding mistress intervened, grabbing Semy's arm. "Hush, child! What makes you speak such nonsense?"

"But, ma'am," said Semy earnestly. "Everybody says—"

"Everybody says nothing. If they do, they're fools. You don't listen to fools."

As the mistress dragged Semy off to her place in the procession, Ren caught the little girl's eye and winked.

At least two dozen women milled about in the passageway, though only eight would accompany her into the main hall. The seamstress, a prune-faced harridan, stood glowering at a distance. Ren had ordered her away. It was hard enough to keep the dagger in her dress hidden without the seamstress fussing about a loose thread or out-of-place pearl.

Breathe, she reminded herself.

She thought of Nadwyn's body hidden in a clothes hamper in the bedchamber. Portia was the only one who'd questioned her absence. Ren had sent her searching for her mistress in a distant part of the palace.

The thick makeup applied to hide her bruises itched. She lifted a hand to scratch her nose, then stopped. The horns had sounded again, this time joined by the steady rhythm of drums. Ren inhaled deeply, and let it out.

Bronwyn had said any wound that drew blood would be enough, but she had to be sure. She pictured the priest's hulking body, with its small mouth and fleshy lips, his repellent touch. She thought of her grandfather, of Abdelar, of the corpses hanging along the Great North Road.

I must not fail, she told herself. I will not fail.

The wedding mistress straightened a hair on Ren's head, then stood back admiringly. "It's time, my dear."

Ren gritted her teeth and nodded. Semy led the procession with her basket of flowers. A chorus of young girls followed, singing "The Bride of Morning," a village wedding song. But the priest had changed the traditional lyrics. "The bride of morning comes to her lover like a flower rising to the sun" had become "The morning bride responds to her master like a flower to the gardener."

The priest had made other changes as well. In the past, flower girls had carried white lilies and golden adelentiums in their baskets, symbolizing the merging of the sun and the moon. Glays did not approve of such concepts. To him the moon was but a pale reflection of the sun, women no more than ancillary appendages of men.

One thing the priest had left unchanged were the routes by which the bride and groom entered the great hall. Traditionally the bride rose from below, approaching through the underground hallway. The groom descended from above, down stairs that led to the wedding dais. In this way the groom was seen as spirit, descending from the sky, the bride as soul, rising from the earth. Glays imagined his descent from above as no more than his due.

Despite the changes, the ritual still carried tremendous power. Ren felt it even before she emerged from the passageway. The great hall, large enough to seat a thousand souls, was filled to capacity. A collective sigh greeted her as she entered.

Could she count on their help? She saw sympathy in their faces, but also fear. She scanned the hall, noting the priest's archers in the balconies above. Templars lined the aisles, ready to quell any dissent.

"Go ahead, dear," whispered the mistress, mistaking Ren's hesitation for fear. "This is a day you'll remember always."

If only you knew, Ren thought.

The priest was already on the dais as Ren approached. Her small entourage had dropped back, nearly out of sight of the audience. Anything that might have reminded people of the Mother had either been removed from the hall or positioned so it looked to be nonessential, even subservient. Glays wore robes fashioned from golden silk, trimmed in burgundy and spangled with jewels.

Templars surrounded the stage. Ren noted their positions, discounting them as threats. They would never reach her in time, though afterward they would have to be dealt with. She couldn't run, not in that absurd dress. It made her feel clumsy, the dagger hidden in her sleeve an awkward weight.

She turned to face the priest, noting with satisfaction his look of irritation when she didn't kneel as she'd been instructed. The drums sounded once more, then fell silent.

The magister appeared in his blue robe. Instead of the traditional three-chambered reed staff, he carried a gilded wooden cross. "Our Lord God Almighty has ordained the union of the Crown Princess Lady Gwyndolyn Ambergin and Lord Glays, prophet of God, steward of Barad'An and protector of Anor."

The magister had been chosen less for his legal knowledge than for the quality of his lungs, for his voice boomed like a herald's.

"We are gathered here to bear witness to the joining . . ."

Ren was fully alert now, ready for the moment when the chalice would be brought and the magister would hand it to Glays. Glays would drink of the sacred haoma, then, in turn, offer it to her. She would strike while his hands were busy with the large cup. For her to accept the chalice would be to accept the marriage. That she must not do, whatever the consequences.

The magister droned on, his voice almost hypnotic in its effect.

"…Agrees to obey her lord and husband in all matters, including those of bed and household…"

Guardsmen shifted nervously at their posts. For a brief moment even the magister's confident voice faltered. Glays himself was either oblivious to the darkening mood of the crowd, or was pointedly ignoring it.

"…Brought together in the eyes of God. Princess Gwyndolyn Ambergin, do you take this man, Lord Glays, prophet of God and steward of Barad'An, as your lawfully wedded husband?"

The words, when they came, caught Ren by surprise. The vows already? No chalice, no offering of haoma.

She wanted to kick herself. Of course he would have banned the taking of the haoma. It went against everything his religion stood for. Why hadn't she considered this?

The hall was deathly silent. It was as if the walls themselves were waiting for her answer. "Don't!" screamed a woman from the back row. "Don't do it, Ren! Don't betray us!"

The priest's mouth twitched in irritation. Two guardsmen grabbed the woman and dragged her screaming away. It was the distraction Ren needed.

She slid the dagger into her right hand and thrust it toward Glays. The magister exclaimed and stepped forward between them. She sliced his neck, the razor-sharp blade cutting through flesh as easily as through parchment. But as she planted her right foot for the crucial thrust into the priest's midsection, her left slipper caught in the hem of the dress.

Slight as the stumble had been, it gave the priest enough time to step clear. His hand shot out, grabbing her wrist and nearly breaking it. "You traitorous bitch!" he shrieked. The knife dropped. His closed fist struck her hard in the face, knocking her backward to the floor.

The magister clutched his throat. The blood leaking between his fingers had turned a ghastly black. He gave a panicky gurgle and fell forward onto the dais.

Glays blanched. "A poisoned blade? You'll pay for this. You'll pay dearly!"

Ren lay stunned. She felt no fear, only great sadness. She had failed; failed herself, failed her people.

Guards arrived, grabbing hold of her arms to drag her to her feet. "Leave her there!" snarled Glays. "I want the godless witch alive."

He lashed out with a leg, the kick landing squarely in Ren's stomach. Instinctively she pulled herself into fetal position, the thick folds of the dress the only thing between her and Glays's brutal attack.

"Watching your friends tortured will be the last thing you ever see!" he screamed. "I'll carve out your eyes myself! I'll give your traitorous heart to Gothmog!"

"Stop!" a man in the front row shouted. "You're killing her!"

Others in the audience were on their feet. "Stop it! Let her go! Let Ren go!"

Glays stopped, his face flushed with fury. For the first time since Ren's attack he seemed to remember where he was. His small, mean eyes glared out at the sea of faces. He'd staged this event to make clear to them who was their ruler, but now half the crowd was on its feet, screaming, "Down with the priest! Let Ren go! Beast! Murderer!"

"Kill them all!" screamed Glays. "Any who resist shall die."

Templars waded into the crowd, cutting down any who stood in their way. Arrows rained down from the mezzanine. Angry shouts soon turned to cries of pain and terror.

The great doors at the front of the hall swung open with a thunderous boom. Templars and citizens alike turned to see a man framed in the doorway. He was drenched head to foot in blood. In his right hand he held a sword, in his left a long dagger. Templars backed away as he strode toward the dais.

"Eanor?"

The name had been whispered, almost as a question. But others heard it, picking up the name and shouting it aloud. "Eanor! Eanor has come!"

Glays stood rooted. Eanor? Impossible. Then he remembered the squire's last words, and for the first time felt the chill of fear. "You'll die beneath a knight's sword—"

"Stop that man! A hundred empresses to the man that kills him!"

Those greedy or foolish enough to take up the challenge were cut down. An arrow flew from the mezzanine, then another. The man's sword moved as though it had a will of its own, easily deflecting them. Behind him dozens of armed men swarmed into the hall from outside.

The priest's slight hope was quickly dashed, for these men were not wearing the white robe. They were dressed in rags, commoner's clothes, some with bits and pieces of rough armor.

"Best we leave, m'lord," urged a guard. It was Borson Brand, his favored captain.

Suddenly Glays remembered Ren, his onetime bride-to-be. Kill her now—that would end it. He looked around, expecting to find her broken and cowering where he'd left her. Instead she was only three feet away, crawling toward him, the recovered knife in her right hand.

"M'lord, watch out!"

Brand's cry came too late. An excruciating pain buckled the priest's left leg. He stumbled backward, collapsing to the dais.

She'd cut him. The witch had cut him. Impossible! It couldn't be. A woman? God would never allow it!

Ren struggled to her feet, preparing for another thrust into the dying priest.

Brand cried, "M'lord, no!" Seeing in the priest's death his own hopes vanishing, the captain raised his sword and ran forward. But before he could strike, his blade was parried. Startled, he turned to face the new threat. "This isn't right," he thought, just before Nick skewered him through the heart and turned toward Glays.

The priest was still staring at Ren. "You filthy little—" he managed before Nick took off his head.

CHAPTER
60

THE FOG SLIPPED OUT of the forest, thick and damp, spreading in great billowing rolls as it approached the city. Some swore it was the work of the morghul who, it was now known, commanded the sirdar's army. It was said such creatures could influence the weather, as well as a man's thoughts.

In the wake of the slaughter at the Ceremonial Hall, Captain Fletcher had managed to bring together what remained of his wall guard. A scarce eighty men now stood watch where once there might have been a thousand. The calls echoed along the wall: "Post three, all's well," "Post nine, all's well."

Nick felt drained as he watched the creeping mist. The madness that had come upon him in the dungeons was gone, replaced by aimless lethargy. Exhausted, he had briefly slept later that morning, his dreams full of nightmarish images. His right arm ached with a deepening chill. The pain had lessened during the past hour, but the numbness that had replaced it was worse.

How many men had he killed that morning? Fifteen? Twenty? Once, he'd called himself a soldier. But now he felt the weight of eternity pressing down on him, as if he'd fought through countless lifetimes. He was tired of the fighting, men killing men, the pointlessness of it all.

Forcing his arm to move, he drew his sword, running the fingers of his good hand along the once-keen blade, now scaly with dried blood, notched in so many places it could be used to saw wood.

It deserved better. He should have cleaned it, but to what purpose? He'd done his job. What moved him now? Duty? Honor? This wasn't his city. Barad'An was a hollow, decaying fortress, fit for little more than the rats in the sewers. He wanted nothing more to do with it.

The death of Glays had ended instantly his hegemony within the city. The priest's men had fled like rodents. Those who fought had easily been dispatched. Others had been killed by mobs holding little sympathy for the men who had filled the oaks with their loved ones.

Bors had been appointed temporary steward. His first act had been to call a council of the remaining knights and captains. There was still the sirdar's army to be dealt with.

The council meeting had gone on for much of that afternoon. Many of those present favored abandoning the city and retreating to the keeps in the south. There was no time left to prepare, and too few able-bodied men to hold the great walls.

Nick agreed with this assessment, though he'd kept his thoughts to himself. The pain in his arm had grown worse, and with it a deepening depression. As the bickering and arguing dragged on into the evening, he'd slipped from the room. Some instinct had led him to the top of the wall. There he'd sat watching as the fog engulfed the city.

"Hoy, lad. Glad I found you." A nebulous shape separated itself from the gloom.

"Ozzy?"

Nick looked up, half annoyed by the interruption, yet glad for the company. "How did you find me?"

"Fletcher trains his lads well. They let you be, reckoning you wanted to be alone. Not much gets by them, even in this soup. Why did you leave the council?"

Nick shrugged. "Not my affair. Will they evacuate?"

"No. They voted to stay and defend."

"Oh. Why did they change their minds?"

"Ren came, bless her."

"Ren?"

Nick hadn't seen Ren since that morning, when Aerindir had carried her off somewhere. Later he'd felt too tired and ill to seek her out. He'd stayed away from most people throughout the day, wearied by the near-awe in which they seemed to hold him. "She's all right, then."

"Some mischief, a few cracked ribs. Bors and the other knights are behind her now. With Cuchulain dead and Artos gone, Ren now holds their fealty. She's certainly proven herself. In any event, it's done. They voted to forego her maturity. She's queen now."

"Queen?"

"Soon as she can be crowned, probably in the morning. And if the queen orders Barad'An to be defended, then it's to the death, if need be."

Nick mulled this over. He was glad Ren would be well. His memories of her were strangely vague, as though he'd heard or dreamt about her, not someone he imagined himself in love with.

"What about you?" he asked. "Will you stay?"

Even in the darkness and fog, he could sense Osmodon studying him, looking for a reaction, perhaps.

"Well now, that depends on you," Osmodon answered slowly. "Though to be honest, if I had my way I'd be on my horse and gone in the morning."

"It's up to you."

"You forget Sianiave, though admittedly this is one of those times I curse having taken the vow. She swore me to look after you. So where you go, I go."

"It's hopeless. They haven't a chance."

Osmodon sighed. It was a weary sound, full of regret. "Aye. Those were my thoughts as well. But Ren has put your name forward as commander. She wants you to lead the defense of the city."

This broke through the grey emptiness of Nick thoughts. "Me? You can't be serious."

"This is no jest. They sent me to find you. They await your answer."

Nick slumped against the parapet. "I'm a stranger here. Bors is better suited. The others must have had something to say. What about Aerindir?"

"Actually they all agree, Aerindir included. You made quite an impression."

"I was out of my mind."

"Nevertheless."

"It's something to do with that name, isn't it? Enor or something. They were chanting it in the hall."

Osmodon hesitated, again studying Nick with that oddly speculative look. "You really know nothing? About Eanor, I mean?"

Nick recalled the grendel's sly whispers, then shook his head.

"Nothing. I've heard the name mentioned a few times, is all."

"People in hopeless situations often draw courage from odd things," Osmodon mused, seeming relieved.

"Who is he?"

"Not is. Was. Eanor lived two thousand years ago, King Ambergin's greatest and most loyal knight. Folk still sing his tales. 'The Lay of Berengard' is one."

Osmodon began to sing. His voice was surprisingly melodious.

"At the king's command the knights set out,
For neither gold nor fame did they ride.
Eanor rode Grenfyr, and Thrandil by his side.
Fifty followed that day, to test the Witch King's—"

Pain exploded in Nick's head. "Ozzy—not now. Please."

"There are some who find my voice pleasing," said Osmodon, feigning hurt. "No matter. I can't remember all of it anyway. But the short of it is this. Ambergin was doing battle with the corsairs in the west when he learned the Witch King was preparing to take advantage by moving on Barad'An. He sent Eanor with fifty knights to Berengard, a keep overlooking Beren's Gate. We saw its ruins in the distance that day in the sledge, if you recall."

Nick nodded, though in truth he recalled no such thing. The pain in his head was too great.

Osmodon continued. "Eanor was to hold the pass until Ambergin could finish with the corsairs. But it took twenty-one days before their fleet retreated. When Ambergin finally arrived at Berengard, he found Eanor alone still standing, so covered in blood it was impossible to tell if he was a man or some dark thing from the hells. A circle of gold cloth under his sword belt was the only part of his garment not soaked red. From that day forward the Ambergin battle colors have been maroon and gold."

Nick lowered his head and sighed. "So that's it. They saw me covered in blood, but there was no circle of gold. People shouldn't put their faith in ancient heroes."

"True or not, that image, Eanor soaked in blood, is fixed in the legends of these people. You came storming into the wedding like that, red from head to toe, wielding your sword with a vengeance. To them, you are Eanor."

"My sword." Nick's reply was bitter. The faces of the men he'd killed that morning were forming in the fog, anguished, accusing. He tried to raise his sword to dispel them, but his arm hung like a dead weight. The numbness was working its way into his shoulder.

The pain in his head was becoming unbearable. The sword fell from his hand, landing with a clatter on the stone. The fog had grown thicker, enfolding him until he could no longer see even the shadow of Osmodon's face.

"Ozzy—"

"Guards!" cried Osmodon, sweeping Nick up in his arms. "Sir Nicholas is down!"

§

When he opened his eyes Nick was lying on a narrow bed. His clothes had been stripped away, and fresh sheets covered him. Ren sat in a chair beside the bed. Her face was cut and bruised, but to Nick she was still achingly beautiful. A glow surrounded her, indescribably intimate. How could he have forgotten?

Others were there, Osmodon and Aerindir among them.

Osmodon was the first to speak. "Good to see you awake, lad. We'd thought we'd lost you. With the Sisters gone, Ren was the only one left with the training."

"What happened?"

"You were poisoned," said Ren.

"Poisoned?"

Nick raised his arm. The skin looked yellow and bruised where the magician's teeth had pierced his skin, but the enervating numbness was gone, with it the emptiness that had filled his thoughts.

He looked around the room, a small infirmary in one of the wall towers. A warm glow from the corner fireplace cut the chill of the night air. Even the stones in the walls appeared to be set in some meaningful and miraculous pattern. For Nick the world once again seemed renewed and wondrous.

This was Barad'An as Ren knew it, he realized, not the rotting carcass of a once-great city, but a place of beauty and harmony, a place of the heart. And he understood the need to protect it, to protect her, for she was Barad'An.

As he looked into her eyes he saw that she was no longer a child, and he mourned the loss. But he also saw a new and unsettling strength, the wisdom of a true queen, and the awareness of her duty, which would take precedence over all else. It was this love that had healed him. But it was a love that he could no longer claim as his alone.

"We need you now, Sir Nicholas," she said.

"I am yours, my queen. I give you my fealty."

He wasn't sure if those were the right words, but no one bothered to correct him. Ren smiled, but there was a deep sadness in the smile, for she knew what his words meant, what they both were forsaking.

"I accept your fealty."

She reached out and stroked his head. "Rest. Let your strength return. You'll need it soon enough."

CHAPTER
61

"YOU CAN STILL CHANGE your mind," Osmodon said.

"You'd have me break my vow?"

"That wasn't a real liege vow. Truth is, I never heard anything quite like it. Besides, you can always say you weren't in your right mind, the poison and all."

Nick laughed. He knew Osmodon wasn't serious. The big man would be the first to lecture him on the sanctity of a man's word.

They were atop a ridge overlooking the eastern plain. Dust clouds stirred up by the approaching army blanketed the horizon. Nick saw for himself what the scouts had reported. The massive force laid waste to everything in its path. With the arrival of refugees fleeing the devastation, the population of Barad'An had easily doubled.

Some seasoned fighters appeared alone at the gate, but others arrived with their own companies, as many as twenty men at a time. Farm folk, woodsmen, traders, even bandits came seeking the imagined safety of Barad'An's great walls. Others came for glory, for whatever the outcome, this battle would be remembered for the ages.

At the height of its power, Barad'An had housed over a hundred thousand fighting men. Long-unused armories and forgotten storage rooms were reopened. Captain Fletcher's archers worked day and night feathering stores of arrows. Water was plentiful and the granaries could supply the city for a year. Livestock and fowl were herded into empty stables, and the city's many gardens, parks, and orchards could supply fruit and fresh vegetables.

"The dust makes it seem larger than it is," said Nick. "It will have camp followers, like any army."

"So long as a morghul commands," observed Osmodon glumly, "every jack one of them will fight to the death. He'll have the sirdar's witch-men with him. Already the air reeks of their sorcery. By Asgar, I hope the Sisters are up to it."

A contingent of forty-four Sisters had arrived that morning, sent by Saolin from the Sisterhood's ancient redoubt at Marduk. They would serve as physicians, and could work against the sorcery of the witch-men. The two hundred or so others who remained at the monastery would, according to Saolin's letter, "join in battle by other means."

The Sisters had gone to work immediately, setting up aid stations in preparation for the coming battle, while doing their best to clean out the debris left in their tower by the priest's men. There would be a ceremony that night to resanctify the temple. Nick had promised to attend.

Low, hovering clouds, the color of bruised flesh, were blowing in from the north, carrying something unclean. Nick had sensed it upon awakening that morning. He was familiar with it now, knew it for what it was: the first wave of the morghul commander's attack. Never again will you control me, for I know you now, Nick thought.

They were outnumbered, twenty to one by some counts. There was no sign of either Ellohir or the desert people, nor any word from Sianiave, though the Sisters said the sorceress had passed through Marduk weeks before, remaining only a night before continuing on toward some mysterious destination.

"Dismal odds," said Osmodon gloomily. "The scouts say at least ten Uruk tribes have joined them, while we have fewer than three thousand men to hold twenty miles of wall. They can surround us, attack anywhere."

They'd been over this a dozen times. As yet Nick had no answer. But Osmodon's remark about the odds set off a memory.

Weren't you the one who always argued that odds don't mean that much?

"Even should Ellohir manage to break out of Gallian," Osmodon went on, "at best he'll bring one or two thousand. It's a matter of numbers."

Numbers, Nick thought. A conversation about numbers. Where did I—

Then it came. They couldn't bring their numbers to bear!

He looked up. "Of course!" Without waiting for Osmodon, he reined Greywind around, spurring him back down the trail. "We have to get back!"

"Now what's gotten into him?" Osmodon asked aloud, then turned his horse to follow.

The trail was the same as they'd taken during their journey to Barad'An. Ten days, and the world had changed. The corpses had been cut from the trees; pyres had burned for days. The scent of daffodils and wildflowers had replaced the stench of rotting meat. The songs of the robins, starlings, and mockingbirds had driven out the screeching of the crows. Barad'An's wall was turning golden in the afternoon sun, and the polluted clouds had not yet crossed over the hills.

Nick was focused on his new strategy. After they'd ridden for some time, Osmodon broke the silence. "I've a confession to make. Should've told you sooner, but the time never seemed right."

"What do you have to confess? You deflowered another virgin?"

"Hardly a thing to warrant confession. No." Osmodon hesitated. "Remember, that night before Gallian when I said I reckoned Sianiave had brought you here so as you could marry Ren?"

"Yes."

"Well, I was wrong."

"Oh," replied Nick, eyebrows raised.

"A blind man could see how you felt toward one another. Still, if I'd used my head instead of listening to my sentiments, I would have worked it out sooner. The truth is, I didn't want to see you hurt."

"Worked what out sooner?"

"If Sianiave meant for you and Ren to marry, why was she so set on finding Artos?"

"Ren's uncle? What does he have to do with it?"

"Everything. You see, he and Ren were—are, if Sianiave is right about him still being alive—betrothed."

Nick felt like he'd been punched. "Betrothed? To her uncle?"

"Has been since she was seven. You see? So long as Artos was thought to be dead, the way was open. But if Sianiave is certain he's still alive, well, simply put, it wouldn't make sense for you to marry a girl already spoken for."

"Her uncle," Nick repeated dumbly.

"Don't take it hard, lad. It's their way, bloodline and all. Anyway, since you pledged your fealty, it's all a bit moot."

Nick struggled to speak. He felt bereft, the world turned on its head. As Ren's liege knight, he wasn't allowed to be her lover, much less marry her. At best, he would be allowed to kiss her hand or wear her token in battle. Despite this he'd held out hope. After all, they'd made Ren queen, despite her age. Things did change. Maybe Artos really was dead, as everyone save Sianiave seemed to believe.

Nick caught himself and laughed. What was he thinking? He'd be lucky to live through the week himself.

"Laughter was the last reaction I expected," muttered Osmodon.

Looking at the big man, Nick had a sudden insight. "You know about these things, don't you? Personally, I mean. It's Sianiave. You're in love with her."

"What? Me? With Sianiave?" Osmodon's cheeks puffed out as if to deny it. Then he closed his eyes and let out a great sigh.

"Of course I'm in love with her. Have been from the night I first laid eyes on her. Clear right off she wasn't the marrying kind. How else to be with her but take the vow?"

Nick shuddered, seeing his own fate.

"By Asgar," breathed Osmodon. "She'll not hear it from you. Promise me!"

"I expect she already knows."

"Your oath. Please."

Osmodon was looking at him with such earnest entreaty, Nick could only nod. "I promise. Sianiave will never hear the horrible truth from me."

"Good." Osmodon straightened in his saddle. "The animals need a run. I'll race you to the gate." Without waiting for an answer, head down, he spurred his horse into a gallop.

CHAPTER

62

THE SPECIAL COUNCIL MEETING Nick had asked for was held in a room in the Left Tower, following the Sisters' cleansing ceremony. The walls were three feet thick and windowless. To remove any taint of the priest and his kind, the Sisters had scrubbed the room with vinegar and alcohol and smudged the air with sage, suph, and kingsroot.

Nick waited, impatient, while the members of the council trickled in: Bors, Aerindir, Captain Fletcher, the old pikeman Ben Shafter, and fifteen others who represented various contingents in the city. They had little time.

Few had seen much sleep the past week. The enemy would be at the gate in less than forty-eight hours. Every member of the council had an essential role in the city's defense.

Last to arrive was Ren. She took her seat beside Nick at the head of the table. Without preamble, she spoke. "I know Sir Nicholas would not have called for this meeting were it not of extreme urgency, so I turn the proceedings over to him."

Ren's resolve was keenly focused, all signs of girlishness gone. Nick stood, nodding to the people gathered.

"I believe I have an alternative to our present plan of defense, one that will give Barad'An a chance for survival."

"A little late for changes, isn't it?" growled a portly, red-faced man across the table. Kamleth Kendren, Nick recalled, once mayor of

Barad'An and a leader among the guilds, or so he'd been told. Kendren had an irritating habit of interrupting, whether or not he knew anything about the subject at hand.

Nick ignored him and continued. "If what I have in mind is to succeed, we must decide on it tonight, before this meeting adjourns."

"Just say what you have to say so we can get on with our real business," sniffed Kendren.

The man's attitude caught Nick off guard. Kendren was annoying, but by all accounts a useful organizer within the guilds. Yet he felt animosity flowing from him like a toxic cologne. If what he was about to say should somehow make its way to the enemy—

He put the thought aside. Irritating he might be, but Kendren was an unlikely traitor.

"The morghul commander is the key," he said. "A morghul's power is said to lie largely in its ability to influence thoughts. This is how it controls its legions."

"You dragged us away from our preparations for this?" sputtered Kendren. "To tell us something every child knows?"

"Be still!" snapped Ren, with a look that froze the man in his chair. He shrugged and settled back.

Nick scanned the room, gauging the mood. Kendren seemed to be the only person present openly antagonistic. He knew that with his next words, that might change.

"We all know the odds. They're overwhelming. With our present strategy, it would take five times our numbers to adequately defend Barad'An. Ellohir's forces are bottled up in Gallian. We've heard nothing from either Sianiave or the desert people. If we don't alter our position in some fundamental way, our chances for saving the city are slim to none."

He received the response he expected. No one wanted to hear the bleak truth spoken out loud, certainly not by him. He could feel their doubt creeping into the room like a physical thing. Yet some in the room understood that he only spoke the truth. The knights in particular were used to facing the reality of a situation, however unpleasant. It came with the calling. Aerindir, Bors, Ilesor, and the others all sat silent, waiting for him to continue.

Ulawyn, the aged representative of the Sisterhood, nodded her head, as though in silent approval of what he was about to say. Osmodon, already his ally, pursed his lips. Nick could almost hear his thoughts:

What are you waiting for, lad? Give it to them. If this thing fails, none of us will live to worry about it.

"You say this new strategy offers more hope," Ren urged. "Please, tell us about it." He could see the trust in her eyes. It weighed on him. He would have preferred doubt. What if he were wrong?

"Get on with it," muttered Kendren.

"My plan is simple," said Nick. "We kill the morghul. Without the morghul to control the army, the sirdar's legions will fail, a snake without a head."

There was dead silence, then everyone began talking at once. "What a marvelous idea," cried Kendren derisively, his voice rising above the others. "Just kill the morghul. I'm surprised no one's thought of it before!"

He leaned forward on the table, his face as red as a beet. "And just how do you propose to do that, Sir Knight?"

"A fair question," someone shouted. "How do we kill it?"

Kendren sneered, "Are you volunteering to sneak into the creature's tent when it's sleeping and slit its throat yourself?"

Nick's arm was throbbing again. He'd been so certain. Now he wondered if he weren't deluded. After all, what did he really know about morghuls? He looked over at Ren and saw the trust still there, and with it a slight nod of encouragement.

"I considered that," he said slowly. "But it's doubtful one man, single-handed, could get into the thing's tent undetected, much less kill it."

"Its tent is certainly protected," said Ulawyn. "The witch-men are not there for companionship. And morghuls have their own means of protection."

"Yes!" cried Kendren sarcastically. "How do you plan to kill a morghul, surrounded by an army and protected by who knows what sorcery?"

"We attack," said Nick.

Kendren's face blanched. "Attack? Are you mad? Attack an army eighty thousand strong?"

The politician turned to the others, his arms raised. "Barad'An's walls have withstood far greater threats than this. If this is his plan, he may as well be working for the enemy."

Nick's hand went to his sword hilt. This had gone beyond rudeness. Kendren was directly challenging his leadership. What was the man up to?

Then, suddenly, the room seemed to fall silent and he saw Kendren as he was, shortsighted and self-seeking. But behind his bluster lay genuine fear. Fear of the enemy, certainly. But more than this, fear of being seen for the trivial man he was.

He was shouting now, pointing an accusing finger at Nick. "Who is this man? What do we know about him? Where is he from? Amra? Where is that? Does anybody know? Has anybody even heard of it? This plan of his is suicide. We must trust to the walls!"

Nick's anger was gone. Kendren was not alone in his fear. Everyone felt it. Kendren was simply acting it out for the rest of them.

Realizing his rant was not having the desired effect, Kendren turned to Ren, pleading. "Your majesty, certainly you, of all people—"

"Sit down, Master Kendren," said Ren quietly.

Kendren froze, his mouth agape. He started to speak, then abruptly sat down.

It was Bors who voiced the obvious question. "How do you propose we attack an army eighty thousand strong?"

Nick let out his breath. The council sat ready to face the truth, without illusion or false hope.

"The morghul may be intimidating, but he's no strategist. He's deployed his forces in a broad front. Ozzy—Sir Osmodon—and I saw it from afar this afternoon. It is impressive, but strategically unwise. The front ranks are thin, no more than four or five deep. It's not a formation designed for defense. I believe its purpose is to inspire terror. It tells us the morghul doesn't expect to be attacked."

Bors nodded. "Easy enough to cut through the line."

"How many men?" asked Aerindir.

"Fifty. No more."

There was a stir. "So few?"

"The odds don't matter. If we move quickly enough, they won't be able to bring their numbers to bear."

"What about the Mongaday?" asked Ilesor, a hedge knight from Amadin. "They're excellent cavalrymen. They move quickly."

The Mongaday were the sirdar's shock troops, Nick knew. A light cavalry force, taken from their villages as boys for training as warriors.

"Fierce opponents," Aerindir agreed. "Abdelar and I fought against them at Ethendel."

"And the Uruks," added Bors. "Less disciplined, but still fearsome fighters."

Other of the enemy's forces were mentioned: Southroners, the Ghaad, Niburian archers, the Maerlings. Nick waved them off. "None of them matter. If we give them time to react we've already failed. Success depends on speed and surprise."

"And the morghul?" asked Ren. "Who will face the morghul?"

"All of us who reach its tent alive."

"Aye," muttered Osmodon, stroking his beard. "Arriving alive."

Bors was thoughtful. "Sir Nicholas, I assume you intend to lead us. What others? There aren't fifty knights left in the city."

"Knights are best in the field," said Fletcher. "Others are better trained for the walls."

"The creature's tent is easy enough to spot," offered the hawk-faced Galwyn, an ex-ranger and their chief of scouts. "It's a great black thing, twelve feet high with five peaks, each flying a red pennant marked with runes of power.

"There'll be pickets," he added. "And the witch-men. We've counted twelve."

Witch-men? Nick hesitated. He knew little of sorcery, less of how it would play in battle.

Sister Ulawyn interrupted. "We will deal with the witch-men."

The aging Sister had been one of Ren's mentors, Nick knew. Sharp-tongued and practical, she drew nearly as much respect as the High Priestess Saolin herself. Ulawyn never spoke without severe purpose. She had something up her sleeve.

"A brave offer," Bors said gently. "And I don't discount your abilities, Sister. But however excellent as healers they may be, I don't see how the Sisters can hope to stand against master sorcerers."

The old woman's black eyes flashed. "Master sorcerers? There's not a first-rate adept among them. A morghul would never allow it. It was sorcery that broke the morghuls' power, and they fear it still. His vaunted witch-men are acolytes, present only to serve as its lens, to channel the creature's own power. You've all felt it. The insidious weight of doubt and failure, hanging like a poison.

"The Sisterhood has always had to deal with the black arts," she added. "One is a poor healer indeed who does not understand the source of the disease. You should know this, Sir Bors, as you were once a student among us."

"My sincere apologies," said Bors humbly.

"We will not be alone, however." The old woman turned to Ren. "Gwyndolyn Ambergin, I ask permission to introduce another to the council. He waits outside."

"He, Sister? A man?"

"Yes. A man."

"If there are no objections, then by all means."

There were no objections. A bell sounded and a man entered, tall and thin, dressed in a stained leather jerkin and faded green tights.

"By Asgar," whispered Osmodon to Nick, "it's the minstrel from Ardendell, Tom O'Something. I knew there was something between him and Sianiave."

Appearing somewhat uncertain, the minstrel approached Ren and bowed. "Your majesty, I arrived only this morning. By chance, I found Sister Ulawyn before I found a room. As I'd come to offer my services in any event, I found the encounter well-omened."

"A minstrel?" muttered Kendren loud enough for everyone to hear. "What next? Dancing maidens?"

Ulawyn glared. "Master Kendren, you would better be served if you listened more and spoke less about things of which you know nothing."

The ex-mayor flushed, but held his tongue.

"A minstrel he may be," Ulawyn continued, turning to the others, "But no common one. He is of the Brotherhood, and it was in Megida where we first met. Then he was known as Maerlis."

A murmur passed through the room. Ren raised a hand and turned to the minstrel. "Is this true? Are you Maerlis?"

The minstrel closed his eyes for a moment, then spoke. "Forgive me. I have not heard that name pronounced in a very long time."

"You forsook the power?"

"I would never do so, your majesty, even if it were possible. I was on an errand outside the walls when Megida fell. With the sirdar's men searching under every bush and stone, it seemed wise to take another calling. Over time I learned to enjoy being a minstrel."

"The Brotherhood is no more, Master O'Canter. Or should I call you Master Maerlis?"

"O'Canter, please. Tom is even better. It's a name of which I've grown fond."

"Tom, then. Yet you come to us willing to help."

"Yes, your majesty. Though to be honest, I wish it were otherwise."

"Why, then? Why at such a time?"

"Many Brothers died at Megida, it's true. But the Brotherhood did not die with them. The Brotherhood is not a physical thing. It exists outside of time, of place. The mantle is never given without a price. Each initiate has made his own terms and time of payment. When the Lady Sianiave came into the inn with these two knights, asking for news of Barad'An, I knew the time had come for me to honor my debt."

The minstrel straightened and seemed to grow younger. "Yes, I will join you in this fight. I have been hiding far too long."

The questions continued for another hour. In the end Nick's plan was set in motion, with the condition that among the fifty men who accompanied him, no more than ten would be full knights. The remaining knights would be needed in the city.

Even Kendren was mollified. Fifty men only, a loss certainly, but not the disaster he'd envisioned. This Sir Nicholas was a glory seeker, like all knights. They were no better than himself, whatever their pretensions.

CHAPTER
63

A SCREAM, UNMISTAKABLY HUMAN, cut through the heavy night air. Somewhere nearby a man had just died a violent death.

"Easy," cautioned Osmodon. "It wasn't one of ours."

Nick was not so sure. He looked at the riders gathered in the darkness. He couldn't see their faces, but he sensed their anticipation and excitement, with no sign of fear.

Of the hundreds who'd volunteered, fifty had been chosen, all seasoned warriors and not a shy heart among them. The meadow where they gathered overlooked the plain and the encampment below. They had come by varying routes to avoid the attention of enemy scouts. Now they waited for the order to attack, knowing that many of them would not live through the morning. Perhaps none.

He glanced up at the sky. The half moon was near to setting in the west. The order would have to be given soon.

Where was Aerindir?

Bors tightened his cinches. Nearby he could hear the creak of leather as men mounted their horses. Aerindir and the minstrel had not yet arrived. The dour knight's absence would be a serious lack.

Nick shivered. The chill seeped its way into his padded armor. He wondered if he were making a mistake not wearing a helm. Bors had offered him one of his. He'd tried it on, finding it heavy and confining, but it would have kept his ears warm.

Several of the older volunteers arrived wearing brass or iron chest plates. Most, like Osmodon and himself, wore the common battle dress of lacquered leather. It was lighter than metal, and nearly as tough.

The horses of Anor had been bred for speed and endurance. Nick still wondered that no one had recognized Greywind, for even among the warriors' mounts, Greywind was exceptional.

The breath of the horses condensed quickly in the cold air, curling away in wisps of vapor. Somewhere an owl hooted. There was little conversation; the time for talk had passed.

Eastward the sky began to lighten. Aerindir or no, Nick knew that soon he would have to give the order. Greywind pulled at his bit.

"A moment longer," Osmodon advised as Nick steadied the stallion. "Aerindir will come."

As if in answer came the sound of horses approaching at a gallop. "Six riders!" came a muffled cry. Then, with relief, "It's Aerindir!"

"Six?" They'd expected only Aerindir and the minstrel.

The riders entered the meadow at a gallop, Aerindir in the lead, followed by the minstrel and four others in hooded capes. Women, Nick realized in surprise.

"Our apologies," said Aerindir. "We encountered four enemy scouts. One managed to elude us, until Tom spelled him."

Spelled him? Nick recalled the scream and suddenly lost his curiosity. "No matter. But these women?"

"The morghul has witch-men, we have these Sisters," said the minstrel. "Besides, the numbers were wrong."

"What numbers?"

"Fifty men. Fives and tens indicate confusion, upheaval. Nine is serendipitous. An end, and a beginning."

"Nine?" Nick had a sudden image of the council room table in Gallian, and the floor in Khagad'Oth. "How do you get nine?"

"Fifty, plus myself and these three Sisters. That's fifty-four. Five and four equal nine."

Nick quelled his curiosity. Now was not the time for a lecture in numerology. "The Sisters can watch from the ridge."

He stopped. There were four women with the minstrel, not three.

Ren threw back her hood. "The Sisters know the danger. They will ride with Master O'Canter."

The thinning moonlight reflected off her flaxen hair. A ripple of astonishment passed through the gathering. "The queen! The queen is here."

"You shouldn't have come. It's dangerous." Nick spoke quietly. "If you were killed—"

"Galwyn's rangers are in the woods," replied Ren. "I'll be safe. It's you who rides into mortal peril."

Nick no longer felt the cold. His impulse was to reach over and take her in his arms, but Ren was their queen. He knew that the other men, each in his own way, felt something of the same, and he understood why she had felt it necessary to come. Her physical presence embodied all they valued in the world.

"Tom and the Sisters? Who will look after them?"

"Don't worry on our account," Tom said. "We're not as vulnerable as we may appear."

Nick studied the minstrel for a moment, then turned away. Sorcery was beyond his understanding, but he recognized courage when he saw it.

"One moment." Ren loosed a slender bundle from her saddle, removing a sword from its blanket wrapping. "Aerindir wished me to give this to you. I would like you to carry into battle."

Nick glanced at Aerindir, who was wearing an uncharacteristic smile. "I have a sword," Nick said.

"Trust me. This one will serve you better."

Nick hesitated, then took the weapon from her outstretched hands. From the moment his fingers touched the blade, he knew he held something extraordinary.

It was light, far lighter than his own sword. Even in the scant moonlight, its blade glistened brightly, the edge so sharp it almost appeared transparent. It was not made of steel, nor of any metal he recognized.

He took a cautious swing. The blade cut through the air with a faint, almost musical sound, like air over harp strings. No swordsmith he knew, in this world or any other, could have fashioned such a thing.

Bors and Osmodon had watched the exchange closely. "Daemonsyr?" Bors asked.

Aerindir nodded. To Nick he said, "It was Abdelar's, brother blade to my own. We hid them in the forest before entering the city. I believe you are meant for it."

"A princely gift," said Bors.

"More than princely," murmured Osmodon. "You could buy a kingdom with such a weapon."

Nick withdrew his recently sharpened sword from its scabbard and handed it to Ren. "Keep this for me, if you will. It's a good weapon."

Ren accepted it. "Until you return."

Nick sheathed Daemonsyr. He'd wanted to encourage the men by saying something rousing and uplifting, but no words came. Ren was there and that seemed enough. He glanced again at the sky. Sunrise was upon them.

"It's time," he said.

Beside him Osmodon repeated the words. "Aye. It's time."

"Bors? Aerindir?"

Both men nodded.

Nick turned to Ren to say good-bye, and instead met her gaze with a resigned smile. Ren understood, returning the smile with one of her own.

He nudged Greywind with his heels. The big horse bolted quickly forward. Osmodon, Bors, Aerindir, and the other riders followed, forming two columns, with the minstrel and the three Sisters bringing up the rear.

No horns sounded, no drums thundered. Struggling to hold back tears, Ren wondered if she would see any of them alive again.

CHAPTER
64

KROSK MORGHUL, commander of the sirdar's legions, could not sleep. The creature was troubled, and uncertain why. They had marched across half of what once had been the greatest empire in recorded history, and had yet to meet serious resistance.

The death of the priest was unfortunate but hardly a disaster. Subduing the city would simply take longer. The priest's reign, short as it was, had left Barad'An in disarray, its king poisoned, its knights dead or scattered. It was not possible for the city to right itself before he arrived.

He had yet to decide whether to settle in for a siege or attack immediately. He was inclined to attack in a frontal assault with ladders and siege engines. The walls were strong and high but, by all reports, only a few thousand remained to defend them. A direct assault would cost men, but this was of little consequence. He was in no mood to wait the weeks, perhaps months, a prolonged siege would require.

He found himself thinking about the strange knight he'd been told about, the one who'd nearly killed Gothmog and released his prisoners. Was it coincidence that he'd appeared at this moment? Were there other powers than Belliol's at work?

Whoever he was, he was still only a man, a hairless monkey. Best to dispatch him quickly. Unfortunately, after Gothmog's hasty retreat, getting assassins into the city had proved difficult. There was new sorcery afoot, bindings he couldn't break, even with the focusing power of the sirdar's witch-men at his disposal.

Krosk peered down at the girl lying unconscious on the bed. Her back was still bleeding from where his nails had torn her flesh, but she was still alive and from this he took satisfaction.

Morganwyn was the child's name, not that it mattered greatly. She'd been found hiding in a cellar at her family's burned-out farm. She'd been a virgin, but was of child-bearing age. Few human females survived his affections.

Two others had lived, though both had gone quite mad. Krosk had ordered them kept alive, at least until it was determined whether either was with child.

He cleared the girl from his thoughts and looked away. The witch-men could tend to her in the morning.

It was too late to sleep, too early to begin the march over the hills. He leaned back in a chair, breathing evenly, almost in a trance, determined to find the source of his strange unease, the anomaly in the pattern.

He was 227 years old, the last of his kind born. Only a handful of others still lived. There were eight that he knew of, and perhaps another half dozen scattered about the Black Mountains, feeding on passing travelers and dreaming of past glories.

Alone of his kind, he had studied the humans. Physically inferior, venal, avaricious, prone to treachery. How had this petty race of monkeys grown to such prominence? Whence came their power? This was the great question.

It was their cleverness, especially in the realm of the Art that was most troubling. Krosk's own kind had a capacity for sorcery far surpassing that of the monkeys, but morghuls as a rule seemed incapable of subduing their personal appetites long enough to complete the arduous training needed to attain true mastery. This had been their downfall.

His own fascination with humans had made him an outcast among his kind. They even had a name for him, *Al agheth-e-benaght*, "the one who mates with animals," and despised him.

After much searching, Krosk had finally encountered a true master, one both willing and able to teach him what he desired. And this master hated the monkeys as much as he did.

The extermination of the race of his birth was a small price to pay. The few who remained were doomed. He and his progeny were the future.

The sound of footsteps brought him back to the present moment. Someone was approaching the tent. He sniffed the air. Gothmog. Who could mistake the little man's foul smell?

Gothmog peered in through the tent flap. His face, never appealing, was now hideously disfigured. His left ear was gone, and the wounds inflicted by the mysterious knight were just beginning to heal.

"Are you asleep, m'lord?"

"Do I look asleep? Why do you bother me?"

Gothmog lifted the flap and entered the tent. He glanced at the girl on the bed, noting only that she still appeared to be alive. "There's been a disturbance in the hills," he said. "Men are gathering there. Several of our spies were discovered and killed."

"They're preparing to ambush the vanguard," said Krosk dismissively. "Don't concern yourself. The captains have been alerted."

"It's not that, m'lord."

"What, then?"

"There was evidence of sorcery."

Krosk straightened. Suddenly the reason for his unease and inability to sleep took form. "The witch has returned. She was supposed to be in the west."

"No, not her. The signature was unfamiliar. The Sisters are involved."

"The Sisters? They're not capable."

Krosk stopped, puzzled. Few really knew what the Sisters were, or were not, capable of. Because the priest appeared to have dealt with them so easily, he'd dismissed them as a threat.

"Wake the witch-men. And bring me a vessel."

Gothmog's eyes slipped away, furtive. "You wish to contact the master?"

"Of course. Belliol will know."

At the mention of his master's name, Gothmog cringed. Unlike Krosk, who believed he knew Belliol for what he was and communed with him almost as an equal, Gothmog saw Belliol as, if not exactly a god, then something close.

The magician preferred to summon Belliol in private, Krosk knew. Perhaps it was the particularly disgusting sexual nature of the relationship. What Belliol got out of it, Krosk could only guess. Likely it was the only means he had to control the little man's vicious and unpredictable nature.

"I'll bring a boy," said Gothmog shortly.

The words were forced. He was jealous, Krosk knew. He himself had no use for such gutless fawning. Belliol had knowledge, which he exchanged for obedience. This Krosk understood. But unlike Gothmog, he saw Belliol as mortal, and therefore fallible. The time was not far off when he would no longer need a master. In teaching him the secret of travel, Belliol had made a grave mistake.

Gothmog left and Krosk settled back into his chair. When the odious little man was no longer needed, he would kill him and eat his heart for supper.

The girl on the bed let out a squeak. Her body shuddered as she rolled to her side.

Morghul and human. To other morghuls the thought of mating with a human was loathsome. But Krosk had decided early on that if a human female could bear him offspring, he would be the father of a powerful new race of beings. Unanticipated had been the exquisite pleasure involved.

The girl was awakening. The pathetic sounds were disturbing his calm. He would summon the witch-men. But a commotion outside— shouts, horns, men running—brought him out of his thoughts.

Gothmog burst into the tent, his face flushed a horrible crimson. "They're attacking!" he cried in panic.

"Attacking? Who's attacking? Where?"

"Here! The knights of Barad'An are attacking here!"

CHAPTER
65

AN EARLY RISING COOK stumbled as he ran to get out of the way. Greywind's metal-shod hooves crushed his chest. A soldier, half naked, his eyes still bleary from sleep, stuck his head out of his tent. Daemonsyr flashed and the head fell into the mud. Horse and rider swept past before the blood spray touched them.

The sun had not risen when Nick's small force began their charge. Sentries, dulled by morning duty, had been slow to react. Minutes passed before any alarms were sounded.

The battle horns, the pounding of hooves, the screams of the maimed and dying—Nick felt caught in time, as if this was how it was, had always been. There was none of the mindless rage that had propelled him up the dungeon stairs. He felt intensely alive, every nerve in his being tuned to one purpose: to reach the morghul's tent.

A soldier appeared to his right, bare-chested, wooden spear in hand. He looked no older than sixteen. Nick parried a clumsy thrust and took off the boy's arm. Later he might feel regret at such slaughter. For now, all he felt was gratitude that their luck had so far held.

Only minutes had passed since he'd given the order for the charge. They'd caught the camp completely off guard, sweeping through the bivouacked army like a storm.

"Can you see the tent?" Nick cried to Osmodon as Greywind leapt over a smoldering fire pit. "We should be almost on it!"

The enemy camp was a maze of crude tents, open latrines, and panicked, half-awake soldiers. They rode over it all, cutting down anyone foolish or unfortunate enough to be caught in their path. But that very disarray also proved a danger. From the hills above it had been easy to spot the morghul's black tent. Not so on level ground, surrounded by chaos. If they missed the tent, all would be for nothing.

"There!" cried Aerindir, pointing with Drakulsyr toward a red pennant visible in the distance.

A huge bearded man clutching an ax lunged at Greywind, his left hand reaching to grab the stallion's bridle. The point of Daemonsyr's blade took him in the neck. He fell back, dropping the ax in a fruitless attempt to stanch the fountain of blood.

An arrow flew past Nick's head. Another glanced off the pommel of his saddle. From here on out it would not be so easy. The camp was coming awake.

Under the clamor of the charge, Nick became aware of another sound, a thin, discordant hum that grew in volume and intensity even as they closed in on the black tent.

Breaking through a final wall of stacked weapons and small tents, he saw the source of the sound. Twelve men in hooded robes stood facing the riders. Their hoods shadowed their eyes, but their lips were visible, calling out in an eerily syncopated chant.

The keening grew in power until Nick's head seemed ready to explode. Horses reared in panic, throwing their riders. Even Greywind was affected, tossing his head as though in pain.

All around, men threw off their helms and clamped their hands over their ears. "Witch-men!" Aerindir cried, fighting to steady his stallion. "Where's the minstrel?"

As if summoned, Tom O'Canter, the three Sisters close at his side, entered the clearing, their horses unfazed by the dreadful sound. The minstrel raised his right hand. A blue glow formed in his cupped palm. He swung his arm as though he were pitching a ball, and the blue light flew toward the witch-men. Three fell to their knees, screaming. Confused, the others drew together in a tight circle.

"Hurry!" he shouted at Nick, his face contorted by the effort. "Finish your business!" The words seemed torn from his throat.

Beside him the Sisters had all grown deathly pale, their eyes closed tight as they rocked back and forth in their saddles muttering counterspells. The horses steadied. Men regained their mounts.

"Barad'An and Queen Gwyndolyn!" It was Aerindir. The knight charged straight into the circle of witch-men, killing three as the rest scattered.

The minstrel leaned forward in his saddle, retching. Two of the Sisters fell unconscious from their horses. The third managed to keep her seat, but her face had turned a sickly green and, like the minstrel, she voided her stomach.

More horns and strange battle cries sounded as horsemen arrived from the army's rear. Lean, golden-skinned men in brown leather armor, curved bows across their backs, charged in with scimitars raised.

"Now we're in for it," muttered Osmodon grimly. "Meet the Mongaday, lad."

"Forget them. We've got to get into that tent!"

Nick leapt from Greywind and in a moment Daemonsyr's blade sliced through the black tent's silk wall. Before Osmodon and Aerindir could follow him inside, they were cut off by the Mongaday horsemen.

§

Osmodon parried a scimitar, grabbed the tattooed hand that held it and dragged the man from his horse. Close beside him, Aerindir spitted the man as he tried to rise. "Ozzy! To the hells with this. We'll be overwhelmed. It's the morghul we have to kill!"

Osmodon hesitated. At the moment Nick entered the morghul's tent, something had become clear to him.

In the first days after the unconscious Nick arrived at Tor Eyrie, Sianiave had tended his shattered shoulder day and night, never seeming to sleep, rarely talking. From her concern alone, Osmodon had known the young man was of no minor importance.

One evening after a long session of healing, exhausted to nearly the limits of her extraordinary reserves, she'd spoken to him of morghuls like the one Nick had tried to fight. "Their strength lies in their ability to see the worst in us," she said. "To feed the Toad. If one is prepared, this can be a blessing, for it forces our ancient enemy to reveal himself. Most of us refuse to even acknowledge the enemy exists. Few manage to defeat it."

Osmodon knew now she'd been speaking of Nick. All this time, in a hundred subtle ways, she'd been preparing Nick to face the morghul, and in doing so to face something in himself: the Toad, the ancient enemy.

The lad had some great purpose beyond this. That was clear.

Around him Mongaday and the men of Barad'An were locked in ferocious battle. Bors was taking on two at once.

"Ozzy!" cried Aerindir as he struck a man from his saddle and spun his horse to face another. "We have to get in that tent! Even Eanor couldn't best a morghul single-handed."

"It's the lad's job," said Osmodon, certain now. "Ours is to hold here until it's finished."

CHAPTER
66

THE TENT WAS ENORMOUS and poorly lit. Nick shifted his eyes, adjusting them to the gloom. The floor was covered in thick carpets. The furniture was oversized, built for a giant. The cloying smell of incense couldn't quite hide an underlying odor of sulfur and something else, a stench he had no words to describe.

A girl lay exposed on a bed in a pool of blood. He was certain she was dead. But she drew her hand to a breast and whimpered.

He started toward her when a mocking laugh from the back of the tent stopped him. "So. It is you. I suspected as much." Nick swayed as pain shot through his head.

"I've often wondered why Belliol sent me to that accursed place. He imagined you a threat." The morghul's voice was sly and insinuating. Nick couldn't tell whether the words had been spoken aloud or were only in his mind.

It was dressed as he remembered in a black leather kilt and high black boots. He could see its features more clearly now than he had that night at Langton Manor. Its eyes were not the fiery red he remembered, but golden, serpent-like. Its limbs were oddly jointed, the head oblong and hairless with small, pointed ears. The slit of its mouth was also that of a serpent. Its tongue, while not forked, was thin and black. It wore a long sword in a scabbard at its waist and carried a meteor hammer, the spiked ball swinging back and forth on its four-foot chain like a pendulum.

"I thought I had done with you. You're the one who killed the priest."

Nick couldn't speak. It took all his strength just to remain standing.

"Nothing has changed, has it? Everything you've done is for nothing. Your life is for nothing. You're weak. Impotent. You couldn't even control your horse. Look at you, shaking like an unworthy slave before its master. Where is your mistress, little monkey? The witch whore. Where is she now?"

Nick fought to steady himself. Time slowed. The clamor of battle became a distant drone. The pain in his head lessened, then disappeared.

The sight returned. He saw the creature as it was: arrogant, vicious, predatory. Behind the cunning lay an essential dullness that accounted for the inexplicable disorder of the camp. The vaunted ability to influence thought was little more than a conjurer's trick. The sly tone, the negative words, the carefully modulated cadence, even the controlled arcs of the hammer, only reflected and amplified emotions already present. Without a man's own doubts to manipulate, the morghul could control nothing.

It was hesitating. Why? Why bother with words instead of attacking?

The answer came from the creature's own thoughts, which Nick found he could read.

Who is this human? Why does Belliol consider him important? His sword is surely a weapon of power. How did he come by it? And the spell that broke the witch-men; even I could find no counter. Was that his doing?

The morghul was uncertain. Deep in its alien mind it knew fear.

Still its words struck home: "A fine sword, little monkey. Do you actually imagine yourself worthy of it? I know who you really are: a failed soldier from an ignoble world. I saw you there, coward. I know your true nature. I know your sins, your weakness. I know you. Tell me if I'm wrong. Tell me!"

Nick couldn't answer. The creature wasn't wrong. It wasn't saying anything he hadn't felt himself. He was weak, an orphan, unwanted. He'd known it all his life, the pain of unworthiness. What was he doing here?

He stood rooted, unable to respond. The morghul chuckled. The arcs of the spiked ball lengthened.

"Nick!"

The sound of his name and a surge of energy snapped him to life. Tom O'Canter stood at the entrance to the tent, hunched over in pain. His face was strained and bloodied, but his eyes were clear and unafraid.

"Don't listen to it. It tries to weaken you. It knows nothing. Only the Earth and the Sky know your true name. And they will not speak it until your last breath is out."

There was a cadence to the words—a spell, Nick realized—that countered the morghul's malign whispers.

The morghul screamed in fury and swung the hammer. But the attack lacked the unnerving speed Nick remembered. Daemonsyr sliced through the meteor hammer's chain as easily as if it had been rope. The spiked ball flew free, missing his head by half a foot.

The morghul tossed the chain aside and drew a sword. "I will enjoy cutting off your legs, little monkey. This time you will have no wizard to help you." Nick glanced over to where the minstrel had collapsed and now lay unmoving. But Tom's spell had helped him steady himself and prepare his mind to ward off the morghul's baleful influence.

The creature was at least two heads taller than he and far heavier. Still, it did not seem so terrifyingly large as memory had made it. Unfortunately its strength was no illusion. The blade it had drawn was longer than his, yet the monster handled it as easily as a willow wand.

It charged in, using the sword more like a club than a blade. The blows drove Nick back toward the bed where the girl lay. He sidestepped, but the morghul turned its blade to cut his arm. It then caught his right wrist in an iron grip, driving him nearly to his knees. Nick struggled to draw his dagger with his left hand, but his fingers felt clumsy and blood had made the handle slippery.

The morghul's slash of a mouth curled into a malignant grin, its golden eyes wide in triumph as it bore down. Its breath stank of turpentine and rotten eggs. Nick rose and drove a knee into the creature's groin. The morghul screamed in pain and its grip released.

Nick pulled away. His right wrist was either badly sprained or broken. Shifting Daemonsyr to his left hand, he regained his balance.

Snarling in fury, the morghul charged again. But its blows were wild and lacked the ferocious will of the first attack. It was flagging. Nick felt a moment's hope. He parried a blow and followed with a sweeping slash to the creature's midsection.

The morghul stepped back in surprise. Taloned fingers felt the wound, and it stared at the blood in disbelief.

Nick waited. He'd been lucky. His right hand was useless and the morghul wasn't the only one tiring. In the distance, beyond the battle raging outside, came the sound of horns. More Mongaday, or Uruks. He had to end this.

The blood seeping down his arm was a bad sign. It was small consolation that the morghul was in little better shape. The creature was breathing heavily and blood flowed from the gash in its torso.

The girl on the bed made a mewling sound and opened her eyes. When she saw the monster she screamed. Absently, as though swatting an annoying insect, the morghul dropped its sword down, severing her neck.

Horrified at the casual murder, Nick took a step forward, then caught himself. It was a trap. The creature was baiting him.

Patience, Nick told himself. Hold the tension. Let him come to you.

No one ever won a battle through defense alone. Where had he heard that? Nick shook his head. Loss of blood was making him light-headed.

The muscles in the morghul's hand flexed as it sought a better grip on its sword.

Almost. Almost. Hold—

A horse crashed sideways into the tear in the tent. Its Mongaday rider was dead. Caught in the ropes and silk of the tent, the horse thrashed wildly before finding its footing and bolting free out the open flap.

At that moment, the morghul attacked. Nick was forced to parry the blow one-handed. Pain shot up his arm.

The morghul turned, bringing its sword around in a sideways slash. Nick's riposte faltered and the creature's blade bit deeply into his left side. There was surprisingly little pain but he knew it was no small cut.

Breathing in labored gasps, the morghul drew back, either too exhausted to press its advantage or knowing there was no need. Outside the horns grew louder, and with them the thunder of hundreds of charging horses. Uruk reinforcements, Nick thought.

A veil was closing over Nick's vision. The morghul swayed on its feet, waiting.

He wiped his forehead with the back of his hand. He felt the blood draining down his side, soaking his breeches, filling his boot. He had nothing left.

He'd failed. Failed Ren, failed his friends, failed Barad'An. A civilization lost.

He blinked, shaking his head to clear the fog. The minstrel lay nearby, unconscious or dead. Nick remembered his words. "Only the Earth and the Sky know your true name. And they will not speak it until your last breath is out."

A fierce anger rose up in him. His last breath was yet to come. He was still alive, and he still held Daemonsyr.

"No!"

Raising the sword before him, he lunged. The morghul, exhausted beyond measure, weakened by its wounds, certain the last blow had ended the fight, did not respond. Daemonsyr's point struck through its ribs and heart.

Krosk looked down at the blade impaling him and shook his head. This couldn't be. It was impossible. He was Krosk, the greatest of the morghuls. Raising a hand as if to ward the blade magically away, he took a last ragged breath, let out a monstrous bellow, and fell heavily to the tent floor.

Nick pulled Daemonsyr free. With his last vestige of strength he swung the blade at the creature's neck. The spray of blood drenched him as the great head rolled free.

The repulsive stench of blood inside the tent was making him sick. He staggered through the torn wall into the open air.

He felt no triumph, just relief and a mild surprise. He'd actually killed the thing.

Outside the battle seemed to have come to an end. Enemies who moments before had been locked in mortal combat stood silent. He saw Bors and Aerindir; Osmodon also, bloodied and afoot but still alive.

The veil of fog was returning. He failed to see the furtive figure creeping from behind the tent.

"Lad! Behind you!"

Osmodon's warning came too late. Even if it had come sooner, Nick was too weak to react. There was a moment's pain as Gothmog's slender dagger pierced his back. Then nothing. No feeling at all. Before anyone thought to stop him, the magician vanished into the tent.

Osmodon was first to Nick's side. "Find a Sister. Bors, Aerindir! Get that little rodent and kill him!"

Bors and Aerindir ran to cut off the magician's escape. Osmodon removed Nick's armor. "Don't worry, lad. We'll get you home."

"Leave me, save yourselves. The horns, Uruks—"

"Not Uruks, lad. It's Ellohir's horns you hear. And Sianiave. She's come with Artos. The desert people also, if I guess rightly."

"Sianiave? The desert people?" It was too much for Nick.

There were tears in Osmodon's eyes. "You won, lad! And only yesterday I was composing my death song. Even the Mongaday are riding off, what's left of them. The moment you did for that beast—well, fearless they may be, but not fools. The others are conscripts and booty hunters. The fear and greed that shackled them is gone. Few will stand now."

"And those who rode with us?"

"Some still live. The minstrel lies unconscious, though not, I think, from any fleshly wound."

Nick closed his eyes.

He heard Osmodon's shouts as though from a great distance. "Sister, someone! Find Sianiave. Get her here. Wake that minstrel! Hurry, Sir Nicholas's life is in the balance!"

CHAPTER 67

AN UNFAMILIAR ROCKING MOTION surfaced in Nick's consciousness. He lay on blankets in the back of a moving cart. Mounted men, grim-faced, flanked the cart, their eyes fixed straight ahead.

One in particular caught his attention: tall, with golden hair, he was fitted with gold and maroon armor. His face was fair and noble, his eyes a startling shade of green. The round shield hanging from his saddle was emblazoned with the seal of House Ambergin: a lion and a unicorn, rampant.

Prince Artos; it could be none other. Ellohir rode with him, as did Bors, Aerindir, Osmodon, Penthys, Prince Bandar, and others Nick did not recognize. The dog, Bear, was also there, trotting alongside the cart, and Greywind was tethered behind. In a column stretching to the forest and beyond rode others, too many to count.

They were outside the walls of Barad'An, nearing the great gate. Horns heralded their approach. The way was lined with people. Maewyn, the tavern wench, stoop-shouldered Gregory, Captain Fletcher, even Wispy Will, dressed for battle. From somewhere came the sound of a woman sobbing.

The crowd was subdued, almost reverential. Why weren't they celebrating? Wasn't the war over? Hadn't they won?

There were other carts with the column, carrying the bodies of the wounded and dead. Perhaps that was it. Respect for the fallen. He felt no pain from his own wounds. In fact, he felt mildly euphoric. Maybe it was Osmodon's goat grease salve, or something the Sisters had given him while he'd been out.

In any event, he felt well again. Not a hundred percent, but well enough to—

He willed himself to sit up, but his body refused to respond. He wondered if he'd been drugged. Certainly he could move his head, his eyes. Otherwise, how could he see what he was seeing?

Abruptly his viewpoint changed. He found himself looking down on himself, at his own body lying on the cart. His clothes were blood-soaked, his hands folded across his chest, the sword Daemonsyr beside him. His eyes were closed. How could that be?

A voice came to him, as though in his head. *You did well, Lieutenant Herron.*

Sianiave?

He saw her now, to the left of Artos, mounted on a white horse. She was in silver armor, her blond hair falling over her shoulders. She looked every inch the warrior maiden.

Don't be afraid. I'm here with you.

The words were spoken with tenderness, but her mouth had not moved. Like the others, her eyes were fixed straight ahead. He wondered that no one else seemed to hear them, for no one turned to look.

Another voice, a boy from the crowd, said, "Is that Eanor, mum? Is he really dead?"

The woman next to the boy laid a hand on his shoulder. "It's true, my son. They're building the pyres now. But his will be the largest."

He saw Ren, riding out from the city to meet the precession. She did not look in his direction, instead falling in beside Artos. Her face was drawn as though in grief, but she sat upright and no tears stained her cheeks.

It's not time! I'm not ready!

The words had surfaced before Nick realized it. It couldn't be true. He wasn't Eanor. And he certainly wasn't dead. How could he be seeing all this?

I'm sorry, said Sianiave.

It was the compassion in her voice that told him the truth. *But I can't die. Not now. I'm almost home!*

This world is not your home, Nick. Not your real home. You have much work yet to do.

Please—

Even I cannot change what is. Have faith. All will be well again. This much I know.

Ren?

And with that last thought Nicholas Herron, lieutenant in the US Special Forces, known as Nick to his friends, and as Eanor by others, passed forever from that world.

§

The pyres were many, though Sir Nicholas's, a man many now called Eanor, was by far the largest. Queen Gwyndolyn herself had replaced Daemonsyr with his own nameless sword, kissing his forehead before lighting the wood.

The minstrel viewed the funeral from a balcony in the Left Tower where he was recovering. As he watched the flames rise, his eyes filled with tears. Of the fifty-four who had ridden into the enemy camp that morning, only nine had returned alive.

Nine living, forty-five passed on. Sir Nicholas of Amra, Eanor—whatever the man's true name—had not died in vain. By killing the morghul, he had broken the army's will.

Nine. An end, and a beginning.

The number would undoubtedly have meant more to the sorcerer Maerlis. But Maerlis no longer existed, and the man he'd become no longer had much interest in such things. He had fulfilled his task and paid his dues. He would live out his remaining years as Master Tom O'Canter, wandering troubadour and sometime poet.

But even filled with sorrow as he now was, a part of him could not help but rejoice. Artos had returned, Barad'An was saved. Once again the forces of darkness had been beaten back. What a song it would make!

In his own long and memorable journey, Tom O'Canter had learned a great secret. A poet, a true poet, is more powerful than either knight or sorcerer. The power to change worlds rests not with those who fight the battles, but with those who tell their stories.

EPILOGUE

Langton Vale
November 1

CONSTABLE JONATHON MCGURDY was baffled. Twenty-seven years with the Yard and he'd thought he'd seen everything. Now, as he whiled away his retirement working as a town constable in one of England's sleepiest villages, he'd come across the strangest case he'd ever encountered.

He stood in the observation room outside the emergency unit at Langtonshire Clinic. Beyond the observation window, a doctor and two nurses were doing their best to revive a man brought in by the local fire brigade. The man was about six-feet-two and well built, with scruffy brown hair and blue eyes.

A passport on his person identified him as Nicholas Herron, a twenty-six-year-old Yank. McGurdy had run the name through Central Identification Services and come up with nothing. The passport bore no UK entry stamp, nor did Herron show up in any database McGurdy could access. And that was the least of it.

At first he'd suspected a prank. An anonymous call in the middle of the night, a wounded and unconscious man, a burning manor house. It was Samhain night, after all. Halloween.

He quickly changed his mind when he'd looked out the window of his small cottage and saw the glow in the distance. When he'd arrived Herron was already being loaded on the gurney. His shoulder looked like raw meat.

But that was hours ago. Other than some nasty bruising, there now appeared to be no physical damage at all. The medics had cleaned it up, of course, but that hardly explained what he'd seen earlier: shoulder and arm twisted, bone poking through deeply lacerated skin. And the blood; there had been lots of it, far more than evidenced by this relatively minor bruising.

The—what? Patient? Victim? Suspect?—was deep in a coma. McGurdy had seen considerable trauma in his career, had stood watching more often than he cared to remember while doctors struggled to save a man's life. He would have bet his pension Herron was a goner.

He turned to the man beside him. "Tell me again, Mr. Winford. How did you say your friend was injured?"

"I've told you twice already, Inspector," sighed Billy. "I really don't remember."

"Constable, if you please. You and your friend drove out here from Oxfordshire to answer an advertisement, you say?"

"In the *Times*. It was left in Isabel, my car, an old Jaguar."

"Yes. Burned when a wall fell on it, I'm afraid." McGurdy consulted his notes. "You arrived at the manor at approximately 11:30 in the evening. It was raining—"

"About to rain," corrected Billy.

"About to rain. Everything was dark. You both got out of the vehicle, and?"

"That's it. We got out, started towards the front door." Billy shrugged.

"And then you remember nothing. Not until you woke up by the standing stone an hour later. You have no memory of how the fire started?"

"None whatsoever."

Billy suppressed a shudder. What he had said was not entirely true. He did remember something, something dark and terrible. Fire. A creature chasing them. Best not to go there.

Billy watched the vital-signs monitor through the observation window. The past few minutes, the illuminated spikes of the sixth line, the heart line, had grown noticeably weaker. The medical staff had gathered around Nick in nervous activity.

The constable's eyes narrowed. "You saw the damage to his shoulder. What do you make of it now?"

Billy didn't answer. When he'd first come to, he'd seen Nick lying unconscious nearby, his shoulder a bloody mess. The medics had arrived soon after, driving their lorry across the field straight to the stone, though how they'd known where to go he had no idea. But the constable was right. Nick's shoulder now appeared nearly normal.

"Samhain night," said McGurdy. "Tricksters. Except this is no joking matter. A squire's house has burnt to the ground and a man lies near death." Clearly the constable did not believe Billy's claim to amnesia, though it was largely true. But Billy was no longer listening.

Every line on the monitor had suddenly flattened. The doctor and nurses shifted into high gear. Oxygen pressure was increased, epinephrine given, paddles brought. Billy couldn't hear through the thick glass, but he could see the doctor mouthing the word "Clear!"

Nick's body jerked. The monitor lines remained flat.

"Again!" Another charge, another jolt. More epinephrine. Seconds passed.

Inside the room, desperation turned to resignation. "Isn't there anything we can do?" a nurse asked. "He's so young." The man on the table was in apparently excellent condition. Not at all like the drunks and pensioners they usually got this time of night.

The doctor looked up, baffled. "Not if we don't know what's wrong with him."

William Niles was a good doctor. This wasn't the first time he'd lost a patient. It wouldn't be his last. But he couldn't get over the feeling he'd somehow failed with this one, missed something important. "Autopsy will tell, I imagine," he said, finishing his thoughts out loud. "Get him cleaned up, would you?"

Ignoring a sign that read *Patients and Medical Staff Only*, Billy burst into the room, pushing past the nurse who tried to block him.

"Sir! You're not allowed in here," she protested.

The doctor, a sad-looking man with grey hair and a kindly face, removed his mask. "It's all right, Nurse Ann. It doesn't matter now."

Gently, he took Billy's arm. "I'm sorry. There was nothing we could do. Other than that bruising, there appeared to be nothing wrong with him. Any information you might have would be welcome."

"Drugs?" Billy asked, remembering the dark thing. It had to be drugs.

Niles sighed. "We're just a small hospital here, a clinic, really. His blood workup came back normal in all categories. We won't have more on the toxicology until after the autopsy."

"Autopsy?"

"Yes. Necessary, I'm afraid, unexplained death and all."

Billy watched as a nurse removed the oxygen tube from Nick's nose, then the IV in his arm. "I'm responsible," he thought miserably. "If it weren't for me—"

"Come along, Mr. Winford. Does no good standing here. The nurses have their work to do."

Billy, fighting back tears, let himself be led toward the door, only half aware that someone else besides the constable now stood in the observation room. A grey-haired woman wearing a floppy hat and brown woolen greatcoat watched Nick through the window. Something stirred in Billy, a memory.

In the observation room, McGurdy addressed the new arrival. "Miss, are you a relative? A friend, perhaps?"

"A friend."

"I'm truly sorry, then. He's just passed."

The woman looked amused. "Passed? I suppose that's as good a word as any."

An odd thing to say, and an odd way to say it, thought the constable. He took another look at her. Samhain brought out all the loons. Her manner irritated him. She expressed no grief, quite the contrary.

"He died just minutes ago," he said.

"Oh, I don't think he's dead quite yet."

Something in her tone—arrogance, or certainty—increased his annoyance. "I'm sorry, madam, but there is no doubt, really. You see—"

Inside the operating room, the vitals monitor gave a sudden beep. The nurse who had been about to remove the monitoring electrodes from the body jumped back in alarm. "Dr. Niles!"

The first beep was followed by another beep, then another. All six lines on the monitor resumed a steady pattern.

The patient opened his eyes. As he looked around the room, he appeared confused.

"Nick? You're alive!"

"Billy? I was worried about you. The morghul—"

Nick stopped. As with a man awaking from a dream, his eyes suddenly sharpened into focus. "Where are we?"

"A clinic outside Langton Vale. An ambulance brought us. Thank God! We thought you were dead."

"The fire—"

"I'm sorry, but I'm going to have to ask you to leave," Niles said to Billy, looking as confused as the rest of his staff. He did his best to regain control of the situation. "He's still a patient. Please."

Nick ignored the doctor. His attention was fixed on the woman standing on the other side of the observation window. "Sianiave?"

"Please, young man. You've been through a rough time of it. If you would just—"

The woman gave a satisfied nod to the middle-aged man next to her and left.

"Sianiave!"

Nick tore off the electrodes still attached to his body, pushed away the doctor's hands, leapt from the bed, and ran from the room before anyone could stop him.

"Sianiave! Wait!"

That late at night, the reception desk was staffed by a single volunteer, a grey-haired matron who stared indignantly as Nick sprinted past wearing only a green surgical gown.

"Young man! What are you doing? Young man!"

Nick burst through the entrance doors and stopped. A heavy fog had settled over the village. Wide steps led down to a brick sidewalk. Some thirty feet away stood a lamppost, its light a pale glow.

Sianiave stood in the circle of light beneath the lamp. She removed a pipe from her coat, tamped it, then lit it with a flick of a finger. She took a puff and looked up. She raised the pipe as though in salute and walked away, vanishing as completely into the fog as though she'd never been.

A crowd had gathered on the steps. Billy was the first to break the silence. "Nick?"

Nick turned toward Billy and the others.

He was smiling.

B.L. Voorhees has lived a uniquely interesting and colorful life. From being in the first graduating class at the University of California Irvine and a member of both its crew and national championship swim team, to becoming a lifeguard in nearby Laguna Beach, after which he became a member of the Air Force Para Rescue Team, perhaps the military's most elite Special Forces unit. He returned to rowing after leaving the military, winning the legendary Catalina to Long Beach World Long Distance Dory Championship, but his hopes for the Olympics were dashed when President Jimmy Carter canceled America's participation that year. Mr. Voorhees went on to complete graduate school, earning an MFA in Professional Writing from the University of Southern California, at the same time traveling the world as an aide to senior members of the Saudi Royal Family. He has studied with many renowned mystics and thinkers, including Alan Watts, Carlos Castaneda, Robert Bly, and Andrew Weil, along with physicist and body expert Moshe Feldenkries and Arica Institute founder Oscar Ichazo. He was also accepted into the Institute For The Study Of Human Knowledge founded by the renowned Sufi, Idries Shah. Mr. Voorhees teaches part time as an adjunct professor of mideastern history and religious studies at the University of New Mexico in Taos. He is also a world-class tournament poker player, if you dare to meet him on the green felt. His new book, The Hollow Fortress, is the first in a series of mystical stories that draw from his Special Forces background, as well as his insights into the nature of the human soul.